Praise for *My Place Among Them*

"*My Place Among Them*, J. Stanion's powerful first published work, is a fascinating historical novel based on her great-grandfather's manuscripts documenting his experiences as a teacher, principal, and superintendent in the federal Indian service on reservations in Arizona, Wyoming, Montana, and North Carolina. Stanion's story revolves around a young man who survived the Lakota Sioux massacre at Wounded Knee in South Dakota on December 29, 1890, in which over 350 Sioux were slaughtered. Those readers who enjoy stories of Indians and the Old West will find this a well-written, most enjoyable read."

—**Bud Shapard**, Retired from the Bureau of Indian Affairs after Twenty Years of Service, Author of Two Nonfiction Books about Apache Indians and Three Novels about the Old West

"First and foremost, *My Place Among Them* is a dramatic epic that I never wanted to end. It's an intimate portrayal of a period in our history when good men believed they knew best, bad men did their worst, and naïve, proud men couldn't tell the difference. The tragic becomes provocative as we see how many shades of gray colored the true story behind the fate of the Indigenous people of America."

—**Fran Lebowitz**, Editor

"*My Place Among Them* is a unique blend of documented Native American history and personal family history compiled from journals, pictures and stories. It creates a riveting read of conflict and resistance, hardships and perseverance, acceptance, and the personal element of loves lost and found. A real page-turner!"

—**Madelyn Rohrer**, Storyteller, Historian, Public Speaker, and Author of Numerous Books, including *Children of the Edict*

"Based on tales from the author's great-grandfather, this close look at Indigenous people, a concerned White teacher, and a promising Lakota student required to attend a government school shows history that isn't taught in schoolbooks. Get an inside look at past struggles from this wonderfully told narrative that includes the teacher's journals as a primary resource."

—**B. Lynn Goodwin**, Owner of Writer Advice, Author of *Talent* and *Never Too Late: From Wannabe to Wife at 62*

My Place Among Them

by J. Stanion

© Copyright 2023 J. Stanion

ISBN 979-8-88824-051-9

All rights reserved. No part of this publication may be reproduced, stored in a retrieval system, or transmitted in any form or by any means—electronic, mechanical, photocopy, recording, or any other—except for brief quotations in printed reviews, without the prior written permission of the author.

This is a work of fiction. All the characters in this book are fictitious, and any resemblance to actual persons, living or dead, is purely coincidental. The names, incidents, dialogue, and opinions expressed are products of the author's imagination and are not to be construed as real.

Some photographs reprinted with permission of The Denver Public Library, Western History Collection, #WH644.

Published by

◤ köehlerbooks™

3705 Shore Drive
Virginia Beach, VA 23455
800-435-4811
www.koehlerbooks.com

MY PLACE AMONG THEM

A NOVEL

J. STANION

VIRGINIA BEACH
CAPE CHARLES

Introduction

The original author of this story, my great-grandfather, worked as a teacher, principal, superintendent, heirship examiner, and advocate for the Indigenous people of America for over thirty years. During that time, he served on reservations from Arizona to Wyoming and from Montana to North Carolina. Family lore tells that his numerous moves resulted from his frequent complaints to Washington regarding what he considered not just unfair but also outright criminal treatment of the Indians in his charge.

Because he was part of the bureaucracy he felt was responsible for the perilous state of the American Indian at the turn of the twentieth century, he did not seek publication during his lifetime. Moving his family was one thing; losing the financial security to care for them was another. Before his passing, he gave the manuscript to his daughter, my grandmother, who was born at "Mission House" on the Pine Ridge Reservation and baptized in the Holy Cross Church where survivors of the massacre at Wounded Knee were taken for medical care.

I grew up hearing my father's stories of his grandfather's letters to Washington and of a mysterious manuscript that revealed the injustices he had witnessed. At my grandmother's death in 1976, the manuscript passed to my father. He transcribed the three hundred hand-typed yellow pages into a computer document in the early 1990s, editing the often difficult-to-read Victorian-style writing. Eventually, cancer stole the time he needed to complete his work, and Dad passed the manuscript to me with the request that I bring to fruition his grandfather's wish for publication.

In 2020, COVID-19 gave me the time not only to locate the original manuscript, letters, records of employment, and family photos but also to begin again the editing process for publication. While there may be words that some people find offensive, I have strived to present the original story as true to my great-grandfather's words as possible. I ask that the Lakota people bear with my calling them "Indians" throughout this book. It is the author's term for all the Indigenous people he encountered. It is also important for you, the reader, to know at least some of the historical context of the story.

In his original draft (approximately 1902), my great-grandfather wrote this introduction:

> History tells us that in the early summer of 1890, a mysterious message spread among the Indians, telling them of a native "messiah" named Wovoka who came from the west. According to his teaching, the Indians had only to perform the Ghost Dance wearing symbolically painted shirts to shield the wearer from harm, and their lost loved ones, their lands, the buffalo, and Indian dominion of the plains would be returned to the tribes, and the white man would disappear forever. Not every individual chose to follow the preaching of Wovoka, but large groups of those who did frightened white settlers, who feared new attacks by the Indians.
>
> Distortion by the press suggested, without evidence, that the dancing would lead to a violent Indian uprising. Military leaders and politicians demanded that all dancing and large gatherings of the Lakota people cease. On December 15, 1890, Chief Sitting Bull of the Standing Rock Reservation, a supporter of the Ghost Dance, was shot dead while being placed under arrest. A few weeks later, Spotted Elk, a chief from the Cheyenne River Reservation, left home with a group of his people to meet with Red Cloud on the Pine Ridge Reservation. Among the families were nearly three times as many women and children as men. They had traveled over two hundred and fifty miles in the dead of winter when they were intercepted by the 7th Cavalry on Porcupine Creek. Within a day's travel of the Pine Ridge Agency, they surrendered willingly to the soldiers and set up camp.

On the morning of the twenty-ninth of December, Spotted Elk's band, totaling about four hundred, was camped on the banks of Wounded Knee Creek, guarded by five hundred troopers of the old Custer command. With soldiers surrounding the camp and rapid-fire guns trained down from the ridge above, the order to disarm the Indians was given. The Indians surrendered most of their guns, but a single shot shattered the frozen air, perhaps accidentally as stories say, and the soldiers were commanded to fire.

An hour later, no standing Indians were to be seen, only those who lay inanimate or writhing in the agonies of mortal wounds. When the final accounting was made, more than thirty soldiers lay dead, many hit by their comrades' bullets in the confusion of the attack. Between one hundred and fifty and two hundred Indian men, women, and children also lay dead or dying, many shot by soldiers shouting, 'Remember Custer!' as they rode. Some of the dead women and children were found as far as two miles away from the field of slaughter where they had been pursued and killed while attempting to escape.

For many years, it was called the Battle of Wounded Knee.

Battle? How ridiculous the writers of history can be.

What would it have been called had five hundred well-armed Indian warriors attacked four hundred practically unarmed and defenseless men, women, and children of the white race with such an awful carnage?

At a time when information is freely available yet it is more difficult to tell fact from fiction, John's story feels more relevant than ever. The names throughout this text are those of real persons existing in family documents from the period 1878 to 1936. Their placement in the story is entirely a work of fiction.

In my great-grandfather's words, "The story of John Iron Horse is born of fact and fancy; the reader may judge of the proportion."

For my dad,
With love.

SOUTH DAKOTA

Home of Chief Spotted Elk

Wall

BADLANDS

Interior

· *Potato Creek*

· *Porcupine*
· *Wounded Knee*
· *Pine Ridge Agency and School*

NEBRASKA

0   12.5   25   37.5   50
DISTANCE IN MILES

I

The Creek

Sitting Bull was one of the principal leaders of the Lakota people. He had fought against white soldiers and settlers for many years, had foretold the defeat of Custer at Little Big Horn—also called the Battle of the Greasy Grass—and even moved to Canada to escape the US Cavalry. Later, he returned to live on the Standing Rock Reservation where an Indian agent ordered his arrest by agency police. When Sitting Bull refused to mount a horse and be led away under arrest, a fight ensued, and Sitting Bull was fatally shot.

CHAPTER 1

Carter's Journal

December 18, 1890

Potato Creek, Pine Ridge Indian Reservation, South Dakota

Murdered! Shot by his own people, if the rumors were true. Sitting Bull, the leader of the Lakota, was dead. It took three days for official word to arrive from Standing Rock. It was difficult for me to comprehend. I thought everyone on the reservation was in awe of Sitting Bull's stardom in Buffalo Bill's Wild West Show.

We'd seen photographs of him dressed in his finery, flourishing his eagle-feather bonnet and war shirt in front of the crowds. We heard of his exploits with Annie Oakley—"Little Sure Shot," he called her. On his trips to visit the reservation, Sitting Bull bragged that while he paraded around the arena at the end of each show, he was cursing the crowds in his native tongue and laughing, but we had heard that the crowds jeered and threw rotten produce at him. The white people paid good money for their tickets, but as was Lakota custom, Sitting Bull gave it away, mostly to the poor. I never saw the show, so I didn't know what was true.

According to Mother's letters, Father saw the show several times and said it was spectacular. He accused me of exaggerating the poor conditions on the reservation in my letters. I wasn't surprised. He disagreed with my choice of careers and questioned everything since I'd chosen not to follow in his footsteps. In truth, life on the reservation was sometimes worse than I described, but I didn't want Mother to worry. Lillian and I focused on the things we had to be thankful for rather than what we'd left behind.

Despite his role in the white man's show, Sitting Bull was considered a great leader by many, both Indian and white, but I believe he was conflicted deep in his soul. He fought white settlers for many years yet sent his own children to white schools and encouraged his people to farm like the white man. He met with President Cleveland, calling him a great leader, but pleaded with the government to stop selling Indian land. He encouraged the Indians to make peace yet condoned the Ghost Dance and invited some of the followers of Wovoka to come to Standing Rock. I knew it wouldn't bode well for peace. As it turned out, it was the only excuse the soldiers needed to accuse him of instigating trouble.

Here at Potato Creek, I encouraged the leader, Iron Horse, to live peaceably with the whites. I didn't want soldiers riding through our camp. Most of the families in the camp were content with their lives. Occasionally, a few belligerent boys played at Ghost Dancing as they walked home from class, but Iron Horse always reprimanded them with a stomp and a gnarly finger pointing them towards home. He understood, all too well, the threat the white soldiers and settlers posed to his people. He'd lost his mother, Plenty Horses, to diphtheria when he was a child. His brother, Fights for Himself, had been killed by a settler trying to collect bounty money. His father, Iron Hand, died supporting Sitting Bull at the Battle of Dead Buffalo Lake.

Iron Horse had long ago resigned himself to the futility of fighting. He chafed at the meager rations sent by the government but refused to ride with me and complain to the superintendent. He still counted his wealth in horses. Knowing the buffalo were gone, he meekly hitched his wagon for the trip to the agency each month and accepted the government handouts without a word, even when the flour was half weevils and he had to share his meat with two other families.

Iron Horse and I spoke often. I saw that many of the people had no hope for the future. The children were forced to attend white schools, often miles away, and when they came home, they were unrecognizable as Indians. It was hard to envision a future for these families. Most of the elderly accepted that their time to leave this life was coming. I couldn't give them hope for anything better anywhere but the spirit world. So, they faced each day in despair, and the loss of Sitting Bull was one more knife in their hearts.

I was thankful for my position in the government system that put a roof over our heads and food on our table, but I was ashamed of how our government treated these people. We were proud of our students' accomplishments and imagined one day they would have homes and families in this beautiful place. Lillian and I prayed we could serve and advise the families of Potato Creek wisely and that those we had come to love would be safe through these uncertain times.

CHAPTER 2

Carter's Journal

December 28, 1890

Potato Creek, Pine Ridge Reservation, South Dakota

I sat outside on that bitter, windy afternoon, fearing for those I had come to think of as family. There was no news. A silent emptiness echoed across the camp. All the Indians had gone to join Red Cloud at Pine Ridge Agency. Christmas had come and gone, and I sat dazed, wrapped in a heavy Pendleton blanket, reliving memories of my childhood and thinking of my family back in Ithaca. It was probably at least as cold or colder back east, but I felt a Dakota storm brewing, and it chilled to the bone.

Our home on the creek doubled as the schoolhouse, but despite it being just days after the holiday, the buildings stood bare of decoration, a starkly shadowed red as the sunlight faded. I allowed my thoughts to drift to the happy years of my childhood in New York. If I closed my eyes, I saw wreaths and ribbons festooning every window. There were decorated trees scattered throughout the house, stretching upwards to the ten-foot ceilings. Each was covered in long strands of popcorn my sisters and I strung onto Mother's sewing thread. Under her watchful eye, we hung brilliantly colored but oh-so-delicate glass ornaments and porcelain angels with soft, spun-glass wings on every branch until the trees veritably sparkled as if each held as many stars as the clear night sky outside the city.

Christmas mornings we spent opening gifts from Santa and each other. There were squeals and laughter at the variety of things the store owners imported for their shops during the holidays. We played for hours, until Mother and Father donned their heavy fur coats to head downtown to do their social duty. Father would bring around our high-stepping chestnut stallion, Roman, covered with brightly striped wool blankets against the chill. Roman always pranced and swished his tail in anticipation, and I would sneak behind the sleigh to see myself reflected in the high, polished back. When Father clucked to Roman, I'd spring away just before the curving iron runners cut the ice, sending shards flying into the air. Off they'd go, carrying mounds of biscuits and ham to feed the hungry in the churchyard.

Later in the evening, we'd gather around the tree, singing the last of the Christmas carols before putting away our gifts and remembering we'd soon return to school. We always slept late the next morning, leaving the warmth of our feather comforters only after we heard Crozier and Feeley's grocers delivering the week's order of fresh eggs, sugar, and coffee. At the sound of jingling glass bottles, we'd race down the stairs, waving to Father as he left for his job as superintendent at the gun plant before piling around the table for breakfast. Oh, what memories!

There were no such holidays on the reservation—no feather comforters, no laden baskets of ham, and no sparkling trees or mounds of gifts for the children. Life here was different from anything I'd ever known, but it was the life of my choosing.

I was the only white man living within a radius of fifteen miles. My wife, Lillian, was the only mixed-blood Indian in the camp. We'd moved to Potato Creek after a whirlwind romance that began at the big Indian school back east. I couldn't face a future in the factory despite our wealth from my father's position there. Against his wishes, I volunteered the metalworking skills I'd learned at the plant in a position as teaching assistant at the school. Though Father railed against my choice, I was happiest teaching the native students. They worked diligently and were fiercely proud each time they mastered a new skill. They often applied their own artistic touches to the pieces we made, and I felt I was making a real difference in their lives. It was rewarding to be away from Father's focus on money and social standing.

At the school, I was often sent across campus in search of materials in the library, or to file documents in the administration building. I took note on occasion of one of the most beautiful women I'd ever seen, walking gracefully across the grounds. Her sun-kissed skin was radiant, and her mahogany hair shone in the sunlight while her entire being seemed to float effortlessly over whatever path she chose. I was smitten and couldn't remove her image from my thoughts.

I found myself taking roundabout routes on my errands in hopes of simply catching a glimpse of her. I had no idea what words to speak and feared my tongue would tangle completely into knots if I actually caught her eye. When it finally happened, I focused childishly on my feet and stammered out the word "library" before I felt a rush of heat in my cheeks and stumbled towards my destination.

Late one Friday afternoon, as I was leaving my classroom, loaded with papers for review, I heard the voice of an angel a few doors down the hall. I couldn't resist tiptoeing to the door of the music room where I realized it was the woman of my dreams I'd heard. I was drawn to close my eyes and lean against the upright of the doorframe, basking in the sound of her voice. In the shadowy light, she appeared a few years older than me. With her hands clasped beneath her chin and her hair falling in luxuriant waves to her waist, she glowed as she lost herself momentarily in the music. It was only then, completely captured by her beauty, that I realized she was neither white nor Indian, for the stark white of her blouse contrasted sharply with her pale, coppery skin.

Realizing she had an uninvited audience, she approached and inquired whether we had met before. I blurted out to the negative before brashly adding that I certainly hoped I could see her again.

Her name was Lillian, and from that moment on, we were inseparable. She was a dedicated student, focused on completing her studies in nursing, but it was her sense of humor and commitment to those she considered her people that convinced me she was the love of my life. Over time, I learned she was determined to return to her reservation in South Dakota. I'd been inspired by stories of the wild West for many years and had never been happy planning a future in my father's footsteps. At the school, I'd seen children from tribes across America. A teaching job on the reservation would allow me to travel west, work with the Indians, and escape the ever-present discord with my father.

Mother tried her best to convince us to stay in the state. She even secured a New York birth certificate for Lillian in hopes she'd work at one of the more prestigious hospitals. Mother's efforts were in vain, however, since Lillian and I agreed it was our destiny to serve her impoverished people on the reservation. After completing the necessary civil exams, we requested an assignment to Pine Ridge, which was granted. We were married at the Holy Cross Church in a traditional Episcopalian service, with the agency superintendent, his wife, and a few Indian women and children the only witnesses present. We were offered positions at Potato Creek Day School, which had a generous allotment of grassland for grazing cattle and an abundant supply of spring-fed watering pools. Living in the school's cottage and building a self-sufficient home while teaching the children of Potato Creek seemed to be the perfect future.

At the time, the federal government hoped that daily attendance by all Indian children at a school with an English-speaking teacher would bring about a cultural change that would allow the government to stop fighting the Indians. Federal policy required that children attend a day school from six years of age until they could be transferred to a government- or missionary-sponsored boarding school no later than the age of fourteen. Day schools like Potato Creek, where children lived at home and attended school during the day, concentrated on the basic elements of education: reading, writing, and arithmetic. The day schools also taught various skills that were necessary for running the school itself, such as cooking, sewing, and carpentry. The objective was for the children to take the fundamentals of the white man's civilization back to the older family members on the reservation and influence their elders to accept a new way of living.

Once Lillian and I arrived, we dedicated ourselves to making the Potato Creek school one of the best on the reservation. We started out believing we were part of a government program marked by efficiency and accomplishment, but over time, we found that every part of the system was run by an impersonal, if not outright malicious, government bureau. If Pine Ridge was any example, Lillian and I understood why there was little hope the Indians could survive the reservations as they were, run by white agents and traders. Soil that hadn't eroded away or been overworked was poor, winters were bitter, and rainfall was anything but dependable. There were few provisions for tools, fertilizer, or other necessities for raising crops. Rations were often late or inadequate, and food was usually vermin infested.

Until forced to live on the reservations, the Indians had been nomads, hunting the buffalo that provided hides for their clothing and homes, bones for utensils and tools, and meat and fats for their diet. They had no knowledge of farming and no tools. The government cattle, if they weren't stolen by cowboys and traders along the route, were a poor replacement for the buffalo, which had been slaughtered by the hundreds of thousands. We prayed each night that we could teach the children enough that they would have no desire to go back to the old ways of life. White settlement was continuing to expand, and we knew these children had to learn a different way of life. Each day, we focused on making our school a beacon for the Indians to see the best of the white man's world.

Iron Horse, chief of the Potato Creek clan, understood the importance of learning the white man's ways and saw no alternative to making peace. I'd encouraged him to travel the sixty-five miles to join Spotted Elk and Red Cloud at the agency and share his insights, but I never imagined he would take the entire camp. Once he decided to go, there was no dissuading him, so I'd begged him to plan a route that would bring them safely to the agency and back in case there was another outbreak of violence.

On this day, Lillian and I awaited their return, hoping all were unharmed. As we considered the recent actions of soldiers and Indians alike, we worried what the future held for our Indian family.

CHAPTER 3

Escape
....

December 29, 1890

Wounded Knee Creek, Pine Ridge Reservation, South Dakota

Twelve-year-old John had slept soundly inside his family's tipi, exhausted from the previous weeks of travel with his clan. Hearing unfamiliar voices, he bolted upright, the thin blanket falling from his shoulders as he glanced around the gray interior to see if others were awake. While his family stirred, wakened by the shouting, he pushed aside the ragged hide that covered the entrance to peer curiously around camp.

His breath crystallized in the air as he realized soldiers were galloping randomly amid the circle of tipis, shouting orders for the Indians to come outside and surrender immediately. As the sun lightened the eastern sky, John's family stepped from the warmth of their home into the dry, bitter air of a South Dakota winter. Bundling their blankets tightly around them, the families of Spotted Elk's clan emerged slowly, glancing around in confusion as they gathered in the center of the circle of tipis. Many of the women held wailing infants close for warmth, and toddlers tightly grasped their mothers' legs.

John had no intention of clinging to his mother like a child, so he eased slowly out of her reach, feeling confident as he worked his way through the crowded circle, trying to get a better view of what was going on. Spotted Elk sat slumped on a blanket in front of his tipi, too ill to lead his people. He was near death from pneumonia and exhausted from their hurried exodus from Standing Rock after the murder of Sitting Bull. They had traveled nearly two hundred miles in the dead of winter to meet with Red Cloud at Pine Ridge.

As he approached the outer edge of the circle, John witnessed several teenaged braves being directed by stern-faced soldiers to toss their weapons on a pile. Once empty handed, the boys stood huddled together, peering nervously at the men who towered over them from horseback. A movement on the hill above caught John's attention. He glanced upward, his courage faltering as he spotted more soldiers, each manning a wheeled, repeating gun.

Back in the crowded center, some of the elders began the shuffling steps of the Ghost Dance. Spotted Elk remained seated, weak and unable to speak to the soldiers or remind them of the group's surrender the day before. Several hundred soldiers had assembled around their camp and now sat rigid in their saddles, wordlessly surrounding the families. Blowing clouds of frosty breath and chomping their bits impatiently, their mounts awaited a signal from their riders.

The boy jumped at the sound of a scuffle that broke out not far from where he stood. A group of soldiers were trying to force a young brave to give up his weapon and toss it onto the pile. As the old men chanted, raising their hands high above their heads, the brave gave one last jerk on the rifle, a treasured gift from his uncle. In the midst of the confusion, a rifle shot shattered the frozen air.

Immediately, the soldiers drew their sabers, brandishing them overhead and spurring their horses forward. As the animals raced towards the Indians, the soldiers dropped their reins to pull Army-issued Colt revolvers from their holsters. The Indian families stood frozen, glancing around in disbelief as the air filled with the sulfurous smell of gunpowder and the ground trembled with the pounding hooves of charging cavalry mounts. Mothers reached out with trembling hands to grasp older children, pulling them into a protective circle even as individuals closest to the hill began collapsing into lifeless heaps on the prairie. Several women screamed for their families to flee, turning away from the oncoming line of blazing guns and blue-gray smoke, trying to make sense of the horrendous scene.

Shouting, "Remember Custer!" the soldiers charged into the group of old men, women, and children, firing their weapons into any Indian that moved and running them down as they fled. John turned and ran for the ravine at the back of the campground. Sheer terror drove his legs as he raced beside fleeing women and children running headlong away from the slaughter. His lungs burned as he ran for his life. Mothers and children fell onto the bloody field around him, and he wondered what his family's fate might be. He jammed his fists into his ears against the rattling of the Hotchkiss guns.

Reaching the ravine's edge, he jumped as far as he could, sailing into the open space of the gulch before dropping into nothingness. Suddenly, his feet hit the glacial waters of Wounded Knee Creek, and he clambered across to the other side. Stumbling along the steep bank, he grasped at tree roots and bulrushes to steady himself against falling into the frigid waters.

Ten wagon lengths ahead of him was four-year-old Red Plume. Her pudgy toddler feet labored through the icy waters of the creek bed as she stretched out her arms to her mother's back, crying to be carried. Short Woman paused to glance back from her flight of terror, black hair streaming across her face. For a split second, her eyes looked into John's and then widened with fear at the apparition closing in behind him. She bent and grasped Red Plume's outstretched hands, swinging the little one to her waist as she turned to flee once more.

Before John could decide whether to trace her footsteps down the creek or seek cover in the tangled mass along the water's edge, the sharp crack of a rifle echoed down the ravine. The young mother pitched sideways into the icy water, clutching at her child as a second shot sounded, knocking the little girl from her grasp. Both settled into the creek, streams of red flowing into the rippling water.

John heard the crack of another shot and felt a searing pain as a bullet pierced his shoulder. The shot momentarily lifted him from the frigid water, legs flailing until he dropped back into the creek, sprawled across the rocky bottom. There he lay still, trembling more from fear than cold as the image of Short Woman and her child lying motionless a few feet ahead played over in his mind. There were splashes as the soldier approached, the jingle of bit chains, and the crunch of steel shoes on the smooth stones of the creek bottom until one black hoof settled into the shallow water inches from the tip of his nose.

Icy droplets splattered on his ear and cheek, and the boy remained immobile, feigning death, afraid to breathe or blink. Any sign of life might draw a reaction from the uniformed man above him. John wondered if the soldier would spur his mount to stomp him into the rocks or simply reach out with his saber to lay open the body of one more Indian for the buzzards to feast on.

Seconds seemed like hours, until a heaving grunt from the bay indicated the soldier was moving down the creek in search of others. Afraid to call attention from soldiers riding the high bank, John tilted his head enough to see the rider continue downstream and peer into the tangled roots and vines before turning and cantering back up the ravine. Pink water splashed around the horse's feet as the soldier passed Red Plume and Short Woman. From above the gully, the sounds of women wailing the death songs of their people and the popping cracks of gunfire echoed through John's ears as he remained still in the water.

Finally, silence fell over the prairie. Not knowing if the soldiers would return, John lifted himself painfully from the icy water, scrambled up the bank, and lurched across the prairie in search of another shelter—never allowing his eyes to look back towards where he had heard the last cries of the women. He moved as quickly as possible across the field. The last snow made a pinto pattern of brown and white as the cutting wind drove it into little mounds against the dry tufts of the short-grass prairie.

He crossed these spaces that offered no shelter, moving towards the cottonwoods growing along the upper section of the creek, their bare trunks presenting only slightly more refuge from prying soldier eyes. His feet throbbed as he floundered along, following a vision of his mother's face, seeking her guidance towards home and family. As the sun set, the snow continued to fall, at times so intensely that he could barely make out the ground before him.

The fading rays of evening slowly yielded to the night, and a blizzard moved in, blanketing the area with snow. John knew it would be difficult to find a path away from what the white soldiers would one day call a battlefield. He staggered towards a decrepit cabin standing in a tiny cluster of oaks, its wooden boards warped and twisted. It had obviously once been a settler's cabin but now stood abandoned by the white fat-takers who could no more farm this land than could the Lakota.

At least it offered some relief from the elements. Bracing against the splintery walls as he sought the sagging doorway, John reached down to scoop aside small mounds of snow, pulling desperately at the red, frostbitten broadleaf plantain leaves beneath. He had fled the creek quickly and failed to gather the soft down of the cattails that would have staunched the flow of blood. There were no horsetail or black root leaves left on the dry stalks of winter, but John stripped bark from the diamond oaks he found beside the cabin. His mother and grandmother had shown him that chewing the bark would bring relief from pain, and the chewed fibers would help stop the bleeding, especially crushed together with the leathery leaves of the plantain.

As the sun settled to the west on his first night alone, John pushed through the doorway, grasping at dusty clumps of long-abandoned spiderwebs and rolling them together with the chewed bark and leaves. Reaching under his shirt, he stuffed the wadded clump into his wound. The wind whistled through the cracks in the walls; the pain eased slightly, and John was thankful for his grandmother's teachings. There was no fresh flow of blood as his body gave way to the numbness of shock. He collapsed to the cabin floor, exhausted, and slept fitfully in the dark cold of a Dakota night, visions of the horrors he had witnessed exploding across his dreams.

A much heavier snow came later, falling silently for hours in the darkness, until he awoke to the sound of birdsong in the gray mist of morning. He checked to make sure no fresh blood seeped from his shoulder, and feeling somewhat encouraged to find that it had not, he struck out on what he prayed would be his journey home. He was unaware he had slept through two days and nights. He had no more idea of what day it was than he had of the distance he had traveled. It didn't take long for fatigue to settle in once more. As the sky grew lighter, John realized the land around him was familiar, but it was not the peaceful valley home he'd been seeking. Instead, his path had been nothing more than a circle, returning him to the scene he had hoped to escape forever.

As the pinks and purples of the morning surrendered to the brilliant blues of full day, John wandered through snow-covered mounds scattered among blackened and leaning lodge poles. Wagons lay in broken heaps across what he recognized as his family's campsite. The soldiers had returned for their dead, but across the open field, a bent knee here or outstretched hand there struck frozen poses from beneath the snow—bodies of the men, women, and children of his people. Grief settled into his soul, joining his body's pain from the gunshot and the frostbite on his feet. He could go no further and collapsed into the mire of snow, grass, and soil. He would find peace in the gift of Grandmother Earth, the land that was the lifeblood of his people. He accepted that this was the time and place to seek the peace of the Great Spirit. He would join the others, the mothers and children, the old warriors sent to their long sleep by the white man's greed for this land.

As his spirit faded, his eyes focused on the dull white of a blanket tossed across the tangled poles of an abandoned tipi frame. He stumbled to the spot, pulling the threadbare fabric around his aching body. Sheltered from the wind in the drooping remnants of the tipi's cover, he knelt to curl up in the snow and prayed for sleep to come.

He didn't see that Spotted Elk, the one the white man called Big Foot, lay frozen where he'd fallen, on the edge of the field. Neither could he know that later that day, white men would come for his chief, gathering almost two hundred of his people to be buried in a single hole dug deep in the frozen soil on the hill where the Hotchkiss guns had stood.

CHAPTER 4

Carter's Journal

December 31, 1890

Potato Creek Day School, Pine Ridge Reservation, South Dakota

Rumors of the massacre ravaged our imaginations. Lillian retired to the kitchen to occupy her hands while I waited in the cold, peering across the clearing towards the empty Indian homes. The school itself was within sight of Iron Horse's cabin and within walking distance of all the members of his band. It was also situated beside a rippling creek, flat and sandy, shaded by a number of cedars, with one last lodgepole pine and several bur oaks shading the hill. Most of the other trees had been cut over the years for firewood, and foraging livestock constantly nibbled at new growth. On this afternoon, it was particularly forlorn, and I suddenly imagined it was probably like any of the twenty-five other schools across this reservation or the nearly two hundred others scattered across our nation.

The government provided funding for the construction and operation of each school. Ours consisted of two small-frame buildings, one about twenty feet wide by thirty feet long that contained a single classroom, topped by a belfry. The other, a slightly larger three-room cottage, was designed as a home for a teacher and a housekeeper, usually a spouse, along with a smaller classroom for the girls. The clapboard sides of the schoolhouse and bell tower had been painted a dull, dingy red a number of years ago by some unimaginative previous instructor at the school. The plain lines of the buildings, the dull-red color, and the forbidding lack of ornamentation served to oppress the minds and spirits of the Indians and, at the same time, to remind all of us that those back in Washington believed no frills were necessary to convince the Indians their lifestyle was inferior.

While teaching carpentry skills to the older boys, I had managed to completely replace the school's shabby, patchwork board roof with cedar shakes made and kept in good repair by my students. Using horse power and the children's labor, I'd also added a substantial and spacious log stable for my horse team and two dairy cows. It included a section at the end for a hennery where we kept a flock of poultry secure from the coyotes and other prairie vandals. When the biddies matured, the boys and I separated them, cocks going into the back pen to serve as food and hens going into a larger coop to brood eggs and raise their babies.

We'd built a large shop structure where I could instruct the boys in the basics of the bench and forge. I had acquired above-average skill in furniture making and metalworking from my many hours at the gun plant. I could make sturdy hinges and latches for use on our buildings, and the boys learned these skills as we designed and crafted things we needed for the school. Two winters earlier, we'd built an icehouse to store chunks of ice we cut from the creek and insulated with layers of straw I purchased from a local farmer. Although it wasn't able to last through the heat of an entire Pine Ridge summer, the ice made for wonderfully cool drinks in hot weather and helped preserve many food products that couldn't be dried or salted.

The previous spring, the boys had helped me frame a small root cellar adjacent to the icehouse, covering it with sod blocks to keep food from freezing in the winter and helping it last longer in the summer. We built both the cellar and the icehouse conveniently close to Mrs. Heath's kitchen door, and she made frequent use of both to supply the children with nutritious meals when school was in session. The spring before that fateful December day, the boys and I had completed a dam across the creek just above the stable, diverting the waters of the stream not just to irrigate our vegetable garden but also to provide sufficient water to grow forage for the horses and cows.

Lillian and her girl students beautified the grounds around the cottage by planting as many wildflowers as they could find space for, beginning with clumps of yellow balsamroot and creeping barberry around the door. Rows of red-and-yellow Indian blanket stood two feet tall with lines of sagebrush buttercup creeping along the rows between. Along the irrigation canal, we could always find indigo bush and purple skunkweed, their arching stems reaching proudly for the swirling clouds that raced across the sky. Around the house they built beds of wild sweet potato, milkweed, and Queen Anne's lace.

Besides the cheerful colors each plant added to the schoolyard, many of them served a purpose as well. The barberry produced edible berries in the fall, and the skunkweed yielded tall stems loaded with black seeds that were used to produce a blue-black dye for cloth. Indian blanket tolerated the worst of droughts and provided nectar for our bees. The children taught Lillian that besides being a tasty herb, sagebrush could produce a lethal poison that Indian hunters dipped their arrow tips in to bring a swift death to their prey; she in turn showed them how to crumble the dried herbs into a savory chicken broth. The point of most significant pride for the entire school, however, was not one but two outhouses we'd built behind the main structures so the children of Potato Creek had the rare pleasure of using separate facilities for boys and girls.

The youngest girls swept the schoolyard daily, leaving the entire area clean and weed-free, inviting to any who came by. Through our efforts, the Potato Creek Day School was a source of pride for all the inhabitants of the camp. It proved an incentive to the children to aspire to better things and an influence that I believe kept the local Indians from joining those who had taken up the Ghost Dance.

On this night, one of the darkest I'd known on the prairie, I made my way into the kitchen, giving Lillian a bear hug as she labored over a pot of hearty beef stew. She laughed, reaching up to tug my ears, then shifted to take hold of my hand. Grasping it firmly, she pulled me down to sit beside her at the organ that had been delivered from Manhattan with help from my father's brother, Uncle Curtis. The gift was priceless since Lillian and I both loved the arts. While I had some talent for playing classical music, it was my special joy to accompany my wife whenever she raised her rich voice in song. It was her voice that had led me to her, and the strains of "Auld Lang Syne" served well to diminish the loneliness that sometimes enveloped us from across the vast stretches of the prairie.

That night, however, her fingers lingered over mine, pressing them one by one to the keys, slowly playing the first notes of Beethoven's "Fur Elise" while tears coursed down her cheeks, our moment of levity forgotten.

I realized the massacre would forever change the lives of the Lakota people. What I didn't know until later was that it would bring into our lives one of the most remarkable young men I had ever known—a young man whose blood kin had been erased, whose memories of the past would be haunted, yet who would become my ideal of a student, a model of civility, and eventually a spokesman for humanity as our leaders worked to erase the very foundations of his native culture.

CHAPTER 5

Haunted Trail

December 31, 1890

Pine Ridge Reservation, South Dakota

Knowing the white soldiers considered Spotted Elk to be a troublemaker, Iron Horse had chosen to travel separately from the main group on the way to Pine Ridge. He knew many of the warriors along the trail participated in the Ghost Dance. He didn't believe in the teachings of Wovoka and didn't plan to travel with anyone who did. As they had approached the agency, he and his family made camp southwest of Porcupine Butte, unpacked their supplies from the wagon, put up their lodges, and established their evening fires more than two days' travel from Spotted Elk's camp. When word came that the soldiers of Yellow Hair had disarmed Spotted Elk and his warriors and then murdered them all, Iron Horse said a prayer of thanksgiving for the wisdom that guided him to camp in a separate place.

After hearing the news, he fasted and prayed yet saw no vision to help lead his people into the future. He was certain their future lay not in fighting the white man, nor in wasting time dreaming of the past, but in seizing the opportunities offered by education and seeking out the best that white society had to offer. Iron Horse had made one trip to meet the great white chief and seen many cities, and he knew the waves of white families swarming over the land were not going to stop. A deep depression settled over him as he faced the reality that he must try to reconcile these recent events with any hope they had for the future.

By the time Iron Horse and his family thought about returning home, the troops who had attacked Big Foot's camp had resumed their routines at the agency as if nothing had happened. Some of them were even awarded medals for bravery, and many were calling it a battle. By the morning of the third day after the tragedy, Iron Horse finally decided to leave his campsite. He struggled to stop the visions of what his people might find as they followed the trail across Wounded Knee and back towards Potato Creek. He couldn't know in those moments of despair just how much what they would find would change his life.

CHAPTER 6

Prairie Foundling

December 31, 1890

Wounded Knee Creek, South Dakota

As they approached the site of the massacre, Iron Horse allowed himself a moment of despair before praying to be blinded to the scenes his mind had conjured. Dangling the reins between his fingers, he allowed his ponies to amble towards home. Despite their being thinner than usual this winter, the old chief was proud of his Palouseye mares, Little Witch and Snow Cloud, the white patches across their hips standing out in stark contrast to their mahogany coats. He pulled his blanket closer around his shoulders and let his chin sink to his chest, permitting a mindless melancholy to settle in.

John squeezed his eyes closed against the increasing brightness of day, tugged the threadbare blanket tighter over his head, and buried his face in the crook of his elbow within the collapsed tipi. Despite the tiny bit of warmth generated by the sunlight, the damp and cold of his self-made cocoon convinced him there was no reason to go on. Had the Great Spirit not sent him here to die by guiding his circuitous steps back to the very spot where it had all begun?

For a moment, he thought it better to drift into his long sleep than to puzzle over the sounds that tickled the edge of his consciousness. He knew he had not heard a soldier pony's iron shoes. His brain worked to reconcile the sound of unshod hooves and the rickety wheels of a wagon with images of the massacre pummeling his brain. He peered through barely cracked eyelids, seeing only winter-killed grasses tipped with glittering crystals of frost.

Always watchful of the world around her, ten-year-old Annie Iron Horse stood in the front of the wagon bed, leaning against her father's back for warmth. Scanning the littered campsite, she spotted a mound lying in stark contrast to the whiteness of the field. Though dirty and dull, the bare blanket indicated that something, or someone, had arrived after the blizzard had blown itself out.

All over the rest of the field, snow-covered shapes appeared as no more than clusters of grama grass for the ponies to graze come spring. The adults in the wagon knew what they were and looked away. Annie knew too but was distracted by the puzzle she saw in the snow. The women in the wagon were happy to let her shout out directions around the blackened firepits, broken lodge poles, and tossed belongings, distracting her father in her excitement to uncover the mystery.

At his daughter's first screech of discovery, Iron Horse jerked hard on the reins, turning his ponies off their homeward trail and towards the object his daughter indicated—the only mound that wasn't covered with new-fallen snow. As he reluctantly steered his ponies closer to the motionless shape, his number one wife, Moves First, cried out, grasping the splintered side boards of the wagon as she half climbed, half fell from the moving vehicle with a speed that belied her fifty-three years. She dragged her own coverings along in the snow as she lifted the edges of the battered cloth, exposing long, jet-black wisps of Indian hair draped over the gaunt cheeks of a child, facedown and pale. He was cool in her arms as she nestled him close and pulled her colorful blankets around them both, but she felt the faintest spark of life reach out to the warmth of her body.

Moves First carried the child to the wagon, lifting his frail body towards her sister, Good Heart, who added one of her own robes to his wrapping and settled him in a heap on the well-worn seat behind her husband. She steadied his limp form and held him close to her side until Moves First clambered back over the side boards and helped settle the child safely onto the narrow board seat between them. They squeezed their arms around the child, tangling all the blankets and robes into a mass of warmth and welcoming the windbreak that Iron Horse provided as he now sat ramrod straight in the driver's seat.

Annie immediately tried to climb from the rear of the wagon, asking a million questions about who he was, why he was lying there in the cold, and where his family was. Good Heart shushed her daughter, reminding her that the remainder of their trip was long, and she should settle into the warmth of a robe or blanket and let the women take care of the boy. Once all were settled, Iron Horse gently nudged the impatient ponies back onto the trail leading northeast and gave them their heads. There was little available grazing along the trail, and he knew they would set a constant pace home.

Iron Horse briefly wondered about the fate of the child's family and his chances of surviving his injuries. As the wagon rolled steadily along, the ponies' hooves treading rhythmically, Iron Horse's shoulders slumped, and he stared unseeing as his mind settled back into a dark melancholy. For the first time in his life, he didn't know how to help his people, worried they had no spirit left to forget the past and look to the future.

Iron Horse's two wives, Moves First and Good Heart, completely forgot their forlorn state and focused on bringing the boy back from death's door. Slowly, a more natural color returned to his cheeks. When they reached the Medicine Root River, the sisters hastily scraped an area clear of snow to set up their tipi, settled their guest on a clean patch of ground under its cover, wrapped him in blankets, and removed the soft, sodden moccasins from his frostbitten feet. They brought in handfuls of snow to mound around his appendages, keeping the bitter cold air from doing more damage. While Iron Horse watched quietly, the sisters transferred their meager supplies from the wagon to the floor of their tipi and set a small, brisk fire in the center. It lit up the inner circle and gave off a welcoming, though tiny, bit of heat.

Outside, Annie danced in excitement, calling her father to unhitch the ponies so everyone could get settled for the night. While he led them to the creek for a quick drink of icy water, she darted back and forth between him and the campsite, wishing he'd hurry back to where the boy lay beside the fire. After tying the ponies securely to the wagon, he tossed them a scant portion of the hay he'd brought along for the trip, watching as Annie squirmed with curiosity about their guest. She knew it was unseemly to ask for details from her father, and for the moment, he almost frightened her in his silence.

Moves First tossed a handful of coffee grounds into their chipped enamel pot and brought the water to a rolling boil in the coals of the fire. She prepared a supper of delicious-smelling soup—the long marrow bone of a steer simmered with ground corn and dried berries. After stoking the fire, she balanced a flat iron pan over the coals and grilled crisp flats of Indian bread while Good Heart gathered dry wood from along the creek bank. She struggled to carry a load that would fuel their fire through the night and keep the coffee steaming.

When all was ready, the sisters laid the boy on a pallet made from the majority of their blankets, close but not too close to the fire. They offered him a tiny bowl of soup that he eagerly scooped into his mouth with a battered metal spoon. When there was no longer fluid enough to scoop, the boy sat and rubbed his fingers over the interior of the bowl, licking them and savoring the flavor of his first food in days.

No one spoke of the massacre or the events that led them to find the boy in the snow. No one asked personal questions of their guest, whom the women secretly referred to as Ghost Boy for the time being. Proper manners, acknowledged across the Lakota nation, prevented direct questioning of a stranger, so personal details had to be acquired other ways. Iron Horse and the women scooped up the remaining soup and finished off the flats of bread, leaving not a drop or crumb. They remained silent until the boy issued a low, involuntary groan and his body spasmed with pain. Annie gasped, fearing it might be the throes of death overcoming him. Good Heart felt the boy's cheeks and checked to see that the bleeding had stopped. Annie assisted the women as they dressed his wounds with cooling mud and mosses from the creek bank.

As everyone settled in for the night, Annie sidled up against the warmth of the child's back, supporting him while he shifted and wiggled to find a comfortable position. The boy drifted into the deep and restful sleep of exhaustion, moaning occasionally as his unconscious mind dealt with the pain of his physical wounds and the agony of his mental ones.

Once Annie, the wives, and their guest had fallen peacefully asleep in their blankets, Iron Horse moved to stoke the fire with wood from just outside the tipi door and replenished his coffee. He pulled a blanket tightly around his shoulders and huddled inside the door, staring into the darkness outside. Focusing on his breath, he let his mind drift to the past. There were happy memories of his people roaming the prairie, free to hunt the buffalo, rich with ponies, satiated with the bounty of the hunt, warm in their buffalo robes and free of diseases the white man had brought. There were occasional skirmishes with other tribes, but these gave the warriors an opportunity to do battle, to count coup, and to raise their rank within the tribe.

The moon passed its peak as the fire burned low and the remaining bits of logs spit and hissed. Iron Horse was well respected and had counseled his people to accept the white man with compromise rather than hostility. He had witnessed the white men digging deep into the Black Hills in search of a shiny yellow metal and seen them fight and kill each other over a tiny patch of land. He was certain of the inevitable loss his people would suffer and encouraged them to accept what he knew they could not change. But as the flames flickered into glowing embers, Iron Horse was overwhelmed with self-doubt.

He questioned whether he'd shown wisdom or a lack of honor in the face of an enemy by encouraging his people to overlook the shortfalls of reservation life. As the embers died and smoke drifted from the circle of stones, Iron Horse pondered the future. How could he lead his people in the white man's civilization when their religion taught tolerance and forbearance yet permitted the murder of women and children because of the color of their skin? How could his people hold on to their freedom while locked inside the boundaries of a reservation?

As the darkest hour of the night gave way to the pale gray of morning, Iron Horse drifted between sleep and consciousness, dreaming he was on the field at Wounded Knee. A multitude of spirit figures—men, women, and little children—danced slowly, rhythmically in his head. A keening chant ebbed and flowed over what gradually became mounds in the snow. Finally, the dancers melted into the mounds, and the sound became a death chant, rising in a crescendo from almost inaudible to a heartbreaking wail that emanated from a single, dull-colored mound.

Suddenly, a nearby scream startled the old man awake. Squinting over the last coals of the fire, he realized it was the boy he'd heard, crying out in anguish and fright for Spotted Elk. As he watched, the child bolted upright, stretched out his hands, and shrieked, "Don't shoot! Hurry, Mother! Run!" before collapsing back onto his blankets, fully conscious and looking deep into the old man's eyes.

Iron Horse knew there would be no return to sleep this day, so he rose from the warmth of his blankets, rekindled the fire, and headed out to tend his ponies. The women, also awakened by the scream, bustled quickly about the tipi, preparing a breakfast of hardtack biscuits. They shushed Annie repeatedly, but she continued to ply the boy with questions he obviously didn't want to answer.

Only when the girl asked if she could do anything for him did he respond: "Water." She dipped some from the bucket her mother had brought from the creek and extended it to him. Annie's face lit up when the boy began speaking slowly as he reached for the cup. His voice hoarse and low, he divulged, "I am John, of Spotted Elk's band, and I have seen twelve winters," as if trying to answer all of Annie's questions at once.

He immediately closed his eyes and slumped back into the warmth of the blankets, but Annie persisted. Her childish questions slowly revealed that the boy had sought safety in the ravine of Wounded Knee Creek, that he had witnessed the deaths of women, children, and unarmed old warriors, and that he had been shot and left for dead. He shared that he had wandered for days before giving in to exhaustion and that when he regained consciousness, he had wakened to the life-giving warmth of Moves First. Iron Horse sat quietly listening. The boy had given no family name in his story. He hadn't said his family perished at Wounded Knee. Most importantly of all, he had never mentioned his father.

After breakfast, the women took down the tipi and packed their belongings in the wagon. Iron Horse brought the ponies to be hitched, and Annie encouraged John to rise and get in the wagon. As he shifted from his knees to his feet, putting weight on his frostbitten extremities, he cried out and collapsed back to his pallet, unconscious. The women wrapped the blankets around him and deposited him against Annie, who by then was ensconced in her own warm cocoon in the bed of the wagon.

Iron Horse clucked to his ponies and relapsed into a deep meditation, his new thoughts bringing relief from the apathy of the previous day. His vision from the night before assured him that the Great Spirit had chosen him to save this child's life. Iron Horse wondered at the certainty with which he felt the boy was now his, that he had finally been given the son for whom he had prayed. Had the spirits finally granted him the awesome responsibility of a man-child who would grow up to be a leader of his people? A man-child who, when Iron Horse glanced over his shoulder to the back of the wagon, looked straight into his eyes, in full charge of his senses and with a peculiar glow, almost of understanding, before closing them tightly and slipping back into a sound and restful sleep.

The two women also rode in the back, their blankets drawn closely about them, a portion of the tipi raised above the rough boards of the wagon to provide shelter as they lurched along. They sat on their feet, finding a comfortable position and beginning an earnest discussion of the recent past. They conversed in a language that was peculiarly musical, their low, softly modulated tones accompanied by the plaintive creak of wagon wheels muting words that were meant for no others to hear.

They talked indifferently of the events of the past few weeks, of their husband's part in it all, and of his recent moods. It was clear that Iron Horse's thoughts now focused on the boy.

Moves First whispered to her sister, "Do you remember when Annie was born and our husband could hardly hide his disappointment that it wasn't a man-child you had given him? Do you remember how many days he waited before accepting that it was the will of the Great Spirit to give him a girl-child? Have you seen his eyes when Iron Horse looks upon the boy, and do you see the same hope as I?"

"Yes, sister," replied Good Heart. "I too have seen the spark of hope in the eyes of Iron Horse, but we must be careful. While our hearts yearn to take him in, we cannot be hasty because we believe he has no family. Though his parents may be dead, others may have a greater claim to him than we. We should hope to restore him to them. Besides, he is grievously sick and may not survive. Let us not encourage our husband too soon to look upon this man-child as his own. Let us take him into our hearts and bring him back to health, and then, if no one claims him, we'll give him to our husband as from us both."

There would be no more learning about his parents for now. John hadn't mentioned them, and it was inappropriate to ask. Instead, the sisters talked and planned, unmindful of the sleeping children, unmindful of the silent figure in front.

As the sun reached its peak, their wagon creaked across the little valley of Potato Creek for about a mile until they crossed near where it joined Little Potato Creek. The ponies' feet moved faster and higher, prancing joyfully as they pulled the wagon up the opposite bank and came to a stop at a low log home overlooking the rest of the valley. From this vantage point, Iron Horse could view most of the homes of friends and family. He noted that no smoke rose from other chimneys, and the emptiness told him that they were the first of their group to arrive home.

The women quickly set about reoccupying their home, setting a fire in the small iron cookstove and seeking fresh water from the creek. The children slept in the wagon until after Iron Horse released the ponies to the prairie. Once the women deemed the single room of their home warm enough, Iron Horse carried the still sleeping boy to a pallet near the stove where Annie promptly awakened him with her solicitations. The women noted the purple tones of his skin were slowly fading to a healthier, rosy copper, indicating they had successfully chased off the bone-chilling cold. As he stirred in response to Annie's chatter, they felt the first glimmer of hope that the man-child called John might make a full recovery.

CHAPTER 7

Carter's Journal

January 2, 1891

Potato Creek, Pine Ridge, South Dakota

I caught sight of Iron Horse just as their wagon slowed to a halt in front of their home. The women began unloading their belongings as a cold dread settled on my heart. I had yet to see Annie and waited impatiently, glad to finally see black smoke rising from the chimney. I knew the cabin was frigid after being empty so many days. The women continued unloading items, and I watched as Iron Horse lifted a bundle from the wagon and carried it quickly inside. I assumed it was little Annie and breathed a sigh of relief.

Not long after, Iron Horse meandered slowly to the schoolhouse. I greeted him at the door, waiting to hear for myself the details of what I'd heard only through rumors. Iron Horse refused to speak of what he had seen at Wounded Knee. Instead, he simply blurted, "I am so disappointed that many of my people refuse to accept the dangers of the Ghost Dance. I do not understand how they believe they can roll up the white man and his animals in their stinking pens and float them away. How can I lead them when their thoughts are so foolish?"

Lillian interrupted, bringing us coffee in her favorite porcelain cups. Iron Horse watched the steam rise, contemplating his words. "The white men write treaties only to break them. I cannot count the treaties our people have signed. But I can count the white camps I see in the Paha Sapa."

With that, he looked earnestly into my eyes as if I held the answer. I could only respond sadly, "My friend, I'm disappointed each time I travel to Washington. The leaders of the great chief do not understand the Indian's relationship to the land. They do not want to understand. They want the Indian to forget his past and live as white men live. I'm afraid they want to own all the Indians' land."

As we talked, he shared details. "The agent at Pine Ridge says it's my fault my people have lost so much. He said I should have learned to read and write the white man's words so I could not be fooled. He is wrong. I never signed a treaty, and I live by the laws of our people." His words poured out. "Now I have chosen a place on the white man's map that he says is mine. There are lines on the paper around where I must live, and the land outside the lines belongs to others. He said I must farm this land unless I want to sell it to a white man. I cannot farm, and if I sell my home, where will I go?"

I knew Iron Horse had no concept of land allotments. To him, no pencil mark could separate the land into pieces. All he knew was that his people believed they were defeated forever. Crazy Horse was gone, Sitting Bull was gone, and the white soldiers were once again killing women and children.

Iron Horse feared that his people would give up—not just their lands but also their pride, their joy in life, and their hope for the future. There were few chiefs left who had experience in battle. There were no buffalo to provide meat for a feast, hides for a tipi, bones for bowls and tools, nor dried meat for the winter. There were few elders left to share the tribes' stories around the fire. Too many children had been taken from their homes and no longer learned the history or traditions of their people. I could only sit and watch as my friend struggled to accept that a single day in December might be the final blow to his people.

At last, Iron Horse lifted his head and shared a vision with me. "This morning"—he looked far off as in a daze—"I arose from a night filled with dreams of dancers calling to the spirits to remove the white man from our lands. As I drifted in and out of the spirit world, my dream ended with a pair of deep-brown eyes staring into my own. Thick, black lashes curled from them upward like the tips of an eagle's wing. I knew they were a warrior's eyes." He paused, thinking I might ask for details, but I stayed silent. He went on, "The eyes were focused, calm, and patient, as if waiting for me to get up and go about my responsibilities for the day."

I listened carefully as he shared the story of the boy they found at Wounded Knee, of how they brought him home and were now praying he would be healed.

Abruptly, he ended the conversation. Lillian brought us a plate of biscuits and freshened our cups with hot coffee. Later, Iron Horse walked back towards Potato Creek. I slumped in my chair, accepting the news of the massacre as truth, wondering what the leaders in Washington would do next, and puzzling over what a vision of warrior's eyes might mean to us all.

CHAPTER 8

Checking on Family

January 4, 1891

Pine Ridge Reservation, South Dakota

Iron Horse spotted his ponies quickly. Their rumps were smooth as mushroom tops, tails hanging still, muzzles buried deep in the tough, overgrown winter grass of the valley. Instinct told them someone was watching. Their heads lifted in unison and turned his way, a nicker of greeting coming from the lead mare. Recognizing Iron Horse's scent, Wichapi raced across the space separating them, and he gladly accepted a nuzzle from the sure-footed bay mare that was his favorite.

He reassured her by rubbing the glistening white star on her forehead that was half hidden by the heavy mane of her forelock. He didn't want Wichapi to think she wasn't still his favorite as he crooked his elbow under the neck of a solid chestnut standing nearby. Iron Horse slipped his rope around Tadita's nose and lifted it over her ears to lead her from the group. He needed her speed and sure step today to cover the expanse of their camp as he checked to see who had made it home and how the families of his tribe had fared.

He'd seen Plenty Bear and White Fox come in late the evening before, but Iron Horse would have to wait to know if any in his camp had suffered. It was obvious from the matted grass and muddy trails through the entry of the valley that others had passed through, but Iron Horse couldn't tell who they were.

He grabbed a handful of mane at the mare's withers and swung himself onto her back, not bothering to use a blanket for padding. He urged the little mare with a squeeze of his heels, and she broke into a steady trot, carrying him to check on his friends and extended family. The district sub-agency was fifteen miles to the southwest on Medicine Root Creek, with its day school and a combination trader's store and post office nearby. Just across the White River to the northeast lay the town of Interior, South Dakota, comprised mostly of white people with cow camps scattered around an extensive range of prairie. To the south on Corn Creek was the neighboring Indian camp with its own day school and trader's store.

Corn Creek was home to Aaron Moss, an Indian ordained as a Lutheran minister. He had attended the day school, then moved on to boarding school and ultimately to seminary. Now successfully settled back on the reservation, he presided over his own church in the community.

East of this was the home of Jake Farmer, a squaw man who had seized and settled the richest portion of the area when many like him had been banished from the reservation years ago. There was no record of how he managed to get his hands on this allotment, but many suspected money had been exchanged under the table. His home included multiple springs, a large growth of cottonwoods, and abundant pasture. Jake had made the most of his opportunity. He had an abundance of cattle that Iron Horse suspected were removed discreetly from various ration deliveries ahead of the herd's arrival each year at the agency.

Iron Horse didn't travel over the entire area. He cared only to know that most of his band was home or safely en route. Hearing no word of injuries or deaths, he gave thanks to the spirit that had protected his family from the fate of those at Wounded Knee and hurried home to check on the progress of the injured boy.

CHAPTER 9

Carter's Journal

Winter to Early Spring 1891

Potato Creek Day School, Pine Ridge, South Dakota

    My training told me that returning to school would help the children get back into a routine that would benefit all of us after the massacre. I knew the twenty-three pupils at Potato Creek Day School both loved and loathed our school at various times. Overall, during my time with them, they were a merry, bright-minded group of pupils just like could be found at any American school of the day. Yet at the close of school hours, I sensed they felt nothing but relief as they hurried home. A few seemed reluctant to come to school each morning, preferring to stay home and sit with their elders, listening to often told but ever new stories of long ago.

    Away from school, the boys were free to gallop their ponies across the prairie, dig wild turnips and hunt for birds' nests in the spring, gather buffalo berries and wild plums in the fall, or trail rabbits and trap prairie chickens in the snows of winter. The girls learned the art of cooking and seasoning food over the fire and caring for younger siblings under the watchful eyes of their mothers and aunts. For generations, Indian children had enjoyed a carefree and open-air life. It was the foundation of their culture, and many of them were reluctant to give it up. But there were fewer and fewer rabbits to hunt or berries to pick, and there was little joy for dancing. Starvation was an ever-present enemy on many parts of the reservation. Because of this, the noonday lunch prepared each day at the school was a welcome exchange for the loss of their freedom.

    The scrawny, spotted cattle delivered to the reservation for beef didn't have enough sense not to wander across the prairie nor wooly coats to protect them through the frozen winter. Seldom did they survive long enough to feed the families, and there was little enough else for the people to eat, especially during years of drought. However, because of monies budgeted for education of the Indians, the school had some form of protein for every meal, whether it came from the lean beef of our provisioned cattle or a plump cockerel plucked and cooked to perfection after fattening on corn in the pen behind the schoolhouse. In the spring and fall, there were fresh vegetables, including lettuce, radishes, peas, and beans picked daily from the school garden. Throughout the winter, there were potatoes, parsnips, carrots, and onions to give a starchy strength to every recipe. The seeds were part of my ordered provisions and not readily available across the reservation, so we ate better than most at Potato Creek Day School.

Even more welcome than the food, though, school seemed to provide the children with a social outlet that many of them no longer had at home. The allotment system left families scattered miles apart, breaking up the social system that was the foundation of Lakota life. Because we had no children of our own, Lillian and I adored each child we encountered and knew our feelings were usually returned a hundredfold. We worked through the year to visit every family and tried to earn the respect of the older Indians as well as build good relationships within the community as a whole. Here at the school, we tried to make everyone feel as if they were family.

With her timid manner, sunny spirit, and fragile constitution, Annie Iron Horse was a particular favorite of Lillian's. In years past, Annie had always been the first to come running to the clanging of the school bell, but on this particular Monday morning, she was still not present when it was time to start our lessons.

I asked Lillian to walk down to the chief's cabin to check on both children while the students and I finished our morning recitations. When Lillian arrived at the door, Annie herself invited her in.

"I'm sorry, Mrs. Heath, but I don't want to come to school today. I have more important things to do."

Lillian sensed she downright resented even the thought of coming to school this particular morning.

"My dear Annie, what could possibly be more important than coming to school?" chided Lillian good-naturedly.

"I must care for the injured boy we found at Wounded Knee Creek. You must meet him," Annie responded pertly, pulling her teacher towards the back room of the cabin. From the expression on his face as they entered, it was apparent that the little girl's sympathies had already formed a strong bond between them. Lillian also realized that the oozing sores and raw, peeling skin on his frostbitten feet would keep him in bed for quite some time.

As Good Heart entered the room to greet Lillian, Annie turned to her mother with a pout. "May I stay home today and take care of the boy? Mr. Heath will not care as long as he knows I'm doing a good deed."

"No, child," replied Good Heart. "Moves First and I will be careful with him, and when you return, you may take over his care. You know how proud your father is that you can read and write. It would grieve him if you missed school."

Good Heart went on to share with Lillian that the boy knew some English but could neither read nor write. Annie was taking immense pleasure in teaching him the names and forms of the letters and adding to his vocabulary. Sure enough, as the older women stood chatting, Annie propped herself on the end of the boy's pallet with her slate and pencil, playing at being his teacher. He concentrated eagerly on everything she said.

Good Heart shared that the children spent countless hours doing this every day. Lillian overheard Annie promise the boy that when she returned from school, she'd bring him a slate and pencil and teach him to write.

"Go, Annie," he instructed her, "and when you come back, tell me all about the boys and girls and teach me what you learn today. Do not forget the slate and pencil."

So, Annie headed back to school with Lillian, excited to tell the others about the injured boy in her home.

Returning home that afternoon, Annie carried the coveted slate and pencil as I walked along with her to see if I could be of service to the family. Upon my arrival at Iron Horse's home, John immediately stepped painfully forward and introduced himself: "Good day, Mr. Heath. I am John," he said proudly before focusing eagerly on the items behind Annie's back. Hearing the name "John," I was sure he'd attended a school at some point where he'd been given a name the white teachers could pronounce. I was impressed by his manners and his clarity in speaking the English language. He may not have known many words, but his enunciation of those he spoke was remarkable.

Seeing no sign of serious illness, I replied cheerfully, "Good day, John. I see you know who I am, and I'm eager now to enjoy your company in my classroom as soon as possible."

The winter days passed quickly, the sun lengthening its path each day across the sky. Annie divided her waking hours between her charge at home and her activities at the day school. Every new detail she learned, she took home to John. He eagerly absorbed everything. I dropped by frequently, watching John as he worked to grasp the letters and words, practiced his writing, and studiously listened to all the rules whenever Annie switched his lessons to arithmetic. It appeared he focused determinedly on learning while blocking any memories of his past.

The boy's survival had to be reported to the agency in order for any living relatives to claim him. I spoke with Iron Horse about the inevitable and agreed to go along with him on the trip. We picked an early spring day to travel to the main agency at Pine Ridge to report his finding the boy. Once the story had been recorded by the government agent, I knew it would become a topic of conversation at every gathering and family get-together across the reservation. The agent assured us that if any family from the clan of Big Foot claimed to be missing a young boy, the agent would tell them where to find him in the camp of Iron Horse.

Back home, I visited the cabin often. As John's feet healed and the layers of his physical injuries peeled away, I saw some of the darkness lift from his eyes. Although he had never shared anything of his experiences, he informed us one evening that his nightmares had ended, and that he was looking forward to what each new day would bring.

Despite many people learning of John's presence in Iron Horse's home, no word came of any others' interest in him. Early one evening, over a steaming cup of coffee, Iron Horse shared with me his hopes that the Great Spirit intended this child to become a part of his family. I couldn't disagree and prayed fervently that it would be so.

CHAPTER 10

John's Adoption

April 23, 1891

Potato Creek Camp, Pine Ridge Reservation, South Dakota

Late spring brought all the glories of the season to the Dakota prairie landscape. The incomparable colors of the native grasses, from the brilliant greens of wild rye to the deep blue greens of the fluffy-headed bluestems, were highlighted by the brilliant orange pollen of the grama grass before blending at the soil's surface with the drying yellows of the switchgrass that had fed the birds all winter. These waves of color had sprung for successive ages from the same mother sod that now gleamed, lavishly decorated with the purples of pasqueflower, the tall pink spikes of fireweed, and the yellow balls of tansy. Added to the dazzling colors, the subtle fragrance of flowers and soil made the whole a statement of nature's eloquence.

The animals grazing the range were sleek and content, giving birth in secluded corners across the prairie now that grazing was secured. Life was easygoing, at least until the heat of summer blasted the plants and baked their leaves to a barely edible crunch. The children at the day school were eager to be relieved of the tedium of the classroom and free to enjoy summer pleasures. Carter divided his time between carefully tending the school garden and checking on those of his neighbors. Little plots of tilled ground around many of the family homes were moist from the spring rains and green with the promise of edible returns.

On a warm, still evening, Iron Horse picked up his ceremonial robe and carefully fingered the beadwork forming a graceful line down the center of the back. It was made from the lighter-weight summer hide of a large buffalo bull and was older than himself. He ran his hand lovingly over the bold reds and yellows of the circular design painted carefully on the shoulder section. The orb radiated out from the beaded center, reaching towards the exterior where red and brown bars and arrows decorated the edges of the entire robe.

Although the evening was warm, Iron Horse added a heavily quilled and beaded shoulder cape over the longer robe, smoothing it over his elbows and down his sides. His news would mark a momentous occasion for his family, and Iron Horse wanted to look his best. He had braided his long hair, wrapping each strand carefully with strips of red trade cloth and finishing with an intricately beaded headband. Brightly beaded leggings and soft moccasins completed his attire. Satisfied with his appearance, he made his way across the creek near his cabin to the top of the butte where he could be seen and heard by all the members of his band.

The sun, settling to the west, cast him in striking silhouette when his deep voice resonated across the valley. "On the third day from this sunset, there will be a feast for all at the dance house below my cabin on the creek."

Those who heard nodded, knowing such an announcement foretold a significant event for the camp. The invitation would be spread from neighbor to neighbor until even the most distant families had heard the news. As soon as he finished speaking, Iron Horse pulled his robe closer and carefully made his way down from the prominence and into his home. He gave no reason for the feast, and no one asked because even if they wondered, it was not the nature of his people to show their curiosity or be rude enough to question another's reasoning.

The dance house sat a short distance from Iron Horse's home in the seclusion of the trees along the creek. Its stacked log walls topped out at nine feet. The smoke hole in the center showed the tips of the long poles that made up the roof. These poles sloped down towards the sides and were supported by numerous forked poles that helped hold the weight of the sod roof covering the rest of the structure. Its octagonal shape easily spanned over forty feet, and Iron Horse knew most, if not all, members of his band would fit inside.

Late afternoon on the day of the feast, the Indians began gathering near the dance house. Those from nearby houses came on foot. Word had spread all across the valley that Iron Horse was hosting a feast. In these times of scarcity, it was an auspicious event. Families from more distant homes and friends from still greater distances came in their wagons with their tipis, prepared to camp overnight. As an evening chill settled in, the older Indians began to make themselves comfortable around the log fire blazing under the opening in the roof. The men set themselves apart from the women. Children played in an open area on one side of the building, and white courting blankets covered the forms and faces of the young men who might seek a private moment with a young woman of their choice.

Eventually, Iron Horse entered, taking a place in the group of men while One Feather recounted an experience from long ago. When One Feather finished his story, he was handed a lit, carved stone pipe filled with fresh tobacco. He inhaled and exhaled several times slowly, releasing the blessing of the smoke to the sky above before passing it on. Hollow Head shared a memory from his childhood as the women settled the children in the back. Moves First and Good Heart, each wearing her finest dress of soft, tanned deer hide beaded across the shoulders, hustled back and forth to the cabin repeatedly, bringing forth a bountiful feast.

Several pots of steaming, savory beef stew and mounds of freshly made Indian bread on large wooden platters sat near the fire. There was also a large boiler of black coffee. None of the preparations performed by the host's wives interfered with the conviviality of the other women. Only when the youngest members of the party were seated quietly among their elders did several women begin assisting the wives of Iron Horse, serving the feast with the cups, plates, and utensils that every family had brought with them.

While the feast was in progress, the families relaxed and exchanged good-natured banter. When the meal was done, the carved pipe was pulled once again from its decorative bag, and the men gathered again to share its blessings. Mothers made comfortable their younger children, most of whom were soon sound asleep.

Plenty Bear, one of the older members and a leading man of the band, took a position near the center of the circle and addressed the assembly, Iron Horse in particular. He told of the appreciation he and those gathered felt for the generosity of Iron Horse in giving the feast, and for the good fellowship shown by all. Plenty Bear raised his hand into the air and spoke to the people.

"When Iron Horse and I were young, we rode our ponies across the prairie and hunted buffalo for our families. We rode with the warriors to fight the Pawnee, stole many ponies, and burned many lodges. We found one of the Sacred Medicine Arrows and returned it to our friends, the Cheyenne. We defended our Sacred Black Hills from white settlers, and both of us have fasted and performed the Sun Dance many times. Iron Horse has traveled to the east and spoken before the white leaders in Washington, and I fought the Long Knives at the Battle of the Greasy Grass."

His words were not braggadocio but rather reminded his listeners that he and Iron Horse were men of standing in the tribe. The stories served to refresh memories from the past and to confirm the leadership skills of Iron Horse and Plenty Bear. At the conclusion of his address, he resumed his seat, and his listeners uttered expressions of approval.

Plenty Bear was followed by two other speakers, who received similar attention and the same token of approval. Finally, Iron Horse advanced into the center with his robe drawn closely about him. He was an imposing presence as he stood silent for a moment before his friends and neighbors, with a bearing and dignity all his own. His people knew him as a man of some years past sixty, tall with a long, slender nose and well-formed though not prominent features covered with rich, bronze-colored skin that showed only a slight wrinkling. His black braids fell almost to his waist, and his deep-set eyes shone with the spirit of integrity and pride that was known and respected in their leader.

He began in a well-modulated voice. "Friends, my heart is glad. It is good to have my friends around me so we can remember the days when we all knew happiness. I fear that time is gone. We are forced to live a new life that is strange to us. When I look across the prairie, I see no buffalo. Our children return from the white man's school speaking the white man's tongue and wearing the white man's clothes. Sometimes, they do not return at all, and we are not told where they've gone.

"We elders cannot forget the old days, nor can we live the life of the white man. We do not want to know his religion, for we have our own, and it is all we need. We must be patient, for it will not be as long as we have already had here on Grandmother Earth before we join the spirits of our ancestors. There will be herds of buffalo as far as we can see, and there we will live the old life and be happy. But our children cannot live the old life. They must live and learn the white man's ways. They must talk the white man's tongue. They must go to the white man's school and learn the white man's books. It is good for them to know the white man's God and his religion. We must encourage them to do these things, but they must never forget they are not white and must teach their children the ways of our people."

Iron Horse lowered his voice. "My friends, I am an old man. Some of us were young together. When I was young, I was a brave warrior and a great hunter. I wanted a son that would be like me and that would live after me. But the Great Spirit did not give the answer I wanted to my prayers. I have a daughter and I love her, but she is not a son.

"You know that I found a boy alone in the snow at Wounded Knee. He was all but dead, and my wives brought him to my home and fed and cared for him. The night we found him, the Great Spirit gave me a vision. I saw the spirits of the dead at Wounded Knee where they died, and I heard their death songs. The Great Spirit made me hear the cry of the boy I had found. I have tried to find his people, for I wanted him to be listed with his real family, but it has been many months, and none of his people have come for him. I know now that the Great Spirit has given him to me for a son. I take him as my own. He will live in my home as my child. He will be brother to my daughter and son to my women. He will be one of my people. That is why I have made this feast tonight and why my heart is glad."

As Iron Horse finished speaking, he looked around the dance house at the stoic faces of his people. No evidence of approval or disapproval was offered by his listeners; it was not their way to show emotion. But he knew in his heart they were happy for the addition to his family, especially a man-child, and he returned to his place among the older men and waited, saying nothing. Finally, Crow Dog, an elder chief from one of the neighboring bands, rose and clasped hands with Iron Horse. He turned back to the group and, in the raspy voice of an ancient one, spoke for those assembled and for all Indians on the reservation.

"I have been friend to Iron Horse for many years, and we have seen many changes in our world. Iron Horse has always been fair and just to his people and honest in his dealings. He has been generous to those in need and wise in his dealings with the white man. For this, he is respected wherever he goes."

Raising his arms above his head, Crow Dog declared as if to the universe, "It is fitting that Iron Horse should have a son to follow him. The spirits have guided him, knowing the people would approve of him taking this child into his home as his son." When he finished his remarks, the heads of all those surrounding them nodded in approval and genuine satisfaction. Everyone knew this was right: so the formal adoption of the boy was accomplished in the traditional way, and he came to be known as John Iron Horse.

CHAPTER 11

Summer Celebration

Summer 1891

Pine Ridge Reservation, South Dakota

The morning bell of the day school ceased its insistent summons, and the Indian children's freedom was at hand. Iron Horse saddled Tadita for the trip to the Pine Ridge Agency to have his son's name officially entered into the tribal rolls. As the mare covered mile after mile at a smooth, tireless trot, Iron Horse wrestled with emotions ranging from the greatest joy to an equally great amount of trepidation. The relationship between father and adopted son grew stronger each day, and Iron Horse feared the possibility that someone from the reservation north of them might still hold a better claim to his custody than they.

Another name on the rolls meant an additional forty acres of land for the head of household as well as additional rations and cattle for the family. A distant relative might claim John in order to enjoy those benefits, but Iron Horse's feelings for the boy had nothing to do with allotments or rations. John had filled a great emptiness in his heart, and the boy's loss would have brought the aging chief unbearable grief. Iron Horse knew too that his loss would bring even greater pain, if that were possible, to his two wives.

But their grief would seem like a smoldering cinder compared to the raging flames of pain it would bring to Annie and John. Such an upheaval would remove the light from their day. It was common to see the two sitting together under the trees, their heads almost touching as Annie pointed out the spelling of a difficult word or posed arithmetic problems to the boy while he gripped his pencil and slate tightly in the struggle to master the lessons. Their companionship reflected their parents' love for the son that had been given to them. In return, John's love for his father was reverential. For the two quiet women who had so readily taken him into their care and then into their hearts, his love welled up from the depths of his soul. He had no memories of another family or home and wished it to remain so.

The wound from the bullet and the damaged skin from the frostbite healed completely, leaving nothing more than a small, round, white scar on John's back, tiny rays of pink radiating from the center like the symmetrical branches of the snowflakes that fell at Wounded Knee. He was growing into a handsome boy, tall with slender proportions and a frank, open countenance that showed intelligence, animation, and a higher-than-average capacity for thought.

The other boys around the camp often discriminated against him in their childish ways, tripping him during races, bumping his arm as he took aim in an arrow-shooting contest, or tossing a rock just as he launched his spear towards a fish in the creek. They laughed at their own tricks and called him names when he failed to respond to their taunts. John wasn't ready to confront anyone and didn't want to complain to his new family, so he kept to himself and found contentment at home in the companionship of Annie and his parents.

To encourage John to be more active and strengthen muscles weakened by weeks of healing, Iron Horse gave him his own Palouseye mare, a blue roan with black spots across her loin and hips, a jet-black mane and tail, and white flecks across her shoulders. She was a valuable horse that would pass on the rare blue-gray color and black markings, giving John prestige within the tribe and across the reservation. She would also be of immense value in the white man's world, for the Palouseye horses were known for their stamina and speed. John named her Hantaywee, or "Faithful," and rode her frequently, galloping with the wind in his face, balancing his seat and grasping her ribs with his long legs. He was at ease on the pony's back, as if he'd spent hours riding in the past, yet he couldn't conjure a single memory of past rides nor of horses he'd ridden before Hantaywee. His only memories of the past were of Annie's smiling eyes and the warmth of Moves First's blanket as she lifted him from the snowy ground.

By July, John had become a familiar figure streaking across the prairie, puffs of dust rising and settling as Hantaywee's hooves pounded across the grassland. Iron Horse took John with him on many trips—out to the prairie to check on their pony herd or to the timber for firewood or to the subagency twice a month for the family's rations. They went on social visits to the neighbors and to several more-distant camps. Wherever they went and whenever he could, John emulated his adoptive father in every way. His erect posture and quiet manner, his thoughtful silence before answering a question or sharing an idea, and the unaffected dignity of his carriage and demeanor would have convinced any who didn't know their story that he was in fact the true son of Iron Horse.

The families of Potato Creek camp always joined the annual summer celebration that coincided with the white man's Fourth of July. This celebration of the summer solstice had actually been held for generations and was particularly important for the Lakota. Many elders carried scars from the skewers that had pierced the skin of their chests when they sacrificed for healing and blessings for their family in the Sun Dance. The government had outlawed the Sun Dance, but the agents could do nothing when the Indians appeared to be celebrating the birthday of an ever-expanding nation.

This year, the celebration was held on Porcupine Creek. Everyone from Pine Ridge as well as visiting Indians from neighboring reservations would be there. Iron Horse, Moves First, and Good Heart knew that in another day or two, Potato Creek would be deserted. But John's new family made their preparations with reluctance. Even though there wasn't a single detail to delay them, the family went by way of a road that was longer than any of those traveled by their neighbors. No one spoke of their hesitancy, but they shared a mutual feeling of apprehension, a fear that their happiness might end if they were to encounter someone with a kinship claim to the boy called John.

When at last they came to the sprawling camp of over five thousand Indians, they set up their tipi in its appointed place and entered into the life of the celebrants with as much joy as possible. The camp was set on a wide stretch of open prairie in the form of an immense circle and contained a riot of color and activity from early dawn until late into the night. The older Indians dressed in their finest attire—fringed leather leggings and moccasins, beaded and painted deerskin shirts with long, fringed sleeves, their shoulders draped with shawl-like necklaces made from pipe beads, leather, intricate quillwork, and the occasional colorful trade beads.

The men distinguished their attire with feathered headdresses that ranged from a few simple feathers wound into long black braids to beaded headbands adorned with eagle feathers secured across the top and into long, trailing tails that draped to the heels of their beaded moccasins. Compared to the men's attire, the women's layered dresses were a cacophony of sound, the smooth leather covered from neck to hem in elk teeth that clattered and clicked with the rhythm of the swaying fringe as they danced in circles to celebrate the season.

The younger members of the tribe dressed in a curious mixture of the old and the new, for many had already spent time away at boarding schools and had more of the white man's clothes than anything like their parents'. The girls wore cotton print dresses, sometimes with ruffled aprons. Here at the celebration, most added a pair of leather leggings beneath their dresses, for they enjoyed the races as much as the boys, and dresses had to be hiked above their hips if they wanted to win a race. Many of the boys wore white shirts and dark-colored trousers, uniforms from school that tore in the rough-and-tumble of chasing rabbits and wrestling.

The ponies were equally glorious in appearance, with brightly painted symbols covering their bodies. Yellow circles around their eyes focused their vision, a sun symbol summoned clear weather for the hunt, and straight painted arrows ensured success on their pursuit. Black or blue handprints indicated their rider had accomplished a mission, but red handprints were reserved for warriors old enough to have killed an enemy in battle. The elders of the tribe rode bareback, while those considered middle-aged draped their horses with deerskin or more precious pieces of buffalo or wolf hide, treasures from the past. These were elaborately beaded, and long fringe dangled along both sides of their ponies. The saddles of the youths, if they used anything at all, were gaudy striped pads of woven wool or cloth from their boarding school.

The tipis at the ceremony comprised a celebration of their own, artistically ornamented to share details of the families' pasts. Whether made of ancient hides or modern canvas, each was covered with paintings of buffalo, herds of ponies and deer, depictions of battle scenes, jagged lines of lightning, or the rising sun. Information was carried from one part of the camp to another by criers running from the open grassland to the cedar and pine forests along the creek and into the moist, low-lying areas, announcing to all the schedule for the day. There was dancing and courting among the young and always something delicious available around the cookfires of the women.

Everywhere were games of butterfly hide-and-seek, teaching the girls to move quietly around others and to leave no trace of their passage over the land; and the bean game, called Vaputta, where rows of young boys and girls tried to guess who held the colored bean, taught all the children to focus on tiny movements as one team took a bean in hand and moved down a row of teammates, sliding their closed hands between the closed hands of the others, dropping the bean at some point down the line and asking the opposing youngsters to guess who had it.

This was Annie's favorite, and she watched everyone closely, trying to see the slightest movement of the hands. There were no prizes for these games other than the bonds of friendship built on memories of fun, food, and everyone together celebrating the sun and their blessings as families.

Some of the games, such as buffalo wheel, where the boys tried to throw their stick spears through the center of a rolling wheel, taught hunting skills. Although John had a good eye and was strong and accurate, he felt he was too old for this game and reminded others that it was not a skill they needed for the future. The older boys and men wagered on the outcomes of games and races, and the losers had to pay up with anything from knives to ponies. Those who participated in the games made fun of John and called him a coward for not competing, but although John knew Hantaywee was fast, he would never have risked her in a race, for he knew her value, and not just on the reservation. He had listened carefully to his father and understood fully the worth of his pony in the white world as well.

Every morning for a week, they renewed the festivities until they exhausted themselves physically and depleted their supplies. When the celebration finally ended, the camp melted away, a long procession of wagons rumbling over the various roads leading away from Porcupine Creek.

Iron Horse and his family headed home with a sense of relief and gratification. Not only had no one stepped forward to claim John as family, but some of the headmen of the reservation to the north had sanctioned the adoption of John, as had the chiefs of the various bands on his own reservation.

As summer ended, one more tradition signaled that school would begin again in a few short weeks. On a sultry Sunday evening, Iron Horse recognized the team of gray ponies belonging to Aaron Moss, the native preacher, coming up the hill from the south as the school bell sounded over the prairie. As far as it could be heard, the tolling bell invited the Indians to come and worship according to the rites of the white man's church and to learn the teachings of the white man's religion.

Aaron was a member of their own tribe and held in high esteem by the older Indians as well as by the young. When he was a small boy, he'd been taken into a missionary family before the end of his first year in boarding school and sent to Augustana College and Seminary, where he finished his education and was ordained for the ministry. After ordination, he felt called to return to the reservation to serve his own people.

He served a large district, and he made the arduous journey across the reservation from his home on Corn Creek as frequently as conditions required and time would permit. He set about teaching the Christian faith quietly and was always respectful of the deeply rooted prejudices of the older Indians. He'd drawn a large number of communicants to his fold. Though most were younger, it was common for him to be summoned to console the older Indians in their last days or to conduct funeral services for those who had never acknowledged his faith. These occasions showed the warmth of the tribe's regard for him as well as the depth of their spirituality.

Everyone gathered at the Potato Creek schoolhouse that warm summer evening, and as the service began, the building filled with Indians of every age. Others, for whom there was no room inside, crowded around the open windows. It was a quiet congregation that listened attentively to the preaching of one of their own, as he told in their own tongue the teachings of Christ. He talked of the truths in the Great Book plainly and simply, avoiding anything that might be taken by his listeners as argumentative. He pointed out the advantages of living from day to day with a desire to serve good and related to his listeners the promise of a better and happier life to come. He stressed the similarities between their native religion and the one by which he lived as he worked to win the confidence of all the people he served. At the conclusion of the service, he visited with as many people as he could. He was eager to meet John Iron Horse, of whom he had heard from others in his travels.

Seeing the boy standing beside Iron Horse in the back of the crowd, Aaron approached, his hand outstretched. "So, this is the son of Iron Horse. I'm extremely happy to meet you, my friend. May you always be a comfort to your father. I pray that you will be as good a man as he."

Aaron spoke slowly and carefully in the Indian way. John appreciated Aaron's respect for his adopted father and for their native religion. Although he didn't yet know which beliefs he would follow in the future, John sensed this was the beginning of a long association with the Christian preacher.

One morning, not long after Aaron's monthly visit to the camp, John and Annie were playing in the shade of the timber around the dance house. There, they could indulge in speaking English without the constraint they felt in the presence of their parents, while remaining within calling distance if needed. To speak in the white man's tongue not only was an insult to those who couldn't comprehend their words but also served as a painful reminder that the old ways of the Lakota would soon be replaced by the ways of the white man.

Despite his limited vocabulary when he first arrived at Potato Creek, John worked hard to show his appreciation for Annie's efforts and quickly became almost as proficient as she. Annie had been in school for five years and loved to converse in the language she'd worked to master. The two spent hours discussing everything from the heat of the day to whether any of their friends had practiced the white man's tongue over summer break. John was curious as to his sister's thoughts of a future away from the reservation. He knew some of the children who went away to school never came home, and he had done much reflection over his own future.

Suddenly, John put a common question to his little sister. "Annie, what are you going to be when you are grown?"

After only a slight hesitation, she replied confidently, "I would like to be like Mrs. Heath. I want to be good like she is, and I would like to teach boys and girls to be good and to do good things. But," she added with a wisdom beyond her age, "I would not like to be a white man's wife, for I would feel that my children would be part strangers to me."

John understood her love for the woman who had taught her a new language and many skills that would be useful in a home like the Heaths', yet he also understood her hesitancy to want a mixed-blood child. He knew that if she became a teacher in the white man's world, she might likely face that decision.

As he pondered her wisdom, Annie returned his question: "And what are you going to be when you are a man?"

Without hesitation, he responded, "I believe the Great Spirit allowed me to live when others died and allowed you to find me so that I could live with Iron Horse and his family and go to school. I also believe he's taken the memories of my other family so that I do not look back and wish for the past. I want to be a good man like our father, who follows the old ways with courage. But I also want to be like Aaron Moss and Carter Heath and seek out opportunities that come from the ideas of the white man."

He had no idea at that moment how these aspirations of a child would become the purposes of the man.

CHAPTER 12

Carter's Journal

Fall to Winter 1891

Potato Creek, Pine Ridge Reservation, South Dakota

Each morning, our pupils set their feet on the path to school—alone, in twos, or in small groups—and their purposefulness, their indifference, or their reluctance to be there was reflected in the manner of their arrival at our door. On one of the earliest days of September, Lillian grasped the school bell's rope, pulling hard. The black iron pealed a message across the camp, calling the children to come and learn.

Their attendance was compulsory, and as in all schools, some welcomed the lessons, while others were indifferently engaged. There were those who were eager to absorb everything and those who were satisfied with an existence that required little to no effort at all. As long as school provided a warm meal to counter the loss of their freedom, they would find contentment putting the least possible effort into their lessons. Unfortunately, to a few, school brought nothing but a sense of irritation and disaffection.

On the first day, Annie and John were the first to arrive. During my visits over the summer, I'd seen they were looking forward to the day. Rather than dragging their feet and weaving along the trail, they stepped quickly and straightaway from their pine cabin to the doorway of the schoolhouse, quickly informing me that they were weary of the tedium of summer and ready for the feeling of satisfaction that comes from accomplishment.

Lillian and I looked forward to our daily encounters with these two. Although we loved all our students equally, it was difficult not to be especially excited about John's first day of school. I'd watched him throughout the summer as he made friends within the community, and, despite the typical teasing of jealous age-mates, he was well liked by everyone. I knew that his attendance at school would help him feel equal to the other children.

Most importantly this year, we were especially excited to know we'd honed our parenting skills in preparation for our own child to arrive. Lillian informed me late one evening as we watched the sun set behind the butte.

Hugging me closely, she whispered, "My beloved, I know you'll make a wonderful father." As I stopped breathing temporarily and turned to face her, she continued, "Yes, dear, after all this time with the Indian children, God will bless us with our own. I believe he or she will arrive by spring."

Speechless and weak-kneed, I questioned, "Are you certain, my sweet? How long have you known?"

She assured me, laughing, "Yes, my husband, I'm quite sure. Haven't you noticed how slowly I rise each morning and how my biscuits don't sit well in my belly?"

I swept her into the air and carried her through the house before settling her carefully on the chaise and proceeding to list off the things she was officially forbidden to do until after the baby's arrival. She simply smiled, reminding me that she had many little helpers to assist her and informing me that I'd best not try to tell her what to do at this point.

Excited to share our news, I wired word straightaway to my family in New York. Rather than sharing our joy, Father demanded we return to New York immediately, expressing concern that the birth would occur in "the hinterland," as he referred to our home. Mother insisted the hospitals in the city were years more advanced than those on the reservation, and Father, as always, expounded on his opinion that my financial situation was insufficient for a family of our status. Tempted as I was to return east for the safety of my wife and child, the thought of my father's disdain for my life choices and concern that Mother would manipulate our stay into a longer time than necessary stopped me from securing my family's immediate return to New York.

Still, the prospect of a growing family increased my focus on a higher salary. Until that moment, I had refused to admit to myself that I was disillusioned with our work for the Office of Indian Affairs. I'd begun studying law several months earlier, imagining that my appointment to a position in Washington might be something Father would respect. Rumors out of Washington indicated that several positions were being reviewed. My superintendent had no insight into the politics involved, and no positions had been posted, but the thought of the increased income as well as direct intervention on behalf of the Indians tempted me to investigate the possibility of a transfer.

I wrote to Mr. Hitchcock at the Department of the Interior, inquiring about openings that offered a significant advancement in salary. He shared, confidentially, that a superintendent's position might become available in Oklahoma but warned that the school was overcrowded and underfunded, and the position would be difficult at best. There were no other openings that he knew of, and I determined for the time being to be content with the successes we'd achieved at Potato Creek.

Once classes began in earnest, I recognized John's unusual curiosity and eagerness to learn. Rather than being bitter after the trauma he'd experienced, John became a role model of living with a good attitude. He dedicated himself to learning everything he could. He proved daily that, despite what many people believed, Indian children were capable of learning equal to any other race and should be expected, and allowed, to take their place anywhere in American society. Seeing John's effort and attitude, I set my mind to proving to those who called the Indians "heathen" that, instead, they could become business owners, artists, bankers, or whatever position in life they chose to pursue.

Lillian experienced the typical mood swings of pregnancy, excited for the baby one moment, concerned for our future the next. My favorite evenings were spent with her leaned against my chest, her hand holding mine as we stroked her belly, overjoyed at the growing child inside. She suffered a few difficult weeks with morning sickness but eventually returned to her cheerful, healthy self. Her figure filled out, but she was adept at sewing and assured me she'd be able to alter her dresses and skirts as needed for several months.

She estimated her time of delivery to be late February or early March. We awaited the day eagerly, thankful the hottest months had passed before she grew too engorged to be comfortable. She walked daily to keep fit, but I forbade her to work in the gardens and flower beds, reminding her that the younger school girls had all the skills necessary and were quite capable of taking over the domestic chores.

As the nights became longer and colder and we were more often confined inside by the weather, I began to feel a bit of melancholy when the children were gone and Lillian preceded me to bed. The dark, quiet hours were my time to complete my records and catch up on correspondence from the East. Although Mother wrote weekly, she mentioned Father less and less. He was disappointed in my career and brooded over it most evenings, she informed me in one particularly despondent letter. She was excited about the baby but shared little about the family or events in New York. Finally, she stopped mentioning our returning east for the baby's christening or to see Father, but always poured out her concern for the primitive conditions of our home.

Another reality I slowly came to accept was that some of my students were prejudiced against our school before they ever darkened the doorway. With their families reduced to living on government handouts, many children saw no hope for anything different in their future. Although I complained to the highest officials at the agency and wrote numerous letters to Washington about the theft of cattle, beans, corn, and flour by the cowboys who delivered the rations or the agents whose job it was to oversee the distributions, my singular voice initiated no action from the bureaucracy. Most of the Indians refused to complain when they received less than half what should have been provided for them. Nothing I said convinced them to speak to the agents about shortages. Over time, I accepted that they were content with whatever was delivered, for half was better than nothing at all.

I also had to come to terms with the reality that my time with John was limited. He would be required to leave Potato Creek to attend a boarding school at fourteen. We worked diligently, and John stayed late many afternoons, for nothing would alter his mandatory transition away from his family. It was my duty to help him overcome his limitations and establish a solid foundation in his coursework. I redoubled my effort to challenge him with hours of work on his diction, reading for understanding, and penmanship. Eventually, John's skill with the English language surpassed that of all my other students. His speech gave no hint of his Lakota heritage, and I was pleased with his accomplishments.

I always enjoyed keeping my students sharp in their critical thinking with oral questioning on a wide range of topics. My favorite activity was to debate their answers, requiring them to explain their reasoning, a skill I felt equipped each of them with an ability for clear, logical, and reflective thinking. With critical questioning, I taught them to think through problems, pick out details and conflicts in writing samples, and complete complex math problems in their heads. This was my legacy to the Indian children and to John in particular.

CHAPTER 13

Carter's Journal

Winter 1891 to Spring 1892

Potato Creek, Pine Ridge Reservation, South Dakota

With its bitter wind and gray days, winter passed slowly at Pine Ridge. Ever grateful for our root cellar, we feasted on parsnips and potatoes seasoned with herbs and wildflowers the girls had dried over the summer. I grew more concerned about Lillian and the baby with each passing day. My wife tried not to gain more than the weight of the growing child, but the size of her swollen belly grew increasingly ponderous within the confines of our cabin. She paced from wall to wall but struggled to navigate the limited space. Heavy snows covered the yard, and her regular trips to the outhouse required me to serve as an escort along the slippery path.

I labored to keep the doorways clear and began to fear a sudden blizzard would limit our ability to seek help. I prayed for an early warming spell, longing for the appearance of dark patches of muddy, melting snow. Lillian remained confident that the camp midwife could perform any procedures needed for a healthy delivery, but I found myself questioning the wisdom of remaining at Potato Creek. Life on the frontier bristled with hazards, but I could not bring myself to ask Father for the money to return to New York. Nor could I accept the defeat of having my first child born under his dominance.

Adding to my worries, a new enemy appeared on the reservation. Despite the massacre of barely a year ago, men claiming to be Ghost Dancers wreaked havoc across the reservation. They habitually stole cook pots and clothing, trampled garden plots, and set fire to cabins whenever they came upon one. Some of their actions seemed to be nothing more than mischief, but eventually they threatened some families' very survival. While official policy identified them as disgruntled Indians, I felt certain they were white or mixed-blood men trying to force more Indians off their lands.

The number of soldiers present on the reservation increased almost daily. As many as three thousand soldiers patrolled the area regularly, claiming the need to bring justice to the miscreants. The government allotted money to compensate the Indians who had settled into reservation life for their losses. As long as the Indians farmed their land and their children attended school, Washington agreed to pay for any damages they incurred. This added to my teaching duties, for I was required to determine if any of my students' families had suffered damages, record the value of their losses, and complete the reports to file grievances against the outlaws.

In the first months, my report listed some unusual and frightening occurrences. At one family's home, the men rode through the front door of the cabin and into the family's living quarters, slashing through pictures on the wall directly over one of the children's pallets. At another home, they rode in circles around the cabin, repeatedly firing their rifles, shooting holes in the walls and shattering doors and windows with no regard to the women and children inside. Camp supplies were dumped into creeks across the reservation. Beef-drying racks were overturned and trampled. Herds of livestock, even from white ranchers, were driven off or slaughtered and left to rot. On my last trip to the agency, I realized that many families were living in tipis because they no longer felt safe in wooden cabins.

The superintendent expected my final reports before Christmas. His final total of claims for the agency was due in Washington before the end of January in order for those who had suffered to receive compensation. Although the monies were intended to mollify the Indians who tried to farm, I was certain the majority would end up in the hands of white ranchers and traders. The exhaustion of the additional work and the worry every time I heard riders in the vicinity of the school wore on my patience as the weeks passed. I tried to be thankful that we hadn't yet suffered damage to what we had built.

By Christmas, Lillian and I realized we had neither the means nor the materials to provide presents for all of the children. Instead, we strung cedar berries on strands of Lillian's sewing thread and tore strips of red trade cloth, tying droopy bows and hanging our motley decorations from the eaves of every structure. Each evening, I enjoyed time to reflect on our lives after Lillian went to bed. I found it heartwarming that despite the occasion being nothing like my New York memories of Christmas, the simplicity of this year's events and the anticipation of our own child would make this one of my favorite Christmases of all time.

In the afternoons, Lillian played the organ and sang with the children. From my view in my rocking chair, she resembled a New England crab stranded on dry land as she reached her arms across the spread of her belly, all while pressing the foot pedals at the base of the organ. It looked terribly awkward, but everyone enjoyed the music immensely. Christmas carols were her favorite, and the Indian children knew most of the songs by heart. They continued to come to the school despite the official holiday, and the schoolyard frequently reverberated with their enthusiastic singing of "Jingle Bells" and "Joy to the World."

We spent a quiet New Year's Eve sipping hot coffee sweetened with honey and fresh cream from our milk cow. Lillian made the most delicious coffee, taking care to serve it in her porcelain cups. I wondered why she risked the delicate pieces, but she reassured me that it made her feel like she was marking a special occasion, and the practice was important to her. In her honor, I grasped the tiny handle of that delicate little cup with my calloused fingers, winking at her over the rim and sticking my pinky high in the air, feeling significant satisfaction as she shook with laughter at my silliness.

Almost at the stroke of midnight, we heard the thunder of hooves and peered out the window to see a mob of riders brandishing torches as they raced in circles around the school. A single, flaming arrow shattered one of the glass windows we were so proud of and stabbed with a thud into the side of Lillian's beloved organ.

Dropping my porcelain cup with a crash, I pulled Lillian to her knees and pointed her towards our bedroom, hoping she could hide safely until the attack was over. As I ran to grab the rifle from its place over the mantle, the riders whooped loudly and steered their horses down the trail towards Iron Horse's cabin. I raced out the door, firing madly and hoping to see at least one of them drop from their saddles. After a few parting shots in their general direction and watching carefully to determine that the riders passed by Iron Horse's home, I dropped the rifle and ran inside to make sure Lillian wasn't hurt.

She sat propped against our bed, face in her hands, sobbing. Seeing no blood, I realized she cried for the loss of her organ and encouraged her to rise and help me extinguish the remaining flames. One curtain hung limply to the side of the instrument, glowing embers eating into the fabric. I jerked it down and tossed it through the now glassless window to land on the cleanly swept grounds outside. Turning, I found Lillian had dumped the remainder of our coffee over the arrow defiantly jutting from the side of her most treasured possession and was now pulling with all her might on what remained of the shaft.

Gripping the wood tightly behind her hands, I helped her remove the offending weapon and reached for a quilt that lay tossed on the floor. I handed her the heavy fabric, and we both held it firmly against the glowing edges of the arrow's entrance into the walnut. Tears flowed freely between us as she lovingly rubbed the wood. We both knew that although the blackened hole did not look like much, the organ was likely beyond repair, and certainly there was no one who could return it to its glory in this remote location.

Finally, we stepped outside, walking with a lantern around the schoolyard, checking for other damage. There were hoof-trodden flowers in the garden and a broken fence behind the barn. Other than those, we found no significant damage. Thankfully, the outhouses had apparently escaped notice. I guided Lillian to our room, helping her settle onto the mattress and snugging the covers tightly over her belly. As she cried herself to sleep, I sat down to record the event in my report and listened breathlessly, hoping never to hear the thunder of hooves in our schoolyard again.

Once the holidays were past, we tried to recapture a sense of normalcy through school and lessons. In my classroom, the students returned to English recitations and arithmetic. Lillian returned to teaching the girls in the kitchen and garden, showing them how to cull rotting produce from the racks on the root cellar before it could affect the rest of our stores. The boys helped me remove the blackened organ and hide it away in the back of the shop. Other than that, our industrial time was seriously curtailed by the number of reports I had to complete. In my absence, the older boys organized repair teams and made daily checks on our fences, ensuring that no cut wires allowed the cattle to escape. The students arrived early each day to feed and water the livestock and chickens, gather the eggs, and milk the dairy cow. The oldest boys kept a steady check on the rooftops of the stable and shop, making and replacing cedar shakes as needed, while the younger boys checked on the elders of the camp, carrying water bowls and firewood to those in need.

After the attack, I stayed close to our home for the remainder of the winter. Lillian struggled to rise from the mattress and preferred resting upright on one of the long, straight benches I brought from the girls' classroom. Occasionally, I found her sound asleep, her head resting between her arms, snoring softly over her distended belly. She assured me she was comfortable and that I shouldn't be concerned for the baby, but my heart stopped every time I saw her hand still as she stroked her belly.

I wondered at how magical it must be to feel a child growing within her. At other times, I would hear loud noises from the kitchen as if the dairy cow were delivering an oversized calf. The first time, I froze at the sound, fearing the baby was jammed in its path to the outside world, but I learned that rushing to my wife's rescue was totally unnecessary; she was surely the most independent woman I'd ever known. Every mad dash ended with my finding her beaming with pride at having lifted her immense dough bowl from its warming position under the stove to the top of the table where she stood, hands propped on her hips, smiling from ear to ear. Over time, I accepted that I was wasting my time worrying over her.

Finally, on a cold, windy day at the beginning of March, Lillian indicated it was time to send the children home from school and prepare ourselves for the birth of our child. She had stacked clean linens beside the bed for several weeks, and there was always a pot of water heating on the stove for that important moment. Unlike her husband, Lillian remained calm, breathing rhythmically in and out, rubbing her hands lightly over her swollen belly. After several hours of pacing and panting, she grasped my arm, sinking her fingers deep. Whispering through gritted teeth, she sent me to fetch Moves First or Good Heart—or better yet, both—to assist with the delivery.

The next hours I spent pacing the length of the boys' classroom, stopping only to listen for the telltale wail indicating my child had entered the world. When it finally came, I realized I'd been holding my breath for far too long. The next sound was a gentle knock on the classroom door as Moves First lifted a bundle towards me before pulling back the blanket to reveal the angry red face of my screaming daughter. Then, whisking her away, the woman signed that she would return the baby to her mother and help Good Heart clean and assist Lillian with nursing the squirming bundle.

I fell to my knees, clasped my hands beneath my chin, and looked up at the solid wooden cross mounted above the chalkboard. I prayed my thank-yous to the Lord for the arrival of my daughter and begged him to keep her mother in good health as well. With a quick "Amen," I hastened across the schoolyard, eager to hold my child. I counted her tiny toes time and again, kissing the velvet of her cheeks until Annie appeared from nowhere, admonishing me for scratching the baby's face with my stubbly beard.

Once news of our daughter's birth spread, all the families of Potato Creek came to visit. None came empty-handed, and our home soon filled with tiny, hand-carved horses, soft, rabbit-fur blankets, rattles, and woven-grass necklaces and bracelets. It was obvious that everyone was excited for the baby, especially Annie, who vowed to be our nursemaid and babysitter forever.

We named our daughter Elizabeth, Elizabeth Lillian. Thankfully, she settled quickly into a routine of nursing and sleeping and being held while adults conversed around her. Several of the older women of the camp came to sit with her, giving Lillian a much-needed opportunity to rest. About a month after her birth, a large package addressed to Elizabeth arrived from New York. I recognized Mother's embellished script and understood the gift was her way of saying it was okay for us to stay on the frontier. She would make sure her granddaughter wanted for none of the finer things in life. Fingers trembling, Lillian opened the wrapping and folded back the cover of the box to reveal the most beautiful green-and-gold porcelain tea set, just the size a toddler might invite her father to partake from on a sunny summer day on the prairies of South Dakota.

It was the first of many such packages we opened, but for the moment, Lillian reached her arm around me, squeezing hard while I squeezed her hand in return, knowing that despite its hardships, our life was blessed.

CHAPTER 14

Day School

Fall 1891 to Summer 1892

Potato Creek Day School, Pine Ridge Reservation, South Dakota

John learned from the agency superintendent that he'd most likely been born in a village too remote for the permanent operation of a day school. Although he'd been exposed to English through infrequent school sessions, and perhaps on trips to the agency with his family, he hadn't had the same daily instruction as the children at Potato Creek. He worried he'd missed too many lessons. In those moments of doubt, he always focused solidly on his desire to please his father and Carter Heath, and his need to prove he was a worthy role model for Annie.

On his first morning at Potato Creek school, John stood frozen at the front of the classroom, seeing the other children seated and ready for class, watching his every move. In his mind, he questioned whether he could accomplish what his heart was set on. It had not seemed so formidable through the summer doldrums, sitting with Annie as she repeated things he struggled to grasp. Now girls and boys much younger than himself were waiting to see what he would do, and suddenly, his abilities seemed inadequate.

Once he settled into the rhythm of daily classes, most days were a source of joy to John. He loved studying the world of the white man. He had the ability to comprehend the details of an idea while quickly assimilating it into his growing store of knowledge. The speed with which he learned and the questions he asked challenged his teacher to maintain a supply of materials for instruction. Carter's teaching methods included a constant back-and-forth of reflective questions that encouraged his pupils to think deeply. Although most of the boys learned only what they found of value, such as basic industrial skills, John soaked up every detail in his lessons, sharing them each evening with Annie, who was proud of his accomplishments.

The day school operated by the white man's calendar; so, for the first time, John celebrated the golden days of fall not with lessons about the moon and stars and setting aside stores for the winter but with a story about Indians and white men eating together and being thankful for the bounty of the harvest. Rather than observing the winter solstice, he learned the story of Christmas about a baby, shepherds, and gifts under a decorated tree. In spring, John learned about Easter rather than celebrating the renewal of life on the prairie.

He appreciated the days out of class sometimes, but the single thought John couldn't get out of his mind was that the white man's celebrations were part of a religion that taught its followers to love one another while forgiving those who killed Indian women and children.

Occasionally, John was discouraged by the demands of the educational process, yearning for life as the elders described it, carefree and idle. At those moments, he would go alone to a sequestered nook along the creek or take a long pony ride across the prairie. In the quiet, he could usually renew his resolve to learn the lessons that promised a better life than his people's hopeless dependency on the white man's handouts. But as the days grew warmer, John began to count down to summer and a long break from the unremitting confinement of school.

Carter, on the other hand, wished he could continue reaching his students throughout the summer; he knew how much would be lost by the months of freedom and indolence in the camp. He had to accept that the children needed time away from his overcrowded classroom, the hard labor of repairing and building at the school, and the rigid curriculum he set for them.

On the last day of lessons, like any thirteen-year-old, John sat eagerly looking out the windows and across the prairie to where the pony herd was grazing. He strained to see the flashing blue gray and black of Hantaywee. Knowing he'd made such rapid progress in his lessons that he was almost as advanced as Annie, he no longer saw himself as a child. He was ready to join the men's life on the reservation. He'd worked especially hard during calisthenics to build muscle and coordination and now stood taller and heavier than he'd been on that first day. He was eager to compete with his classmates in their summer games and contests.

As Iron Horse's children headed home that day, Annie trudged along reluctantly. In addition to missing her time in class, she knew in her heart she'd no longer share her brother's companionship as she had the summer before. Ambling towards home, the two discussed their plans for the summer.

"I'll stay at home to help the women, of course, and I hope to learn more of the beadwork my mother makes. But I dread the days when there is nothing to do, and I'll miss you when you're out with your friends instead of doing lessons with me under the trees."

Feeling only a little guilty, John replied, "I'm going to ride horseback with my friends every day. We'll explore the Bad Lands and follow the creek south. Maybe we'll even go to the White River to see what we can see." The White River marked the end of Indian country. "Of course, I'll help our father with the ponies and other work, but as soon as my work is done, I'll spend time with my friends on the open prairie. It's my favorite place."

Annie's shoulders drooped lower.

The first week of summer flew past. On several of his rides, John felt a sense of familiarity, as if he'd been to a spot before, but he steeled his mind against the memories, reminding himself that he was on a path he was destined to follow. Sometimes he ran footraces against the older boys, once winning a Palouseye colt and proudly adding him to the family's herd. John and his friends ventured into the Black Hills, but after two days of camping on hard ground, hunting prairie chickens, and searching for firewood, the boys decided there was nothing left of the beauty of that sacred place. Deep cuts into the earth, mud-stained creeks and streams, and the dirty camps of white miners scratching for the last few grains of gold so disheartened them that they returned early to Potato Creek.

After that, John's thoughts turned back to the promise that education held for his future. He had no idea what jobs existed in the white man's world, but he knew that being a teacher as good and caring as Mr. Heath would serve him well. He prayed nightly, even to the white man's god, that he could find the strength to learn everything possible until he was ready to follow in his teacher's footsteps.

CHAPTER 15

Difficult Conversations

Fall 1892

Potato Creek, Pine Ridge Reservation, South Dakota

Before summer was half over, John was weary of the summer's idleness. When school resumed, he entered his second year with a new eagerness that pleased his teacher tremendously. Although he wouldn't have described Carter as handsome in an Indian way, John recognized that his teacher was intelligent and respectful. Despite the precious nature of materials for the school, there were no outbursts of anger if a student cut a board wrong or broke a hinge from improperly tempering it at the forge. Working closely with only that student, Carter would quietly ask simple questions until the boy discovered, as if on his own, where the mistake had been made. The result was a student who learned from his mistake without being humiliated, thus building his confidence and enjoyment of the work.

John was most fascinated by the fact that despite being surrounded by Indians and married to a mixed-blood, Carter appeared to be totally comfortable in his own white skin. One afternoon, when he stayed late for extra lessons in arithmetic, John boldly inquired, "Mr. Heath, do you ever wonder what it would be like to be an Indian?"

Carter was serious by nature, and the question caught him off guard. He stopped writing on the board, pausing with his hand poised to finish the math problem he'd begun, before he turned to John and answered matter-of-factly, "No, I've never wondered what being an Indian would be like. I know the history of the Indian people and the tragedies that have been set upon them by the white man. But to wonder what it would be like to be an Indian, I would have to think that it is something different for a person with red skin to suffer than it is for a person with white skin."

As John pondered that response, Carter asked back, "Do you ever wonder what it is like to be a white man? I assure you I love the smell of Lillian's fresh biscuits, and my stomach grumbles when I haven't had one early enough in the morning. Doesn't yours?"

John scowled, trying to link this response to his original question, but when he looked up, Carter's contagious smile reassured him that the question had come from the heart.

"Of course," he responded quickly, "doesn't everyone's?"

Carter challenged, "Does your stomach grumble more because your skin is red, or is it more likely because you are growing tall and strong and need more food than your aging teacher?" Carter's quick wit was a trait the Indians particularly appreciated.

John laughed and retorted, "Surely it's because I'm younger and stronger than my teacher."

"I think that's the end of our math lesson for today, John. There is much more to talk about," said Carter. "Why do you ask?"

Pausing to organize his thoughts, John replied slowly as if thinking through every word before allowing it to escape into the room. "I don't know many white men, but I've seen many white soldiers, and most of them simply want to kill Indians. They ride past me, looking straight ahead, and don't acknowledge me when they pass. It's as if I'm not even there. You tell us the agent at Pine Ridge doesn't give us all our rations. Jake lives on Indian land, and when his sons are grown, they'll be given land that should belong to our people."

After a heavy pause, John continued, "You don't seem very different from me except that your skin is white and you were not born on a reservation. You have all the qualities I respect in a man. You are kind to everyone you meet. You are fair and honest with those you deal with. You weren't afraid to leave a city in the East and come here to the reservation to teach. You are educated and have traveled many places. You encourage your students to become educated and go out into the world. You've shared with our class that you may take a job away from Potato Creek because you need more money for your family. You called this a goal and encouraged us to set goals for ourselves."

Carter interrupted him, "But these things have nothing to do with the color of my skin."

John inhaled slowly before responding, "Don't they? I try to be fair, kind, and honest. I work hard in my classes and plan to go as far in my education as I can. Will I be able to travel as you have when I am through with school, or will I be expected to return to the reservation? If I work for a white man, will I be able to change my job when I wish to have something better?"

His teacher remained silent, so John continued, "You love your daughter, the same as Iron Horse loves Annie. Those things are the same no matter the color of our skin. It comes from our heart. All fathers feel these things, just as a stallion protects his family when the foals are born. I want to know how it would feel to be free to choose the other things in my life as you have been able to do."

Carter sat quietly, considering the truth of everything John had said. After several minutes of reflection, he stood slowly and reached out his arm to place it warmly around John's shoulder. He carefully brought the conversation to a close. "John, you always ask questions that require much thought. We'll talk about this many more times before we find our answers. Perhaps, working together, we'll learn more about how it feels to live in another man's skin."

John smiled widely, knowing it was the best answer he could have for now.

CHAPTER 16

Carter's Journal

Spring 1893

Pine Ridge Reservation, South Dakota

Lillian and I enjoyed our life as parents immensely, despite the changes it brought. The spring after our daughter's birth was a blur as I tried to teach both the boys and the girls while Lillian recovered from giving birth. In the afternoon classes, the older boys taught the little ones, and we maintained steady progress in the upkeep of the school. But for the girls' classes, I often ended up sitting in the schoolyard with the baby and rocking her continuously to stop her caterwauling while Lillian disappeared with the younger girls to point out which weedy sprouts should be ripped by their roots from her precious gardens.

Having been raised in families where siblings had cared for younger children since the beginning of time, the older girls were natural caregivers. Since they were usually busy cleaning the kitchen each day after lunch, I entertained our daughter until Lillian finished her lessons with the younger girls.

Unable to grasp the intricacies of a cradleboard to carry the baby while she worked, Lillian wrapped the baby in linen blankets, finishing the bundle with a decorative woolen shawl positioned as a sling. The pièce de résistance to the outfit was a ruffled bonnet tied tightly around Elizabeth's ears with a bow nearly as big as she. Off the two of them would go, the baby slung under Lillian's breasts, perfectly content. Even the youngest of the girls quickly learned to carry the child comfortably so she could be passed among the students. Despite my humor at the attire, it worked well. Meals were prepared, vegetables preserved, eggs gathered, and cows milked. The school grounds never looked finer—all as if no one had been distracted one whit with the care of an infant.

In the evenings, however, Elizabeth suffered what my mother diagnosed from a distance as colic. Her tiny face wrinkled and red, Elizabeth would start squalling as soon as we nestled her into the cradle. I'm sure Mother would have insisted she was simply spoiled, but holding her made no difference. In spite of our cooing and rocking, she continued her fits, sometimes gasping for air until she finally fell asleep in the wee hours of the morning. Lillian and I were exhausted from our duties at the school and desperate for a good night's sleep, leading me to inquire of Iron Horse if there was an Indian woman willing to serve as a nanny for our daughter.

Early the next morning, he entered the schoolhouse with a young woman at his side. He introduced her as Rosa Long Soldier, daughter of one of his friends at Corn Creek. She wasn't married and had just returned from the Indian school back east. He assured us she was trustworthy, skilled at childcare and competent in other domestic duties as well. She spoke fluent English yet had managed to retain her native tongue and assisted by translating for the older women of the camp who dropped by frequently to help with the baby's care. We welcomed Rosa with her gingham dresses and neatly sewn leather boots into our home. Her cheerful smile and singsong manner of speaking seemed to soothe Elizabeth's fretful attitude. Lillian and I were confident we'd found the perfect caretaker for our daughter.

As package after package of lavishly ruffled gowns arrived from New York, I feared that Mother and Lillian would suffocate the child in satin. In May, Elizabeth was christened at the Holy Cross Church, the lace of her gown reaching almost to the floor and her rosy cheeks hidden by layers of ruffles on her bonnet. Of course, she screamed throughout the ceremony until the priest handed her back to Rosa, who promptly began a gentle rocking motion while singing a melodious chant that effectively sent our daughter into dreamland.

CHAPTER 17

Rustlers

Summer 1893

Pine Ridge Reservation, South Dakota

Wichapi, one of Iron Horse's favorite ponies, was missing, and John and his father rode hard in search of her. They'd traveled several miles west of their home, it was near midday, and waves of heat rose from the plain, blurring their view of the horizon. Streams of white lather ran down the necks of their ponies, whose sides heaved from hours of hard riding. As they topped a ridge looking down into a small valley where there was shade and water, Iron Horse motioned stiffly for his son to stop.

Iron Horse's skill as a warrior served him well. From the ridge, he had spotted a number of cattle in the shade of some cottonwoods and accompanied by three unknown riders at the water hole. At first, John and his father were curious, then cautious as they watched the group from their place of concealment. It was obvious from the thickness of their horses and the hats tilted away from their faces that none of the riders were Indian. This was not the time for the fall roundup of cattle on the reservation, and this remote, unfrequented valley lay suspiciously outside the cattle's usual range. The riders were resting but watchful.

Iron Horse whispered, "I'm afraid those men are up to no good. I can't identify them, but I don't believe those cattle are theirs. Wait here without being seen, and I'll take a closer look."

He handed his pony's rope to John and slipped behind the ridge, working his way along the creek bed towards the group of strangers. Iron Horse remained shielded by the tall bunch grass as he cautiously gained a vantage point from which he could determine the identity of the men—and possibly of the cattle as well.

Iron Horse took his time, and when he returned, John was peering at the strangers with such intense interest that his father was able to pull his pony's rein from John's grasp before the boy was even aware of his presence. John gasped in surprise.

"Shhh. Always watch with eyes behind as well as in front," Iron Horse chided his son.

Although his father had spoken with a twinkle in his eye, John flushed with embarrassment. He knew the traits that all Lakota took pride in and realized he had made a childish mistake by focusing only on the strangers he could see while forgetting that enemies could come from all sides. Iron Horse had made the experience a lesson for his son.

"A wise man always has one ear to the ground and is never taken unawares with his gaze fixed in one direction," Iron Horse said in a fatherly tone, dispelling John's feelings of humiliation. "It's always wise to look into the future with one eye on the past."

John was curious what his father had learned from his reconnaissance but knew it was rude to inquire directly. Instead, he began, "I looked closely and am sure I've never seen any of those men on the reservation," giving his father the opportunity to tell him what he had seen.

"No," replied Iron Horse, "when I got close enough to see their faces, I learned they are strangers. Their actions are suspicious because they didn't dismount from their ponies, and they watched all approaches into the valley. I'm sure that some of those cattle belong to Jake Farmer. When we get home, you must ride to his ranch to tell him what we saw."

Arriving home by midafternoon, Iron Horse secured a guide string in Tadita's mouth while Good Heart prepared a trail lunch for her son. After a brief rest and cool drink of water, John headed for Living Springs. He was excited and honored to be given this responsibility. He knew that if Jake Farmer's cattle had been stolen, there could be no time wasted in recovering them.

Jake was about fifty years old and had come to Indian country as a young man seeking adventure. He took an Indian wife, securing his right to reside on the reservation. When they received the allotment for their household, he selected the section known as Living Springs. It was one of the most desirable locations on the entire reservation with its never-failing water and access to rich pastures in the valley and open areas held in trust by the federal government. In a suspiciously brief time, he had built a well-established ranch where large herds of cattle grazed, their red-and-white markings displaying the white-faced Hereford influence that had made its way across the frontier.

Jake was a large, rough man with coarse features that matched the coarseness of his nature, bristly gray hair that fell past his shoulders, and a scruffy, unshaven look that always made him appear slightly dirty or unkempt. He affected an air of joviality and habitually talked in a loud, boisterous voice, but the Indians called him "Big Talk" and didn't hold him in high esteem.

As John rode up to the rancher's home, Jake and his two sons were driving into the corral with a load of hay. John told them what he had seen, and Jake ordered his sons to unhitch the team and saddle their ponies. Within minutes, they were all riding hard to the west, securing gun belts around their waists and whipping their ponies to a frenzy. They didn't bother to see if they were missing any cattle, for any time spent on that task would give time for the thieves to drive the stolen cattle into the Bad Lands, making them nearly impossible to recover.

The sun had disappeared from the sky when John, Jake, and his sons rode up to Iron Horse's home. After speaking with Iron Horse, the ranchers galloped on, following the path that John and his father described. The ranchers trailed the thieves all that night and came upon them the next morning. After killing one of the rustlers, the ranchers rounded up the herd and headed home.

Two days after John and his father found the rustlers under the trees, Jake and his sons returned to the Potato Creek camp, slowly driving the recovered cattle down to the creek. As it turned out, the cattle proved to be thirty of Jake's best cows. Once watered, they rested quietly in the cool shelter of the trees while their owners enjoyed a warm meal provided by Carter and his wife. After dinner, they unrolled their bedrolls and settled in for the night with the herd.

At dawn the following morning, the cattle started towards Living

Springs, lowing for their calves and eager to return to their home range. Jake rode up to Iron Horse's cabin where the family was eating breakfast.

He called to John in the Lakota tongue, "John, you have done me a mighty good turn and saved me a lot of money, and I appreciate it. Down in the timber by the dance house is a young heifer that's about to have her calf and cannot take another step. I'm giving her to you for your own. She'll probably return to her home range when her calf is ready to travel, and if she does, I'll brand her for you. If she remains here, my boys will come back and brand her for you so that everyone knows she belongs to you and is not one of the government ration cattle."

John was elated. His first thoughts were of the great feast his new possession would enable him to give, and he attempted to thank the gruff cattleman in a jumbled combination of English and Lakota.

Jake responded, "It's all right, boy, just remember that Jake Farmer never forgets a good turn," and with that, he rode off to catch up with the herd.

John and his father immediately walked down into the timber to view his new possession. After a brief search, they found a two-year-old heifer standing quietly, heavy with calf, in the seclusion of a cluster of box elders. She was distinctively marked, deep red in color with a clearly defined, nearly perfect circle of white on her left flank. John experienced a feeling of prideful pleasure along with a sense of reluctance to think of her as part of a feast. Later that morning, he went to the schoolhouse to share the story of his good fortune with Carter.

With his teacher following behind, John eased back to the shelter of trees along the creek, needing to see her once more just to be sure it was all real. They found the expectant mother in the trees exactly where John and his father had left her. Carter suggested that she remain there undisturbed and instructed John to keep careful watch over her for a day or two. When the calf came, they would decide what to do next.

John made many visits to check on her, always so quietly that the heifer never sensed his presence. As he walked along the trail on each visit, he pulled tufts of grass, leaving little mounds scattered near the heifer, encouraging her to move about as if grazing but not wander too far from her hideout. Several mornings later, John was up before the others and went to the spot to find that his wealth had doubled overnight. He now owned a second, tiny heifer, with identical markings to her mother. With enthusiastic joy, he watched the calf gain strength and coordination over the following days. She was quick to jump and peer this way and that, watching the world around her. John named her Sparrow after the tiny bird that lived its life jumping and peeking at the world. Before the end of a week, she was capable of running circles around her mom as they eased into the open and down to the creek each day for water, and John began to consider the possibilities of being a rancher as well as a teacher.

CHAPTER 18

Carter's Journal

Summer 1893

Pine Ridge Reservation, South Dakota

Over the next few days, John checked on the pair constantly until, a little over a week after Sparrow's birth, he went to where he normally saw them only to discover his two cows were nowhere to be found. He burst through the schoolhouse door, gasping for breath, his brows furrowed.

Once his breathing slowed and I knew he was listening carefully, I prompted, "John, have you forgotten what Jake said about the pair probably returning to their former home at Living Springs? Remember how Wichapi returned home when your father thought she was lost?"

I saw a look of relief, then clarity and finally determination as he told me where he'd be heading next.

"I'll be glad to ride along with you. We can search as we travel," I added, hoping I wouldn't end up consoling John if we found the pair had met an untimely demise.

Being an ardent sportsman and knowing prairie chickens abounded in the vicinity of Living Springs, we set out for Jake's house with guns loaded. I had an ulterior motive to speak frankly with John about the future. Based on what we knew of his past, John would be, if he wasn't already, fourteen years of age. I'd received a letter from the agency office several days ago that advised me he'd be required to attend the boarding school at the agency in the coming year.

This was part of the assimilation process, the primary goal of the government school system. He had to leave—and stay away from—his home in the hope he would forget the ways of his elders. I'd been expecting the letter, but it was still upsetting to read that John would be leaving. There was no choice. Rations or other supplies were cut to families who didn't send their children to school. I kept my feelings hidden until I couldn't put off the inevitable. I knew John would find the news unsettling, but he deserved to know as soon as possible.

We rode towards the ranch at Living Springs, guiding our ponies with our heels as they ambled in whatever direction the birds were flying. We were in no hurry, so I allowed John to guide our conversation, talking about how much his mothers would appreciate a fresh bird in the evening's cook pot and teasing each other about our poor aim. We were completely distracted until we found ourselves in the center yard of the cattleman's home where the family had gathered for their noonday meal. Although I desperately wanted to get back to my conversation with John, prairie custom required that we accept an invitation for a meal with the rancher and his family.

During lunch, one of Jake's sons reported that he'd spotted John's cow with her calf making her way back to her home range that morning. The rancher turned to John, speaking emphatically. "Boy, it'd be wise to leave her where she's content to ensure her own and her calf's well-being for the first several months. If you move her and she returns again, the calf may be lost."

Speaking on John's behalf, I asked the cattleman, "Will you brand the cow for John?" I added hurriedly, knowing that only a unique brand would guarantee his ownership in the future, "And will you forge a specific design that will indicate that John is the owner?"

After a moment's thought, Jake replied, "How about a J lazy horseshoe? Would that suit ya?" He drew the brand in the loose dirt with a stick, "J C," so that John would have a clear image of his brand. We agreed it was a suitable design, and John thanked Jake again for his gift.

As we rode slowly homeward that afternoon, I sensed that John felt a certain disappointment that we were not taking the heifer and her calf with us.

"The animals will be much better off among other cattle on a familiar range," I reassured him. "They'll be cared for with the others. More importantly, it won't be quite as tempting to the older members of the tribe to feast on your animals when winter rations run short." I reached over and patted John's shoulder as we rode. "In a few years, John, the two animals and their increase will grow into a herd, making you, young man, a cattleman in your own right. I'll record your ownership of the cow and her calf with the sub-agent at Medicine Root."

John smiled, elated to know that his name would be included on the tribal roles with an official list of his possessions.

I held the supervision of the interests of all the families in camp with particular gravity. Unable to read or write, the elders could be cheated by unscrupulous traders or agents. I made special effort to keep records of all these things in our camp, whether it was foals born in the pony herd or the number of ration cattle delivered each spring.

As we rode in no particular hurry back to Potato Creek, I steeled my emotions and began, "I have news, John, that is both good and bad. You've done well with Iron Horse and his family and grown tall and strong." John straightened his shoulders to sit taller on his pony's back. I continued, not wanting to share the news about the school but knowing I could no longer put off the inevitable. "Although we don't know the day of your birth, based on what you told Annie when you were found, you are fourteen years of age." I saw questions deepening in John's expression and finished by blurting out, "As you know, it's required that you continue your education at the boarding school at Pine Ridge. It will all be new, and you will most likely be expected to attend there for several years." Looking down, I waited, unable to hide my disappointment.

I saw that this revelation saddened John tremendously even before he realized he'd be leaving his home and family. As that fact entered his mind, his shoulders slumped, his face became a mask of stone, and he uttered gloomily, "I must leave the place where I have learned so much and sacrifice the time I have to be home with my mothers and precious Annie in the evenings. I will lose my evenings riding across the prairie and sitting with my sister under the trees by the creek, whispering our secrets in the white man's tongue and dreaming of the future." Kicking his horse to run ahead of mine, he shouted back at me, "All to live with strangers and try to become a white man. This is not freedom as we have learned it in your class, Mr. Heath!"

I spurred my horse to catch up with him, adamantly arguing, "Don't forget, John, this is just the first step on your path to the outside world. You're a capable student, and once you've finished your term at the agency school, the big schools will offer you opportunities you cannot imagine."

I continued, "Don't forget your dreams of living a better life than you'll find on the reservation. Here, when you turn eighteen, you can take your cattle and choose a piece of land for grazing. You're smart enough to realize that most of the good grassland has been settled by the white man. How will your cattle fare on poor soil when the rains don't come ?" I pressed on, "Who will help you protect your herd from predators—or worse, from theft, as happens so often on the reservation? How will you feed them in winter if the summer is dry and there isn't enough grass? These are the things you must consider if you plan to be a rancher."

John continued to ride without responding. I resolved to add one final detail to my argument: "There are already young men who can't make a living on their land. They're dependent on rations from the white agents. Many are hungry, even starving, and some are trading anything of value for bottles of the white man's whiskey to escape their misery. Have you forgotten why so many of your people danced the Ghost Dance?"

I went on, speaking softly. "John, you must not listen to the words of the old men of your tribe. They have lost their dreams, and their talk will poison your mind against a future in the white man's world. You must remember that there are good people and bad people everywhere, and you are free to choose to be either good or bad."

I could see John beginning to take my words to heart; at last, he pulled his horse to a stop, turned, and looked squarely into my eyes as if accepting the truth of everything I'd said. I persisted with the words that John needed to hear the most.

"Once you have gone to the outside world and finished your education, you cannot return to the reservation and live a life of dependence on the government. There's no money here to pay you for the skills you'll learn in school. You must be free of the constraints placed on you here: never to leave the reservation, trying to grow food with no tools or seeds, waiting and hoping for the delivery of everything you need to survive. There is no way to better yourself from that life if you stay on the reservation."

Sitting like a stone astride Hantaywee, his voice trembling, John began, "I am saddened at the thought of leaving the home that means so much to me. I know how unhappy my father and mothers will be at my leaving. It will break Annie's heart. Not only does she love me as a true brother, but we have been partners in our studies, and I am her favorite student." We smiled warmly at each other, knowing that he was her only student and hoping she could fulfill her dream of teaching many others.

John went on, his voice husky with emotion, "I understand your words. My father has said that I cannot live in the past. I've been blessed by the spirits, and I must honor them." With that, John turned his pony towards Potato Creek, kicking her sides and riding off with a new focus.

Upon learning that John would be required to attend the boarding school at the agency, Iron Horse made no comment. I watched the old chief slowly climb to the top of Signal Butte, where he stood motionless, looking towards the east until he became as one with the late evening's shadows. Despite knowing he'd encouraged the boy to accept the white man's way, John's absence from their home would leave a void in his father's world. He had lost so much in the past, and having just found the joy of a son, he needed, I knew, solitude to resolve the conflict in his heart.

II

The Agency

CHAPTER 19

Carter's Journal

Summer 1893

Pine Ridge Reservation, Pine Ridge, South Dakota

John and I had infrequently chatted about the school at the agency, and I had told him, more than once, what the government policy for Indian education was. In his heart he knew he would have to leave home to further his education, but he had been unwilling to talk about anything past the Potato Creek school and his lessons with Annie.

Until that day riding home from Jake's, I hadn't realized he wasn't thinking about what was coming next because he was so focused on learning everything I could teach him. He was also not taking life with his family for granted. I realized that if he'd given no thought to going away to boarding school, then he'd probably given even less thought to whether or not he'd return to the reservation. So far, his interests in being a teacher or rancher had resulted because of events at Potato Creek, and I knew he wasn't envisioning a future that expanded beyond the people he loved so dearly. I also believed the buried memories of a family lost were driving him to build his happiness around those he loved in the present.

When anyone shared details from beyond the reservation, John was intrigued by the differences he noted between that world and his own. Returning students told stories of platters with meat and fresh, warm rolls and bowls of vegetables the students could grow at the school because water was always plentiful. I shared with him that the boarding schools brought water to their gardens and barns like we did at Potato Creek.

Boys who went away to school returned wearing stiff leather shoes and thin, high-collared white shirts. They spoke of the industrial shops with rows of tools for making furniture and wheels and machines that rolled and bent tin into lanterns and kitchen tools. They told stories about plowing large fields, caring for massive horses that pulled plows that cut deep into the dark soil, and growing enough to feed everyone at the school. John wasn't sure many of the things they learned had any use on the reservation, but he was curious just the same.

The girls talked about pressing wrinkles from clothes with a hot iron before folding and stacking them neatly on shelves in the dormitories. They showed off their neatly stitched clothing and spoke of washing and ironing large sheets of fabric that wrapped the beds where they slept. Of course, this was nothing new to Lillian and me, but the older women babbled among themselves and looked amused at the stories. After several years at school, some of the girls went away to the East, living and working in homes far away. Whenever anyone mentioned those girls, John was concerned for his sister because he couldn't picture life away from her family as a bright future for Annie.

On the other hand, we talked about the boys who went off to boarding schools and learned the skills to become successful laborers. I told John that a young person could attend an institution of higher education, even Harvard, before going on to medical or law school as Aaron Moss had gone to the seminary. But I was compelled to share that not all children returned and explained that hopefully they were earning a good salary in a new world. Secretly, I prayed it was this and not that they had died and been buried far from their homeland, a reality I knew happened all too often.

John acknowledged the truth in my words about there being no future for him on the reservation. He'd helped his father slaughter the skinny cattle on ration day at the agency. More and more often, families had to share a single cow because there weren't enough for every family to have their own. He'd heard Moves First grumble that there wasn't enough to make stew every night and how tired she was of bone soup. He watched her struggle to dry the almost hairless hide and cure it to make new moccasins for Annie and knew the feeling of his own toes poking through one of the moth holes in the lightweight wool blankets the government sent each winter.

As we strolled about camp, John commented that the cotton dresses the girl wore weren't warm enough to protect them through a snowy Dakota winter. It was laughable, but sad, to see their dainty shoes covered in mud after a trip to get water from a rain-swollen creek. When John asked why the girls were taught domestic skills, I always repeated the official reason: so that they could run an efficient home when they returned to their families on the reservation. John commented that little efficiency was needed to manage the meager rations each family received. I did not acknowledge the accuracy of his statement; nor did I share that I suspected the real reason for the training was to provide domestic help for the wealthy back East.

After one such conversation, John acknowledged the futility of having an education only to return to the reservation. He accepted that he would have to be brave enough to follow my advice, get the best education possible, and perhaps one day move his family to a new home where there was plenty of food. He steeled himself to the time away from Annie and his mothers and father, and I told him he would have to be brave enough for us all.

I couldn't bring myself to share that the entire system, all the money, all the manpower, was designed so that the pupils returned home and shared their knowledge of the white world with their elders. I had come to understand that educating the Indian was not a benevolent government at work but rather an effort to remove any vestige of native culture from the younger generation. I could only encourage John to focus on his goals for the future, knowing that he would do anything to provide for Annie and to build a life for himself that did not end on a bloody battlefield.

CHAPTER 20

Off to School

Fall 1893

Pine Ridge Agency Boarding School, Pine Ridge Reservation, South Dakota

Early one morning, under the yellows, oranges, and reds of the leaves of early September, Iron Horse and his family prepared for the trip to take John to the agency school. In the bed of the wagon was a small, tin-covered trunk purchased at the trader's store and carefully packed with his belongings. In addition to clothes, there were soda crackers, store cookies and candy, and a generous portion of the sun-dried beef and wild cherries pounded together that the people had made for generations from buffalo meat. They had adapted as best they could when making it from the stringy beef of the white man's cattle. Tough and chewy though it was, Moves First and Good Heart prayed it would keep John strong.

The ponies dragged their feet as they started on the trip, and the women seemed especially melancholy, sitting huddled behind the driver's seat. The wagon and food were evidence of the people's uncomplicated way of life, but the care with which it had been packed was proof of the love and support that endeared his family to John. His heart was heavy as he took his place beside his father on the worn wagon seat.

The trip was marked by sadness, and when they camped that night on Porcupine Creek, their tipi was filled with gloom because it would be their last night together for many months. Iron Horse had killed a single prairie chicken behind the dance house at the creek, and Moves First boiled the last ribs of a scrawny beef into a watery broth to moisten the bird. Good Heart made a large pan of John's favorite, fry bread, to dip in the broth as well.

After dinner, few words passed between them for fear of bursting into tears, and everyone headed to their blankets early. It would be a long night as each reflected on what tomorrow would bring: a lost study partner and confidant, a child away from home during perilous times, and a long-awaited son living far away from his adopted father. For John, tomorrow's trip meant being miles from a sister he'd come to treasure, missing his favorite meals with his mothers, and, most importantly, losing time to learn from the two men whose influence he valued the most, Iron Horse and Carter Heath.

The next day, they passed the spot where John had been found near the field of slaughter at Wounded Knee, towards which the older Indians never looked. John too looked away, hoping the nightmares wouldn't return. He steeled his heart to the unknowns of his past, for he knew had his family survived, they would have come for him long ago. He accepted that the Great Spirit had brought him to this point.

The family's dejection deepened as they drove into the agency. They rode past the office and over to the boarding school where his mothers carried the trunk into the building while John and his father reported to the superintendent's office.

The school itself was a forbidding two-story structure in the shape of the letter *H*, sitting in the midst of open prairie that looked empty otherwise. The center structure was made up of an office, two identical classrooms on either side, as well as a large kitchen and cafeteria. The uprights of the *H* comprised the dormitories, males on one side, females on the other. No children from Potato Creek besides John were of age to attend the boarding school this year, making John feel especially lonely as his eyes rose to take in the full height of the building. The stark, clapboard sides were painted a milky white. Large windows all around and five dormers across the outside roof allowed fresh air to drift through in the summer and copious amounts of sunlight to shine in for warmth in the winter.

Scattered about on all sides of the main buildings were various smaller camps consisting of a mixture of tipis and tents. These served as living quarters for Indians or mixed-blood individuals who worked at the school as cooks, caregivers, or laborers. Each camp had its own collection of tattered wagons with an old cannon here and there sitting on steel-rimmed wheels as if to be rolled at any moment to face the school and fire away. Moving among the tents and tipis were several older women, heavyset, with shawls about their shoulders and covering their heads. They stood and watched the comings and goings of the boarding school with hidden curiosity, and John wondered if these women were the mixed-blood wives of some of the soldiers assigned to the garrison that was part of the agency.

Once John was signed in, his father and mothers and Annie turned abruptly and hurried back to the wagon and drove away. They did not say goodbye or embrace, for their hearts were too full, and such a display of emotion would not have been considered appropriate. As they pulled away, Annie could no longer restrain her sobs, and the mothers chanted of parting with a low, keening song. Iron Horse sat upright on the rigid wagon seat, his hands clutching the reins until his knuckles turned white, straining to keep a tear from slipping down his cheek.

John watched as the distance shrank them and the rigid figure of Iron Horse passed from view. He felt the pangs of loneliness, and his shoulders slumped. He was one of the first pupils to arrive, giving him an afternoon of idleness, free to wander about the buildings and grounds. The empty feeling in his heart increased to the point that by early evening when he went to bed in the dormitory, he cried himself silently to sleep under the coverings of his bed.

During the next few days, the superintendent of the school assigned John to simple tasks with two other boys about his age. The chores occupied his mind and distracted him from feelings of emptiness. At the same time, they provided him an opportunity to learn his way around the facility and meet the people he'd be dealing with in one way or another. Mr. Butterworth, the superintendent, was a kindly man, rather portly and gray haired with a massive, drooping mustache. After a single day, he had determined John was one of Carter's pupils. Because of John's excellent English and the correctness of his pronunciation, Mr. Butterworth appointed him as his messenger, and not for the first time, the young man felt a sense of gratitude to his former teacher for providing him the skills that put him in a position of responsibility in a new place.

By the following Monday, the dormitories were filled to overflowing. Most of the students settled quickly into the routine of rising by the morning bell, lining up for roll call before breakfast and another roll call before going to the classroom, another roll call before marching to dinner, afternoons in the classroom or industrial work, another roll call for supper, and again a roll call in the evening before going to bed. Every roll call was signaled by the tolling of an iron bell, larger and deeper in tone than the one at Potato Creek. The repeated roll calls allowed school personnel to quickly discover runaways and initiate pursuit. For John, the routine took a toll, as he recognized that here he was just one among a hundred other boys.

By the end of the first week, the grind had crushed John's spirit. He began to doubt whether he would survive the unfeeling and unforgiving nature of the drudgery. He struggled to focus on his goal of achieving the best possible education, reaching out nightly to stroke the little trunk as he thought of how much he was loved by his family and what his success might mean to them. As the weeks passed, he forced himself to concentrate in class, whether carpentering, ironworking, marching in step, calisthenics, or games, and managed to get through the daily regimen with tolerance if not enthusiasm. Eventually, he began to earn the regard of his teachers.

Late one afternoon, after dismissing John's class from several hours of marching on the field, Mr. Winslow, the school's drill instructor, pulled John aside as the group headed back to their barracks.

"John, I wanted to take this opportunity to applaud the efforts I've seen on your part since school began."

John looked down at his feet, ashamed that he had just moments before been mumbling to himself about how boring and useless the exercises were.

"Sir?" he responded, looking up and straightening his shoulders.

"I know the long hours of marching are exhausting," Mr. Winslow continued, "but your efforts in calisthenics and the concentration you apply to your marching are definitely making improvements in your performance. I've noticed some of the other boys beginning to watch and follow your example."

Surprised, John inhaled sharply, realizing he now had an opportunity to be a leader like his father. "Thank you, sir," he replied with a smile. "It is indeed challenging some days."

"Well, keep it up, young man. You're making a difference," Mr. Winslow finished with a pat on John's back. Ultimately, regular recognition from the staff boosted his morale, and John found increasing encouragement as some of the other boys began to turn to him for leadership, not just on the field but in class as well.

Though he kept busy during school hours, the shorter days of the approaching winter weighed on John's cheerful spirit. The long nights allowed him time to reflect on the skills he was learning, the things discussed in class, and the entire staff's absolute focus on all things of the white man. He found himself questioning the usefulness of learning the art of ironworking when there was little iron available on the reservation. Despite not seeing a use for the skills he was learning, the pride he felt when teachers noticed and commented on his efforts was enough to elevate John's spirits day by day.

He enjoyed the challenge of learning and was fascinated with what he could build, but so far, he'd found no one with whom to have a reflective conversation such as he so often did with Carter Heath. In class, there were no verbal challenges to his answers, no questions that made him think deeper or reflect on possibilities. The students were expected to learn nothing but simple facts. Other than being told how to do things, there were no conversations about *why* things were done or how certain skills could be applied outside of school.

John saw no way to improve the lives of the Indians living on Potato Creek. The teachers never discussed opportunities for selling the items they made or how they would be useful for farming or ranching on the reservation. Everything focused entirely on being successful at the school. It seemed the teachers' only goal was to erase his memories of the Indian ways. He continued, more and more often as he settled beneath his bedcovers, to longingly stroke the tin trunk beside his bed, the last tangible connection to his family on the reservation.

Every morning, as John went about preparing to start the day in the quiet of the dormitory, listening for the bells to report to breakfast, report to class, report to drill, all the students following the bell without thinking, he realized how much he'd come to depend on the adoring looks from Annie to inspire him. He missed the quiet communion with family over a meal at the fireplace in their cabin. Here, meals were taken in silence, the disciplined quiet revealing nothing of the personalities or feelings of the students who surrounded him.

On Thanksgiving Day, they had an abundant feast for the midday meal. Later that evening, since art was an important part of the curriculum, there was piano playing and accompanying singing performances given by the students for the agency personnel. John was part of the group who showed off their painting skills with a large mural on the cafeteria wall they had completed, but he wondered at the futility of all these things. A holiday celebrating the things he should be thankful for simply made John aware that it would be months before he saw his home and family again. There was no one to confide his feelings to, no one to laugh with when he questioned why the white man celebrated everything with eating—never dancing, just eating. Slowly, John realized his sense of humor had wasted away from lack of use. Everything here was serious, driven into his soul to smother Indian thoughts. He found no joy in this school and needed to get away.

John determined to escape. At the end of a massive meal of turkey and gravy and pies interspersed with prayers and speeches about all they had to be thankful for that evening, John imitated the stoic expression of his teachers as he sneaked several pieces of bread into his pockets. Returning to his room for roll call, John curled contentedly in his bed to convince everyone in the dormitory he had drifted off to sleep.

It was quite a surprise the next morning at roll call when John was nowhere to be found. He had waited still and quiet until all he could hear was the even breathing of his schoolmates as they slept before sliding from beneath the bedcovers and carefully rolling the pillows beneath them and tucking the edges tightly. To anyone who awakened and glanced about, the form would convince them that John was sleeping soundly under the quilt, when in reality he had slipped noiselessly along the hallway, down the stairs, and out the back door.

Using only the stars for direction as he had so often done when riding Hantaywee, John covered the intervening sixty-five miles between the boarding school and his home in about fifteen hours. How he did it on foot none but his father could tell, but his instinctive sense of direction took him by the most direct path, avoiding the common trails and taking advantage of the contour of the country.

Late that afternoon, he appeared in the door of his home on Potato Creek, much to the astonishment of his family as they gathered around their evening meal. Annie, seated so that she faced the door, was the first to see him. Rushing to grasp his hands, she squealed much like she had on the day she first discovered him in the snow at Wounded Knee.

"Oh, John! You're home!! We've missed you so!"

His mothers rose from their seats and hugged him warmly, saying only, "Our boy, our boy! It's so good to have you home!"

Iron Horse took the boy's hand, a questioning look in his eyes as he remained silent. John had completed the trek despite the chilling November air and now huddled close to the fire, rubbing his arms briskly. The smell of fry bread reminded him of his grumbling stomach.

Taking his place in the family circle, he stated simply, "I ran away for I could wait no longer. It would have been the middle of summer before I could ask for permission to visit, and my heart could not wait so long to see you all."

His family each nodded in agreement; they understood his feelings completely. There was no teasing as they sat around the fire for the rest of the evening. Instead, they focused on the joy of their family after finding him, retelling stories of John's time with them until he fell sound asleep with Annie at his side. For another several hours, the adults enjoyed the quiet communion of their family reunited.

The next morning, before the others had awakened, Iron Horse went out to the prairie and secured his team of ponies once again. By the time the others began to stir and breakfast was prepared, he'd harnessed them to the wagon. Iron Horse took his place on the driver's seat immediately after their meal, and John wordlessly sat beside his father. Back over the long trail they traveled without stopping. Not a word was spoken until they approached the gradual slope leading down to Wounded Knee Creek, at which point Iron Horse spoke from his heart to the boy who had become his son.

"My son," he began, "it is over two years since you were born to us from these prairies. You came to us through the agonies of our people who tried to oppose the inevitable. Since then, you have grown into my heart as if you were my own. Your mothers love you as their own, and your sister thinks no more of us than she does of you. Your coming to us last night made our hearts glad, for it showed the love of a son." Lowering his voice, Iron Horse continued truthfully, "Yet it also made us sad. All things change, and life is full of parting. We must learn to accept the changes as they come, and to bear the partings."

Iron Horse paused here to give John a moment to absorb what he had said.

He started again, slowly, in the solemn voice of a chief of his people. "I want you to always feel that, though you are away from us, we think of you, and you are always in our hearts. I am growing old, and I know that soon the long parting will come for me." John inhaled sharply, pained at the thought, but Iron Horse continued, "I hope that when I go on the long hunt, your heart will still be nearby. Although you must never forget who you are, it is best for you to go to school and learn. You should remember the old ways. But you must learn to think in the new ways. You can talk in the white man's tongue. Always think good and talk with a straight tongue, and you will have many friends."

John nodded, looking down so his father wouldn't see the tears coursing down his cheeks. "Father," he returned lovingly, "your words have pierced my heart, and I will do as you have counseled. I will not run away again. When I am lonely and homesick, I will remember that you are thinking of me. I will be good and will always speak with a straight tongue." As the wagon trundled on, they talked of more indifferent things until they drove into the boarding school grounds late that evening.

The next morning, after sleeping in the back of his wagon, Iron Horse sought assurance that his son would not be punished for his delinquency, then headed back to Potato Creek. John resumed his place in the life of the school, remembering the words of his father. His visit had been comforting. More importantly, Annie's love and his father's belief in his ability to succeed in the world of the future were inspiring. As never before, the surroundings at Potato Creek made him starkly aware of the difference between the old and the new and brought a quiet sense of reconciliation akin to resignation.

It wasn't long before John regained the confidence of his superintendent and teachers, and he settled confidently back into the school routine. However, when the Christmas season brought some of the students' families to visit, a deep melancholy set in, making it difficult once again to resist the lure of his home on Potato Creek. He worked overtime doing calisthenics and studying his lessons, exhausting himself physically to ensure a deep sleep each night. When the balm of early spring inspired the prairie larks to sing in the morning and the peepers along the creek to trill their seductive songs in the evening, his memories of Annie tugged at his heartstrings, and once again, he found comfort in the feel of the tin trunk and the memories of the dried beef made by his mothers and sent along to give him strength.

As the prairie spring bloomed, John recognized the last days of the school year were approaching. Class time was a rush of completing projects. Reviewing his own works, John felt a certain amount of satisfaction. In the classroom, he'd established himself as one the best students at the school. He had entered wholeheartedly into sports and other contests. Dreaming of the possibilities with his cattle back home, John had worked his hardest on the school farm. He regarded Mr. Brun, the six-foot-tall German agriculture instructor, as the most knowledgeable farmer he knew. Under the kind man's direction, John had acquired many skills and was eager to apply them to his own herd. Despite his self-doubt in the beginning, John recognized that his achievements amounted to more than what some others had managed to accomplish. He felt a growing pride in his abilities as the end of his first year approached and determined again to succeed in the white man's world.

The day for closing school was set, and word was sent to the furthest corners of the reservation. On one of June's last days before the heat of summer set in, wagons lumbered towards the boarding school to bring the Indian children home. John waited hour after hour for his father and passed up several rides offered by other families. He was certain his father would arrive soon. As the last wagon rumbled away, John realized it was evening and he'd be forced to wait until the next day to head home. But when Iron Horse's wagon failed to arrive the next morning, John started out on foot, expecting any minute to meet his father along the way. That hope kept him going as he crested ridge after ridge with no sign of the familiar wagon and colorful ponies.

CHAPTER 21

Brush with Death

Summer 1894

Pine Ridge Reservation, Pine Ridge, South Dakota

Trudging over the lonely road, John tried to envision the cabin at Potato Creek, surprised to find the memory dim. His disappointment changed to apprehension as the distance between him and the school grew. He was helped on his way by several wagons. Sundown found him near Porcupine Butte where he rested briefly and ate with a family who were camped along the trail. He didn't tarry, for his apprehension had grown into a sense of foreboding. He continued his tiresome journey through the dark hours of the night, one foot plodding in front of the other, hoping that nothing was amiss with his family.

Just as the gray dawn displaced the darkness of the night, he quietly entered his family's cabin without disturbing the sleeping occupants. Accustomed as his eyes were to the darkness, he saw that Iron Horse slept in his usual place, as did the others. Perplexed, he didn't awaken them but instead secured a blanket against the chill of the morning and fell asleep in his own corner of the room. When he awoke, the sun was well across the sky, and the women were up and about—all but Annie, whose still form showed that she hadn't moved from where she was when he arrived.

Without disturbing his sister, John stepped outside to find his mothers chatting softly around the fire. Iron Horse was nowhere to be seen. The two women welcomed him with a wrinkle of worry in their brows and explained that his father had left early for Corn Creek to find the doctor. Annie had not been well since early spring. A cold had settled in her chest and worsened until she was forced to quit attending school a few weeks ago. The mothers tried their own treatments and called on the medicine man, but nothing worked, and Annie's condition had not improved. Even Carter Heath's medicine and his wife's care did not have their usual effect, and several days before John's homecoming, her condition had begun to cause them grave concern.

Carter had persuaded Iron Horse to send for the agency doctor, but when Iron Horse reached Medicine Root, he learned that the white medicine man was seeing other families further away. Iron Horse spent two days driving from one camp to another, only to find that the doctor had gone to yet another distant camp. He'd returned home for a few hours of rest the night before and exchanged the cumbersome wagon for Wichapi, his fastest pony. He was well on his way to Corn Creek by the time John awakened.

Having heard the details of Annie's sickness and believing his father would return with the doctor, John reentered their cabin to find Annie still lying as he'd first seen her.

Good Heart spoke softly. "Your sister has been like this for several days. None of our medicine has helped." Annie's shallow breathing and occasional moan frightened John. Anxiety changed to dread and then to anger as the day progressed and no one arrived to help. John found himself viewing the old life from the perspective of the new. At school, he'd grown accustomed to regular visits with the doctor and had learned the power of the white man's medicine. Fearing for his sister's life and frustrated by a feeling of helplessness, he headed to the day school to confer with Mr. Heath. When Carter offered no further advice, John returned home to wait at Annie's side.

When he could sit no longer, John left the house, making his way to the prairie to find Hantaywee. Like Iron Horse, he was determined to find the white doctor and make him come to Annie, whether he wanted to or not. John secured his pony with a guide rope about her neck and leaped on her back. Whispering for her to run like fire through dry grass, John leaned over her neck and raced across the prairie with a savage impulse. He felt its strength and did nothing to throw it off. Fearing he might need the rifle Carter had given him long ago to force the doctor to come to

Annie's aid, he circled back to the cabin to find that the doctor had arrived; a haggard pony was tied to the wheels of Iron Horse's heavy wagon. John jumped to the ground, releasing Hantaywee as he ran inside to find the doctor at Annie's side, a somber look on his face.

His mothers stood beside Annie's pallet of blankets, distrust mixed with hope on their faces. John grabbed the rifle and stomped outside to wait. He positioned himself near the doctor's buggy where he could see through the open door to where Annie lay with the doctor at her side. He couldn't tell if the man had brought medicine nor whether he was treating Annie or just waiting for her to die, but he was confident the doctor would come outside eventually.

When he did, John was surprised to see a young man, who, he later learned, had come to work among the Indians less than a year before to get away from the demands of hospital work in a large city in the East. He'd volunteered to come, loved his profession, and worked zealously to relieve the suffering he witnessed. However, here on the reservation, the bureaucracy had refused to provide any assistance, and with no history of his patients and little time to study symptoms, he was forced to make cursory diagnoses and hope for the best.

The doctor approached John, who whispered hopefully, "Will she get well?"

"The sickness is very bad, but I'm doing everything I can to help her."

Hearing no hope in the comment, John gave in to his desperation and fear that a white doctor would not give his best effort to an Indian child. John grabbed him by his shirt and growled, "You go back in there, Doctor, and make her live; for if she dies, you die as well," staring into the doctor's face and shaking the rifle threateningly. With a smile of understanding, the doctor turned to reenter the house and resumed his place by the frail girl's pallet. It wasn't the first time fear had caused an Indian to threaten him with harm, and he understood their distrust of the white race.

Despite her shallow breathing, the doctor was confident Annie was not in imminent danger of dying. He'd seen similar cases back east where the poverty was equal to what he'd seen here. He knew a mother's poor nutrition during pregnancy affected her baby. He also knew the Indians had been exposed to a number of illnesses by the coming of the white man and how those illnesses could impact the health of an infant. He pondered on Annie's case, sitting through the night, his fingers on the child's pulse, forcing a sip of nitrate potion, a new heart medicine, through her lips at regular intervals and watching expectantly.

The young man found this to be an unusual and interesting case. The girl's heart seemed naturally deficient in strength, as if it were already the heart of an old woman. Annie, with her intense efforts to learn everything possible, had taxed her heart her whole life. Burdened by the bitter Dakota winters and a diet lacking in nutrients, her existence on the reservation had lowered her odds of living to adulthood. She might be restored briefly by a lengthy period of hospital care, but on the other hand, she might even now be approaching the inevitable end. He watched and waited through the long hours of the night. At moments, he would discern an improved strength and definition to her heartbeats, and his own heart responded with hope, but at other times he was saddened when the tired little heart barely fluttered in response to the demands of her body.

John and Annie's mothers succumbed to their need for sleep while the doctor maintained his vigil. Iron Horse had not returned, and John stood watch outside the cabin door in the fresh night air. Both men fought a rising apprehension when the hours drew near to the shadowy time of early morning when it seemed easiest for the soul to release itself and return to the unknown. But as daylight broke the darkness and Annie shifted her sleeping body into a more natural position of rest, the doctor felt a touch of hope.

When the morning sun slanted over the prairie and shined through the uncurtained window, touching the bed where Annie lay, the doctor beckoned John, who still stood rigidly at the door. The doctor resumed his seat and felt for a pulse while John stood by his side, gazing down into the face that meant so much to him. Even to his untrained eye, it was clear that Annie slept a more natural sleep, and his fingers relaxed their grip on the gun for the first time in hours.

As the sunlight warmed her face, Annie opened her eyes. Smiling weakly, she whispered, "Oh, John, I'm so glad to see you," before closing them again and returning to a restful sleep.

No word passed between the doctor and John when they saw the light of recognition in her eyes. John watched the doctor keep a touch on Annie's pulse and noticed how his face lost the strain that had been etched on it throughout the night. For the first time in many hours, John felt the tension flow from his shoulders, hoping the doctor's ease meant there was hope that her heart might heal. As before, John's mind filed away the benefits of the white man's ways.

CHAPTER 22

Carter's Journal

Summer 1894

Potato Creek, Pine Ridge Reservation, South Dakota

Despite the gloom cast over the camp by Annie's illness, our home on Potato Creek was filled with joy. Liz, as we now called our rapidly growing toddler, followed Rosa's every step around the cabin and schoolyard. Her hair was a riotous crown of cinnamon curls, not quite long enough for the bows and ribbons Lillian preferred but far too frizzy for Rosa to twist into braids. Lillian gave up dressing her in ruffles and frills, trading in the luxurious gowns sent from New York for a sturdy pair of overalls over a rough cotton shirt with plenty of room to grow into.

Indoors, Liz's favorite activity was to perch on the round stool that served as a bench for a piano we'd purchased from a run-down saloon in Nebraska. Though far from the beloved instrument of Lillian's memories, it served us well to expose our students to the music we all adored. Liz found nothing more entertaining than banging her hands on the keys before spinning the stool to face her audience, grinning from ear to ear and applauding her own antics as we stood by, praying she wouldn't be slung across the room.

Outdoors, Liz was everywhere around the schoolyard, most often under the feet of whatever animal she could find. Her favorite was Madge, my riding horse, who stood still so as not to trod upon this helpless creature with her trail-hardened hooves. When I lifted her to the saddle, Liz would cackle with joy and kick her feet as if intending the horse to race across the prairie as the Indian children so often did. Rosa took her on several rides about camp, and we looked forward to the time we could get Liz a pony of her own.

We'd made friends over time with the superintendent at Pine Ridge, Mr. Edwards, and his wife, Ann. He checked regularly on our progress at the school and delivered several of the packages sent for Liz from New York. He'd first brought his wife to meet Lillian during her pregnancy, and they became fast, though distant, friends. The couple had two small children who I believe would have been wonderful playmates for our daughter had it not been for the distance between Potato Creek and the agency. As it was, the occasional visit from someone who understood the isolation we sometimes felt was always welcome.

Despite our best efforts at providing nutritious food for our students, we found ourselves increasingly surrounded by poverty among the families we served. The government continued to shortchange the Indians, forcing them onto the least productive areas of the reservation and cheating them of rations and supplies while white settlers encroached frequently, hunting what game remained and stealing any cattle they found.

Despite our love for the Lakota people and respect for their traditions, I knew we must expose our daughter to the same curriculum she'd be learning in a school in New York. I vowed she would have an education, not just in the ways of the prairie but in the things that would allow her to return east if that was what she desired. I wanted her to be free to choose her own destiny, as I had ultimately done despite my father's interference. Besides, I'd yet to meet a man on the frontier whom I'd accept as her suitor, and if she returned east to find a husband, she would need an excellent education. Even if she chose to follow in her parents' footsteps and teach on the frontier, she would need a better education than could be provided here. To this end, I inquired often into opportunities to place myself in a worthier position as to salary.

Liz would be two within the year and was bright and inquisitive. Lillian and I wished to enroll her in a regular school rather than having her spend time with only Rosa and ourselves. We were busy with the Indian children throughout each day, so our daughter already knew more of reservation life than she did of the ways of white society. The freedom of our camp was a wonderful place to grow and run as a child, but there would be a need for her formal education to begin at some point.

Our daughter spoke Lakota as well as many of the younger Indians. It was obvious she thought and spoke in both languages with ease. Sometimes, she would burst into our schoolrooms, excited to share her latest adventure, babbling in an incoherent combination of English and Lakota that no one could decipher.

She had just done the same thing in our kitchen as we were cleaning up from dinner when Lillian stooped down beside our daughter and, taking both tiny hands tightly between her own bigger ones, quietly asked if Liz knew the Lakota word for baby. While Liz stuttered and stammered for the word in her Indian tongue, Lillian gazed over her head and directly into my eyes, smiling as her question settled into my consciousness. I hugged them both tightly, glancing around at our three-room cottage. I couldn't deny that my first thought was that I wanted this new baby to be delivered somewhere other than Potato Creek. I was eager to improve our future.

Rumors of a new position piqued my interest. After multiple fires at the Fort Peck Indian School in Montana, a new school had been opened, the Fort Shaw Industrial Indian School. I wrote to Mr. Hitchcock, secretary of the interior, requesting a transfer there. Among other amenities, the school had a hospital of its own. I felt I'd earned an appointment as superintendent after my work here at Pine Ridge and requested the appointment. Weeks later, I received a copy of a letter forwarded by Mr. Kelly, Department of Indian Affairs, that he'd sent along with my request for transfer to Washington. In his recommendation, he called my work eminently satisfactory, describing our progress with the children as unflagging and noteworthy. We waited eagerly for news of my promotion.

According to Mr. Kelly, the facility at Fort Shaw had been altered from fort to school. The superintendent was housed in the commanding officer's quarters with his own bedroom and dining room as well as a room for servants. I was sure Rosa wouldn't want to leave her home on Potato Creek but was confident we'd be able to find a local woman to work as Liz's nanny. We planned to establish her in the servant's quarters to be available to Lillian and the soon-to-be two children at all times during the day and night.

With a staff of twenty at the school, I hoped there would be accommodations made for educating the children of the staff. Otherwise, we planned to hire a tutor from the East, using the garret room for her personal quarters. The sitting room would be suitable for instruction. I learned there were a number of other white children who would benefit from a well-trained tutor and requested the salary be included as part of the budget for the facility. We awaited word from Washington in hopes that we'd be transferred before Lillian's time of delivery.

CHAPTER 23

Gates of Heaven

Late Summer 1894

Potato Creek, Pine Ridge Reservation, South Dakota

John watched Annie's eyes flutter open. The light of recognition shining into his own brought a rush of relief from the fears he'd suffered through the night. Passing noiselessly outside, he headed for the trees by the dance house where he and Annie had spent so many hours practicing their English. There, he threw himself on the ground and gave vent to his emotions in sobs that had been denied him except in solitude, for no Indian man ever wept in the presence of others.

As his torment flowed out, John vowed he would never again lapse into the primordial state that had allowed him to consider violence as a solution to any problem. When he finally returned to the house, the doctor was buckling his horse's harness to the buggy. Once done, he rested his head in the animal's soft mane, telling himself he must drive to the school for some breakfast and much-needed rest. The man retied his horse as John approached. Putting his arm around the young man's shoulder, the doctor directed their path towards a knoll some distance from the house.

Seating themselves on the ground, they faced one another in the warmth of the morning sun.

"John," the doctor began, "Annie's heart is too weak for her body to grow without making it work overly hard. I don't know if her heart was weak when she was born or if she suffered an illness that weakened it as a child. All I know is that it is not a child's heart anymore, but that of an old woman who has worked too hard for too long."

John listened attentively despite already hearing the part he dreaded most; Annie's heart wasn't strong enough. His own heart broke as he waited for an answer to his only question: "Will she live to grow up and become a wife, a mother, and a teacher?"

Trying to conceal his sorrow, the doctor responded with the truth. "I can't promise, John. My medicine can't make her heart young again. You must appreciate her presence now, help her rest as much as she will, and love her while she is with you on this earth."

When the doctor returned to his buggy and drove away, John watched him disappear into the distance before whispering, "I accept that I must help Annie rest and love her as long as she lives on this earth. There is nothing more I can do." John slipped into the house and found Annie awake, her mother crooning to her in the soft cadence of a mother's tongue. As he looked on his sister's sweet face, he felt a new responsibility to those around him. He took on the mantle of a warrior—not to fight but to live a life of service and love for others.

Days later, Annie was able to leave her bed inside and spend a few hours in the shade of the bowery behind their cabin. She wasn't gaining appreciable strength from day to day, though she once walked as far as the school to visit Mrs. Heath. She was still the same sweet spirit but, having studied the teachings of Aaron Moss's heaven, now showed a resigned acceptance that came from glimpsing a better life to come. John was her constant attendant, his watchfulness tempered with the tranquility of acceptance as well.

Iron Horse finally returned from searching for the doctor. He'd heard of the doctor's visit and entered quietly to see his daughter. Though he struggled to remain stoic, the love of his child and the recognition in her eyes warmed his heart until he could no longer repress a tear that glistened in his eye.

Not wanting his father's hopes to build too high, John wrapped one arm around Iron Horse's slumping shoulders and led him towards the same knoll where his own heartache had begun.

"Father, the doctor shared with me that the white man's medicine cannot help our Annie. We must love her and celebrate the time we have with her here on the earth."

Iron Horse turned a quizzical look at his son. "I don't understand. She seems better and simply needs time to recover."

Shaking his head gently, John denied his father's hope, praying they would all learn to accept the workings of the Great Spirit. As the days passed and Annie's lassitude confirmed the doctor's prognosis, John seldom left the immediate vicinity of his home. He sat for hours in the shade of the pine and cedar branches near the sister he held so dear. Annie enjoyed his being close by, seeming to accept her fate with such unwavering graciousness that he came to love her more dearly each day.

She left her bed less and less as the hot days of July were succeeded by the oppressive days of August. She slept most of the time, though she roused easily to accept the attention of those who cared for her, engaging them in conversation that was bright and cheery. She loved to talk about school, or of Carter Heath and his wife, and often of Aaron Moss, for whom she had earlier formed a great fondness and to whom she now turned in hope. She loved hearing his stories of life in a place called heaven, of angels singing and streets of gold where everyone was healed of disease and sadness.

Late one morning, she awakened with difficulty. After taking some broth, she asked, "Please help me to my place in the shade so that I may lie quietly and enjoy the prairie once more." With half-closed eyes, she turned to her father and whispered, "I wish Aaron Moss would come."

"He will, my child," he replied, rising quickly to go for Tadita. At midday, an unusual restlessness came upon Annie suddenly before disappearing once again. As the afternoon wore on, she was conscious less and less. To those watching intently, she seemed to shift frequently between moments of death-like stillness and periods of peaceful sleep, her breathing steady and deep.

In one of her moments of wakefulness, she expressed numerous Indian endearments to her mother. Turning to John, she witnessed softly, "Oh, John, it's so beautiful. I think I see all the good spirits that Aaron Moss told me of," before lapsing back into that state they'd all come to dread. A pallor came over her face, and Good Heart asked her sister to hurry to the school and fetch Mrs. Heath. As John and her mother sat beside her, Annie opened her eyes and with a smile of transcendent sweetness said, "It seems so wonderful." Moments later, with her eyes closed and a smile still on her lips, she repeated the English lines she'd learned in school as though reciting them to herself.

> I wish my heart was a tiny cloud
> On the sunset edge of even,
> That tenderly bears the children's prayers,
> Through the open gates of heaven.

Her last words, spoken in the adopted tongue she loved so well, were a tribute to her loving nature. Her mother asked John to interpret them for her understanding, and as he spoke, a long sigh recalled their attention to the child. They realized that with that sigh, the spirit that had been too fair for earth had flown—just as the last rays of the sun gave various glowing colors to the clouds that rode low in the western sky.

It had all come so much as the doctor had said it would that John was lost in wonder and did not instantly recognize his grief. When Annie's mother realized that her child was gone, she seized the long knife that hung just below her waist and began to slash the hair from her head and to gash her face and arms. Despite knowing it was a traditional part of grieving, John put a restraining hand on her shoulder.

"No, Mother, Annie would not have you do this."

She stopped at once, knowing what he said was true. As she replaced the knife in its sheath, she fell to her knees by her daughter's side and with her face in her hands gave vent to her grief in a tremulous wail. It was heard by her sister and Mrs. Heath as they came from the school, and they knew what it meant.

It was heard by those in the camp as well, and they also knew. As the night deepened, the two mothers went out on the hill and the unearthly, plaintive wail of an Indian mother's song of grief was heard throughout the night while John and Mrs. Heath watched beside the body. Later on, as Aaron Moss and Iron Horse came over the ridge to the south, they heard the song of sorrow, and they understood. The darkness permitted tears to flow from a father's eyes without restraint, for no one could see them but the stars.

The following day, Annie was tenderly borne to a spot across the creek where she could face the day school that had meant so much to her. As they returned to the emptiness in their home, Iron Horse felt he was much nearer the time that old men look forward to, knowing that death would reunite them with their loved ones in the spirit world. John spent many hours sitting on the hill beside Annie's grave. As far back as he could remember, she'd lived her life joyfully enthusiastic about learning and loving. She'd been frail—not in spirit but in body—as long as he'd known her. He found peace in being thankful for having been given the time to learn and love with her in his new family. Ultimately, he accepted his grief as something he would carry forward as a reminder of the pain of loss—not as a burden but as a gift along the road to maturity.

CHAPTER 24

Carter's Journal

Fall 1894

Living Springs Ranch, Pine Ridge Reservation, South Dakota

Just days before his scheduled return to the boarding school, John asked if I knew how his cows were getting along at the ranch near Living Springs. We were all struggling with Annie's loss, and I was glad John expressed an interest in the future. I recalled an encounter with Jake Farmer some months earlier when I'd asked him how John's cattle were doing, and he'd simply replied that everything was all right.

John's question prompted me to suggest we ride over the next day to see for ourselves. He was eager to see his increased wealth. He had told Mr. Brun, the agriculture teacher at the school, about his cow and calf, and the man had shown interest in John's growing herd, teaching him the intricacies of being a cattleman until John developed a fondness for the animals and an excellent understanding of their care. Mr. Brun suggested that according to the general rules of increase, John could assume that his cow and calf should have grown into a herd of five by the addition of at least a yearling and two calves in the time since John received the first pair from Jake Farmer.

The following day, as we rode towards Living Springs, we shared thoughts about the general goodness of things at the time. John would have enough cows to start his own herd, and the summer had been mild with plenty of rain. Within sight of the cottonwoods marking Jake's ranch, we spotted him across the prairie, riding among a number of grazing cattle. We rode out to him without disturbing the animals.

"Good morning, Jake," I shouted as we rode up.

"Mornin', Mr. Heath. Mornin', John," responded the ranchman.

"Hello, Mr. Farmer. How are the cattle doing?" John inquired. "The grazing seems mighty abundant for this late in the season."

"Yes, the grass is good, and the cows are getting fat. We'll be cutting hay before long. I'm thinking of shipping my fat steers to Chicago this fall."

"How are the J Lazy Horseshoe cattle coming on?" I asked.

"Mighty fine," replied the ranchman, "getting fatter every day. I just saw her on the other side of that hill."

"Saw *her*?" I queried, not satisfied that I had heard correctly, considering John's calculations of how many cattle he should own by now. "Did the calf die?"

"No, the calf is with her mother and also has a calf at her side."

"That's what we expected," I ventured, "and how many head has John now?"

"Why, he has the cow I gave him, and she is branded as I agreed," Jake sneered.

At this response, John's eager expression changed to mirror my own unbelieving and sinking feeling. The word "she" indicated there was only the one, yet John knew both the heifer and her calf had survived.

"I see." I began an angry summation. "You know what the practices of the cattle country are: the offspring of any animal belong to the owner of that animal, not to the person on whose land they graze. John owns the heifer that you gave him because you thought she would die when you left her exhausted on Potato Creek. Yet the calf she had there and the calves that both of them have had since are marked with your brand instead of his. Is that what we are to understand?"

"Well, I only gave him the heifer, didn't I?" replied the man defensively, balling his fists around his reins. "I'm sorry if there has been a misunderstanding," he added in a vain attempt at conciliation.

I continued my summation of the rancher's actions. "There has been no misunderstanding. You owed this boy for a service he did for you. You made a pretense of showing your appreciation, but it turns out you have robbed him. And," I continued in an even tone, although I made no attempt to hide the contempt in my voice, "you led this boy to believe in you, yet you have betrayed his confidence from the beginning. What do you think any respectable cattleman of this country will say when they know of this?"

With a clear understanding of what he knew would be the sentiment of the other ranchers when they learned of his treatment of the boy, Jake sought to placate John and me by saying, "If that's the way you feel about it, Mr. Heath, I'll pay John the value of the cow if you ride to the house with me."

I glanced at John, who shook his head and whispered harshly, "I do not want his money. I trusted him with the care of my cattle."

Understanding his feelings of loss not just for an animal or two but also for the lost potential for his future, I watched as the young man's resentment and disgust grew into an expression of stoic acceptance. Unable to control my anger at this injustice so soon after the boy's loss of his sister, I leaned over from my seat in the saddle until I could feel the man's breath and enunciated simply but firmly, "Mr. Farmer, I'm proud of this boy for his self-respect. I want you to know I think you're one of the most contemptible human beings I've ever known. What if I'd been the one to find your cattle stolen? I think—" But I was interrupted by the cattleman, whose blind fury had taken control over his better judgment.

Jake rose in his stirrups, shaking his fist in the air, and roared with an oath, "I want you to know that no man, least of all a damn school teacher, can come on my range and tell me what's what!" As he spoke, his right hand lowered as if reaching for the gun in the holster on his belt.

I straightened in my saddle, looked steadily into his eyes, and spoke in the vernacular of the range. "Jake Farmer, you don't have the guts to shoot me." Then, after a second's pause I sneered, "Or anybody else in the open."

Following that statement of truth, Jake fingered the grip of his pistol momentarily before settling back into his saddle, jerking his horse harshly around, and spurring him towards the house. Obviously, there would be no further communication.

We watched as he continued to whip his horse angrily into the distance. Not wanting to be sitting in the same spot if the rancher decided to come back shooting, we turned and rode slowly homeward. As we traveled, I spoke the only words of consolation I could offer.

"John, I'm sorry—sorry that you lost your cattle, sorry that your plans as a rancher have been set back, and most of all sorry that such a skunk has white skin like mine. These days, you will find it is often so.

You have a right to take the branded heifer with you. If that's what you want to do, I'll help."

John pulled on his bridle to slow his pony's steps. "No, Mr. Heath. I will take this as a sign that I should heed my father's words and look for a new way to live." After a moment, he added solemnly, "So it will be," briefly nodding his acceptance of fate before we encouraged our horses towards the schoolhouse.

CHAPTER 25

The Gift

Late Fall 1894

Potato Creek Camp, Pine Ridge Reservation, South Dakota

On his way home, John stopped by the cabin of Running Fox, a longtime friend of Iron Horse who had many children and grandchildren. John shared his experience with the old man. He told how Jake had promised to care for the cattle and then gone back on his word by branding the calf and all subsequent animals with his own brand. Finally, John followed through on the intent of his visit.

"I believe it will be easy to identify my cow and her offspring. I have studied about the markings of animals and how they are passed from mothers to their offspring. She and the calves I saw have the same red coloring with a circle of white on their flanks. I believe any others would carry the same marking. There should be five head that rightfully belong to me."

His voice devoid of enthusiasm, John finished, "I promise that I have no intention of trying to recover my cattle from the likes of Jake Farmer. If the Indians of the camp want to secure them, they may do so and use them as they please—a gift from John Iron Horse."

With that, he headed home, resigned to the loss of his future as a cattleman. Gradually, he reflected on the smile that remained on the older man's face as he rode away and consoled himself that the family of his father's friend would not go hungry over the coming winter.

That evening as they sat outside their cabin, John told his father of the encounter with the cattleman and his visit to the home of Running

Fox. After several moments of thoughtful silence, Iron Horse weighed in. "I am sorry for your disappointment, but you will find bad men wherever you go. There are white men who will lie and steal, and there are Indians who will do the same. Soon, you will go away from the reservation. You will see many white people. You will live among the white people. Some of them will be good like Mr. Heath, and some will be bad like Jake Farmer. You must learn to know the good ways and not follow the bad ways. I'm sorry you told Running Fox that the Indians could have the animals from the white man's range. Our people do not steal cattle, but next winter they may act on your words."

Taking a deep breath, he continued, "But it may be right. Perhaps it is meant for you not to dream of being a rancher on the reservation. You'll have to choose your future among the white men."

Hearing his father's words, John understood he would return to the boarding school at the agency for another year.

In midwinter, there was a severe blizzard, and Iron Horse heard many stories of hardship among the families in the camps. The snow blanketed the range, with ice covering the water holes, making it necessary for the white ranchers such as Jake and his sons to give their cattle special attention. Aaron Moss shared with Iron Horse, who later shared with John, that he had seen the sons of Jake Farmer spend an entire day chopping ice from the watering places and scattering hay on top of the snow to feed their cattle. It reminded John of the hardships he might have endured if he had become a rancher, and he smiled thinking of how well the families of Running Fox would be eating over the winter.

Weeks later, Jake dropped by the cabin on Potato Creek to inquire if Iron Horse had seen John's cow. In a hateful voice, he stated more loudly than necessary, "On returning to the house late yesterday, my sons told me they haven't seen the J Lazy Horseshoe cow for several days. There may be others marked like her gone as well, but we're certain we haven't seen John's brand." He added snidely, "You don't reckon your son knows where she might be, do you?"

Hearing the unspoken accusation in the rancher's voice, Iron Horse replied calmly, "It would be strange for her to drift away in the blizzard, for she was born on this range. Perhaps she'll turn up in the spring roundup."

But when spring arrived and all the cattle were rounded up, Jake Farmer and his sons complained to the superintendent that not only the J Lazy Horseshoe cow was missing but also four of her descendants. Hearing the gossip, Iron Horse's eyes twinkled, knowing that throughout the winter the Potato Creek families had enjoyed many feasts at the dance house where a rich beef stew was served in unusual quantities, and the name of John Iron Horse was popularized by repetition in the council.

CHAPTER 26

Moving On

Fall 1894 to Summer 1895

Pine Ridge Reservation and Agency School, South Dakota

John's life following Annie's passing was marked by the transfer of his mentor and friend, Carter Heath, from the day school at Potato Creek to a boarding school in Montana. John returned to the agency school with his sorrow still poignant. He felt for his parents, whom he had left behind in their loneliness, yet he welcomed the necessity that took him away from everything that reminded him of his loss.

He accustomed himself to the changes that summer brought and derived some satisfaction from the realization that he was now one of the older and larger boys at the school. He entered into his work with an eagerness that became habitual, and soon earned a place high in the confidence and esteem of all his teachers. He frequently sought out the company of his teachers rather than spending time with other students his age, for he sensed in many of them a desire to return to the reservation as quickly as possible. Instead, John spent time with Mr. Brun, learning about record-keeping, or honing his body to its highest level of fitness with the calisthenics instructor.

When spring finally arrived, some of the older boys found employment working cattle at nearby ranches for the summer, but John no longer had any desire to become a rancher. A few of the girls left for an off-reservation school in hopes of becoming seamstresses and finding employment in the East. Several of the oldest girls had fallen in love with local drovers and convinced themselves they'd be happy raising a family on the range. It was a hard life, but there were no jobs for Indian boys on the reservation, and the drovers lived in nice cabins on large ranches. As the second year of his attendance at the agency school drew to a close, several of his teachers recommended he leave Pine Ridge for one of the larger, non-reservation schools, but John wouldn't consider such a step without consulting his father.

As expected, Iron Horse arrived on the closing day, his ponies pulling the creaky old wagon to the front of the school. Along the way home, John told Iron Horse of his accomplishments and shared his feelings of success. In the course of the conversation, he mentioned casually, "Father, shall I go back again to the boarding school at the agency, or shall I go to a big school far away?"

Iron Horse replied simply, "You must follow your heart, my son."

John didn't question his father's answer. When they arrived back at camp, he walked slowly out to where he knew he would find the pony herd, seeking the companionship of Hantaywee and the quiet of the prairie to make his decision. Late that night, Iron Horse prayed that his son would find the courage to leave the reservation behind.

Summer was a disappointment to John. The mentor of his youth had gone away, and despite frequent letters, John missed their heartfelt conversations. He had little inclination to hang around the Potato Creek camp since being around the day school only served to remind him of Carter's absence. The other youth were content to idle the days away, dozing in the shade of what trees remained, but John chose to spend most of his time in the company of Aaron Moss, whom he visited frequently at Corn Creek.

John often remained for several days at a time, accompanying the minister on his long drives. Aaron gave the kind of questioning answers that Carter had used, and John relished the opportunity to tax his mind with details as they discussed the intrigues of the Christian religion. John appreciated the belief in doing good to others and being honest in his dealings, for those were the same beliefs that were taught by the elders of his tribe. On the other hand, a religion that taught these things while establishing schools that punished Indian children for following the teachings of their elders was perplexing to John. Until he resolved that puzzle in his mind, he couldn't bring himself to commit to a belief in the goodness of this religion, and their conversations usually circled back to the weather or John's plans for his future in teaching.

CHAPTER 27

Carter's Journal

Fall 1894 to Spring 1895

Fort Shaw Indian Industrial School, Poplar, Montana

After almost five hundred miles of rattling trains, rocking coaches, and a rolling ferry ride that resulted in the loss of many of our personal possessions, my family arrived at Fort Shaw exhausted but in awe of the vast green vistas and flat-topped mountains such as we had never seen. Originally, I was disappointed to learn I'd be transferred here not as superintendent but as a teacher under the supervision of Mr. Doyle. However, my salary was higher and included a stipend to cover the expenses of my family and purchase new teaching materials. The additional monies along with the beauty of the area were enough compensation for us to be content for the time being.

Upon meeting Mr. Doyle, the superintendent, I surmised him to be a man of efficiency and dedication, though not particularly sociable. Just as Potato Creek had been, the school was well organized and established to serve both the staff and students in a way that brought pride to everyone involved. Mr. Doyle informed me that we were anticipating an enrollment of up to 250 children and were expected to be fully self-supporting this year. This would require the Indian students to produce all the needed food, clothing, and construction materials necessary for the running of the school at the same time as they worked to master the English language. I could only hope this was possible.

My family was assigned one of the former officer's quarters as our home, a place of white-plastered walls and wide glass windows that brought a joyous dance from Lillian as we entered. The structure was quite expansive compared to what we were accustomed to at Potato Creek. Besides a front and back room that served as our parlor and bedroom respectively, there was a small garret room that we turned into Liz's bedroom. There was enough space for a crib on the wall opposite her bed, and we had our own kitchen as well as a servant's room.

The only distressing aspect of our living arrangement was that we had to share a common dining room with the adjoining quarters. Our neighbors were a surly couple from Wisconsin, a teacher and his wife who seemed to find endless reasons to complain about the school. He was a man whose teaching philosophy required nothing more than his oversight of a group of students laboring for what he considered was their own good. It was obvious he felt they should be grateful for what the government was "giving them for free," in his words. His wife found countless amenities missing from the comfortable life she had left behind in the city and endlessly reminded her husband that it was his duty to elevate his status in the bureau so that they could be transferred as quickly as possible back to Washington where they would find a suitably lavish home on the river.

Despite the unhappy attitude of our quarter-mates, Lillian and I found the school itself to be a glorious place. There was a small chapel as well as a library, and—most importantly to Lillian, with the ever-increasing demands on her bladder—multiple outhouses, several of which were considerably closer to our quarters than those at Potato Creek. We discussed at length the importance of our children having an education at least equal to our own in order to ensure their success in whatever career they chose in the future. After a particularly lengthy conversation about a tutor for all the staff's children at Fort Shaw, Lillian stated firmly, "I wish for Elizabeth to be exposed to the more cultured refinements, art and music as well as embroidery and household management. Any sons must learn not just reading and arithmetic but a modicum of business management, logic, and something of politics."

I could only shrug. I was committed to teaching the Indian children to the best of my ability; it would be up to Lillian to raise our children and manage our household.

"My dearest," she continued, "I know that a school for our children will require planning. I realize every empty room on the fort is being used for instruction of the Indians, but I've also noticed they're completely empty in the afternoons when the Indian children labor at their industrial skills in the gardens and stables. There's no reason we can't bring a tutor for Liz to the school by spring."

I knew better than to argue with my pregnant wife at this point in my career.

Among the amenities at the school was a small hospital building where the superintendent, who was also a physician, operated a medical clinic that regularly served the needs of both Indians and staff. We were particularly thankful for his presence as both Lillian and I found it necessary to call upon his services often. Once again, Lillian's pregnancy was cumbersome, and she struggled with fatigue and discomfort. The doctor examined her and informed us that everything appeared normal. However, his recommendation of rest and quiet was almost impossible without a nanny for Liz. There was none of the closeness with the Indians as we'd had at Potato Creek, and despite my best efforts at getting to know the families of my students, we were unable to locate a woman who suited us as Rosa had.

In addition to Lillian's discomforts, I suffered from fever and chills off and on for several weeks, accompanied by an excruciating pain in my abdomen. The doctor examined me and prescribed repeated soakings in a tub of salts and steaming water. Thankfully, water was easily available from tanks outside that were fed by wooden pipes coming from the river. Despite that convenience, the mountain water was icy cold, and either Lillian or I had to fill buckets and carry them inside to fill a large iron pot to be heated over the cooking stove. Between the buckets and the armloads of wood required for the fire, my soakings were not an easy chore. However, the practice brought instant relief. The doctor prescribed a diet with abundant vegetables, and Lillian enjoyed taking advantage of the wealth of produce found in the school gardens. Thankfully, I began feeling much better once I established a regular schedule of trips to the outhouse.

Teaching in Montana was quite different from Potato Creek, where all the children were of the same tribe and had families nearby. Most of the students here were far from their home camps and were classed by skill, not age. Each class had students ranging from five to eighteen years of age and included as many as twenty or more.

For teaching English, I was required to make the students memorize English phrases and recite them daily in front of the class. The younger students, of which there were only five, were adept at memorizing the words. At that age, their brains were like sponges. The older students, however, had more difficulty and quickly lagged behind their younger counterparts. While they were all forbidden to speak their native languages, they often lapsed into various phrases I couldn't understand at all. I could only imagine what it must have sounded like to anyone listening in on my classroom; at any given time, there might have been three or more languages being spoken at once.

The students were a mix of several tribes, including Shoshone, Blackfoot, and Crow, among others. They also varied tremendously in dedication to their studies. A few seemed content to be at school and applied themselves—if not with Annie and John's enthusiasm, at least cheerfully—to learning a new language. On the other hand, the vast majority were either quietly distant or openly sullen. I heard rumors among the staff that the reason my position came open at Fort Shaw was because the former teacher was dissatisfied with the government policy of forcibly removing children from their homes to attend school. After I repeated the rumors to Lillian one evening, she observed, "It must be true, for that would explain the recalcitrant behavior of your students' parents towards us all. Perhaps it's why we haven't been able to find a nanny for Liz."

Not long after our arrival in Montana, we received a telegram from Aaron Moss updating us of events around Potato Creek and of John's progress in school. Though I've instructed many students over the years, John held a special place in my heart. Aaron's wire was simple: *"John summered here* STOP *Doubts my teaching* STOP *Ever hopeful* STOP."

I hadn't realized how much I missed the thought-provoking conversations with John and his father's insight into the behavior of the Indians, but Lillian and I had to settle into our new home and establish our own routine. I wrote John to update him about our lives as he approached the end of his student days at Pine Ridge. Several weeks later, Aaron was kind enough to wire John's response: "*Congratulations* STOP *Must leave Pine Ridge* STOP *Where* STOP."

Without leaving the telegraph office, I sent back immediately, "*Carlisle* STOP *The best* STOP *Where I found my love* STOP."

We celebrated the birth of our son, Ralph Carter, at the end of February. Lillian did well with the delivery and appreciated the presence of a physician. But she immediately missed the presence of John's mothers, who had stepped in to help clean up, wash linens, and comfort the baby when needed. There was no such assistance here, and my hands were full keeping up with Liz. Several days later, I found time long after Lillian, Liz, and little Ralph were asleep to write John a letter informing him of our son's birth and wishing him our best.

Dance house at Potato Creek

Elizabeth Lillian at one month

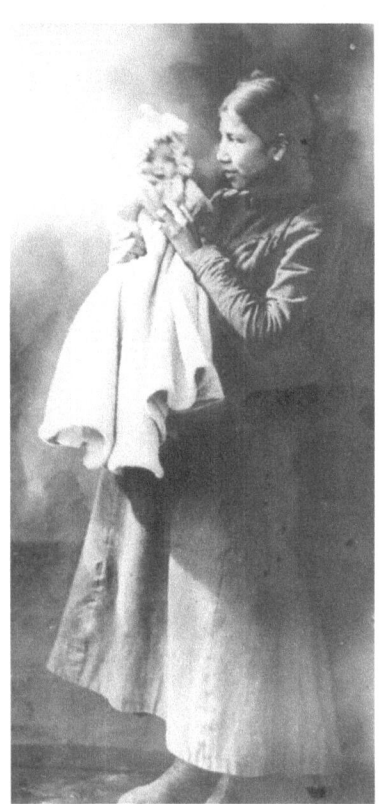

Liz with Rosa Long Soldier

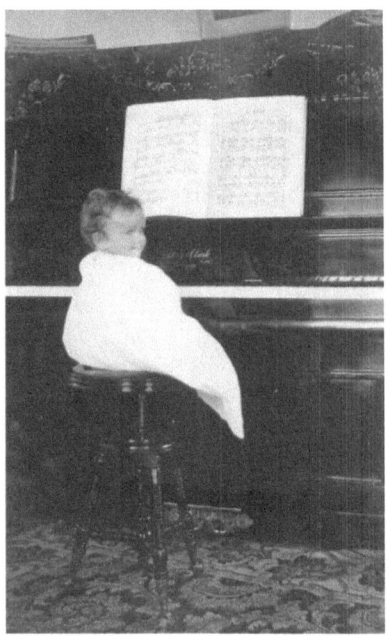

Liz at the piano

Liz with Spotted
Horse's wife

Liz's play wear on
the reservation

Fourth of July crowd at Pine Ridge

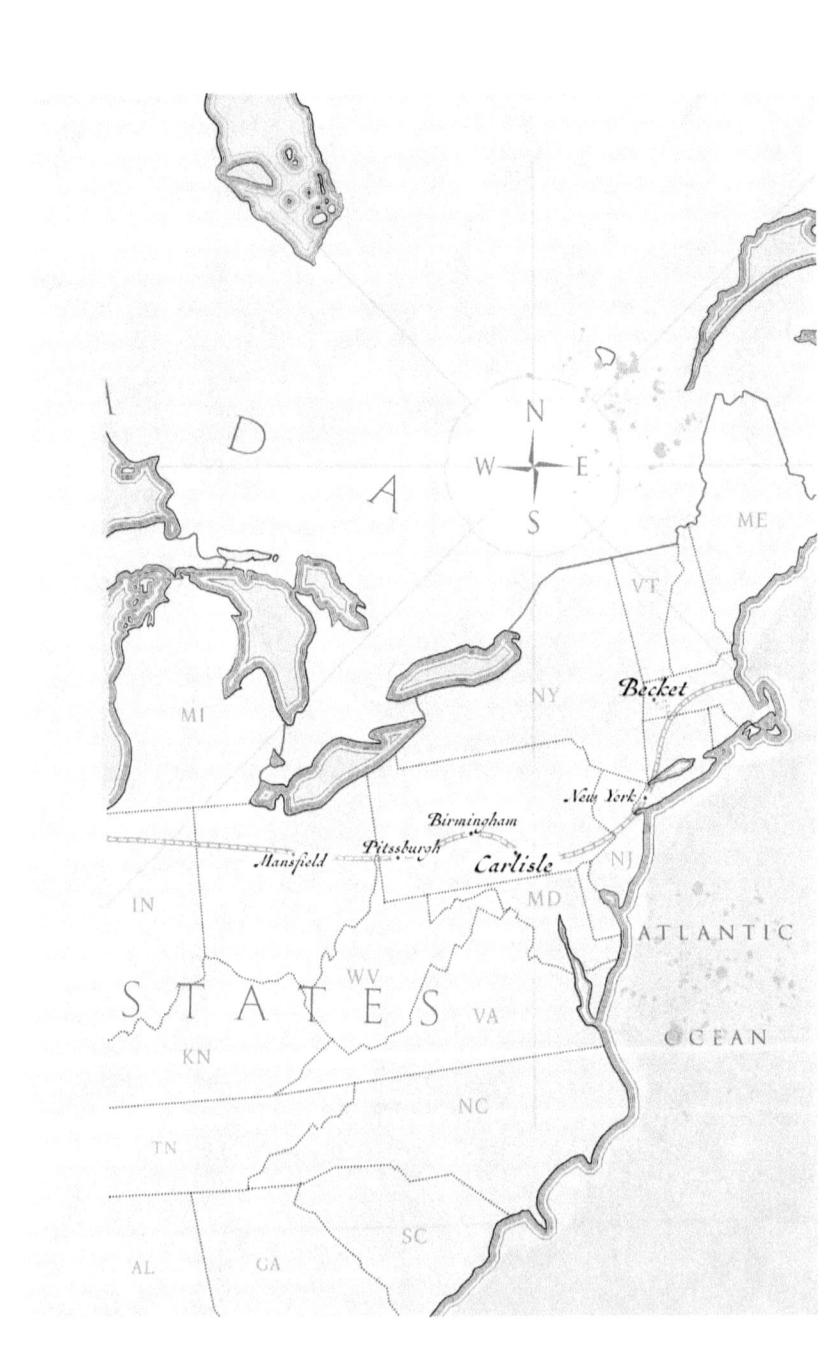

III

The Big School

CHAPTER 28

Carter's Journal

Spring 1895 to Summer 1896

Fort Shaw Indian School, Montana

Fort Shaw was much larger than Potato Creek. It was difficult to help Lillian and get my lessons prepared each day. Besides our time in class, numerous meetings were scheduled by our superintendent where we were told how things would be done rather than being able to work a schedule that fit my family's needs. Without a doubt, I was overwhelmed. The care of two small children and Lillian's subsequent pregnancy, her third, was almost more than I could handle. Unlike Potato Creek where we visited with the families of our students regularly and I had frequent discussions with Iron Horse about their needs and wants, here we felt stranded and alone.

The faculty was substantial in number but distant and unfriendly. Those who taught the industrial subjects kept to themselves. They seemed more like foremen of work crews than teachers, most of them pacing silently beside the students as they worked on various projects necessary for the operation of the school. The occasional "Do it again!" or "Get it right this time!" was all the instruction I witnessed during their classes.

I would have been happier teaching construction or metalworking because the academic classes focused almost entirely on teaching the students English. The female teachers occasionally inserted harsh lessons on etiquette at the table or complained their laundry wasn't clean enough. It was as if there were a school and a work camp, each with its own separate goals. Back at Potato Creek, I taught math while doing carpentry work, and the children improved their English skills by learning Christmas songs and poetry. Here, there was no such cooperation, and almost no art or music, only sports.

The girls stayed busy until sunset each evening, working in the gardens, making butter, sewing, or crocheting. The boys worked constantly on the upkeep and maintenance of the stables and outbuildings, shoeing the numerous work horses and mules, building furniture, and maintaining the water lines and tanks that serviced the school from the river. All of their energies were directed towards these tasks, with little emphasis on skills that would be useful when the students went into the world after completing their education.

There were large, productive gardens, but virtually all our other food, especially meat, had to be brought in. It appeared that what wildlife might have been here in the past had been hunted to extinction for miles around. Occasionally, an elk or black-tailed deer wandered close and provided a tasty meal for the lucky hunter, but there was no water in the soil, so there was no grazing for livestock of any kind. We were lucky to get the occasional prairie grouse or rabbit, and the cost of my family's food, taken out of my salary, forced Lillian to budget our remaining funds carefully.

I missed our herb garden, the root cellar, and the ration cattle that grew fat on our grazing allotment. Most of all, I missed Rosa Long Soldier and her quiet solicitude towards Liz and Lillian. Because of the inflated cost of everything at the post, there was no hope of affording a nanny for the children or a tutor for Liz. As her pregnancy progressed, Lillian could no longer care for Ralph. He was an active child, squirming in her arms when she picked him up or wiggling his way off the bed and onto the floor when she put him down. Although he wasn't walking yet, he was able to scoot over the hardpan floor, smearing dirt on his clothes and getting out of doors so quickly that Lillian couldn't keep up.

Liz became a petulant child, crying as easily and loudly as when she was an infant and always demanding to be the center of attention. My mother's good intentions in lavishing her with gifts early in her life caused difficulties in this remote location. Her fascination with horses would have been a godsend if only we could have enlisted the services of someone to watch over Ralph. Relieved of that responsibility, I could have found time to explore the area on horseback with Liz, but as it was, I struggled to finish my daily lesson preparations while holding Ralph and trying to entertain Liz with poetry readings and stories of the Indians.

Unfortunately, I began to suffer again with fever and chills along with painful cramping deep in my belly. The doctor suggested I follow my previous practice of soaking in salt baths, which relieved the discomfort temporarily. I learned to eat only the blandest of foods: warm milk poured over toast for breakfast, potatoes creamed with butter from the school dairy for lunch, and chipped dried beef creamed and served over warm bread from the student bakery in the evenings. These meals were hardly sufficient to keep up my health under such a rigorous schedule of teaching and childcare.

To my surprise, Mr. Doyle received several complaints saying that I was impatient with the children and more concerned with my own business than that of the school. When he called for an investigation, I felt certain the source of the grievance was my disgruntled neighbor. His lassitude towards his teaching duties was evident. He didn't seem to comprehend that the children would advance to the level that was demanded of them. As a result, his students lagged behind those of the other teachers in their comprehension of reading and did very poorly when reciting English phrases to an audience. I believed he was unable to inspire them because he found nothing of value in what he did. He disliked the Indians and wanted only to collect his check and move up the ladder of bureaucracy.

The investigation uncovered nothing to substantiate charges against me, just complaints from an unhappy employee. I had never failed to perform my duties, but the entire affair was unnerving. Late one evening, after the children had finally drifted off to sleep, Lillian whispered, "I don't know how much longer I can stay here," and then rolled away from me, pulling the covers tightly over her head, shutting off further conversation.

The following morning, I requested a transfer back to Washington as a copyist in the General Land Office. I had already passed the civil exams required and felt the move was the only answer to our predicament. I wired several former acquaintances at the Department of the Interior, seeking letters of support, and wrote a missive to John, telling him of the beauty of this land and sharing the news of our growing family.

For the next few weeks, there were rumors of my transfer to Chamberlain Indian School as superintendent. Although it would have meant a significant raise, it was still a remote location. The only concern was that my health inspection revealed that I had missed more work days than I realized and, at five feet, nine inches tall, weighed only 140 pounds, significantly under the recommended body mass for a man my age.

Thankfully, after a number of letters of recommendation were delivered to the assistant commissioner of the interior, Mr. Richards assigned me as a clerk in the Office of the Attorney General in Washington. It was a position I would not have sought but was more than happy to accept. I was sorry to learn of the death of Mrs. Lewis, the former clerk, but her position was one I felt perfectly suited to our needs at the time.

In addition to receiving the notice about my new position, we received a long letter from John, sharing his adventures and excitement about his decision to attend the school I had recommended.

CHAPTER 29

A New World

Fall 1896

Pine Ridge Reservation, South Dakota

The time had come for John to leave the reservation. Representatives of different schools came to the agency to solicit John's enrollment. Each gave his own glowing account of the advantages at his school, but in reality, their greatest interest was in what prestige or winning record John might bring to their school to increase funding from their supporters. Winning teams in football and baseball drew a great deal of financial support from private donors, but debate teams and track and field success made the news as well, bringing in additional contributions to the Indian schools.

He could pursue any number of programs, from law to medicine, business to art. The representatives described the possibilities for social life and emphasized special comforts in the dormitories and dining rooms they thought might appeal to prospective students. Boys were especially interested in the freedom allowed for visiting nearby towns and the potential for jobs in whatever area each school was located. Every new pupil added federal funding to the coffers of the schools, and the representatives were superb salesmen.

John's heart was set simply on attending the best school. After listening to each representative, the young man had asked to seek the guidance of his father, Aaron Moss, and Carter Heath. Despite Iron Horse's encouragement to learn the white man's way, John feared his father would want him to go to Chamberlain or Rapid City, both closer to his home and family. On the other hand, he knew Carter and Aaron understood his long-term goals. Having received each of their counsel, John enrolled for a term of five years at Carlisle Indian Industrial School in Pennsylvania. The five-year agreement guaranteed him the privilege of returning home to visit family at the end of three years, but no sooner. It was the government's intent to remove the students from any Indian influence for as long as possible.

Arrangements were made for his transfer as soon as he passed a physical exam. He traveled to Corn Creek to visit Aaron, thanking him for helping fill the void left by Carter and Lillian's departure. Later that afternoon, he dropped by the day school, sitting quietly on the knoll above Annie's grave and reflecting on lessons learned from Mr. Heath.

Back at his family's cabin, the tin-covered trunk was packed. Once again, it would carry the love of his family and serve as a reminder of his life on the reservation. His mothers were especially sad as they contemplated the loneliness that would come to them by his going away not just for one year but for at least three. It was required by the white man's law, and his parents knew it had to be as it was. That night, as he lay in his blankets, John was filled with regret and sorrow yet excited for his future—regret at leaving the home that had been so dear to him, sorrow for those who would be left behind, and excitement as he considered the wonders in the outside world of which he had heard but never seen.

He thought of the great iron horse that drew trains of wagons over miles of steel tracks, of towns and cities where white people were as many as the grasses on the prairie or the needles on the pines. He tried to imagine buildings as high as the sky and rivers so broad and deep they could only be crossed on bridges built of timber and steel. He thought of lakes that no one could see across and forests so dense and thick that no one could see through or beyond them. John wondered if this could all really exist.

Sunup the next morning found the family well on their way. They stopped at the agency, where John met several other boys and girls traveling to Carlisle. After securing his ticket and completing the paperwork for school, the family stayed overnight before heading to the rail station at Rushville. For all anyone knew, it might be their last trip together as a family. Three years was an eternity on the reservation, and many young people never returned from their first visit to the white man's world.

Once in Rushville, the students were scheduled to board a train that would carry them across the country. Iron Horse understood the enormity of the journey, for he had made the trip to Washington in 1875 as one of the delegates with Red Cloud who spoke with the white leader, Ulysses Grant. The chief had not forgotten that the president ultimately broke his promises and betrayed the Indians, yet Iron Horse was confident John was making the right decision.

As the horses plodded before the wagon, Iron Horse counseled John, his voice filled with sadness. "My son, I feel this is the last ride we'll take together, for I am old, and not much time will pass before I go to the long sleep. Remember, my spirit will always be with you. While you are among the white men, do as they do. The world is good if we are good, and it is bad if we are bad."

John solemnly nodded his understanding.

As they entered the town of Rushville, its rail station standing quietly beside tracks that disappeared over the horizon, Iron Horse turned, grasped John's hand, and pledged hoarsely, "When you go away tonight, my heart goes with you."

There were no words for John to respond as he nodded, blinking over and over, both hands squeezing tightly onto his father's.

Having no plans to return home in the darkness, Moves First and Good Heart set up their tipi as the men said their goodbyes. The women wouldn't embarrass their son by displaying their tears publicly, so they settled into their blankets, crying softly. When the call came for boarding, John paused and stared wordlessly at the massive engine. Steam hissed, and the engineer blasted three short whistles, giving the final signal for all to get on board. John reached out one last time, grasping his father's hand and feeling his father's powerful grip in return. With that handshake, John left his family and turned to greet the representative from the school, Mr. Cornish, who had been sent to escort the new students on their journey.

John settled into his seat and fell asleep to the rocking lull of iron wheels on steel tracks. He felt the sensation of speeding through the darkness and a sense of loss at leaving his family behind. Once a deep sleep overtook him, he had a vision of a land he'd never seen. There were undulating hills, widespread trees, fields of beautiful green and gold, large, comfortable-looking houses, and huge barns. There were horses and cattle different from those on the prairie, and everywhere people with kindly faces among whom he felt at ease. Throughout his vision, there appeared a presence that was spirit-like and vague, but just as John felt he might recognize the identity of the spirit, he was awakened by the cheery voice of Mr. Cornish asking if he wanted to go to breakfast when they arrived at their first stop.

It was bright daylight as the train approached Sioux City, where it would wait while they had breakfast. John became absorbed in watching the changing panorama. They passed stacks of hay and grain so immense that he wondered if there were enough horses and cattle to eat it all. The fields were vast and bordered all around by trees such as he had never seen. As the train slowed and drew into the station, he felt sure the building must be one of the most beautiful in the world. Its shape was not unlike the *H*-shape of the agency school, but it was built of solid, deep-red brick with huge, white-framed windows all around, more than John could count. The metal roof was highlighted by what appeared to be an enormous bell tower that John imagined must keep everyone on schedule. People bustled in and out of various doors, brightly dressed and hurrying as if they too were going on a great adventure.

Mr. Cornish showed him a small lavatory, where John quickly cleaned up, growing hungry as he realized he had not sampled any of the delicacies his mothers had packed for the trip.

After a breakfast of ham and eggs, biscuits, and coffee, he had a few moments to observe the huge iron monster waiting on tracks that stretched out of sight in both directions. As he heard the pulsations of the monster's heart and saw its breath emerge in gasps of impatience, it seemed the creature possessed the very breath of life. It was a product of the civilization into which he was going and of which he was to be a part, and he began to feel that he would never be content to go back to a life that found glory only in the past.

In his mind, he compared the lavish portions of ham served with breakfast to the meager strips of beef his mothers were forced to use for every meal. The verdant forests here made the windswept prairie look dry and dead. The pastel greens and blues of the grasses where his ponies grazed seemed faded compared to the verdant fields that stretched to the horizon here. Neatly folding a soft cotton coverlet and draping it back over his seat, he could almost feel the dirt and grit he would have shaken from his blankets on Potato Creek before pulling them tightly around himself and falling asleep on the floor.

When the train resumed its journey, John sat apart from the others where he could watch the changing scenes. He saw the open range of the great West give way to fields of corn, orchards, and cultivated farms in rich valleys fed by wide streams of water. The wonder of it caused him to forget time, and he realized it was afternoon when he caught his first glimpse of a mighty river. The train followed its course for mile after mile, now on its very bank, then lost to view behind fields planted with crops unknown to John. He was overwhelmed by the scenes and drained from trying to absorb it all at such speeds as the train traveled.

There was more to come as they entered the outskirts of Dubuque, the train slowing to thread between houses set so close together that he could not see between them. Suddenly, they were passing great buildings so high he couldn't see their tops from his position by the window. Bell clanging and steam whistle blaring, the train finally slowed to a stop, ending inside a huge structure that surrounded the entire train and cut off John's view of the blue sky and clouds. He felt a sense of relief when Mr. Cornish came to tell him they would have time to leave the train for a while to rest and find refreshment.

They left as a group and went out into the pandemonium of the great station, forcing their way through crowds of hurrying, jostling people who wore purposeful expressions. The food in the station restaurant was delicious and different from anything he could have imagined. He had a choice of a small beefsteak with rich brown gravy, a thick-cut pork chop drizzled with maple syrup, a large slice of pink, smoked ham, or thick slices of liver with chunks of bacon crumbled over a thick onion gravy. In addition to the choice of meats, each meal included a bowl of steaming, maple-sweetened oatmeal with fresh cream, a huge slab of fruit pie, and large, fluffy wheat cakes with butter and syrup. The snow-white porcelain plates with *C. & N.W.* gilded across the top, the silver place settings and starched linen napkins, the black-dressed waitstaff that filled and refilled, whisking away used plates and bringing fresh dishes, comprised a show of abundance beyond his comprehension.

At the end of the meal, Mr. Cornish handed a number of carefully folded bills to one of the waiters and guided the travelers back into the crush of people. His action was repeated at each point in the trip where food or services were provided, and John began to understand that it was all part of the cost of his government education.

To resume their journey, the group navigated another section of the depot and boarded a different train that drew slowly away between enormous buildings. Mr. Cornish took a seat beside John, for he was intrigued by the young man with his quiet maturity. He explained the things they'd seen along the way, relieving much of the anxiety that had built up as John tried to absorb it all in a single day. The train snaked towards the great river again, gradually climbing on rails that rose higher and higher on massive piers of wood and later stone and steel sunk deep into the riverbed, until the whole of the train was above the roiling waters.

John was more impressed than afraid. The sheer volume of water that flowed into the distance and the huge timbers of the bridge were an awe-inspiring climax to the day's experiences. He sat silently, gazing at the vast expanse below and on either side, but he was glad for the deepening shadows of evening and soon enjoyed the oblivion of sound slumber.

When he awoke the next morning, he was again in a country such as he had never seen. It was flat and level, unrelieved by hills or noticeable landmarks as far as he could see, and it appeared to John to be one vast, interminable field of corn. Soon, the towns became more frequent, and it was not long before Mr. Cornish came by with his cheerful morning greeting. It was apparent they were again coming into a large city. The track they were on merged with others, and again they passed houses, small and scattered at first and gradually getting larger and closer together. The train slowed to traverse a massive jumble of tracks, until suddenly they plunged into darkness amid the clamor of clanging bells and thick, smoke-filled air. Finally, they saw the light of day again as they came to a stop among an unbelievable number of long trains of cars and other hissing, throbbing horses of iron.

This was Chicago, one of the world's great cities. They had three hours to stroll about the city, giving John and his companions relief from the tedium of their journey. Passing under the twenty-six-foot-high domed ceiling with its ornate columns and marble floors, the group moved through the crowded station to the street filled with people and amazing sights.

Mr. Cornish took great pains to show them as much as possible. The students were intrigued by the black covering of the streets that didn't shift or make dust when they walked, the great skyscrapers that appeared to touch the sky, and the street cars that seemed to move along by magic, dinging their bells to warn pedestrians to move quickly or be mowed down. They stayed clear of the massive, lathered horses that drew enormous loads and the carriages that moved without apparent power, honking their horns and clattering as they traveled. All along the streets, the bottom floors of the buildings were filled with shops displaying an infinite variety of products in beautifully decorated windows. Street vendors with colorful carts and umbrellas offered unknown fruits and wares along the curbs of the paved streets.

Mr. Cornish led them into a gigantic store, where they experienced marvelous exhibits of candies and clothing and shoes such as they'd never seen, finally boarding an elevator that whisked them up to another level of the store and left them with indescribable sensations of fear and wonder mixed with a touch of having their stomachs turned upside down. When at last they returned to the station from which they were to depart, they were filled with the spectacle of it all.

They left the city and found themselves again in open country. They passed the indigo-blue waters of Lake Michigan that stretched into the distance. That night, John settled into sleep with the knowledge that he would be at his destination in the morning, but for a moment, he wished he could go back to the cabin on Potato Creek and start over, just to experience it again and know that it was all real.

CHAPTER 30

A Different World

Fall 1896 to Spring 1897

Carlisle Indian School, Pennsylvania

John woke as the train slowed to a stop, shaking his head to dispel the cobwebs of slumber. He glanced out the window and had a sense they were in a massive valley, for he saw rolling hills in every direction. Close to the station were small, irregular fields and clusters of massive trees like he'd seen in his vision on the first night of the train ride. He wondered if this could be the land that had come to him in his dreams.

As John contemplated the possibilities, Mr. Cornish came to his berth.

"Well, my boy, we're nearing our journey's end and will depart from the train momentarily."

When John stepped from the train, he was impressed by the quiet of Carlisle in contrast to the clanging bells and shrieking whistles at previous stops. It was a welcome change. Following Mr. Cornish's soft-spoken directive, John stepped from the platform into a second vehicle and took his first ride on a mysteriously propelled coach that ran along its own trail of steel across the city. Beautiful homes surrounded by spacious grounds lined the streets and were shaded by spreading trees like those he remembered from his dream.

As the coach slowed, John peered forward to see the entrance of the school. Tall, straight columns of red brick standing on white granite bases and topped with carved granite globes stood guard over a curving drive that flowed across landscaped grounds and well-trimmed trees. Numerous young people sat around the grounds in the shade of massive trees or stood on the porch of what Mr. Cornish informed them was the dining hall. Its neat, white, clapboard exterior, wide front porch, and massive windows were complemented by ornate white trim work all around. Nestled behind the dining hall stood another building with wide, white-trimmed porches, airy windows, and a widow's walk above the porch. The overall appearance of the entire grounds was clean, well cared for, and inviting. John felt the stirrings of hunger and wondered what meals would be like in such an attractive place.

Mr. Cornish led John, along with two other boys, directly to the front steps of what he explained was the administration building. Set apart from the other, larger buildings, its exterior walls were burgundy-red brick with wide porches that wrapped around the front and sides, while the rear wall was covered in climbing ivy vines that revealed its age.

Inside, the young men were introduced to Major Mack, the superintendent of the school. He was a military man who had taken part in many of the early Indian campaigns as an officer in the Army. Unlike many in similar positions, he'd seen the goodness and humanity of the Indian people. After much effort, he'd succeeded in getting a school established based on the tenets of the Hampton Normal and Agricultural School of Virginia, a facility founded to educate freed slaves so that they could support themselves after the Civil War. He believed a similar program would help the Indians adjust to life in the white world. His motto was "Kill the Indian, Save the Man" for he believed the Indians' only hope of survival was to give up their native culture and assimilate as a people into the white man's world.

Of course, his motto suited the government completely. After years of bloody battles with the tribes, the government had decided it would be easier, and cheaper, to educate the Indians rather than fight them. If the children were denied their native culture, the old ways would die with the elders. Ultimately, the government's goal was to send them not into a new world as educated individuals but back to the reservations to change life there while saving the Army the embarrassment of losing any more battles as Custer had.

The major refused to acknowledge the difference between his own goals and the government's and focused only on the good he believed he was doing. Like Carter, he threw himself wholeheartedly into his school. It was understood that no student would be enrolled or discharged without being brought to him for his greeting or to receive his Godspeed on their journey into the world.

Major was taller than the average man, about fifty years of age with military erectness and carriage. His graciousness and dignity were reflected in his face, and his kindly nature shone through his deep-set eyes. He looked intently into the eyes of each student as they were presented to him. When his hand closed over John's, the young man felt a firm but gentle pressure, suggestive of a personality he hadn't felt since Carter Heath's. When the major placed a second hand over their joined ones, John could feel the extra pressure. He looked deep into the major's eyes and recognized a spark of personal interest, then returned the intensity of the handshake, feeling he had found a kindred spirit in the director of his new school.

By now, John was about eighteen years old and a full six feet tall, with proportions and a carriage that could have served the most exacting artist as a model for the ideal man. His face expressed a quiet reserve and sincerity. His deep-brown eyes bespoke intelligence and inherent gentleness. His nose, though not prominent, was full and straight, and his mouth slightly wider than most, with thin lips that gave the world notice of his determination at a glance. His cheeks were not so high as to detract from the symmetry of his face, and his jaw showed strength. His unblemished skin was light bronze, glowing evidence of his physical good health. He returned the major's greeting and replied to his questions with characteristic composure and a facile use of English spoken with an intonation that was indistinguishable from any white man's.

John left the superintendent that morning with a feeling of admiration and respect. When John found his assigned place in the dormitory later, he was amazed to see that someone had kindly brought his tin trunk in and placed it squarely beside his bed. He sat on the military-style cot and reached out to stroke the top of the trunk, briefly sensing the presence of Iron Horse in this place far from the reservation. Knowing that his father's spirit was indeed with him as promised, John sponged himself clean and dressed in the uniform that had been laid across the bed when he arrived. He placed the military-style cap on his head, tucking loose ends of hair behind his ears and pulling his braids over his shoulders to the front. He rubbed his palms over them as they lay flat along the full length of his chest, wondering how long it would be before he could expect to see them cut.

It was all part of accepting the white man's way, but that knowledge brought little comfort in the quiet of the empty room. Shaking his head, feeling the weight of his tresses, John inhaled deeply and mentally accepted what was to come. He understood it was necessary to achieve his goal of completing the education he needed in order to be successful in the world of the white man. After that brief moment of gloom, John strolled out onto the campus that was supposed to be his home for the next five years.

The year was set to begin with a full enrollment of six hundred boys and girls and an employee force of more than sixty. The students ranged in age from those not even in their teens to some who were in their mid-twenties. Some, like John, had begun their education at a day school, moved to a boarding school on the reservation, and were coming here to complete their education off the reservation. Others—orphans and children of families who had surrendered their children to white agencies—had lived there most of their lives.

All across the Western territories, government agents had worked to ensure the Indians believed in the benefits of the white man's ways. Some convinced Indians that they wouldn't have lost their lands had they been able to read the treaties their leaders signed. Some persuaded parents to send their children, no matter their age, to off-reservation schools, telling them that bigger schools provided greater opportunities for food and jobs. Some threatened parents with the loss of government provisions if they didn't send their children to school. The worst believed that Indians were simply too primitive, giving the government not just a reason but a right to remove their children, forcibly if necessary. Regardless of the reason, Indian children were sent away to schools where they succumbed to disease and depression, many never to be heard from again.

John knew none of this history as he strolled the grounds and open buildings. He saw students with every degree of Indian blood, from the darkest-skinned full-blood to the yellow hair and gray eyes of those with the smallest fraction of mixed blood. As he met more of his fellow students, he learned there were Indians from nearly every reservation in the country, including Eskimos from Alaska and mixed-bloods from Maine, New York, and other sections where the Indian had long since been lost as a distinct part of the population.

Despite the relaxed atmosphere, John knew that life at the school was organized in a military manner. It gave the students an orderliness and discipline that helped prepare them for learning without questioning. The curriculum was designed to train them to live what the white man considered a better life. It included English, math, various courses in history, drawing, and writing composition. The students produced their own weekly newspaper as well as other publications.

In addition to academics, they were required to devote half of their time to work in the industrial departments, where the boys learned farming and manufacturing skills while the girls learned sewing, cooking, and gardening. Since there was significant demand for domestic help in the homes of wealthy families in the East, the girls were expected to master home management, etiquette, and the laundering, repair, and ironing of clothes made of fabric. Some students stayed at the school after graduation in order to attend courses at Dickinson College or Dickinson School of Law, all paid for by a government that was willing to spare no expense as long as the younger generation of Indians did not continue to fight for their ancestral lands.

The school offered a top-notch music program, and the award-winning band, orchestra, and choral groups were evidence of the natural talents of Indians from across America. Carter had told John that the school was ranked highly in athletics, and their ball teams frequently competed with such prestigious schools as Harvard, Cornell, Yale, and Dartmouth. John looked forward to making use of his height, physical strength, and hours of calisthenics against these other teams.

On his second day at Carlisle, John had time to walk through the various buildings, into the shops, and out to the farm fields, experiencing much the same feelings as when he had walked into the well-ordered schoolroom of Carter Heath. He also felt the same loneliness that possessed him on the first day at the agency boarding school when he sensed the coming change in his life and was unsure and afraid.

Later that day, the transition in the students' identities began in earnest. The boys' braids were cut, falling heavily to the floor beside the barber's chair. The remaining hair was clipped short above their ears and neatly shaped across the top. The girls' flowing black tresses were cut at or above shoulder length with short bangs across their foreheads and then topped with massive bows tied and drooping along the sides of their tear-filled faces. Back at Potato Creek, John had never questioned the difference between his and Annie's names and those of his adopted family, but now he learned how lucky he was to already have a name that was easy on the white teachers' tongues and to have already become proficient in the white man's language.

Here the teachers couldn't pronounce most Indian names nor understand the languages of the students from various tribes. Furthermore, they made no effort to learn, and as a result, the students were forced to take on a new identity. If a student had been exposed previously to the education system and understood English, they were given the opportunity to modify their Indian names. Otherwise, they were forced to choose a new name from a list that was easy for the white teachers to pronounce and remember. The first two boys John had met, Lone Eagle and Dancing Fox, became Ethan Williams and Preston Smith. The boys picked Ethan and Preston from a list on the chalkboard and were given surnames the teachers chose because they sounded something like the Lakota words for eagle and fox.

Once their names were recorded, the students spent the next few hours getting familiar with their new identities. Those who had been at the school for some time helped the newcomers adjust, speaking comfortingly to each, calling them by the white man's names and reassuring them that they too would become accustomed to the change. Former young warriors sat pensively, running their fingers through shortened tresses, continuing over the collars of their uniforms as if the hair were still there, then glancing at the others in embarrassment at the mistake.

John quickly looked away after seeing a single tear fall between Ethan's fingers where the young man's face was buried. Ethan sat dejected and alone under one of the massive oaks on the school's parade ground. Rather than walking towards him to offer solace and let his new friend know his tears had been seen, John turned and walked away.

Several children spoke no English. They sat wide eyed and confused, tears flowing silently for fear of discipline from the attending teachers. Sitting as straight and proud as they could, the little ones held tightly to the ends of their freshly shorn locks as if pulling them hard enough would miraculously make them grow back. Most had seen others return from school with short hair, but the actual loss of their own was a devastating blow.

Having accepted the loss of his braids as part of his journey to the life Iron Horse and Carter Heath encouraged him to seek, John walked slowly back towards the dormitory. He was uncomfortable with such raw emotion on display. As he crossed the parade grounds, John passed where the girls had gathered in much the same way as the boys. Those who had been at the school longer sat beside the new arrivals, their saggy hair bows falling across their foreheads like rivulets of sweat as they reassured the new girls of their beauty and tried to emphasize the freedom and cleanliness of shorter hair.

Most of those who had just lost their tresses sat hunched over and sobbing, their fingers sliding through the short, loose strands that ended at the jawline. Some few tugged at the ends like the boys and younger children, willing the length to increase with every tug, while others sat, their backs ramrod straight, braiding what hair they had left as tears streamed over their cheeks, dripping into dark, widening circles on the navy fabric of their skirts.

On his third morning at Carlisle, John awakened to the sound of reveille and entered into the routine of life at the school. It was regulated and timed by bugle calls. The interest he felt in that first day's work intensified as the days passed and he gained self-assurance and purpose. He found himself well advanced in scholarship according to the standards of the school and was told by one teacher that he could pass the requirements for graduation in three years, possibly two, despite having agreed to a term of five years.

He was assigned to work in the tin shop in the industrial department, but as he engaged in the work of a tinner's apprentice, he found humor in learning this trade as if he could continue it on the reservation. He laughed at the thought of earning income by repairing the nonexistent tin wares of the housewives on Potato Creek, where the creek itself was the washpot, empty five-gallon coal-oil jugs served as tea kettles, and coffee pots were nothing more than salvaged containers for a lard substitute. He imagined equipping the run-down cabins with gutters and downspouts or replacing tipi coverings with tin laid upright over the lodge poles. When the futility of it finally replaced the humor, John sought Mr. Cornish and asked to be assigned to work on the farm.

At the opening of football season, John practiced with other newcomers. Running with speed and agility had served him well in his years at Potato Creek. However, nothing had prepared him to toss a hard leather bundle into the arms of a running teammate, let alone catch it when it was thrown high in the air in his general direction. Despite his dedication to practice, John didn't make the team, but he had earned the respect of many of the boys. When the baseball team went to New England for one of its most important games, he was taken along as a substitute because of his speed. Hitting a flying ball with a stick was similar to some of the hunting games he'd played as a child, and the hand-eye coordination he'd learned helped him score a run for his team.

He attained the office of first sergeant in his drill company, an unusual achievement for a first-year student. He took an interest in many other activities, winning numerous debates with students older than himself thanks to Mr. Heath's practice of making his students defend their answers, right or wrong. John had an obvious gift of speechcraft, common among a people who valued their oral history and shared important traditions in story form for their children. As the year advanced, both teachers and students recognized John as one of the most dependable students in the school, and his classmates took to calling him "Chief" in a respectful but joking way.

One day in late spring in Miss Sharp's English class, a large, mixed-blood boy named Ben Rowland, known by everyone as a bully, refused to rise from his seat when making a recitation. It was standard classroom policy for him to stand, a fact Miss Sharp reminded Ben of in her sweetest voice. A second soft-spoken request from the teacher prompted an insolent sneer as Ben announced loudly, "I don't have to stand, and you can't make me!"

Timidly, the teacher asked him to report to the disciplinarian, to which Ben loudly and forcefully bellowed, "You can't make me."

John had seen the teacher's discomfort and went to stand at her side, hoping his presence would encourage Ben to do the right thing. Instead, Ben squared his shoulders and thrust his chin forward belligerently. John asked the teacher to repeat her request, hoping Ben would comply, but was sorely disappointed when Ben lifted his head higher, balling his fists on the desktop and shaking his head defiantly. Angered at the disrespect being shown to his teacher, John strode towards the bully. Ben wrapped his fingers around the wooden seat, his knuckles white, afraid John might try to remove him bodily from the desk.

John realized the uselessness of such a struggle but didn't want to back down and leave both himself and the teacher at the mercy of this bully for the remainder of his time at Carlisle. Recalling the effectiveness of a well-placed punch from his boxing lessons, John struck a single blow that landed directly on the point of Ben's jaw. The bully crumpled out of the desk, falling unconscious into the aisle. John bent down to grasp Ben around his chest and dragged him out of the classroom.

The fresh air brought Ben to his senses. As he regained his feet, John calmly directed him, "Do not speak. If you want to go to Mr. Cornish by yourself, go ahead. If not, I will go with you or take you. You're a student here, and Miss Sharp is your teacher. Her position deserves your respect."

Without further comment, Ben stomped off in the direction of the disciplinarian's office. Details of the event soon spread to the entire student body, and he was cheered by boys and girls alike. However, when he was summoned to the disciplinarian's office that evening, he expected to be punished.

Alone with John in his office, Mr. Cornish spoke slowly, contemplating each word as he spoke. "John, what you've done today is certainly out of the ordinary and could ultimately have a negative impact on your future. I don't know if Major Mack knows of it yet or if he'll approve when he learns what happened. But, for right now, I want you to know that I consider your action a personal service to me. I appreciate what you did in standing up for your teacher's authority.

"Every now and then there comes along a student who must be dealt with, and that is part of my job. However, I admit I've been dreading for some time the necessity of making an example of the young man you so effectively whipped today. He is larger and stronger than I, and although I'd heard more than one story about his bullying, I didn't relish the thought of trying to discipline him. Had he chosen to ignore my commands as he did Miss Sharp's today, I couldn't have done what you did, and my control over the rest of the boys would have been lost. Your actions saved me that embarrassment. Please treat what I'm telling you confidentially. I believe your respect for our faculty and school merits my saying thank you, man to man."

At first, John could only look down at his hands clasped tightly in front of him while his mind absorbed the full meaning of Mr. Cornish's words. Once it did, John raised his head to see a twinkle in the eyes of his counselor.

Still unsure if a reprimand was coming, John began, "I apologize for my actions, Mr. Cornish, but when I saw Ben treating our teacher as he did, I had to do something. All I could think of was what my first teacher, Mr. Heath, would have had me do, or what he would have done had he been there. Although I never saw him raise his hand to a student, I know that discipline was an important part of his school program. My father taught me that a bully is nothing but a coward who uses fear to control others. Most bullies have never known discipline or been shown respect by others. They only know fear, so that's how they influence others.

"Perhaps that's why Ben is a bully. I don't know what his life has been like. I'm thankful to have had a loving father who showed me that standing up to fear is the only way to lead. He also taught me that people who are afraid are difficult to lead. Sometimes you must show them the right way because they won't listen to your words. Ben was not listening to anyone, so I used the boxing skills I learned to convince him to make the right decision. I'm glad my actions helped you as well. Perhaps Ben won't be a problem again. I don't believe he has a bad heart; he's just very unhappy."

Mr. Cornish patted John warmly on the shoulder. "Not all those who've come here were given the same guidance you've had. Like many others, Ben struggles to accept the changes being forced on him and his people. He's bitter. Perhaps you can help him find some goodness in his future."

CHAPTER 31

The Superintendent's Office

Spring to Summer 1897

Carlisle Indian School, Pennsylvania

A notice to report to the superintendent's office came several days later. It was John's first such summons, and he wondered if the major had finally learned of his actions and was displeased. His stomach tied in knots and his heart pounded as he proceeded towards the vine-covered building.

Even though he'd been justified in his treatment of the bully and had also received Miss Sharp's whispered thank-you when he returned to class without Ben, John had no idea how Major Mack would view his conduct. As he walked to the office, he wondered if he could bear being censured by a man who reminded him so much of Carter Heath; but he accepted that he would have to suffer whatever the consequences might be.

When John entered the office, the major was busily scanning some papers at his desk. He glanced up in his kindly way, asked John to be seated, and continued with the task at hand.

John felt his self-assurance evaporate. A lump rose in his throat without warning. After what seemed an eternity, Major Mack placed the papers to one side of his desk, removed his glasses slowly, and looked at the boy with a tiny smile teasing the corners of his mouth. Rubbing his glasses on his sleeve, he drawled out, "John, pull your chair closer here. I need to talk with you," and John was afraid that all his fears had been justified.

The major clasped his hands together on his well-worn desk and leaned forward, bringing John's total concentration to his face. "Young man," the major spoke clearly, "your first year in this school is coming to an end. Your conduct has been exemplary, and your presence here has been a benefit to the entire school. I'm particularly impressed by the way you kept away from associations that might have lessened your accomplishments. I've spoken with many of our teachers and staff, and the report of every employee has been favorable."

The major continued, "As you know, many of our students are sent on outing activities each summer in order to further their education and let them see the opportunities available off the reservations. It's been customary to retain the first-year students here at school for their first summer to provide sufficient labor to accomplish work that must be done on the farm and for maintenance of the school buildings and grounds. We're currently making the list of outing students for the summer, and I'm compelled to add your name for a position that's special to me on a personal level."

John realized he'd been holding his breath. Exhaling slowly, unable to believe what he was hearing, he whispered, "Yes, sir?"

The major continued, growing more animated as he spoke, "I have an old friend who owns a large farm in the Berkshire country of Massachusetts. When I first became interested in Indian education, my friend, Mr. Hall, had no interest in my goals. When I decided to place boys and girls in desirable homes during the summer season, he guffawed in my face. When I argued for the benefits the students would receive from their experience at his farm, I couldn't interest him in taking an apprentice to help him with the summer farmwork even though he'd often complained about not having sufficient help. After years of trying, I finally convinced him to tolerate—as he put it—'an Indian for a season.'"

With that, the major laughed and glanced through the window into the distance before continuing, "That was fourteen years ago, and he's not been without one of our students on his farm since. He's almost as dedicated to the Indians as I am. I've made it my personal business each year to see that one of our most deserving young men is sent to Mr. Hall, not only out of consideration for my friend but also due to the fact that his home is one of the most desirable locations.

"You should know, John, that Mr. and Mrs. Hall have with them a young lady who will also remain in their home for the summer. She can't do the general labor of the farm that's needed, so they need a young man to help as well. However, it must be a young man whom they and I can feel every confidence can be trusted to be a gentleman as well as an industrious worker. So, John Iron Horse, I'm going to send you to the Berkshires when the first outing pupils go in that direction. That should be in a week or two, and I trust you'll appreciate the opportunity and justify the confidence I'm placing in you."

John sat speechless, a smile beaming over his face. He'd come here expecting a reprimand and instead was being given a unique and challenging learning opportunity. As the major continued talking, John focused on every word, all the while feeling a lump in his throat, but for a far different reason. Obviously, the major didn't know about Ben. John's vision blurred as tears began to form, and he struggled to regain his composure.

The major babbled on about details of what John would be doing on the farm this summer until John could listen no longer. Instead of the words of thanks he wanted so much to say, he blurted out, "Major Mack, the other day I had a fight with a boy in Miss Sharp's classroom. I can only believe you haven't heard of it and don't know the details if you're considering me for such an advantageous assignment. I'm so sorry for my outburst. I simply couldn't stand by and—"

The major interrupted calmly, as if there were nothing further to discuss. "Yes, John, I heard all about it. If I were to reprimand you, it would only be because you didn't . . ." He paused, followed by a mischievous smile. Knowing it had all been accepted as an appropriate intervention by the other students, he continued in a military tone that ended further comment.

"That's all past." Changing the topic completely, he added, "How are the folks at home, John?"

More than willing to put any thought of disciplinary action to rest, John responded happily, "I've had letters from Carter Heath and from Aaron Moss on Monday about my family and the reservation. Aaron says that many of my people are hungry and that he prays for the enlightenment of our elders so their hearts do not break as they grow old. I last heard from Mr. Heath in winter; his transfer to Fort Shaw proved regrettable, and he was transferred again to Washington. He said everything was as well as could be expected with two children and another on the way, but I have the feeling there was something he wasn't saying in his letter. I hope all is well."

John continued, "Mr. Moss shared that my father seems to be growing old amazingly fast. I sometimes wish to be back there with him, but I know I must be well educated to succeed in the white world. He wishes the same for me. I plan to live always looking towards the future but never forgetting the past."

"I know Aaron and Carter both very well. I met your father years ago when he stopped on his way to join a Lakota delegation that met with our leaders in Washington. They came to discuss the Great Sioux Reservation and our government's plan to remove the Indians. Though I'm sure the group argued for the preservation of Indian lands, your father believed that simply moving the Sioux to Indian territory would cause more fighting. He gave one of the best talks I've heard before or since, encouraging our students to learn everything they could before finding their own place in the white man's world. He's an incredibly wise man."

John nodded in agreement, and the two men, one young, one old—one red, one white—looked across the massive mahogany desk respectfully at one another. The office was still as they wordlessly accepted there might be more similarities than differences between them. Then, John nodded abruptly and left the superintendent's office, saying only, "Major Mack, I thank you for it all."

In his work from that day on, John found new focus. His feelings for the major developed beyond respect for his position to almost the camaraderie he'd come to feel with Carter. He no longer felt a requisite distance between them as he'd felt with the teachers at the boarding school at Pine Ridge. There, he'd been forced to keep his personal feelings to himself, always reminded he was a student of the white man's way but never a member of the community itself. Here, he felt perfectly welcome to seek guidance from the major about things he would previously have spoken about only to his father.

About two weeks after his interview in the major's office, John found himself among a number of boys and girls boarding a train for various points in New England where they would spend the summer. Although there were no packages of dried beef or store candy, his uniforms had been neatly folded and packed, and John felt the comfort of his father's spirit in the little tin trunk that carried his belongings. The group would be overseen by Mr. Cornish, who would assist the students with introductions to their summer hosts.

John was particularly glad to have extra time with Mr. Cornish because he knew the trip would be more interesting under this man's guidance. John was determined that Major Mack would have no reason to regret the confidence placed in him. For the past two weeks, he'd tried to imagine the possibilities of a summer spent so far from home. He would see New York for the first time, one of the greatest of all cities, as well as the waters of the ocean. All these things he'd only read about until now.

On a brilliantly blue morning in early June, the train wound in and out among the hills of eastern Pennsylvania, carrying John further from the reservation. He saw mines whose buildings seemed to grow parallel with the sides of mountains, rising straight yet crooked from a hole in the ground to the top of a hillside stacked with great mounds of coal awaiting transport to the cities. There it would furnish energy for lights and furnaces, huge steel mills and factories, and so many unimaginable things that were part of the great industrial life of the Northeastern states.

Later, they traveled along the seaboard, where the cities seemed to merge into each other, until they arrived at the edge of the great water, which washed repeatedly onto sandy shores and stretched endlessly to the horizon in the opposite direction. Mr. Cornish escorted the students as they left the train and boarded a boat that seemed so big it was impossible for it to float, yet from its deck above the water, John saw a great harbor filled with boats and ships of all kinds, sizes, and descriptions.

After disembarking, their group mounted an apparently impenetrable wall of stone and brick before entering the circular, multibranched train station of New York. Inside, they passed hordes of people before boarding another train and escaping the city. Finally, the train rumbled into open countryside and the farmlands of old New England. The group that had started together at Carlisle began to disintegrate along the way as members were met at various stations and taken to their summer homes—some returning to the warm welcome of friends already made, and others to the opportunity of making new acquaintances.

Late in the afternoon, they came to the station at Becket where John was to disembark. Mr. Cornish barely had time during the stop to introduce John to Mr. Hall, who met them as they arrived. Mr. Hall was a jovial man in the garb of a well-to-do farmer, and John was made to feel at ease by his greeting: "Well, son, I'm mighty glad to see you."

He led the way to a light buggy hitched to a single, shining bay horse, and they began a conversation that continued throughout the hour-long ride, John sharing details about his family and Mr. Hall filling John's ears with plans he'd made for projects to be completed on the farm.

They drove over the winding road through hills and woodlands interspersed with fields of richest green, bordered by streams. Each hilltop looked down over land that was bejeweled here and there with little lakes of sky-blue water. Mr. Hall graciously gave John a respite from conversation, allowing him to soak in the beauty of the scenery. As they traveled, John's posture revealed a deepening sense of relief and contentment after the turmoil of the journey.

As the shadows lengthened into evening, they turned from the road onto a lane that wound between two rows of spreading maple trees towards a spacious white house. It reached upwards for two stories, with matching chimneys and dormers on either end. A covered porch began just to the side of a wide door, stretching across the front of the house and along one side until it disappeared around the back. Tall windows bordered by deep-green shutters graced almost every other exposed piece of the house, and a tiny second-floor landing and staircase gave access to the upstairs from the porch.

John stated, as if in answer to a question Mr. Hall had not asked, "This is it. This is the country that came to me as a vision while I rode the train my first night on the journey from the reservation."

Mr. Hall turned towards John, eyebrows raised in surprise, but before he could ask for an explanation, their conversation was interrupted by a sweet-faced, smiling woman to whom Mr. Hall said as they stopped, "Mother Hall, this is John."

John had already focused on the latticework around the base of the porch, noting repairs that needed to be done. Glancing up quickly at the introduction, he found himself looking into a round, pink-cheeked face surrounded by the most unusual blue-gray curls he had ever seen. Mother Hall stood before the wide-open front door, leaning lightly against the porch railing and dusting her hands on her apron before self-consciously smoothing the curls around her face.

"Oh, my dear, you must be exhausted after such a long journey," she said cheerfully as she hurried around the end of the railing and reached out to clasp John's arm, maneuvering him up the stairs. "We're so happy to meet you and to have you here for the summer. We'll have a wonderful time these next few months, but first, there's someone you must meet." Turning towards the open front door, she called out loudly, "Stella! Stella, come here please."

Moments later, a girl of about eighteen appeared from around the other side of the house, holding a pan containing remnants of grain as if she'd been feeding chickens in the back. She held her head poised halfway between looking down at her feet and peering at the dark-skinned stranger from beneath long, sooty eyelashes. Tucking one ankle gracefully behind the other, she curtsied to acknowledge the introduction. She was tall and slim with a wealth of dark auburn hair that curled tightly around her ears before disappearing into a thickly knotted twist at the top of her head. A sprinkling of freckles dotted her nose, and her wide, expressive mouth curled into a lopsided smile before she looked bashfully away.

In a serious tone, she responded, "Very pleased to meet you, sir," then turned to Mother Hall and added, "I must finish feeding my chickens before I can help you in the kitchen. I'll be done quickly." Her voice was low and formal, and John strained to hear her comments. He wondered what relation she was to the Halls and whether he'd see more of her over the summer.

As soon as the horse was unhitched and John had been shown to his room where he deposited his trunk, they all sat down to supper in a cheery dining room. Mr. and Mrs. Hall shared the many activities they'd planned for the summer, from trips to town for supplies to enlarge the livestock barn to picnics and fishing from the large farm pond. Later in the evening, the conversation turned to more personal topics as they sat together on the wide front porch. Mr. Hall lit his meerschaum pipe, its odor instantly reminding John of the many nights he'd sat atop the butte above Potato Creek while Iron Horse enjoyed a smoke.

John learned to his surprise that Stella was not Mr. and Mrs. Hall's daughter as he had first assumed but was in fact the young lady of whom the major had spoken. She disclosed she was a graduate of the school at Carlisle, piquing John's interest immediately as that meant she carried at least a trace of Indian blood, though it did not show to look at her. She'd spent several successive summers with the Halls and had been with them continuously for the past year. Stella questioned John intently about the past year's happenings at Carlisle and shared that she expected to return in the fall to continue her studies nearby at Davidson.

Following up on John's comment about seeing the land before, Mr. Hall inquired, "John, as we came up the driveway, you commented that this appeared to be the country of your dreams. Your tone made me feel as if you'd seen this place before, but if I'm not mistaken, the major said this was your first year away from the reservation."

Not knowing how Stella might react to the news of his coming from the reservation, John looked quickly towards the ceiling to hide the heat that came to his cheeks. For a split second, he remembered sensing a presence he hadn't recognized that had danced across the land of his dreams. He waited, hoping for some inclination that this girl might be the personification of that spirit. When she made no comment, he hesitantly shared with them the vision that had come to him on the train.

The words flowed from him—of his fascination with the abundance of water and the lush greens of the forests and fields. What he had seen, both in his dream and on this farm, was in sharp contrast to the golden, dry hues of the grasslands and the multiple years of drought they'd recently experienced.

After a light supper and general chitchat about John's trip, everyone seemed ready for a good night's sleep before the business of summer began early the next morning. Sitting on a soft mattress in the open, airy bedroom, John rubbed his hands over the lightweight, ruffled bedspread, mentally comparing it to the rough blanket he'd tucked tightly under his mattress each morning back at the school. Minutes later, he slipped between the crisp cotton sheets, pulling them up to his chin as he considered the vision he'd seen on the train. Iron Horse had spoken often of visions and had used them to guide himself and his family. John wondered if the similarities between the land of his vision and the land where he would spend the summer was a portent of success in the white world he had entered.

In the last moments before he drifted into the dreamless sleep of exhaustion, John wondered why he felt drawn to this fair-skinned, part-Indian woman when none of the beauties he'd met so far in his life had ever drawn his interest. For a fleeting second, an image floated before his eyes of himself with a partner in a flowing cotton dress, looking over the grassland from the butte above Potato Creek.

CHAPTER 32

Carter's Journal

Winter 1896 to Fall 1897

Office of Attorney General, Washington DC

The move to Washington was a significant deviation from mine and Lillian's early goals to serve her people on the reservation. I was certain we could return to one of the larger schools out west when there was a suitable opening.

Perhaps the most convincing argument I'd made for the move east was the possibility of hiring a full-time nanny and a French-speaking tutor for Liz. Once decided, we couldn't arrive in Washington fast enough. As soon as I sent notice that I would accept the position, we learned my appointment had been confirmed. I was especially pleased to be named as clerk to the assistant attorney general rather than a copyist in the General Land Office.

I was tempted at the time to notify Mother of our new residence but hesitated, feeling pangs of guilt for not having shared with her my discontent in Montana. The salary of 1,000 dollars per annum was significantly better than the 720 I'd been paid at Fort Shaw and higher than the 900 offered for a copyist. A per diem allowance for travels required by the position was an added enticement and totaled to a salary I'd have been proud to share with Mother and Father.

Washington was beautiful, with wide, open spaces along the river, squarely delineated streets, and easily navigated intersections. From our room in the National Hotel, we strolled down the Mall, awestruck by the massive granite buildings of the Department of Agriculture, the National Museum, and the Bureau of Engraving and Printing where our money was made. As we approached the new Washington Monument one afternoon, its almost white obelisk shape reaching towards the sky, Liz immediately noticed the color change in the stones some one hundred feet above the ground. Lillian and I simply stared, captivated by its beautiful simplicity, noting that it was indeed a fitting tribute to the man it honored. We were thankful its construction had been completed after delays from war, bankruptcy, and the death of its designer. We were happy to have the chance to see it.

As we approached the base, I couldn't resist the opportunity to discuss with Liz how stones from various places were different. She reminded me of John with her ability to absorb information and ask thought-filled questions in return. She commented that the rocks in the monument were more like the ones where we picnicked in the Bad Lands rather than the soft ones that crumbled where she and Rosa played in Potato Creek. Later, we rode the elevator to the top and enjoyed the vista of the entire city. I couldn't resist the urge to impart another lesson and lifted Liz as high as I could to point out the home of President McKinley and the beautifully domed building where our senators and congressmen were most likely meeting at that moment.

That movement proved to be my downfall; a stabbing pain shot through my side. I felt a rush of cold chills as had always accompanied a bout with my problematic bowels, but this was the worst pain yet. We departed the monument and, knowing I couldn't walk the distance to our hotel, called a carriage and returned to our room. The pain was unbearable. Lillian called for a physician, who after a brief examination of my abdomen informed me that surgery was my only option. He feared my appendix was not only inflamed but might have burst, leaving me with an infection that could end my life.

Lillian was distraught at the doctor's pronouncement, and I feared she would go into labor. The physician handed me a small bottle of laudanum and departed to schedule with his office a time to proceed with the surgery. His diagnosis included several months of leave from work under the best of circumstances, and if infection was present, I would be lucky to return after a year of rest and recuperation.

I was forced to send a note asking for sick leave from my job and—against my commitment of the past—a telegraph to my family in New York, seeking their financial help for the care of my wife and children. Within hours, the stress of the day sent Lillian into labor, and our wonderful son, James Henry, was born in the National Hotel under the watchful eye of Dr. Carrol and three young nurses who happened to be staying on the second floor of our hotel. They assisted Lillian and watched over Ralph while the hotel staff cleaned the room and brought in a bassinet for the baby.

The following day, my supervisor, Mr. Holcombe, paid a short visit to inform me that my leave had been granted, unpaid, for up to a year. He seemed put out by the whole affair, having lost a clerk as well as having to take time out of his day to make an official visit to the bedside of the offending employee. Looking steadily out the window of the hotel, he pretended to be concerned for me, reminding me to focus on my recovery and giving assurances that my position would be reestablished upon my notice to his office that I could return to work full-time.

There were no allowances for part-time labor within the bureau, and I had a sick feeling that he had no intention of keeping any promises he made. To add to my discomfort, albeit not surprisingly, there was not a hospital to my mother's standards in Washington, so she took the liberty to secure a physician, Dr. George Sternberg of Lebanon Hospital in New York. To his credit, he scheduled an emergency procedure for immediately upon my arrival, and Father wired money straightaway. Mother booked my family direct passage by train in a sleeper car for my comfort without any discussion from me or my wife.

Dr. Carroll returned to check on me and agreed to assist with our short trip to the rail station. He even allowed one of his nurses to accompany us on the journey and return the next day at Father's expense. We arrived in New York without incident until my sisters came rushing across the platform, their arms raised high and squeals of welcome ringing through the station. After I enveloped my mother into a singular hug, my sisters greeted me with a bear hug before turning and reaching for Liz and Ralph and swooping James from Lillian's arms, giving her a sorely needed respite. Father's absence was apparent.

A transom awaited to carry me to Lebanon for surgery the following morning. To my surprise, Mother announced that the largest portion of our party, besides her and me, would be reboarding the train for an overnight ride to our home in Ithaca. She planned to serve as my escort and caretaker. I supposed Father remained at home to ensure the house and staff were ready for two toddlers, a newborn, and my wife. I prayed it was so. We waved the train off, Liz's face showing through the window, her brows wrinkled with concern. Mother and I proceeded to meet with Dr. Sternberg.

What a strange experience. The first aspect I noticed upon entering Lebanon was the cleanliness of everything in sight. The city of Washington was beautiful, but here, the floors sparkled, the walls appeared to have been hand-washed and shined, and even the bright lights above showed not one speck of grit, grime, or soot. Quite a contrast to the world we'd left behind at Fort Shaw and Potato Creek. I feared for an instant I'd been brought to a sanitarium and that Mother had no intentions of allowing me to return to the West. *What a jest*, I thought briefly. It was for my own sake everything was so clean. After being laid out on a rolling bed to go for the surgery, I remembered little. An attractive nurse placed a mask over my face, smiling as I breathed slowly and the world went black.

My pain upon waking was significant but localized. There was no bloated, throbbing sensation across my entire abdomen—just a sharp, severe pain in my right side. Dr. Sternberg dropped by to inform me the surgery had gone well, and there was no sign my appendix had ruptured. He added, however, that during the procedure he'd noted several swollen segments of my intestine, dark in color and distended in a way that indicated there might be other factors contributing to my discomfort. He prescribed a small bottle of laudanum, plenty of rest, a diet rich in vegetables and grains, no alcohol, and plenty of fluids. I realized my mother was still at my side, resting on a cot I assumed one of the nurses had brought in.

One week later, I was released from the hospital with a warning not to pick up any of our children, nothing else heavy, to refrain from stressful interludes, and to drink a half-teaspoonful of my laudanum only if the pain was unbearable. The doctor hinted that such pain would merit notifying him for a recheck of the surgical site.

Within six months of the beginning of my medical leave, I was informed by telegram that my position as clerk in the Attorney General's Office had been exchanged for a Mr. Myers's position at the Arapaho

School in Oklahoma. He needed to be in Washington in order to be close to his dying mother. Although angry at the exchange after the assurances I'd been given, the new position promised another two hundred dollars per annum, and I was eager to return west after the extended period in my father's house. Though stressful, my time there wasn't wasted. I'd completed sufficient readings in law and had applied to take the bar exam.

During my recuperation, I received numerous short letters from John that brightened my days and kept me abreast of events in his life. I was delighted he was going to the Halls' farm for his outing experience. Although I didn't know them personally, their reputation was one of both integrity and innovative thought. John would learn a great deal about cattle, both in efficient feeding and breeding selection. Mr. Hall's animals were well known across the Northeast, both in the show ring and on the plates of some of the finest restaurants. Sadly, I wasn't punctual in responding, not even with brief notes as he'd so diligently sent to me. Between studying for the bar and quarreling with Father, I felt not only depressed and distracted but also guilty of failing in my duties as mentor as well.

CHAPTER 33

The Halls

Summer 1897

Snow Hill Farm, Becket, Massachusetts

John Iron Horse could never have foreseen his fortune at being placed with the Halls as an outing student. Not only was their home overflowing with refinements and culture, but Thomas Hall was, much like Iron Horse, a man who believed in a well-planned future. His father, Oliver, had made a fortune sawing the forests that covered the rolling hills of the Berkshire area. Thomas focused on cattle instead, selling his first animals to the tanneries until turning his interests to meat production for an ever-burgeoning population in the East.

He devoted his time to breeding a strain of purebred cattle and took considerable pride in their colorful lineback patterns, the deep blue-black or mahogany sides showing starkly against the sparkling white of their back lines and bellies. Thomas enjoyed exhibiting them at fairs and stock shows in the region; the breed had a reputation for high-quality meat, which brought premium prices, and the animals were easy to handle. His ideas and business acumen earned him the respect of neighbors and businessmen across the region, while his wealth allowed him a certain amount of influence in the state.

He had represented his district in the assembly in former years, but he found the unscrupulousness of politics repugnant to his nature and developed an absolute distaste for public life. Born and raised on the farm that was his home, he'd graduated from one of the country's leading universities as a classmate of Major Mack, and their friendship continued well past their school days. Thomas married a childhood companion, and besides one instance, their lives were as complete and happy as anyone could ask for.

They shared a single incalculable grief: the loss of their first and only child in infancy. After several years, it was apparent they'd be denied other children, so Major Mack had reached out to them regarding his work with Indian children. Eventually, they felt drawn to be a positive influence in the lives of young people so far from home, and Major Mack began placing one or more boys and girls with them each year. At first, they requested only the youngest pupils from the school, but as the years passed, they chose boys and girls of more advanced age. John and Stella were about the age their own child would have been, and the couple felt a kinship to them, a link almost to their departed child.

For several years, Mr. Hall had not actively worked his farm but leased most of the arable sections to his neighbor, Mr. Parkins, a tenant who lived at the foot of the hill with his son, Hiram. In recent years, despite Mr. Hall's best intentions and the help of several students from Carlisle, everything about the farm was beginning to show its age. The lawns were well kept, but flower beds and shrubbery in every nook needed weeding or pruning. The grove of hardwood trees behind the house was littered with fallen branches and underbrush, and some of the fence boards needed a well-placed nail or two to be put straight.

Mrs. Hall had managed, with Stella's help, to keep a fastidious home. The furniture gleamed from regular polishing with linseed oil, and the draperies filtered sunlight that entered through crystal-clean windows. But her step was getting slower, her eyes missed the wisps of cobwebs drifting from the lofty ceilings, and she was quicker to sit down to rest her knees, as she always told Stella.

Early morning the day after John arrived, Mr. Hall took him over every inch of the farm, explaining the various things the young man would need to do. They strolled around the corrals to a massive barn where the patriarch of the herd was standing deep in a straw-filled stall; through the garden with its luxuriant vegetables; to the orchard, just coming into the earliest fruits; to the piggery with its blue-blooded Cheshires; and out to the pasture among the cows and calves that were their owner's pride and joy.

All along the way, John took mental notes, just as he had been taught by Carter Heath, of loose boards or shingles, vegetable rows that needed weeding, and signs of insect bites on budding fruits. Mr. Hall meticulously explained every detail of the work, and as they turned at the lower end of the pasture to retrace their steps, he continued, "You know, John, it is said that cleanliness is next to godliness, and order is heaven's first law. A pasture, an orchard, or a garden can be kept clean and orderly just as well as a house, and a piggery or barnyard as well as a barn. That is my foremost rule of farming."

He went on to explain, "Recently I've depended on Hiram Parkins to do all that's necessary except in the summer when his father needs his help on their own farm. I'm not sure he's as intelligent as many of the other young men in the community, and I've noticed he tends to prefer sitting to working. For all his deficiencies, though, he's been the only adult on which I could depend." Mr. Hall added resignedly, "I suppose he's done fairly well. The present condition of the place is largely a result of his efforts, albeit I'm sure you've seen numerous places that need improvement."

Finally, he admitted, "I confess, I'm not much of a hand to direct or follow up closely, so I'll depend on you to make use of your education. Tonight, you'll have an opportunity to meet Hiram. I hope you two can get along." After a pause, his eyes twinkling, he added, "I might advise you, however, never to swap jackknives with him, because if you do, you'll lose by your trade." With a wink and a chuckle, Mr. Hall headed back to the house, leaving his newest charge to ponder exactly what a jackknife was and why he might swap one—and which job he would tackle first.

John worked the remainder of the day while Mr. Hall drove to Becket, about five miles away, as was his custom. After finishing his evening chores, John dressed for supper in the uniform he'd brought from school. Having finished their meal, the group retired to the porch, and John indeed got the opportunity to meet Hiram Parkins.

Hiram was a tall, angular, stoop-shouldered young man of about twenty-three, with coarse, straw-colored hair and the sharpest features in the smallest face John had ever seen. Among the Indians, Hiram would have been called "Coyote Face." The very thought forced John to look away, covering the grin that flitted across his face. Glancing back to the group, John realized Hiram had taken a seat on the steps as close as possible to

Stella, who had settled into a large rocking chair. She immediately tensed and straightened in her seat, obviously uncomfortable as he spoke in the high-pitched, nasally drawl that was common in parts of New England.

"I've moved the sheep to graze the weeds between the apple trees and checked for cracking in the cherries since we've had several rains recently." He chortled as if he himself had some brilliant plan to stop the moisture from damaging Stella's favorite crop. She drew her arms tightly against her waist and simply ignored his comment, staring down at the stones closest to the doorway. She dared not contribute anything that Hiram might interpret as an invitation to conversation.

Sensing her distress, John distracted Hiram by extending his hand in greeting. "My name is John Iron Horse, and I'll be assisting with work on the farm for the summer."

Without returning the gesture, Hiram continued, not to John but to impress upon Stella his self-imagined importance to the Halls' farming operation, "Soon, I'll be bringing in the calves for weaning and beginning the harvest of what I'm sure will be our best peach crop ever."

John discerned immediately that Hiram's only real topic of conversation was himself. Whether or not it informed or included anyone else besides Stella mattered not one bit to Hiram. As this realization settled in his mind, John knew for certain that he didn't like Hiram Parkins. Furthermore, John perceived that Stella was uneasy in the man's presence and determined quickly that it would be his responsibility to ensure Hiram kept his distance if that was what Stella wanted.

The first week passed pleasantly for John as he learned the details of cattle and pig handling and the management of orchards. He had never seen anything like the fruits growing here, and he had much to learn about which branches to prune on the different trees, from cherries to apples. Mr. Hall showed John new things daily, calling his attention to projects and possibilities. Mrs. Hall showed him her dairy and fruit cellar with pride and described in detail her plans for a strawberry patch.

On the other hand, John was mystified by the young woman whose very presence made him feel queasy inside. He knew she spent much time in the care of her chickens, yet no matter how many questions he asked about chickens or eggs, Stella never responded with anything more than the simplest, most direct answer. If he shared an idea to improve the chicken coop behind the house, Stella politely resisted asking for details and declined every offer to assist her in the building of it. Other than that, his time at the farm was enjoyable and educational except for the whiney drawl of the ubiquitous Hiram on his frequent evening visits.

One day in the early part of the haying season, John was in the far corner of the orchard, gathering some windfall apples and throwing them to the pigs, when he saw Hiram walking towards him across a field. John had almost completed the task by the time Hiram sauntered up, innocently asking, "John, do you allow that you'd help me pitch and stow a load of hay that I've hauled up to the barn? We were cutting hay just below the house there," he said, pointing towards their tenant house in the lower field, "but Father broke our mowing machine and has gone to town for repairs. If you help, I'll pay you back."

With nothing pressing to do for the remainder of the afternoon, John agreed to help, and in a brief time Hiram's hay was safely stored in the barn, protected from the shower that was threatening over the mountains. After resting a few minutes, Hiram inquired casually, "Can you fish, John?"

John responded, "There's not much to catch in the fast-running streams of prairie country, and they're always small. Maybe a frog or crayfish, but I'd rather hunt rabbits."

"Do you allow you could take a break and go fishing with me this afternoon?" Hiram wheedled. "I can't do anything until Father comes back with the horses, and if you go, I'll show you where and how to catch the big ones. The lake over yonder is full of bass and perch, and I know it like a preacher ought to know his Bible," he continued, one eyebrow cocked upward as he looked sideways at the young man in the doorway. "That'd be one way I could pay you back for helping me with the hay. There's plenty of fishing gear here in the barn," he added, making John wonder if perhaps Hiram wasn't such a bad sort after all.

After a few minutes of digging worms in the garden nearby and supplementing them with grasshoppers caught on the way, they arrived at the lake at the far end of Mr. Hall's pasture. Hiram showed John just what size and color of worm he considered best for perch and which to use for smaller bass that were tamer than the big ones. He described which worm to use for the medium-size fish and what kind should be used to catch the wily large ones. Hiram went on to explain, "Some days the fish will snatch almost any bait you offer 'em, while other times they won't bite nothin' at all."

John thought it was all gibberish to talk about different kinds of bait only to tell him the fish might or might not bite despite all. He couldn't help but wonder why Hiram had wasted so much time giving him details that were apparently useless.

After more explanations of all the various and secret ways to hook the particular fish he recommended for John, he continued, "I allow, John, that over yonder by that old beech log on the south side is the absolute best fishing on the lake. If you want to go there, I'll go to the north side where the water's a little rough and the fishing is harder." Hiram grinned. "But I don't mind since I've been here before."

John couldn't know that on the south side, his shadow would fall across the water, allowing the fish to easily spot the fisherman. Nor had Hiram mentioned that the foul smell of a sulfur spring nearby might also impact his luck. John's inexperience left him without an inkling that the rippling water on the north shore that Hiram had allotted to himself created the best possible spot on the entire pond, something the scheming Hiram knew well after years of practice in these very waters.

Several hours later, when they met to return to the farm, John was surprised to find his string of eight puny perch compared unfavorably with the eighteen platter-sized perch and two big bass his companion had caught. Later that evening, when the family gathered around the supper table, John shared the story of how he'd helped Hiram unload his hay and how he'd been instructed in the art of fishing by his neighbor, though he didn't share all the details that Hiram had told him were top secret.

As he told his tale, John thought he detected a look of vexation on Mr. Hall's face, but it gave way to a glimmer of amusement as the older man leaned away from the table, finally bursting into laughter until he had to remove his glasses and wipe the moisture from his eyes. When he was sufficiently recovered, Mr. Hall turned to John jovially.

"I told you, John, never to swap jackknives with that Yankee, and that if you did, you'd get the worst of the trade. Our lake abounds with bass and perch. In fact, it's one of the best fishing lakes around," he continued. Taking a more serious tone, he added, "Several years ago, the privilege of fishing there was abused by your partner of this afternoon, so I was forced to make the rule that no one be permitted to fish there except in the company of one of our family. Hiram, I believe, would rather fish in that lake than do anything else on earth. For that reason, I've always insisted on his sleeping and eating at home when he works here so as not to be able to consider himself family. Today, however, he took advantage of someone I look upon with particular favor." He continued with another laugh, "I've never found it convenient to invite him to go fishing with me, nor has Mrs. Hall, and I do not believe that Stella has either; have you, Stella?"

"No, I haven't," replied the girl, confused, for she heard Mr. Hall's humorous tone but didn't enjoy his teasing about Hiram's persistent attentions, for they were not welcome, as both the Halls knew well. "But," she added, gathering her confidence and flashing a mischievous smile directly at John, "I might one day."

John felt chagrined at being fooled so easily into allowing Hiram to fish without Mr. Hall's permission but had the grace to join good-naturedly in laughing at himself. His embarrassment was somewhat diminished when Mr. Hall said whimsically, "I could be angry that Hiram used you, John, both to unload his hay and to fish in my lake without my consent, but I'm confident you'll learn from this and not fall for such a scheme again. You couldn't have known the devious nature of Hiram. Don't concern yourself, John. We'll all go fishing the first good evening, and you can put into practice what you've learned this afternoon."

It was no surprise to John that fishing wasn't mentioned when Hiram joined them on the porch that evening, and John was confident the neighbor wouldn't be joining them on any future excursions.

Several days passed with Mr. Hall helping John pick the choicest cherries of the season while his wife and Stella preserved them in the kitchen. By midafternoon, the biggest tree had been stripped of its fruit. While dipping cool water from the well near the kitchen, Mr. Hall called out, "Mother Hall," using her preferred nickname since the long-ago birth of their child. "If you and Stella will pack a lunch, John and I will gather bait and tackle, and we'll go down to the lake to fish and eat supper there."

"What an agreeable proposal!" Mrs. Hall beamed. "Stella and I will be glad to escape the heat of this kitchen for the rest of the day, and I'll even wager that the two of us can catch more fish than you and John," she continued with a laugh.

"I'll bet you don't," he retorted happily, striding purposefully to find John so they could gather the fishing supplies and a bucket of worms. By the time Mrs. Hall and Stella finished their preserves and prepared lunch, the men were waiting. Reaching the lake, they deposited their hamper in the shade of an expansive walnut tree where they could later eat their supper. They divided the bait, gathered their poles and lines, and proceeded to a place of each one's choosing. Mrs. Hall was an expert fisherwoman, such that her husband could never be sure his catch would outnumber hers.

John worked his way around to the old log from which he had fished with Hiram, catching only a few small perch. On second thought, disgusted with himself for returning to the spot where Hiram had fooled him, and with fishing altogether, he ambled back to where they'd left the hamper. Finding no one there, he baited his hook and tossed his line into the water. Setting his pole on the bank, he secured it with two forked sticks and threw himself lazily to the ground.

Almost instantly, his line straightened out towards deeper water, so swiftly that it suggested his pole was about to follow. After a struggle that bent his pole into an arch, John landed a good-size black bass on the bank. Suddenly, his interest in fishing was revived. He continued dropping his line in the same spot with what he thought was significant success until Mr. Hall ambled around from the other side of the pond, dangling a catch that was more than double in both number and size.

When Mrs. Hall and Stella joined them a few minutes later, Mrs. Hall had one more fish to her credit than her husband, and Stella had almost as many. Already sampling the delicacies from the hamper, Mr. Hall teased his wife by claiming his catch would outweigh hers, even though she had one more fish.

Suddenly he wrinkled his brow and turned to John. "Why in the world did you choose to start fishing from that old beech log, John?"

"Well," John admitted slowly, "Hiram told me that was the best place." Slapping him heartily on the shoulder, Mr. Hall fell back on the picnic blanket, laughing heartily at a joke John didn't understand. Finally, Mr. Hall gathered his composure, explaining, "You see, John, there's a well-known sulfur spring close by that log. I'm surprised you didn't notice it. There are many sections of the pond where the fish find much more to feed on. Any little distraction, such as your shadow from the afternoon sun, sends them slipping away from your bait."

Finding little consolation in the details, John nodded his defeat, finally understanding the swap he'd made with Hiram Parkins.

The group enjoyed sitting in the gathering dusk around a cozy fire. The conversation lapsed into the silence of reflection, until John disengaged from his private thoughts and asked sincerely, "Mr. Hall, it's been said that Indians are naturally vengeful and they never forget a wrong. Do you believe a person can undertake to repay a wrong or injury in kind without being resentful or vengeful?"

"I'm not sure I quite understand you, John, but if you have Hiram Parkins in mind, I'd say that if he played upon my kindness as he did upon yours, and then repaid it by insulting my intelligence and abusing my trust in him, I would certainly repay him in kind if the opportunity ever arose," responded Mr. Hall truthfully.

"And so I will," muttered John as though to himself. When the moon rose to light their way, the group returned to the house. As the elderly couple lagged behind along the path, John glanced to his right to see Stella stepping carefully, deep in thought. How beautiful she appeared in the moonlight, her arms swinging gracefully as she carried the picnic basket back to the house. Wordlessly, John adjusted his pace to match hers, prepared to assist if she stumbled.

As she matched her steps to his precisely, he noticed there was no tightening in her shoulders as he'd seen in Hiram's presence. The light near the porch showed the curve of a smile. He couldn't help but wonder what she was thinking, and when he went to his room later on, John gave not one passing thought to Hiram Parkins but instead focused completely on his memory of the young woman by whose side he'd walked for the first time that night.

CHAPTER 34

Carter's Journal

Late Fall 1897

Darlington Arapaho Indian School, Darlington, Oklahoma

After months of arguing with Father, I left Ithaca immediately upon receiving my medical release. Rather than having Lillian and the children travel with me only to arrive as we had at Fort Shaw, with plans and hopes that were quickly dashed, I went alone to my new assignment. I was excited to return to the plains and life in the West, but more importantly, I needed to secure control of school funds and establish my position as the decision-maker. The school was small by comparison to others where I'd served. The current superintendent had developed a fever in his brain, and it was my understanding he'd already given instructions for his burial at the agency, so his demise was imminent.

The school was located at the intersection of the old Chisholm Trail of cattle-driving fame and the North Canadian River, a beautiful site with tall shade trees interspersed among multiple buildings of similar wood construction. I'd heard there weren't many Indians at the school but learned upon my arrival that the situation had changed significantly with the extermination of the buffalo. Originally, most of the Cheyenne had moved by choice to reside on the western side of the reservation, as far from other Indians, and whites, as they could go. They'd continued subsistence hunting and living the old ways for as long as possible, even going to war with the buffalo hunters several times. As the herds were hunted to extinction, the Indians had been forced to move closer to the agency and were now fully dependent on government rations and annuity payments.

I had two concerns from the first day. Would the former assistant be willing to accept my assignment as his superior? And what provisions could be made for the education of my own children in such an overcrowded and remote location? The fait accompli for this destination was that there were no medical services within less than forty miles, a detail that was insurmountable considering my family situation. I saw no future in planning to remain at Darlington permanently.

The job of distributing rations and supplies wasn't difficult. Most of the families lived in camps near the school, an area encompassing less than sixty acres. The remainder of the reservation, if I'd been told correctly, had been claimed by settlers during the land rush of 1889. My greatest difficulty was ensuring the rations arrived in a timely manner and were properly distributed to each family. No matter the number of telegraphs I sent to Washington inquiring about cattle herds, the small number of Indians and well-populated white settlements virtually guaranteed that many of the ration cattle didn't make it to the reservation.

Another observation I made was that the Indians here were uniformly much darker skinned than many I'd dealt with before and far more traditional in their behavior. I could only surmise there were considerably fewer mixed-bloods due to the previous remoteness of the Cheyenne camps. The people on the reservation were most likely from two tribes, Cheyenne and Arapaho. The children of each demanded to be segregated, to the point that I had to suspend a blanket on a lariat across the classroom in order to prevent children of the different tribes from seeing each other. It made my work of educating them exceedingly difficult.

Unlike at Pine Ridge and Fort Shaw where instruction in the English language was paramount to the school program, the program at Darlington focused on teaching religion using Bibles written in English. I suspected had the Bibles been written in French, the natives would have been learning to speak French. I saw no evidence of regular arithmetic lessons, nor of calisthenics nor of agriculture. Although there was sufficient water for gardening, and I saw several staff members working in vegetable plots, there had been no effort to teach the Indians farming techniques. This left the Indians totally dependent on the government for food. A nearby town operated two cotton gins, and there were large tracts of cotton growing around the reservation, but they were all worked by white men and their families, leading me to believe the Indians had leased or sold their allotments from the reservation, leaving them penniless and jobless and waiting on each month's government distribution of provisions.

While going through annuity records and school rosters, I found that several of the allotments had mineral rights as well as water rights. I'd heard from several friends in Washington that the sale of the entire reservation had been discussed frequently. Obviously, the rights to both water and minerals increased the land's value significantly, but such a sale would force the Indian school and all their homes to be moved. I didn't have the political connections to influence a decision in this matter and was further convinced that there was not much of a future for me or my family at Darlington.

I was awarded the Juris Doctor degree and became an official member of the Oklahoma bar. I was legally qualified to handle land transactions and other property matters, but there was no word from Washington naming me as superintendent. With my family comfortable in New York, moving myself and my scant belongings wouldn't be complicated, so I posted a letter to Washington requesting a transfer to the position as superintendent at the Rosebud School in South Dakota. Because of the size of the reservation, the position would bring a considerable increase in salary.

Lillian wrote, "Your mother's given James Henry a beautiful silver bowl and place setting much like Ralph's, and Liz is very happy in the private school she's attending here. She's learning French and has become quite skilled at tatting lace. She longs for a pony to ride, and the boys need more time outside enjoying some rough-and-tumble activities such as your father simply doesn't tolerate. We walk along the streets to the park each evening, but it isn't the same as climbing trees and racing across the prairie.

"The evenings are cool, but there's always a blazing fire when we return to the house, and your mother reads to each of the children before tucking them contentedly into their beds. Life here is nothing like that on the reservation. I so miss the rugged beauty of the frontier and the satisfaction of helping my people through these challenging times. I wait eagerly to hear of our coming move to Rosebud."

CHAPTER 35

Tensions

Summer to Fall 1897

Snow Hill Farm, Becket, Massachusetts

August was drawing to a close. The farm benefitted from John's time there and from the construction lessons he'd learned from Carter Heath. John's youthful strength enabled the two men to cut timber from the hills, carry the logs by wagon to the sawmill in town, and bring back smoothly sawn boards and posts. As his outing time ended, John and Mr. Hall completed the addition of a shed on the side of the barn for hay storage.

John enjoyed the trips to town for supplies like nails or shingles or the occasional box of pickling jars for Mother Hall. Mr. Hall always introduced him to important business owners where they shopped, and John reveled in walking down aisles of shelves stacked high with such variety as he'd never seen. There were rows of bottles of molasses, pickled herring, and syrup. There were huge bags of rice and potatoes, three varieties of flour, small bags of salt, tins of lard and dried cod, as well as stacks of hoes, rakes, or shovels at the end of each aisle.

John had not been able to resist touching the beautifully colored rolls of delicate fabric, imagining how each might look as a dress for Stella. Although John had a feeling that some of the shopkeepers watched him carefully, he didn't encounter any anger against himself as an Indian like he'd witnessed repeatedly among the white men on the reservation. In fact, some of the business owners looked to be mixed-blood Indians, and John made a mental note of their success.

John also enjoyed his time around Stella, infrequent as it was. He offered to build a larger coop for the chickens, but she graciously indicated her hens had no need of more room since the Halls wouldn't increase the size of the flock if she returned to school. Sitting around the table for their evening meal, she always laughed demurely when he shared stories of funny things that happened during the day as he and Mr. Hall worked on projects around the farm. While everyone avoided it in conversation, they all knew that the time was coming when John, and probably Stella as well, would return to Pennsylvania. It was to each of them an unwelcome thought, for they had enjoyed the summer together very much.

Stella had won a warm place in the Halls' hearts from the beginning and would be sorely missed even if just for the school year. During a visit, the major had shared with John that when Stella first arrived at Carlisle several years ago, several of her closest friends had just succumbed to one of the many illnesses that killed children at boarding schools across the nation. The major had never asked for details nor sought answers from St. Joseph's Indian Industrial School in Wisconsin where she'd come from. She was reticent to reach out to other girls at Carlisle, so he had brought her to the Halls, hoping she'd find some semblance of the family she needed and start to recover from the losses she'd endured. Over the years, the Halls had come to look upon their house as her home in the fullest sense of the word, and she'd become part of their lives as no other student before.

While they were loath to see her leave, the Halls knew she should seize the advantages of the education the government was offering. Her staying with them for an entire year and skipping a year of school had been in response to her emotional needs, but Stella had long shared her dream of completing her education at Dickinson College and becoming a faculty member at Carlisle. Teaching offered the security of a well-respected career for an unmarried woman, with housing as well as income. The Halls were careful now not to expose their own feelings for fear of dissuading her from her dreams.

John showed himself repeatedly to be of good character. His willingness to work long hours on a project, his intelligent and reflective solutions to problems with the animals, and his creative approach to building projects made the Halls hold him in the highest regard. John immensely enjoyed the older man's counseling, for his thoughts and philosophy in life overall reminded the younger man of another example of manhood whom John had come to love in the cabin on Potato Creek. Mrs. Hall had won his heart by her unfaltering motherliness, much like the two women who had saved his life on the prairie. His devotion to Mother Hall showed in his striving to do whatever would please and help her.

As the summer wore on, however, both Mr. Hall and his wife noticed that despite what sometimes seemed to be a growing friendship between them, John and Stella just as frequently ended up at odds with one another. One evening at dinner, when John began a story about how he and Mr. Hall brought in a group of cattle to wean the calves, Stella gazed off into the distance as if not caring to hear any more. As John finished his story and Mr. Hall pointed out that without John's help, he would never have gotten all the calves into the barn, Stella remarked brusquely, "But you sorted all the calves last spring with no help from John. Surely it's not that difficult."

Mr. Hall chided her gently, "Yes, I did get the job done last spring, but not without spraining my ankle and having to mend two gates in the corral."

John continued in an effort to appease Stella, "We added a gate that has a large spring on it, like Mrs. Hall's kitchen door. Once the cows walk through, the spring pulls it closed so they can't come back to look for their babies." Both men were obviously pleased with the success of their design, but Stella didn't seem impressed.

She glanced out the window, adding in a derogatory tone, "I suppose it worked, but sorting calves is only done once a year. It seems a lot of trouble to build a special gate for that one day." John shrugged, giving up on breaking down the barriers she constantly put up. He wondered how she could be so pleasant and gracious one moment, yet so condescending the next. He wasn't sure he wanted to bother with understanding her behavior; but there was no denying his attraction to the girl.

A few days later, as John came down the stairs towards the kitchen on his way to help Mr. Hall, he overheard Mrs. Hall and Stella chatting as they worked together in the kitchen.

"It's going to be lonesome for us this winter with you gone, and Mr. Hall hates to lose John. Don't you think he's a fine young man? I hope we'll have him with us again next summer."

"I suppose he's fine, Mother Hall," Stella conceded, but after a beat she added, "I just think he's conceited, like all full-blooded Indians."

As John froze in mid-step, his eyebrows raised in shock, a stupefied Mrs. Hall retorted sharply, "I think, child, you mistake his reserve for conceit, which I believe it is not. Why do you always disparage the Indians of full blood? You carry Indian blood in your own veins. Do all mixed-bloods judge others so harshly?"

John waited, his face red with anger. Stella's answer came after a brief pause: "I suppose all mixed-bloods, and whites alike, are inclined to look down on full-bloods."

John lowered himself to sit on the stairs.

"I know it's so on the reservations and in the schools," Stella continued with a touch of bitterness. "I don't understand why, for the smallest part of Indian blood makes us all Indian to some."

John pondered the truth in that statement.

Stella continued somberly, "Perhaps it depends on how we're taught. For me, it's difficult to be neither one nor the other."

Mrs. Hall asked Stella to bring the eggs from the basket by the door, cheerfully adding that it was time to start making dessert. The girl remained quiet as she picked up the basket, returning to where the elderly lady waited patiently for further comment. John could tell it wasn't the first time they'd discussed the topic and knew they weren't saying everything but rather choosing their words carefully. He wondered why they believed not giving voice to the truth was the best way to solve a problem. Iron Horse had taught him to always speak the truth. The quiet told him each of the women was waiting, hoping the other would change the subject.

Instead, Stella probed, "Mother Hall, is it right for a man of one race to marry a woman of another?"

"Why, Stella, I don't know how to answer your question," replied Mrs. Hall kindly. "Since we've been involved with the Indian school, we've seen children from many different tribes. As I see it, the trouble in such marriages, if there is any at all, is apt to fall upon the children. Whether they be part white or a mix of different tribes, they must learn to walk in two worlds."

"Yes," added Stella, pensive, "I know that many mixed-bloods are not respected because they do not honor traditional ways. The whites do not respect them simply because they are part Indian. My teachers say that all the ways of the Indian are bad. I believe the children of any mixed relationships will be confused, for they must live in two worlds yet belong in neither."

As he remained seated, unheard on the steps, John thought he heard Stella's own pain in that simple statement. He had no idea of her parentage and only devised her mixed blood from knowing she was a former student at Carlisle. He wondered if there was something important he didn't yet know.

"Surely that's not always so, Stella," Mrs. Hall continued.

"Not always, but usually," Stella said firmly. "I don't expect to ever marry, for should I marry a white man, my child might be dark like my mother and remind its father every time he saw it that I was an Indian. Neither would I want to marry a mixed-blood and have to worry that my children might inherit the worst part of either parent. Yet," she added almost tearfully, "I've always wanted a baby so much."

Mrs. Hall exclaimed, reaching out to place her arm gently over the girl's shoulder, "Child! I think you worry too much about things you can't change. We have nothing to do with our coming into the world, but we can do much to make our journey pleasant by being good and considerate of others and by taking our place in life with grace. There's always hope."

Then she continued, her tone lightening, "Just think of Jean Baptiste Charbonneau, who fought for our freedom against the Mexicans, and of Jane Johnston Schoolcraft, who is half Ojibwa and whose writings you've probably studied at Carlisle. Some of the greatest minds of all time have been contained in bodies that were a mix of two races."

"Thank you, Mother Hall," replied Stella, hugging the woman affectionately. "You are such a loving person and always find the best way to look at our troubles!"

With that, the two women scuttled busily around the kitchen, pulling out bowls for potato salad and a pan for frying chicken. Afraid of being caught listening in, John scurried up the hallway and out the front door, calling out to Mr. Hall that he was on his way. Despite a busy day around the farm, though, his mind could not erase what he'd heard.

"How dare she call me conceited"—his voice rose as he walked to the field—"when it was she who always looked down her nose at me, ignoring my presence in the room during those early meals together. Does she think she's better because she carries some trace of a white man's blood?

"I might look down on her because her blood is not as pure as mine. And yet I cannot deny that her quiet dignity reminds me of Moves First, who saved my life, and her sparkling smile is so much like Annie's. Stella is intelligent like Carter's wife, who is also mixed-blood and who has given so much to the Indians at Potato Creek. Carter himself is white, yet he gave me the gift of oratory that has opened many doors for me. I refuse to believe there's any real difference between us despite our skin being different colors."

John knew now what he felt for Stella and pledged to give her plenty of time to sort out her feelings as he approached Mr. Hall and took over the task of cleaning the horses' stalls.

For the remainder of the day, Mrs. Hall fretted over the fears Stella had expressed about her future. She couldn't imagine such a lovely young woman avoiding marriage in order to escape imagined difficulties over the race of her future children. That evening, Stella bade the family good night just before Hiram was due to make his appearance, and John retired shortly after. Hiram had obviously not come to visit Mr. and Mrs. Hall, for he left quickly, giving Mrs. Hall a chance to tell her husband the details of her conversation with Stella.

Mr. Hall responded with the sincerity of a farmer who saw life simply. "She's such a good girl, and I feel sorry for her sensitive nature." Then he added wisely, "In most cattle, it is no matter if the parents are purebred or crossbred; the mother raises her calf. The calf cares not about the pedigrees of its parents. Stella needs to forget such nonsense about judging people by the degree of color in their skin."

A few days later, Mr. Hall said to the others as he started to town, "Mother Hall, I may bring a friend from the village this afternoon who wants to try the fishing. If I do, he'll stay overnight. Stella, I'd appreciate if you could spare a couple of your good frying chickens, and, John, if you'll have the bait and tackle ready, we'll try for some bass."

Mrs. Hall, John, and Stella relaxed in the rockers on the front porch of the house that evening, watching curiously for Mr. Hall's return. He was later than usual. As he drove up the hill and turned in to the lane, they saw he was indeed accompanied by a guest, but John didn't recognize the genial face of Major Mack until the buggy pulled into the yard. After hearty greetings all around, Mrs. Hall chided her husband for the deception of the morning while with the air of a mischievous schoolboy he explained as best he could. He knew how much John respected the major and wanted to surprise the young man with a visit from his mentor.

It was a new experience for John to see Mr. Hall and the major, freed momentarily from the cares of the outside world, enjoy the company of old schoolmates. Mrs. Hall took pleasure in repeating her share of stories, for they were all dear friends. For many years, Major Mack had made a point of spending a few days each summer at the Halls' home. Nowhere else could he find relief from the worries of his everyday life, and he abandoned himself to nothing but enjoyment as they lingered over the wonderful supper prepared by the ladies. Later, as they all sat together on the porch, John and Stella joined in the laughter as the three old friends giggled and guffawed like youngsters while sharing memories of times gone by.

Long after the others had retired for the night, Mr. Hall and the major sat discussing the growth of the school. "I know you have your doubts, Thomas," said the major, "but I'm convinced the most help I can be to the Indians is to remove the last vestiges of their former lives. They must accept the white man's way of living."

"Major," interrupted Mr. Hall, "I understand immersing them in the white world to teach them the skills they need, but to be forbidden any connection to their former lives must be extraordinarily difficult for the youngsters."

"It is indeed, but it's the only way to make such progress in the few years we have them at the school. This business is costly, and it's my duty to ensure the younger generation has no remnant of their native culture when they return to the reservation," the major said emphatically. "Otherwise, they'll simply forget their training and start fighting us for the land again."

Mr. Hall had serious concerns regarding the government's policy, but for the moment, he wasn't sure how to phrase his doubts without upsetting his friend, so he simply listened, nodding as if in agreement.

When their conversation turned naturally to John and Stella, they had no idea how clearly their voices carried along the polished wood floors of the farmhouse, straight to the door of John's bedroom where he lay, wishing he couldn't hear their voices.

"Yes," Mr. Hall concluded, replying to a question from the major, "John is certainly one of the best young men I've ever known. He's dependable and interested in all our work. I don't believe the place has ever been in better condition than it is at the present time."

"I'm gratified that my confidence in him is justified," the major replied. "I've been impressed by many of our students, but none has ever stood out to me more than John. Without being asked, he completes his work, including doing things he sees that need to be done even if they're not part of his assignment. He shows compassion to everyone, including those who've been unkind to him. He's calm and patient regardless of what goes on around him, raising his voice only when it's needed to provide leadership. For some reason, he sees every side of a question, not just the side that might benefit himself."

He continued, his zeal for his cause resonating, "No one's been able to tell me how he came from Spotted Elk's group to such a forward-thinking family at Potato Creek, nor how he learned to speak our language so clearly. I know Carter is an exceptional teacher, but how could the boy possibly learn so much in such an abbreviated time? What motivates him? I've met his father, Iron Horse, on more than one occasion and still wonder what made him accept that his children should learn the white man's ways when so many other leaders have not. Up to this point, John seems like a sponge that has no limit to how much it can absorb. Why can't all the Indians be like him?"

Struggling to control his fervor, the major lowered his voice. "One cannot, however, judge conclusively by a single year's observation. I felt considerable concern over his coming here on account of Stella, for there's always a risk in such close contact as they've had for the past two months."

"Their association has been nothing to be questioned," Mr. Hall replied quickly and reassuringly. Then, at length and with some amusement for them both, he related how he was convinced that Stella admired the young man but was afraid to let it show, so she pursued a course of studious avoidance, while John, for all his reserve and dignity, was afraid of rejection and determined that stoicism was his best plan of action.

He continued ardently, "It's been the most fulfilling and enjoyable circumstance for the missus and me. Mrs. Hall adores Stella and has her confidence as few mothers have with their own daughters. John has been an intelligent and diligent companion to me over the entire summer, and we've accomplished many tasks I thought were impossible." Mr. Hall hesitated before adding, "You know, Major, over our long hours in the field, he's told me a great deal about himself—his home, the reservation life, his goals."

Knowing there might not be another opportunity to express his concerns, he jumped onto a more difficult train of thought. "We're old friends, and I don't mean to question your life's calling, but I'm more convinced than ever, Major, that you're wrong to send these boys and girls back to their Indian homes after immersing them in the white man's world.

"From what John has told me about the reservation when he left, even the strongest character with the fixed habits of civilization can hardly be expected to live an acceptable life in his homeland. Particularly, I think a real wrong is done when they're made to go back against their every inclination. John's lived through hardship, hunger, and the loss of loved ones. He's seen it all and left that life behind. Through his experiences at school and with us, he's seen a different life and has no wish to return to the reservation. Many of your students are adapting as you intended. Why send them back to live in a world where there's no place for who they've become?"

Shaking his head, Major Mack responded somberly, "I see your point, Tom, and deep in my heart, I believe you're right. The policies of which you speak are no longer my own and may be outdated. Soon there will be more young, educated Indians than old ones who battled our government so fiercely. But the wheels of government turn slowly, and the policies have not changed. The school has been my life's work. It has grown and requires much funding, and now I find myself torn between what I believe and what it takes to garner the favor of Washington from whence the money flows.

"When I began work on the school, I believed the best hope for the Indian was to become white, learn to live in our civilization, and give up their past. I wanted to believe it was best for them to go back to the reservation and try to change it. Now I don't believe that's possible. Yet as school costs have increased and the need for land has grown, the Indian schools have attracted the attention of misguided and misinformed interests.

These people see themselves as philanthropists, and they build their own egos by convincing themselves they're doing good. Unfortunately, they also believe their money gives them power, and that's where I'm caught."

Here, the major rose from his chair, pacing, before he went on in a fervor, "My donors believe the educated Indians should return to their reservations as living examples of the white man's civilization. They've read stories about the West but have never actually been there. They envision the reservation where the buffalo roam," he added with a chuckle, "and cannot imagine a home where meals are cooked over an open fire instead of a stove. They can't envision a woman cooking in an old oil can or breaking open cow bones to cook out the marrow because it's all that's left.

"They have no concept of the primitive conditions and can't comprehend there's no use for many of the skills we teach. All the bureaucrats understand is that settlers want more land, which means more battles for the Army. Somehow, Washington believes we can educate the Indians out of fighting." His voice lowering almost in defeat, he concluded, "It's a sad cycle, and I've been driven to the brink of melancholy by the contemplation of it all." He poured himself a brandy and sat subdued on Mrs. Hall's favorite velvet chaise.

When he looked up again at Thomas, his friend asked hesitantly, "What are you going to do with Stella and John?"

As if the question didn't need an answer, Major Mack replied with a smile, "Why, they're coming back here next summer if you'll allow it."

In his lowest-pitched, most sincere voice, Mr. Hall responded, "The missus and I will be exceedingly glad. We're eager to have them with us again." With that, the two old friends shook hands warmly before bidding each other good night.

John had listened to the first few minutes of the conversation before forcing himself to ignore the voices and try to drift off to sleep. Despite a guilty conscience for eavesdropping, John relaxed in knowing that he was held in high regard by both men. His thoughts turned to Stella; that she too would be returning brought a warmth to his chest.

As he lay there, still feeling the sting of her sometime disdain, he remembered her patience with her chickens scurrying beneath her feet as she struggled to keep from stumbling over them. Smiling in the dark, he called up the memory of her excitement at catching the biggest bass of the summer, how she danced and laughed, her pearly teeth reflecting the firelight. Wasn't that the same excitement any youth would feel? What about as they strolled back from the lake to the house that first time, stride matching stride, a smile gracing Stella's face as their arms swung in unison. John couldn't bring himself to believe she wasn't happy in those moments. How could she express that happiness in his presence if all she was thinking about was the color of his skin?

As his eyes blurred into sleep, John remembered his teacher's question about being hungrier for biscuits because of the color of his skin. He wondered if there would be opportunities for he and Stella to share the same kind of conversation in the future. He hoped for more time with her during the upcoming year at Carlisle. His last thoughts were a reflection on Mrs. Hall's implication that Stella had feelings for him but chose for the moment not to show them.

The major remained with his friends for three days, enjoying the exercise of his skill as a fisherman, the restfulness of their home, and the companionship of its inhabitants. When the time came for his vacation to end, the major invited John to return to Carlisle with him the following day.

John lay awake long after he'd gone to bed, thinking about his last night in the cabin on Potato Creek. Life had been so simple there: helping his mothers, studying with Carter and Annie, and spending time with his adopted father as he traveled around the reservation. John remembered how happy he'd been rather than that there wasn't an abundance of food or of firewood in the winter. He felt the same keen regret for the parting that was to come, yet also a new excitement for the opportunities that lay ahead. He thought of the goodness of Mr. Hall and the kindness of his wife. He felt pride from a job well done and peace from the knowledge that he'd return next summer.

The next morning, his trunk sat nestled beside the major's canvas bag on the back of Mr. Hall's buggy. Mrs. Hall handed each a neatly wrapped gingham bundle that was warm and smelled of freshly baked gingerbread. As John bade Mrs. Hall and Stella goodbye, his regret about leaving was lessened by the fact that he was returning to Carlisle in the company of Major Mack. He was thankful to be invited to travel with someone as important as the major and hoped to learn more about the school on their trip.

As the buggy turned from the lane onto the big road, John looked back and saw Stella still waving slowly as if she regretted their leaving.

CHAPTER 36

Return

Fall 1897 to Spring 1898

Carlisle Indian School, Pennsylvania

Once they boarded the train and settled in for the ride back to Carlisle, John carefully broached the subject he'd overheard the evening before between Mr. Hall and the major. He wanted to believe he could convince the major to see things differently.

"Thank you for inviting me to join you on the trip back to school. I enjoy the train and getting to see more of the white man's way of living in the East. My father believed that our young people should go into the world upon completing their education," he began. "I'd like to put what I've learned to use in the world beyond the reservation, perhaps build a successful farm like Mr. Hall's or open a business like I've visited with him on our trips to town. I'm not sure I see a future for myself if I go back to the reservation."

After several moments with no comment, the major sighed deeply. Without turning to face John, he replied, "I'm not surprised your father believed that. He's lost much over his years, and he's a wise man. He knows the Indians must change in order to survive. You're an outstanding student and have made excellent use of the opportunities that have been provided, but most of our students must return to teach their parents and grandparents. It's the founding principle of the government's education program. Furthermore, my heart is in what I've built at the school, and I can't go against government policy. I'll reflect on your thoughts, but for now, John, I'm sorry. I was up quite late last night and need to rest." With that, the major ended their conversation, crossing his arms and resting his chin on his chest as if settling for a nap.

They rode in silence for the remainder of the journey, John staring blankly out the window as the landscape shot past. He wondered if it had done any good to open his heart to the major. As the train pulled into the station, the major stirred and gathered his things, then glanced at John, who still sat deep in thought.

"Thank you, John, for joining me on this trip. Perhaps, one day, I'll speak to my superiors in Washington about a change." Turning to disembark, the major hesitated before adding, "By the way, here's something Mr. Hall asked me to give you." He handed John an envelope.

"Thank you, sir," the boy replied, his brow furrowing slightly. The major hustled up the sidewalk towards the school, ending further conversation.

John strolled slowly towards his dormitory with the trunk that had accompanied him from Potato Creek. When he finally opened the envelope from Mr. Hall, he found a check and a note.

My Dear John:

I enclose a check in payment for your summer's work. It is drawn in such amount as Major Mack and I have agreed is fair compensation, and I trust that you will find it satisfactory. We thoroughly enjoyed having you with us this summer and want you to know that your work and your efforts to do your best have been appreciated. We will, of course, look forward to your return next summer.

Trusting that your summer's success will continue and extend throughout the school year, I am,

Yours sincerely,
Thomas H. Hall

After reading the note three times, John felt a burst of pride course through him. He was glad to know he could elicit the commendation of those he respected. The check, which represented the first money he'd ever earned, gave him an assurance that was worth more than the entire summer's experiences. It was more money than he'd ever possessed in his life, and in its possession, he felt the conviction that he could work—and by his work, live.

After depositing the check in the superintendent's office for safekeeping the next morning, John went straight to Mr. Cornish and asked if he could work with the carpenters instead of on the farm as he'd been doing.

"Are you sure?" asked Mr. Cornish in his usual quiet voice. "I've been thinking of making you one of my student assistants. The position includes a small salary. You could continue your schoolwork and help me during your industrial hours. But if you're sure, of course you can work on the carpenter's detail."

"I've enjoyed working with you, Mr. Cornish," John said, smiling widely, "and certainly I'd like to earn the money. But I worked on the farm last year as well as while I was at the reservation boarding school. I don't particularly want to learn the carpenter's trade, but this summer at Mr. Hall's, I saw many things around the farm that need to be repaired. When I go back next year, I want to know how to fix them right."

"You have the right idea, John," Mr. Cornish said proudly. "I'll be glad to help you any way I can. Later on, if you want to work with me, I'll be glad to arrange it."

As the year progressed, John's interest and dedication to learning became so much a part of him that he achieved high honors in every one of his classes. He continued to go to football practice as the season wore on, hoping to make the team eventually. John accepted that he'd probably never be a regular member, but he continued to sit on the sidelines, giving encouragement when needed and learning whatever he could of the game.

Towards the end of the season, Carlisle faced Dickinson College, best known for two of its alumni: James Buchanan, fifteenth president of the United States, and Roger B. Taney, chief justice of the Supreme Court. Their football team was undefeated, but so was the Carlisle team. Because the final standings for the season depended on this game, there were large delegations of fans from neighboring colleges and universities.

Dickinson's team came out for the pregame warm-up and showed off their impressive ball-handling skills as well as their formidable physical appearance and colorful uniforms. Coach Warner simply advised the Carlisle team to hold the other team to as few points as possible. As they ran onto the field, the cheers from the Carlisle side seemed to signify moral support more than any real confidence their team would win. The game dragged on, the enthusiasm and confidence of the white team never quite overwhelming the skill and determination of the Indians.

Several of the Carlisle players suffered injuries, and in the final minutes of the game, John was called in to play. Racing onto the field to his assigned position, John found himself right beside none other than Ben Rowland, the bully. As play commenced, Dickinson's quarterback made an outlandish attempt at putting the score out of reach of the Carlisle team. Overly confidant, he lost his hold on the ball, sending it tumbling right into Ben's outstretched hands. Ben took off, racing towards the goal line with John blocking for him all the way. Ben crossed the goal line and in the next play held the ball for John, who kicked it squarely between the opposing team's goal posts, luckily scoring the winning point just as time ran out.

The combination of a touchdown and the point afterward brought victory to the Indian school against a team made up entirely of whites. Furthermore, it assured their school's status as the number one college football team in the East. The two young men threw their arms around each other's shoulders and raced to the center of the field, where Ben shouted, "I couldn't have done it without you, old friend!" shaking John's hand exuberantly. Most of the other members of the team remembered the boys' previous confrontation and understood the feelings behind that statement. Huddled together in the center of the field, the team reveled in the knowledge that the championship established their team as one deserving respect from all competitors, regardless of the color of their skin.

However, John counted as his greatest success an encounter with Stella as he was leaving the field. She approached him, eyes alight with pride, and shouted, "Oh, John! I'm so proud of you!" Immediately, his self-assurance deserted him, and looking down shyly, he could only mutter, "Thank you" before hurrying away to his dormitory. Once his heart stopped pounding and the reality of the day settled in, John was elated she'd noticed and praised his efforts.

The rest of the year was a series of accomplishments for John. He was appointed head of the junior class and ensured a place among the graduates the following year. He pursued his work with dedication and purpose. Commencement was set for the first week in May to allow graduates and those whose enrollment had ended to return to their homes at a pleasant time of year. It also allowed the outing students to go to their summer placements.

Preparation began weeks before the event. Buildings were cleaned, the grounds were groomed, and preparations were made for the entertainment of important guests who might attend. There were exhibitions ranging from athletic contests and military drills to band concerts and literary programs, and finally the commencement exercises themselves. Many people would be in attendance. Donors came from far and near—some out of curiosity, some to cheer for winning teams, and some to support the education of the Indians. The donors were given the choicest seats, beside the officials and directly in front of the podium and stage.

John recognized that this was a time when those who called themselves philanthropists came to look on complacently. Many of them had never been to a reservation and had no idea about the lives of those who lived there. Watching them stroll about the grounds with an air of disdain for others, John wondered if they got involved because they had more money than they could spend or if they felt better about themselves just knowing someone else was worse off. He knew their motivation was seldom a genuine interest in improving the lives of the Indians.

At every event, speakers impressed upon the graduates the need to do their duty to their people, to hear the cry of their reservation, to serve by returning to help remediate the conditions back home. Among the graduates were Julia American Horse and Abram Lone Bear from John's reservation. They'd both been at the school for five years and had received the honor of speaking at commencement. Abram was to deliver an oration titled "Taking Civilization Back to the Reservation," and Julia was to read an essay on "What I Propose to Do for the Indian Women Back Home."

John was disheartened to learn they hadn't been allowed to choose the topics of their speeches. He'd seen students return to the reservation and wondered if Abram and Julia would go back physically and then go back to living the reservation life as so many others had done.

The words "go back" were significant. John had seen young people leave the reservation and return wearing white men's clothing and sharing white men's ideas, resolute in their determination to bring change to the reservation. Within a few months but never more than a year under the demoralizing influence of no tools, no jobs, and little food, they would "go back" to the camp style of living, back to the abject poverty of a lost culture, lost language, and lost land.

The biggest social event of commencement week was a reception given for the graduates, alumni, and invited guests. John was among the invited members of the underclassmen. For this occasion, the gymnasium was decorated in the colors of the graduating class, and a band played.

As his eyes swept the room, John spotted Stella amid a small group of alumnae. Not only was she beautiful, with her auburn hair and slender figure, but she was intelligent. John had watched more than once while she coached a debate team for Carlisle. They worked in a room that he passed on his way to shop class three days a week, so he'd made a habit of standing in the hallway outside the door, listening to her during class discussions. Sometimes he was amazed at her knowledge of the outside world. Her graciousness also showed in her classroom, and in how she treated not just her friends but also those who were mere acquaintances, people she passed on the sidewalks or sat down beside in the dining hall. All who knew the school at all knew Stella Nelson. Those who knew her respected her; those who knew her well admired her; and those who knew her best loved her.

For the reception, her hair was fastened atop her head, and she wore a dainty dress fashioned in the plain and simple lines she always chose. John watched her exchanging small talk with those around her, laughing off a compliment or extending a pleasant word to someone she was meeting for the first time. She exhibited the identical traits he had admired in Moves First and Good Heart—the kindness, the quiet support, the genuine interest in others around her. But he had also seen her resolve, her anger, and her determination. In a flash, John thought about how close they both were to finishing their education and wondered if it would be possible for her, or himself, to ever "go back."

His reflections were broken when something brushed lightly against his shoulder. Turning, he realized Stella stood beside his chair, smiling as if waiting for him to make the next move. He rose to his feet, shifting his weight for balance, and extended his hand to offer his seat, but she paused and looked sideways as if hesitant to be seen sitting beside him. Then, suddenly, she was grinning happily before taking the seat he'd offered. She'd reverted to the Stella he knew in the Berkshires, relaxed and confident.

"I'm exhausted. Sitting here with you is the most restful thing I can think of. It takes me back to Mother Hall's."

John found himself wondering if the Stella he saw sometimes was a mask, meant to keep others at a distance. For all the haughtiness she was capable of, there seemed to be a frightened child inside. Keeping these thoughts to himself, he commented excitedly, "I'll be back there in less than a month," before continuing with genuine interest, "What about you? When will you return?"

"Not before the latter part of June, I'm afraid. The college year doesn't end until then," she stated gloomily. In a heartfelt tone, she added, "I wish it were over now. I'll be so glad to get back. I want to stay there for always."

"I feel the same and didn't even realize it," John blurted, surprised at himself. "I've been content with my success here at school, but I miss the peace and quiet of the farm and the feeling of accomplishment when Mr. Hall and I complete a project."

He continued, his heart on his sleeve, "I've sat here all evening where I can see without attracting attention. I've watched the graduates and listened to their speeches about going home and teaching their families what they've learned. How can they teach farming to people who have no fertilizer and no plows? What use will their mothers have for dainty stitches and ironed clothes when they cannot buy fabric at the trader's store? What use is a punched tin pie plate when there's no fruit or sugar?

"I see past graduates here, with their false smiles and insincere handshakes. I want to scream at them to share the truth of what they know about the reservations or at least encourage the graduates to seek a job in the white man's world. I know that Iron Horse was right. I don't want to go back, ever. Not to the reservation as it is today. It became clear to me when you told me your feelings about the farm. We are the same."

"Why, John, how wonderfully you talk!" Stella responded in amazement.

John reached out and took her hand as they sat there together.

Remembering the conversation he'd overheard last summer between the major and Mr. Hall about the school's goal not being to send the Indian children into the white world, John now faced the real reason the school was sending so many of its graduates back to the reservation. Meanwhile, Stella wondered aloud, "Are there enough jobs for these students on the reservation? If not, why don't they encourage those who have valuable skills to find a job in the East in the white man's world?"

John answered truthfully, "I fear the goal is not to teach us so that we can enter the white world but rather to show us a better life so that we might teach our elders to desire that life so they'll quit fighting for their land."

The two became so absorbed in their discussion about school, government policy, and jobs that they were oblivious to the passing of time. At last, they were recalled to the present by the raucous departure of the crowd. When he left Stella at the door of her dormitory, John wondered if she'd think of him when she regained the seclusion of her room. He couldn't know that when she did, she would feel a chilling sense of foreboding as she recalled their conversation about going back to the reservation.

For hours, she sat curled on her bed, comparing him to others she'd known, wondering what drew her to him. She thought of the traits she admired in any man, and as the night passed, she became thankful that he'd been made a child of Iron Horse, the companion of Annie, and the pupil of Carter Heath. They were what had shaped him into the man she knew. It wasn't whether or not he was Indian or white or mixed-blood. It was who he was as a man.

As John drifted to sleep, replaying his memories of the last picnic with her at the Halls', Stella shook off her doubts, accepting finally that regardless of the color of his skin, John Iron Horse was a good man who had seized every opportunity provided to him in life. Those were the things her heart found attractive.

CHAPTER 37

Sweet Revenge

Late Spring 1898

Carlisle Indian School, Pennsylvania

On a walk to the school from town several days after commencement, Abram Lone Bear shared his concerns with John about the future. "I leave for the reservation tomorrow, and I confess I don't care to go nearly as much as I thought I would. For a long time, I looked forward to going back, and I've thought of all the old things I can do when I return. But now that the time's here, I find it's not so appealing. When I know that in three days I'll be back there, I can't help but see things as they were when I left. I've been away so long that I'll have to talk to my own parents through an interpreter," Abram said sadly.

"I think I know how you feel, Abram," John sympathized. "There's so little on the reservation for the returning student. Are you planning to stay there?"

"I don't know. My folks will be glad to see me. They'll want me to stay because my mother didn't want me to go away in the first place. My father's more progressive and would support my staying here for another year or two. I'd like to get a law degree, but I'm being sent back to the reservation because there's no job for me at my summer outing home. They wanted someone younger, who could be with them for several years," Abram said wistfully. Coming back to reality, he added, "Maybe I'll find work at the agency or at one of the traders' stores. Certainly, I'll try, but there are so many returning students and not enough jobs."

John wondered aloud, "Would you be going back tomorrow if you'd been encouraged to remain here in the East?"

"No," Abram replied after a moment or two. "I enjoyed my summer outings when I worked and made my living. If I'd known their plans, I would've looked for other jobs. I love the farm in Connecticut where the rain is plentiful. Maybe I'll come back to school."

"That will be hard," John stated simply. "You'll hurt your mother by leaving again. Parents want their families to be together as in the past. Students who have stayed want others to do the same. If they're happy, they want you to be happy. If they aren't, they may wish that upon you as well."

Abram sorted through his own thoughts as John continued, "There are things that hold you to that life: the beauty of the prairie in spring, the freedom to do as you choose, even be lazy, because you have no employer or teacher telling you what to do. I've tried to see my life both ways—if I return to the reservation or if I do not. I know there'll be no barns to build on the reservation, no fat, spotted cows for me to care for. No one will tell me what project I'm to work on for the day. There'll be no family to go fishing and picnicking with or fruit trees to tend or stores in town with bounteous shelves from which I can pick any number of items to buy.

"On the other hand, on the reservation, I'll be close to my adopted father and mothers and be able to visit Annie's grave and walk along Potato Creek as in my youth. But I'll worry that my parents don't have enough to eat and that there may be no medicine to help if they become sick in their older years. I loved my life with Iron Horse, but I don't think that's enough for me anymore. I don't believe I'll go back, except perhaps to visit," said John as they turned onto the school grounds. Glancing towards Abram, he realized his companion was deeply depressed over their conversation.

The following day, Abram and Julia were among a group that left the school for various reservations far away.

Three weeks later, John was on his way to the Berkshire country, the first journey he'd ever taken on the railroad by himself. He found it absorbing and derived great satisfaction from being on his own.

His itinerary provided for a stay of several hours in New York, and he felt the enormity of it as he threaded his way alone through the vast throngs on the streets, wandering at will and without any purpose except to see it all. He almost lost track of the time. Heading back towards the station, he turned up one of the more congested thoroughfares and found himself amid a crowd surrounding the cart of a street vendor. While John had seen similar things in Carlisle, he was curious, and as he listened to the hawker expound on his wares, his curiosity changed to interest.

"Here you are, ladies and gents, the purest, best soap on the market today. Just a few left. Only ten cents per cake. One dollar for the box of twelve in assorted colors. With every box, I give a solid-gold-plated watch worth five dollars of anybody's money. Thank you, sir. Now, who's next?"

John stepped forward with a devilish smile, produced his dollar, and received a box of the purest, best, and most highly perfumed soap, along with the watch, which the vendor set by the one from his own pocket as he handed it to John. "Thank you, young man. The watch is right to the minute and well worth the money, for it cost you nothing. Now, who's next? Only a few more left."

As John took the watch, he imagined Mother Hall's surprise at his gift of the colorful soaps, but he rubbed his fingers carefully over the gold plate of the cheap watch, pleased with the opportunity it would provide to avenge an insult. He thought about the cost of the watch, smiled mischievously, and planned his revenge.

Mr. Hall met John in Becket that evening with a warm welcome, repeated by his wife when they drove into the yard an hour later. As John settled into his room that night, he knew that the world could be as good to an Indian as to anyone else.

He began his work around the place in the morning, and late in the afternoon he made it his purpose to go down to the house at the foot of the hill and greet Mr. and Mrs. Parkins and Hiram. He intentionally overstayed his time just a little that he might have reason to take out his new watch to support his declaration that it was time for him to return and begin his evening chores. He noted with inward satisfaction that Hiram showed great interest in his new possession.

From that time on, John made it a practice to carry the watch whenever there was a likelihood of seeing Hiram, and invariably he took the occasion to look at it in Hiram's presence. It otherwise reposed unwound and unused on the dresser in his room.

About three weeks after his return, while making repairs to the chicken coop and thinking how pleased Stella would be, John chanced to see Hiram coming towards him through the orchard. He retrieved his watch at once and was back to work by the time his neighbor arrived with an unusually pleasant, "Howdy do, John."

John responded with a "Howdy, Hiram," and kept steadily at the work at hand.

"John, I come over to see if I could borry the big crosscut for a spell this afternoon."

"Why, of course, Hiram. It's hanging in a tree out in the grove, near that big maple the wind blew down the other night."

John glanced at his watch and remarked that it was later than he thought.

"I can find it without any trouble, I guess," replied Hiram, eying the flashing gold timepiece in the Indian's hand. "That's a good-looking watch you have, John."

"Thank you. It was a present to me."

"I don't allow that you would care to swap it, would you?" asked Hiram as though feeling his way.

"No, I don't believe I do," replied John after a hesitation that suggested uncertainty.

"Would you sell it? I have a notion that I would not mind owning a good watch."

"I would miss it a good deal if I let you have it," said John with reluctance.

"If you would sell it, what do you allow you'd take for it?" inquired the artful Hiram.

"Oh, I don't know." John adopted a casual tone. "I couldn't take less than ten dollars for it."

"Can I look at it?" asked Hiram, and John handed him the watch, letting it swing briefly and sparkle in the sunlight.

Hiram studied it critically, held it to his ear, and tried the winding stem, and as he handed it back said, "I'll give you seven and a half. It doesn't look like solid gold to me."

"Well, Hiram, it may or it may not be, but I'll tell you what I'll do. I'll let you have it at your own price, just to be neighborly."

Grinning, Hiram took the exact amount from his pocket and handed it to John, saying, "A bargain is a bargain." He put the watch carefully in his pocket, turned, and went back the way he'd come with no further thought of the saw that'd been his excuse for coming over.

A few days later, John was making some improvements in the grain bins when Hiram Parkins appeared in the large open doorway.

John looked up with the usual greeting—"Howdy do, Hiram"—but saw at a glance that his caller was perturbed. He'd been expecting this visit ever since Hiram purchased his watch and had carefully prepared himself for every contingency he foresaw. Hiram replied to his greeting with a "Howdy do," then came inside and stood in silence for a moment while John continued his work. John was putting into practice some of the carpentry skills he'd learned the previous year, and he continued as if his neighbor's presence were commonplace.

"John," Hiram began, trying to appear at ease and at the same time plainly showing his insecurity. "I've come to the conclusion that I do not allow to keep your watch, so I've brought it over to swap it back."

"Why, Hiram, I have no watch. You bought the only watch I had the other day," replied John as if he did not completely understand.

"Yes, I know. That's what I mean," said Hiram with a show of excitement. "The watch is no good, and I have no use for it. I want my money back."

"Well, that's strange," returned John mildly. "It was a good-looking watch too. What's the matter with it, Hiram?"

"Why, it won't run unless I wind it every hour or two, and the paint is all worn off, so it looks like brass."

"You didn't drop it, did you, Hiram?" asked John.

The question exasperated Hiram, but with an effort he maintained a semblance of self-control and resolved to pursue a course of conciliation as long as there seemed any chance of recovering his purchase price, for he was notoriously cheap. He said, "No, I didn't drop it, and it is just as it was when you sold it to me."

"That can hardly be, Hiram, for when you bought it, the watch kept time and looked like a good watch, as you yourself said."

Hiram saw that his chances of recovery were not good, and after another struggle with his increasing anger, he said, "I'll let you have it back for five dollars, John, and you'll have two and a half dollars of my money for nothing."

"No, I don't feel I ought to take your money for nothing, Hiram. I didn't swap the watch. I didn't even try to sell it to you. You bought it at your own price. You made your own bargain, and you know, a bargain is a bargain."

Hiram detected a note of banter in John's tone. As he recognized it, his anger gained control and he blurted out, "Well, I don't want it. It's no good, and I have no use for it!"

"Why not try it for bait, Hiram, fishing for some of those big bass in the hole by the beech log?" John replied, letting a big grin spread over his face until it lit up his eyes with a roguish light.

Hiram knew! He knew that he'd recover no part of the money he'd paid for the watch, and he knew that John had squared his account. He knew, too, that the account was just and that he'd been toyed with by an Indian, even as he had played on that Indian's trust and inexperience. "Doggone you, Indian, you cheated me, and you know it." Then, giving way to his rage entirely, he added, "I never knew an Injun that could be trusted."

A ringing laugh from the doorway broke in, and they both looked up to see Stella standing there as though she might have heard it all. She'd returned from her year of college study moments earlier and was strolling around the farm, incredibly happy to be there, when she heard their voices.

"And to think that I'm just such an Indian," she commented as she looked at the two young men, one with amusement and the other with contempt.

"You're all alike!" cried the infuriated Hiram, starting for the door. At those words of insult that included Stella, a hard look replaced John's smile, and he closed his powerful hand around Hiram's arm.

"You lily-livered loser, you apologize!"

But Hiram, despite his ungainly figure and awkwardness, was a man of exceptional strength and unsuspected agility. He wrenched himself free of John's grasp and delivered a hard blow with his fist to the side of John's face.

Stunned for an instant, John launched into a tackle he'd learned during weeks of football practice and brought Hiram to the ground in what rapidly devolved into a wrestling match with no holds barred. The contestants were evenly matched in weight, strength, and size. They struggled fiercely for a few minutes without advantage to either, and both were beginning to tire when John secured a hold that enabled him to slam Hiram to the hard-packed dirt floor. When John set himself for a resumption of the contest, he was startled to find that the prostrate Hiram made no effort to get up but lay where he'd fallen, motionless.

At the first blow, Stella had hurried to the house to get Mrs. Hall, and the two entered the barn just in time to see Hiram's hard landing on the floor and to hear the ominous thud with which his head hit. Stella was relieved it was Hiram on the floor and glanced quickly towards John to be sure he wasn't seriously injured. Hiram was breathing, but his eyes remained closed, and there was no other movement. John stepped closer to his prostrate form, reaching to assist his nemesis if he attempted to rise.

For several minutes, Hiram remained as he was, mostly ashamed of being defeated in front of Stella and trying to gain as much sympathy from both her and Mrs. Hall as possible. Slowly, groaning with even the slightest motion, Hiram regained his wits and struggled upright, propping his back against one of the large timbers that supported the floor of the loft above. Mrs. Hall sent Stella to the house for water, and as she returned, Hiram rose, keeping his reddened face to his chest. Without a word, he walked unsteadily out of the barn, moaning and supporting his left arm as if every movement caused unbearable pain. For a passing second, John hoped Hiram had not suffered any significant injury. He watched as the young man made his way towards home without so much as a glance back.

As they sat together on the porch that evening, John, worried the Halls might be disappointed he'd fought with Hiram, reminded them of the incident the previous summer when Hiram had gained access to the lake and imposed upon John's trust and inexperience. Assured there was no anger from his host and hostess, John shared how he'd sought for a year to find a way to repay Hiram without resorting to any unfairness or taking undue advantage. Everyone laughed when he shared his encounter with the soap vendor on the street corner in New York, revealing how he planned to engage Hiram in a trade he was bound to lose and how it had all come to pass as he'd hoped.

Stella added her own tale to the evening entertainment. "Why, John, I suppose now we've both gotten the best of Hiram. When he last asked me to be his wife—for the sixth time, I remind you—he was adamant I'd never be happy on this farm again, and now here I am, not only here and happy but also as witness to his inglorious defeat by an Indian."

Holding his belly, Mr. Hall sat back in his chair and laughed so long and heartily that he must have been heard clear to the house at the foot of the hill. The other three joined in with relish. Their laughter must have been understood as well, for although John felt a miniscule amount of pity for any injury he might have caused and worried that he might not have heard the last of Hiram Parkins, from that time on, evenings were enjoyed without the company of their unscrupulous neighbor.

CHAPTER 38

Loss

Summer 1898

Snow Hill Farm, Becket, Massachusetts

Because of his eagerness to find ways to improve his farm that summer, it became normal for Mr. Hall to consult with John rather than merely direct him from day to day. John was always finding ways to make improvements, and the farm looked better and better each week. Mrs. Hall grew dependent on him around the house, whether reaching for objects on tall shelves or shifting furniture for cleaning. Since the encounter with Hiram Parkins, Stella had begun to show a strong attachment to John, seeking out his presence each evening on the porch. There were still brief moments of aloofness that distressed his heart and puzzled his mind, but he hoped they were growing closer day by day.

It was a wonderful atmosphere for John and Stella's relationship to develop, and the Halls enjoyed the feeling of family they feared had been lost long ago. The days were filled with the joy of accomplishment, and their evenings with close companionship. Mr. and Mrs. Hall felt their regard for the young people grow into parental affection, and in their private conversations always spoke of them as "the children." John and Stella returned their affection wholeheartedly. John's attitude towards Stella was outwardly much the same, for he concealed his attraction to her lest she spurn him, but in his innermost heart he kept thoughts that weren't shared with any other.

Mrs. Hall's instincts told her that Stella's emotions for this young man caused a conflict in her heart. They'd spoken of his virtuous character, and at times Stella's conduct hinted something of the warmth of her feelings towards John. Still, she always stopped herself just in time to prevent any disclosure of her true feelings. Mrs. Hall had asked her once if she thought she might ever have serious feelings for the young man, but Stella's response was puzzling.

"Mother Hall, I sometimes wonder if what I'm feeling is true love as all young women dream of, yet too often in the quiet of my room there comes a vague, indefinable feeling when I try to imagine our future. It's not frightening, but the only word that describes it is a sense of foreboding of things to come."

"Dear, dear, don't be concerned about such," Mrs. Hall reassured her. "Every young woman feels a bit of trepidation when wondering about a choice that will hopefully last a lifetime."

Although their work on the farm kept them busy, both John and Stella had books to read and sketchbooks for relaxation, and they enjoyed quiet evenings by the pond where they shared feelings and dreams. Stella would shake off her leather slippers and run her bare toes through the deep grass, stretching her legs full length as she sat along the bank and gathering her skirt hem to tuck under her knees. John couldn't resist taking a long stem of bluegrass and stroking it up the middle of her bare foot until she erupted in squeals of laughter. His body flushed with warmth whenever she tugged on his arm or leaned into his shoulder, looking into his eyes and smiling happily.

Over the course of the summer, it became the norm for John and Stella to fish here and there along the water until settling down so close together that they showed a single silhouette to anyone observing from a distance. Sometimes he would sit behind her, stretching his long legs neatly beside hers, and she would lean back against his chest and settle into his embrace as he wrapped his arms around her waist.

"I could sit here forever," John whispered one day as he pulled her closer, hoping she wouldn't take offense at his nearness. "I want to forget my time at Carlisle will end soon and there may be no more summers such as this. I fear I know more of what I *don't* want than of what I do want for my future. Do you ever think of what you'll do when you finish college?"

Stella basked in the sound of his voice and wanted to know more of his plans. "I've also thought more of what I don't want than do. I've always wanted children but can't imagine myself married or living anywhere away from the Halls."

John remembered her long-ago comment about not marrying and hoped it had been erased from her thoughts. He delighted in listening to her voice when it was for him alone, so he queried, eyes twinkling, "But you have to be married to have children! Have you thought about the kind of man you'll marry?"

"Of course," she teased softly. "He'll be extraordinarily strong and tall, and he'll work hard for our family." She looked quickly away so he couldn't see her blushing cheeks.

Sometimes their conversations drifted into confidences, even intimacies, and sometimes they became so absorbed that Mr. Hall would stroll down to the pond and light a fire to bring them back from their dreamland. Sometimes their lines became entangled in the water. Not that it mattered about their lines, for there were few fish in the area, and it wasn't fish they sought. Afterwards, when Stella returned to the seclusion of her room and questioned her own thoughts, she always had the same premonition—the same feeling of darkness, of John waving to her from a distance—and the following day would conceal her emotions and try to stay aloof.

"Mother," said Mr. Hall, using her pet name for emphasis, "I'll be a little late this evening, and I'll again bring a friend who wants to fish in the lake for a day or two."

The major brought his usual cheeriness that evening, yet he was conscious of a sentiment he couldn't quite identify. The jolly spirit that usually prevailed was missing, and finally the major turned to John and Stella.

"What's the matter? You two don't seem very glad to see me."

Stella replied impulsively, "Of course we're glad to see you, Major," then, looking across to John, added, "but it's been such a wonderful summer." When she fell silent, Major Mack read her feelings far more than she wished, and John added simply, "We're always glad to see you, Major Mack."

"That reminds me, John," returned the major, taking an envelope from his pocket. "Here's a letter from the folks back home that came to the school yesterday."

When Mr. Hall and the major went out to the porch, John remained behind to read the letter. It was from Aaron Moss, and read:

My Dear John:

    I know that you will be intensely grieved to learn that Iron Horse died yesterday. As you know, he had been failing for some time. He went to the long sleep cheerfully and patiently as he had lived, and his last little while was much like Annie's. I was with him when he went away, and his last words were for you. "Tell him," he said, "that my spirit will always be with him." We laid him on the brow of the hill across the creek beside your sister, facing the camp and the distance into which he so often looked with you on his mind. He was a good man, John, and I know that his soul rests in peace, whether in the red man's happy hunting ground or the white man's heaven, and may God bless his memory and you.

Your affectionate friend,
Aaron Moss

    At first John didn't comprehend the contents of the letter, but as he finished reading, it all came to him in one surge that gripped his heart with intense, convulsive pain. Although his face didn't betray the intensity of his emotion to Stella, who had remained beside him, it was clear to her that he'd been cast into the very depths of sorrow. He made his way stoically out of the house without a word or sound. As she watched him disappear into the trees of the orchard with the letter clutched tightly in his hand, she felt a great pity well up and wished she could comfort him.

    When the after-supper work was finished and Mrs. Hall joined her husband and Major Mack on the porch, Stella walked out past her chickens at the back of the house, on to the garden, and through it to the orchard, impelled by something that seemed a part of her. She didn't have to search for John but went straight to the far side where she found him seated against one of the larger trees, the letter crumpled in his hand. He gazed unblinking at the glow that still graced the western sky.

    When he gave no heed to her presence, she asked softly, "John, can I help?"

    He handed her the letter without a word, his gaze still fixed towards the west. As Stella read, tears came to her eyes, and she sank to the ground beside him. Her voice trembled in an effort to hold back the tears when she said, "John, I'm so sorry. I know how much you loved him, and I know what a good man he was."

They sat together in silence, her heart yearning to comfort him. Gradually, he accepted her nearness and the consolation she offered. She welcomed the pleasure of giving solace. A long while later, he rose and extended his hand, lifting her to her feet, and they returned to the house through the gathering shadows. They felt a deep sense of togetherness for the first time, but he entered at the side of the house to go to his room, where he could be alone with his sorrow. Stella went out to tell those on the porch the news of Iron Horse's passing.

Mr. Hall had heard so many stories of Iron Horse from John, and of the boy's love for his father. He said, "Poor boy. I'll go and comfort him."

Major Mack put out a restraining hand. "Not tonight, Tom. Stella has done all that's possible for now. You don't know the Indian nature as well as I. It doesn't care for pity, and our sympathies will be more acceptable and effective in the morning." Mrs. Hall wiped her eyes as Major Mack eulogized Iron Horse and spoke highest praises of John. As they parted for the night, they all felt the chastening of the spirit that comes through sorrow.

John sat a long time alone, oblivious to everything but the vacancy in his life because of the going away of one to whom he owed so much—even his very life. He thought of his first memory of the man when he regained consciousness in the cabin on Potato Creek. He remembered the night in the dance house when he was recognized as the son of Iron Horse, of the many times they'd been traveling companions, and of the rare goodness of his father's heart. He recalled the watchful care, wise counsel, and inspiring messages Iron Horse had given throughout the time of their relationship, down to the last handclasp on the train platform in Rushville. John felt its pressure as surely as he breathed, and he envisioned the tipi set up in the yard by the cabin on Potato Creek, his father's wizened form lying inside, waiting patiently and cheerfully to hear the cry to the long trail. John heard his father's words—"Tell him my spirit will be with him always"—before Iron Horse got up and journeyed into the night to let his spirit find peace under the stars.

When they assembled for breakfast the next morning, Mrs. Hall returned from John's room and announced that he wasn't there, his bed hadn't been disturbed, and his room and belongings were in perfect order. As she spoke, John appeared in the doorway with the suggestion of a smile hovering about his lips. Everyone beheld the sorrow in his eyes, and there were lines in his face that could only have come from suffering a great loss. They all rose with respect, but before they could utter the words they each wanted to say, he looked at them with a quiet serenity.

"Although my father's body has returned to the earth, I feel his spirit with me as he told me it would be so long ago. It was my greatest desire that he and my sister, Annie, be proud of my accomplishments, so I have studied hard and worked diligently to learn all I could. I will have the education he wanted for me, but more importantly, I will have the memories of my father to guide me.

"I still see his proud stance on the butte above the village and feel the softness of his painted buffalo robe. I still hear the wisdom and love in his voice when he told me to keep one eye on the future and one on the past. I see him in my mind, smoking the pipe before sharing stories with his friends, and sitting balanced astride his pony as we raced across the prairie. His stories of our people will never leave me. His spirit will stand beside me at the ceremony, and I will share his wisdom with all those I encounter in the white man's world. I am at peace."

Stella appreciated the goodness of the heart that spoke through the newly lined face and accepted that she could love this man—and that she did.

CHAPTER 39

Carter's Journal

Spring 1898 to Spring 1899

Rosebud Indian School, Rosebud Reservation, South Dakota

I was thankful to receive news of my transfer away from the Darlington School. Having received my shingle as a lawyer, I wanted to investigate the sale of water and mineral rights on land that belonged to Indian families to make sure they'd been properly compensated. Despite multiple requests, however, I was never granted leave to question individuals who might have been victims of fraud and was kept busy instead with petty squabbles among the tribes. I felt distinctly that I was being distracted until I could be moved.

Upon arriving at Rosebud, I received a wire from Mother informing me that Lillian had suffered several attacks of vertigo for which her physician recommended a mastoidectomy. I set about arranging a trip back to New York, but before the plans were complete, I received a letter from Lillian assuring me it was a common surgery and everything had gone well. I was grateful for the news but regretted I'd been unable to be with my wife through such a procedure.

Not long after the surgery, Mother wrote that Lillian was suffering bouts of dizziness and depression. She suspected the depression resulted from the fact that Lillian was losing her hearing. I wondered if the surgery had caused some damage, but of course, Lillian refused to accept this possibility and insisted she was simply too tired to play the piano or sing with the children in the evenings.

Not long after this news, I was devastated to receive notice from John of the loss of his father. Although there were many miles between them physically, John knew his father supported him, and the young man shared that he was comforted in knowing his father's spirit would remain with him forever, but I knew the loss hurt deeply.

There had been numerous complaints to Washington that the nuns at Rosebud were using interpreters to help them teach Catholicism to the Indians rather than teaching the Indians English and other core subjects. Rumors had spread that the ladies endeavored so earnestly to teach religion that they resorted to the use of abusive punishment on any children who lagged in their studies. I was to investigate the allegations.

Because I was given direct responsibility over all monies, I was required to post a surety bond of fifty thousand dollars. I couldn't procure the papers on the reservation, so I wrote Father at length, describing the need for the bond and asking for his help in securing the needed materials. Not unexpectedly, he thought it was his chance to force my return home by refusing to help. After indulging myself with a full day of anger towards him, I wired directly to Mrs. Watkins in Washington, who secured the bond.

I requested freight shipping of my household goods to be covered by the agency budget in order not to request a cash advance from my family, but the comptroller general's office denied my request. I struggled to grasp the irregular assignment of monies for people affiliated with the Indian schools. It seemed at times that money flowed abundantly from Washington, while at other times, it was a mere trickle that strained the purse and conviction of those of us who served.

Another issue that stressed me was the inordinate number of disgruntled employees within the bureau who filed grievances or instigated investigations in order to advance their own causes. I had seen it in almost every setting, and it was no different here.

Sister Cecilia was timid and quiet but excellent with the children, especially the girls. She was able to calm them when they arrived at the school and get them to eat. She helped them work through nightmares and depression, and eventually most of them settled in well. Sister Margaret, on the other hand, was coarse, loud, and harsh tempered. The children feared her and preferred hiding under the covers to talking with her. One day, she insisted we turn away a little girl about eight years of age who came to school thin and sickly. The child died less than three months later, and I found it difficult to forgive Sister Margaret's decision. In the end, I assigned Sister Cecilia to oversee all the female students, angering her cohort and starting an endless stream of complaints from Sister Margaret.

Not long after, a wire arrived from Washington that I was under investigation for being cold natured and unresponsive to the needs of the Indians. I suspected that Sister Margaret was the source of the complaint.

Days later, a missive arrived from Lillian.

> My dearest Carter,
>
> Liz can now read the newspaper aloud to her grandfather, an activity he seems to enjoy immensely. She's also speaking French almost as well as she spoke Lakota when we lived at Potato Creek. She enjoys riding her pony, playing school with her brothers, and dressing up, the more ruffles the better. However, her favorite thing is the latest black patent slippers your mother purchased at the new Macy's store downtown. She's seven going on sixteen and growing more strong-willed by the day. Ralph is starting to talk and busily getting into every closet and drawer around the house. He keeps both your mother and the nanny on their toes and no doubt irritates your father as well.
>
> I must confess, I now feel as uncomfortable around your father as I did in the earliest years of our relationship. His stern manner and brusque conversations make me feel unwelcome at the very least. He seems unhappy with the children under his feet and angry that we're here in his household. I've worked hard to keep the children from being a bother, but admittedly, three children can disrupt the quiet of any evening. I wish the nanny could be here each night as well, but your mother enjoys playing with the children and helping Liz with her lessons. She can easily entertain any one of the three but is too exhausted in the evenings to handle them all. I confess your mother is more tired than she should be, and I'm worried something more serious may be causing her lack of energy. The children miss you terribly, especially Liz, but sometimes I fear little James hardly knows you at all. We pray

nightly for your safe travels on the reservation and hope for success with your students as well.

Forever your adoring wife,
Lillian

A second envelope was delivered as well, properly addressed and posted. Upon ripping it open, I found the most beautiful cursive writing in a letter that simply read:

I love you Daddy,
Elizabeth.

I missed my wife and children terribly. James was a healthy one-year-old, becoming more mobile every day, and I'd hardly seen him since he was born. I wished they could be with me, but the situation simply wasn't suitable.

On a happier note, I'd been instructed to purchase a number of dairy cattle from Carlisle to be shipped to the school at Rosebud. My plan was to arrive at Carlisle in time to visit with John and attend his commencement. I was determined to recognize the completion of his education and congratulate him for being valedictorian of his class. Lillian wired a message informing me that she'd managed to secure funds for herself, Liz, and Ralph to meet me at Carlisle. No doubt Mother appropriated the funds from her household budget. I was thankful. I knew a visit with this young man and introducing him to our children would lift my spirits tremendously.

CHAPTER 40

Graduation

Fall 1898 to Spring 1899

Carlisle Indian School, Pennsylvania

John and Stella returned to Carlisle from their second summer in the Berkshire countryside. They brought with them memories of afternoons strolling through the orchards, evenings spent fishing, and hours spent whispering secrets to each other. John also brought back his grief, which Stella shared. It pushed him to work harder on his lessons, and he again chose to work with the carpenter crew rather than accept Mr. Cornish's offer to take a position as one of his student assistants. Staying busy distracted John from the pain caused by his father's passing. Knowing his father's spirit was always near was John's greatest incentive. His goal of graduating at the top of his class would soon become a reality.

Stella entered into her work at Dickinson College with enthusiasm, focusing on a degree in teaching. She had a wonderful voice, and her singing was often in demand among various churches and social organizations. Because she'd attended Carlisle, many ladies of the community knew she had Indian blood. Even in that environment of religion and higher education, she was sometimes hurt by those women, though never by outright unkindness so much as by thoughtlessness. She couldn't help but notice when some of the women pulled their children away when she approached, as if they might be sullied by her Indian blood. Others might enjoy a cup of punch with her outside the church doors but never invited her to sit with them around the tables of refreshments with their friends and families.

At those times, Stella would withdraw and remain quiet, keeping her thoughts to herself. John struggled with her aloofness but came to understand it was her way of dealing with unpleasantness in the world. She was too full of pride and dignity to acknowledge the hurt, so she pulled a shell around herself until she found the strength to smile at the world again. Then, he would laughingly remind her that anyone who treated her unkindly was simply jealous of her talent and beauty and trying to make themselves feel better.

John's graduating class was the largest in the history of the school and included some of the brightest and most promising students who'd ever attended. He'd completed five years' work in only three years, all while keeping the highest scholastic average among his classmates. He was proud of his position as a leader among his fellows. He had two more years to work as an outing student for the Halls and could perhaps take classes at one of the local colleges during the school terms. Despite being confident of his future at the Halls, John and Stella discussed the possibilities of teaching if there wasn't a permanent farm manager's position available.

As valedictorian, John would be giving a speech to the other students, and he readied himself through long hours of consideration of his words. He chose what he believed to be the most important advice Iron Horse had ever given to him and prepared to share it with the students of Carlisle. He practiced for hours, speaking to an imaginary audience, enunciating each word carefully, his voice deep.

"My fellow Indians, today is a good day. We've completed a long and difficult program of work. We have learned a new way to live, to speak, and to dress. We have changed our names and the way we look. We have lived in a way that is different from our fathers' ways and traveled to places our fathers will never see. I know that many of you plan to return to the reservation, where you believe you will make a difference. You have been told you owe a debt to your people and that you must go back and teach them the new ways. You've been told you will be betraying your loved ones if you don't return, but I tell you we cannot live the new way among the old men.

"It is good to remember the old ways and find value in doing right. You must be proud of your heritage and stay Indian in your heart by keeping all the good things of our fathers: think good thoughts, have confidence, speak with a straight tongue, and be honest and fair to all people. Only then will your life be worth living. But for now, a profound change has come to our world and to our people. Your mind must think of new ways to provide for yourself and your children in the future. You must use the skills you have learned and adapt to a life that doesn't depend on the buffalo. We must learn to think differently and seek unfamiliar places to live in the world. Today, let us go out into the world and live our best lives!"

Despite his best efforts before submitting the speech for approval, it was returned purged of the words he had spoken from his heart. His entire speech had been rewritten so that it no longer expressed his beliefs but was instead a discourse that seemed to come from a misguided bigot determined that all Indians should be satisfied with living on the reservation. John was shocked his counselor expected him to publicly support educating young Indians for the sole purpose of sending them back to the reservation. John argued as persuasively as he could, using every debate skill he'd learned, but his objections were to no avail, and the counselor said he must report to the major for any further discussion.

"John, I know how you feel," said the major. For the first time, John sensed condescension as the man went on, "But the duties life imposes on us are not always of our own choosing. Sometimes, we're subject to control from an authority higher than ourselves. We may not understand, but we must accept that control when it is part of the inexorable demands of destiny. I'm sure you can say the words that will benefit the school. For me."

John stood befuddled, his arms hanging at his sides in rejection. The man he had respected above all others at the school was asking him to express thoughts and sentiments that were completely at odds with John's own. And he was asking John to do it as if he were owed a personal favor.

John squared his shoulders, drawing himself as straight as he could, and stared out the massive window towards the manicured lawns. He knew he had to be willing to compromise because this was what his father had taught him. Turning again to the major, he replied, "I will do my best, Major Mack," but even as he spoke, he felt unable to voice words that reflected a view he did not share. As he left the major's office, he knew he couldn't doom the best of the Indian youth to a world that would never move out of the past.

Mr. and Mrs. Hall traveled down for the ceremony, and John and Stella enjoyed every possible moment of their company. As the hour for the public ceremony drew near, the auditorium filled to capacity. There were officials from Washington, representatives of various societies and organizations with an interest in Indian work, visitors from the nearby towns and colleges, and alumni who had experienced commencements past. Here and there throughout the assembled crowd were Indians with clothes that ranged from the traditional, brilliantly colored blankets to the latest styles of the day.

The graduates in their neat uniforms, with their animated faces and proper demeanor, were particularly handsome as they sat on the stage with the superintendent and various dignitaries. John sat in his place of honor, scanning the faces of the audience until stopping at the seats occupied by Mr. and Mrs. Hall and Stella. Suddenly and joyously, he realized that Carter and Lillian Heath, with three of their children, were seated with the Halls. He waited for the moment he would deliver his address. As he stepped forward to conclude the afternoon's exercises with his valedictory, he was at peace.

He stood before the assembly, a striking figure—tall, erect, and possessed of unstudied natural poise. Every line of his face and figure evidenced both great suffering and great dignity. He stood for a moment with the attitude of one who listens to something far off, hearing that which may not be clear to others. The room stilled, and when he began, his full, rich voice went forth without conscious effort, without his will, and without his power to constrain. In low, musical tones he uttered strange syllables with emphasis, giving the speech he had planned from the heart. As he continued, the audience's wonder changed to astonishment. John focused his eyes on Stella, her expression a mixture of fear and pride. Suddenly, he heard the words he spoke and realized he'd been speaking in the language of Iron Horse, a language he'd been forbidden to use in public for over five years.

While consternation ruled him, his face showed nothing but calm. Shaking his head slowly to clear it, he paused for a moment. His self-possession returned, but try as he might, he could not recall a single syllable of the valedictory written by other hands. He'd spoken the words that Iron Horse had spoken to him as a child, and he wouldn't betray his father's counsel. He looked over the sea of surprised faces and then back to Stella. The realization came that he had a message for these people, and here was an opportunity to deliver it.

With the same smile that accompanied his greatest efforts, he spoke again in the language of the white man, and his words resounded in the silence of the room. Sometimes, there were no white words that expressed the meaning with the same depth the Indian words could express, so John articulated his thoughts in his native cadences with conviction. Like the life he'd been living, his message needed a combination of both worlds, sometimes in terse, forceful sentences, sometimes in quiet tones. His syllables were so distinct and the silence so profound that there was no one in the audience who didn't hear.

With only slight reference to himself, he talked of "the Indian." He spoke of how "the Indian" had always been a problem for the government; how "the Indian" had antagonized the government but had also fought on the country's behalf in every war it had with other countries; how "the Indian" had been treated as a ward from the beginning and how "the Indian's" status as a ward had been set for all time by the country's highest tribunal. He related how "the Indian" had been pushed further and further westward and kept just beyond the edge of civilization until there was no place left to which he could be pushed, and finally how "the Indian" had been confined to the reservations. Then, he shared how "the Indian" had been dealt with on the reservations with handouts and dishonesty and how "the Indian" personality had been so disregarded that individual identity was all but lost to him as a trait.

John spoke of the occasional generosity with which the government issued the necessities of life but remarked that these could never function as a civilizing medium, for they were subsistence at best. He told of the conditions on the reservations and of the utter impossibility of "the Indian" making advances in lifestyle under the conditions so many of them were in. He praised the school facilities that were available to boys and girls alike and the government generosity that made it possible for every young Indian to acquire an education, but he reminded them of the futility of it all when the youth were educated for no purpose other than to go back to the reservation, how the schools urged and influenced them to go back, constantly reminding them that they owed it to their people. He encouraged the audience to conceive a new course, and to give the Indian students the same chances that other students had, without every influence bearing upon them to go back to where there was no way out.

When he concluded, there was a long pause—like a sigh—followed by an outpouring of applause that swept through the building, leaving many eyes welling with tears of sympathy and approval. Not until he returned to his seat did John pause long enough to think that the major might feel he'd been betrayed. That fear persisted as he walked across the stage to receive his diploma—until, with a puzzled smile, the major reached out, placing John's diploma in his left hand and grasping his right hand in a hearty shake.

In measured tones, he spoke. "It's all right, John. I should have known you could only say what you truly feel."

As John walked to where his extended family waited, he was relieved to hear Mr. Hall's hearty "Fine, my boy, fine!" and delighted when Mrs. Hall added enthusiastically, "Oh, John, we're so proud of you!"

Carter grasped his hand, shaking it exuberantly, his face beaming with pride. "I knew you were destined to become a spokesman for your people, and you have exceeded my greatest imagining. Your father would be so proud."

Stella said nothing, but the tender smile that graced her face and the glowing look in her eyes told him everything. Later, she shared how grand it had been to see him standing so poised and confident on the stage and how proud she was of him. She admitted she'd been afraid for him at the beginning, yet when he recovered himself, she'd known the validity of his words and felt that others in the audience recognized the truth as well.

John hugged Lillian and was introduced to an older Elizabeth and to Ralph, who hugged him tightly and chattered away at once. They all enjoyed a celebratory lunch at the school's cafeteria, after which John walked Carter to the dairy barn, where he introduced his former teacher to Mr. Tutwiler, the farm manager. They strolled through the open-air barns, discussing the heifers that Mr. Tutwiler exhibited for Carter to choose from. The man had gathered a large number of animals, some of the highest quality and others that were hardly better than average. Admitting he knew more about pianos than cattle, Carter deferred to John's expertise for selecting the best ten animals from the group. Carter enjoyed listening to the persuasive techniques John used on the older gentleman as they negotiated the price. When the deal finally closed, John had convinced Mr. Tutwiler that the school in Montana would benefit greatly if an additional two animals were sent along at the same total price just in case any of their first choices were lost in transit to the reservation.

While the manager completed the paperwork for the transfer of the cattle, John and Carter enjoyed a quick but heartfelt reunion. Knowing John's love for his Indian mothers, Carter shared his recent worries over his mother's fatigue and his fear that her doctors might be missing signs of a serious illness. John revealed his and Stella's plans for returning to Snow Hill for the summer and their secret dream of remaining there together after completing their education programs. Carter compared Liz's success in the classroom to his former student's and was bragging on his daughter's riding skills when Lillian reminded him that their train would be departing shortly.

Rising from their seats on the bench in front of the barn, Carter reached for John's hand. Instead of taking it, the young man threw his arms around him, squeezing tightly and thanking his teacher for coming to the ceremony and for all the things Carter had done to help with his education. Carter returned the hug mightily before turning and heading in the direction of Mr. Tutwiler's office to pay for the animals and arrange for their delivery to Rosebud.

John walked briskly back to join the Halls and Stella, brushing a single tear from his cheek and inhaling deeply, his confidence restored at having shared a moment with his mentor. Mr. and Mrs. Hall were to return to Becket the next day, and John planned to go with them for his final summer outing. Stella would follow as soon as she completed her current courses at the college.

Mr. Hall and Major Mack sat late into the evening on the porch of the major's quarters, talking of the events of the afternoon. The two shared a common interest in John and Stella, but the major was concerned with John's outburst of feelings against going back to the reservation.

"No, Tom," the major said forcefully, "I won't approve of John's remaining at the farm beyond the summer period just because he's completed his course of study. You know he committed to five full years when he enrolled. He's been here only three. He may have completed the coursework, but I expect him to fulfill his entire obligation. When he returns in the fall, I'll give him a position worth his while, perhaps as an assistant on the faculty or managing a carpentry crew repairing our buildings."

"And after the two remaining years to help the school?" inquired Mr. Hall.

"He'll be free as far as I'm concerned. You have my promise I won't retain him after that. He could have gone home this summer because he agreed to three years without a visit. Had Iron Horse lived, perhaps he would want to go now, but hearing his thoughts this afternoon, I wonder."

"Perhaps he'd have been more inclined to go a year ago but knew it wasn't allowed," agreed Mr. Hall. "What about Stella? I don't think either of them will be intimidated by the world outside of school at this point."

"I feel that Stella belongs to you and Mrs. Hall, Tom. She feels that way too. She's always been a puzzle to me, though a pleasant one. She's an intelligent and talented young woman. When I brought her here some years ago from one of the smaller reservations in Wisconsin, I entertained the notion of adopting her myself but had to consider how it would reflect on the school, considering I was unmarried and many years her senior. I've never shared her history with anyone until now.

"Her grandfather was one of the early fur traders, back when it was common for a white man to marry an Indian. Her father was an Irish drunkard of exceptional mentality but questionable morals. He became quite wealthy in the fur trade and had no intention of putting up with a girl-child. Her mother had passed, I know not of what, so she was an orphan with no relatives as far as I could ascertain.

"Looking at her, it doesn't seem possible she's a quarter-breed. It's easier when you know her history to understand her auburn hair, fair skin, and regular features. It will be good for her to know her past. Perhaps she'll come to feel as if she's your daughter and comfort you in your older years. I'll leave it for you to decide when you feel the time is right to reveal her story."

Major Mack continued, slowly, "I still have some reservations regarding John and Stella. Do you think there's any danger of impropriety there, Mr. Hall?"

Mr. Hall's smile stiffened, and he shot back, "I don't know exactly what you might be implying, but I have every confidence in both John and Stella. I'm certain there's no danger of any such thing."

The family with John and Mr. Tutwiler at Carlisle, John's graduation

CHAPTER 41

Customs

Summer 1899

Snow Hill Farm, Becket, Massachusetts

John returned to Becket with the Halls, with the understanding that he'd return to Carlisle for the next school year as first assistant to Mr. Tutwiler. Stella arrived in Becket a month later. Her premonitions about John had all but faded, though in her dreams she occasionally saw him as if she were standing on a hill, waving lovingly to him as he waited for her in front of an old schoolhouse. It was disconcerting that she could never go to him, but she was comforted by the look of love on his face.

She and John had come to think of the Berkshire farm as their home, referring to it as such between themselves. They never spoke of Mrs. Hall except as Mother Hall, nor of her husband as other than Papa Hall, always with love and respect. The older couple had grown so accustomed to looking at the young people as their own that, in their minds, their home was complete only during the summer months when John and Stella were there.

The successive days of summer were marked with increasing joy for the couple. John and Stella knew in their hearts that their feelings for the other had been proven by time, trial, and experience to be more than friendship. Although as yet unspoken, they felt secure in the reciprocity of the other's love and respect. Still, they chose not to divulge their feelings publicly. Mr. and Mrs. Hall had watched it all with questioning at first, but as they better understood the young people, their pasts, and their possible futures, they were at peace with what they saw.

The days before John planned to return to Carlisle for the opening of school were dwindling to only a few. Stella was undecided on whether she would return to the college or remain with Mother Hall. They all headed to the lake one evening for perhaps the last time together for the summer. Mr. and Mrs. Hall fished in their favored spot on the north side, and the approach of dusk found John and Stella not far from the old beech log. She sat between two outgrowing roots of an old elm, and he rested full length on the carpet of grass beside her.

He lay where he could look at her and still reach the poles, which were propped up with lines dangling into the water. They talked of the past, the present, and the future. John stated as simply as possible, "I know I have to return to Carlisle to fulfill what the major feels is my obligation to the school. I'm not sure I'll be able to hide my thoughts on what the future holds for any Indian who returns to the reservation. If I speak my heart, I'm afraid he might not reassign me to the Halls for my outing time. I couldn't bear if you remained here and I was unable to return."

Stella pondered his comment. "John, you must be true to your heart in both words and actions. I'm so happy here with you, and I don't want us to be parted. You are bound to return by the term you agreed to. Neither do I want to be at the college where I'll be away from you for days at a time. Perhaps I could find a position at Carlisle so that we could be together every day."

They shared their deepest feelings, always focused on the imminent parting. John held it too sacred a question to pose without knowing if it was acceptable to Stella. He realized the material obligations she should consider: no Indian brave ever asked for the hand of a maiden without a gift of horses for her father. What did he have to offer? He thought wistfully of his beloved Hantaywee and the colorful colt he had won. They would have been an acceptable gift, but John shook his head, freeing his mind of the memories; he hoped his horses ran free on the prairie. His heart wanted him to speak, but he could not. Finally, the glow of the fire on the opposite shore reminded them that their evening was all but ended. John rose and wound the lines about the poles, extending his hand to help Stella up. As she stood close to him, their hands touching, a thrill passed between them. He knew that if he didn't speak then, what was in his heart might go unsaid forever.

John broke the silence. "I've told you of the courting robes that our young men use on the reservation. Now they're made of the muslin that enters so much into the Indian's domestic life and that's commonly used for many things, but in the old days the courting robes were made of antelope skin tanned to a wonderful softness and sewn together with long fringes cut around the edges. They were beautiful, and they had a sentimental mystery attached to them."

He and Stella had often spoken of the reservation and tribal customs. She had said more than once that she wanted to visit the place John had called home, but he usually dismissed her comments, not unkindly but as if it were a trip for far in the future.

She whispered, "Yes, there are many beautiful things about tribal customs. The use of the courting blanket is not the least of them. I can imagine a young man stealing quietly to the tipi where the maiden of his choice sits among her family. Without confronting her parents, he'd sing a song, or whistle or play a melody on his flute. She would know it was him and slip out of the tipi and into the folds of his courting blanket, walking slowly with him in the dusk of moonlight—a single silhouette."

Shrugging as if to wrap an imaginary blanket tighter, she went on, "I can imagine being wrapped in a blanket, drawn close so that no one can hear. I think it would be easy to pour my heart out within the security of the courting blanket and your arms."

Reaching out, enfolding her in an imaginary blanket, John put his arm around her and whispered softly, "Stella, I want you to be my wife." He couldn't wait more than a moment. "Will you?"

She allowed him to pull her closer within their make-believe blanket and murmured back, "John, I've known for a long time that I would be." When she lifted her face to him, he laid his smile upon her lips with great tenderness.

Arm in arm, they sauntered towards where the Halls were waiting. John confidently kept his arm around her as they continued whispering, pledging their love to each other. When they were near enough to see the faces of the Halls in the light of the little fire, John asked, "Shall we tell them?"

Her face aglow, Stella thought a moment before answering, "Not tonight. I want to cherish this moment as my own and let it sink into my heart. We can tomorrow."

In their joy, the couple overlooked the fact that their courting blanket was entirely imaginary; they'd come fully into the light of the fire, and Mr. and Mrs. Hall saw their expressions and the closeness of their embrace and knew, without words passing between them.

The young people made a pretty picture as they stood in the glow of the fire. His arm was around her waist, and her face shone with conviction. The glow of a woman in love was in her eyes. He stood, smiling, his self-assurance telegraphing to all that he felt he had conquered the world. Finally, Stella released herself from John's arm, went to sit with Mother Hall, put her arms around the older woman, and kissed her. Nothing more. No words were needed.

Mrs. Hall didn't pester them with questions. The next morning, while busy with their usual work, Stella excitedly told her all about it. When the major came a few days later, they all talked it over, agreeing that John would return for one year's work as an employee of the school. At the end of that year, when they returned to the Berkshires, Stella and John would be married. Even so, the major insisted John fulfill his five-year term and expected the couple to return for a final year of service after their marriage. He assured them there would be positions for them both for the full year, and John would be free of further commitment at the end of that year.

The major winked to his old friend. "After that, Tom, you can do with them as you please, but I'll still insist on the privilege of coming to fish every summer just the same."

CHAPTER 42

Carter's Journal

Spring to Winter 1899

Pawnee Indian School, Pawnee, Oklahoma

It was a terrible blow to learn of my mother's passing upon my arrival home in New York after John's commencement. Father had tried to contact me when I arrived at Carlisle, but the large crowd and absence of officials from their offices during the ceremony prevented the message from reaching me. Blissfully ignorant and elated after a wonderful meeting with John at Carlisle, I'd enjoyed a restful ride on the train.

After hearing the news, I struggled to comprehend what it meant for my future with three children and a full-time job on the frontier. I learned later that Mother had failed to mention anything in her letters about never fully recovering from a severe case of influenza last fall. Lillian felt this was the reason for Mother's fatigue. Apparently, burdened by weeks helping with the children, running the household for the holidays, Christmas shopping, and keeping up with social obligations associated with Father's position, Mother had been unable to fight off an infection in her lungs. The very evening Lillian and the children left to join me at Carlisle, she collapsed. Nothing the physician administered helped. She passed away of pneumonia in the peaceful quiet of the following morning. Father was beside himself.

On top of that devastating news, Lillian found a telegram from Indian Affairs on Mother's writing desk that had been delivered two days earlier. It curtly informed me of my immediate transfer to the Pawnee Indian Agency in Oklahoma to serve as field agent at large. I wired Washington and requested two weeks of leave in order to deal with Mother's arrangements.

Father was in total denial, but Mother, always the matriarch, had written her final wishes long ago. Thankfully, Lillian found them neatly folded inside the front cover of our family's Bible. Somehow, I wasn't surprised that after managing our home all those years, Mother didn't burden anyone with her wishes or wants. She simply carried on as necessary to the end.

The house overflowed with flowers. Stacks of condolence cards from around the community sat unread beside Father's chair. Numerous people from the factory, from various charities where Mother had volunteered, and from the school we attended as children brought food, managed the domestic duties in Mother's place, and looked after James until we arrived home. Thankfully, Mother wished only for a simple service at St John's Episcopal, followed by burial in the family plot at City Cemetery.

I was granted three days of leave rather than the two weeks I requested. Later, though, I confessed to Lillian that I was relieved to return west rather than remain in New York without my mother's intercessions into Father's dark moods. He returned to work at the factory the day after her service, and the housekeeper assured me she would follow Mother's example in caring for him in the following weeks and months. I had no regrets other than not telling Mother how much I loved her and appreciated her patience with the long-running feud between the men in her life.

Although not exorbitant, my new salary was sufficient to care for my ever-growing family. In addition, there were funds for traveling expenses, including the use of a sleeping car when duties took me away from headquarters. The tribal accountant sent his assurances that I needed only to list the equipment I required and it would be sent at agency expense immediately. He also informed me that I was free to hire a clerk and a cook. The school agreed to provide a matron to assist Lillian with the care of our children and to tutor the few white children present on the reservation. All the employees' salaries were guaranteed through the agency.

I was responsible for probating the estates of deceased Indians leaving trust estates in the state of Oklahoma. The agency included the Pawnee, Ponca, Otoe, and Tonkawa tribes. I had been asked to arrive posthaste as there were already some sixty cases awaiting my action. I was a member of the Oklahoma bar and confident I could perform these duties. As superintendent, I also collaborated closely with members of the Pawnee tribal administration and was responsible for maintaining all records for the school.

The facility at Pawnee was far more comfortable than any place we'd served. I was eager for Lillian and the children to arrive. There were boys' and girls' dormitories, a spacious classroom building faced with sturdy, red, ashlar sandstone, as well as a commissary and carpenter shop. My assigned living quarters were large enough to serve as both office and home, two stories with a wide, wraparound porch. It also included its own kitchen with a smaller room attached that served as quarters for Mrs. Cooper, the matron I'd secured.

Recurring pains in my belly occasionally deprived me of my favorite activities, such as horseback riding, and I enjoyed hot salt baths frequently. Soon after arriving in late spring, I developed a cough that the physician hinted might be a precursor to problems with my heart, but he promised not to include that diagnosis in my health report to the agency. I was certain it was simply spring allergies on the prairie and that an opportunity to rest, with the clerk to assist with the stacks of papers accumulating on my desk, would cure my ills. As I looked forward to the presence of my wife and children, the tribal administrator informed me they'd been told my appointment was for six months only. I assured him that I'd been told I was to hold this position for several years, perhaps even to retirement.

Lillian and the children arrived by train and immediately took to the open prairie as wildly as the Indian children I remembered at Potato Creek. There were numerous trees about the facility: large, spreading bur oaks as well as loblolly and pinyon pines. In the hollow below our quarters, a massive American elm struggled to defeat the elements. After being knocked over at its roots, its massive trunk had sent up three branch shoots, forming perfect handholds for Liz to climb to a seat on the top of the trunk. Several other children joined her in her play place, turning it into a favorite hideaway for us all. Even Lillian took to sitting on the lowest end, propping against the upright branches to read in the shade of the afternoons. At peace and enjoying the company of my family once again, I looked forward to picnics there for years to come.

We stayed our projected six months at Pawnee and continued in service. As I toiled over issues caused by the allotment system, my anger increased each time I witnessed the Indians being dealt with unfairly by our government. If a head of household received an allotment in 1887 and had five children and fifteen grandchildren, the land, still a single parcel, had twenty owners at the time of my arrival at the agency. Even more of a test of both my patience and my legal capacity was tracking down and verifying the claims in these heirship cases. Many of the original owners could neither read nor write, produced no will, and simply passed the land to their heirs verbally.

There were copious records, detailed and difficult to read. By the end of each day, I was often troubled by throbbing headaches. Word from Washington was that restrictions regarding the sale of land in the area would be lifted in a matter of months, allowing settlers to purchase allotment properties. The bureau expected me to have all these records organized by then, but the situation was a stressful mess that buried both my clerk and me for days on end. I couldn't see how we would ever keep up once the first parcel sold.

At the end of one particularly stressful day, Lillian stood in the doorway when I arrived home, twisting her hands in her apron, obviously in distress. "Dear," she began in a tone that set me back briefly, "I hope we can find a way to deal with one more little one on the way."

I can't say it was a joyful announcement, but seeing her furrowed brow, I tried to reassure her. "My beloved, we've struggled often over the years to make ends meet on my government salary, yet somehow we've always managed." Smiling as broadly as I could, I added, "So now we're going to be a household of six, with three under the age of four. We're in for some very busy days and probably many long nights. I'm sure our love will see us through."

Hustling quickly past her towards my office, I couldn't help but worry how I could possibly fulfill my duties to the Indians or, for that matter, pay our bills.

Thankfully, Lillian didn't suffer morning sickness as she had before but was fatigued daily and dependent on the matron to assist with everything from tutoring the school-aged children to cooking meals and doing laundry.

Liz was slowly wearing out the generous wardrobe purchased for her life in New York. The beautifully caped jackets, frilly dresses, colorful stockings, and flowery hats did not hold up well to the rigors of reservation life. She'd never given up her penchant for riding and frequently raced her horse, Maud, about the yard and around the trees, jumping the leaning elm and racing to the creek. She ultimately reverted to the wardrobe of her toddler years: stiff canvas overalls, a fluffy white shirt, and a beat-up, dirty cowboy hat.

The boys grew steadily, needing new clothes every few months. They spent most of their days playing under Mrs. Cooper's feet or sitting on Lillian's ever-expanding belly, waiting patiently for her to recite nursery rhymes or sing one of their favorite songs. Because they seemed content inside, Lillian insisted on dressing them with pert caps and long coat jackets, even though James was struggling to walk. They were adorable with their bow ties and white shirts buttoned tightly under their chins; however, their appearance by the end of each day was quite different, and Mrs. Cooper barely kept up with the laundry.

Lillian appeared to grow weaker with each passing month of her pregnancy. She picked at her meals, moving the food around on her plate and trying to look as if she were enjoying it. In reality, she often left most of the food uneaten, regardless of what Mrs. Cooper prepared. When I realized it had been many weeks since I'd seen my wife sitting in her favorite seat on the elm tree to read, I insisted she walk with me as many evenings as she could muster the energy. We strolled hand in hand at a leisurely pace, pretending we were young again on the prairie at Potato Creek, gathering wildflowers and enjoying the brilliant blue of the Oklahoma skies.

I hoped that exercise would improve her appetite, but over time, we went out less and less frequently. Worried for the baby since Lillian was obviously not eating well, Mrs. Cooper often brought a glass of warm milk in the evenings, and Lillian would rock on the porch while I finished whatever paperwork I could complete.

Lillian went into labor with our third son, Charles, in the wee hours of the morning while everyone was sleeping. From the start, I knew things were not going as they should. Lillian looked pale and weak as Mrs. Cooper struggled to push her distended belly from side to side. All the while, Lillian strained and cried out in agony. I had no idea what to do or who to turn to for help. Oh, how I missed the loving hands of Moves

First and Good Heart! As soon as the baby was born, Mrs. Cooper passed him into my arms, screaming, to be bundled into a soft blanket. As I sat wiping his face and shushing him over and over, not knowing how to comfort him, Mrs. Cooper continued to reach for blankets and sheets as the bed became saturated with Lillian's blood. I felt my very life drain away as I watched the blood drain from her body. I prayed, sobbing, my tears falling to mix with those of the tiny boy I held.

Slowly, Lillian's beautiful skin turned ashen gray as our son continued to struggle against my grasp. I paced the floor until the infant collapsed into an exhausted sleep, just as his mother passed quietly from this world.

My heart was broken. There had been no opportunity for me to caress or comfort my love in her last moments, and now she was gone. I forced myself to accept the reality of the night before sending Mrs. Cooper to find a wet nurse for the baby. It fell to me to care for a newborn and distract the others as they awakened. After what seemed an eternity, Mrs. Cooper returned with Pretty Woman, wife of Long Knife, who had lost her infant son earlier to diphtheria. She took the infant, settling him momentarily while Mrs. Cooper quickly bundled the other children off to one of the teachers' homes.

Pretty Woman nursed and cared for Charles while Mrs. Cooper tried to keep the other children's lives as normal as possible. In a daze, I arranged for Lillian to be buried at Highland Cemetery and ordered a simple square of rose-colored granite for her grave. The service was small, with only a soloist singing "Amazing Grace," a bugler from the fort playing taps, and the Indians beating lightly on their drums in the background as we walked to the grave. Two days after Lillian's death, I wired my father, asking for train transport for Mrs. Cooper and the children to his home in New York. I didn't know what else to do.

CHAPTER 43

To Have and to Hold

Fall 1899 to Summer 1900

Carlisle Indian School, Pennsylvania

Stella didn't stay with Mrs. Hall that fall, nor did she return to Davidson. Instead, she chose to return to Carlisle as a teacher in order to stay near her husband-to-be. John assumed his responsibilities under Mr. Tutwiler, enjoying his position as assistant manager and planning numerous improvements around the facility. He wanted to install a new weaning gate, such as the one he and Mr. Hall had built at Snow Hill. He shared what he had learned about various grains, including barley to feed the cattle, and made other contributions around the school through the year. The superintendent was pleased with his work.

John and Stella found ways to be together during most of their leisure hours. Their love increased day by day. They discussed the advantages of returning to the Halls' farm as soon as John's time at Carlisle was done, for both had now long considered Becket their home. Having no children of their own, the Halls needed someone to continue the work of the farm and to assist with maintenance of the house and grounds. Stella fretted over the wedding ceremony, for neither had family who would attend. The death of Iron Horse had cut off John's connection to the reservation. His mothers could neither read nor write, so there'd been no communication between them since John learned of his father's passing through Aaron.

The last they'd heard, Carter was somewhere in Oklahoma, overburdened with responsibilities and devastated by the loss of his wife. John missed news of his friend but had no way of knowing if his letters reached his mentor's hands. Waiting for communication from Carter would delay the ceremony. The couple had no concern for others besides the major and the Halls to witness their vows.

Both John and Stella wanted a family of their own. They shared their thoughts about the future with all its problems and possibilities. Would they build their own home? Would Stella want to teach in town? Yes, they were accepted as members of the Halls' family, but would they be accepted as independent members of the community once they were married? After all, John was a full-blood Indian. They talked of these things many times, and yet by the time they headed back to Massachusetts, it was easy to forget their concerns.

The day after school closed for summer break, John and Stella accompanied Major Mack to Snow Hill. Early in the morning of the second day in Becket, in the place that already felt like home, they were married in the presence of those they considered family. The guests included a few special friends of the Halls and several well-wishers John had met on his trips to town. After the ceremony, Mr. and Mrs. Hall traveled with Major Mack to New York and from there on to spend a few days with friends in the eastern part of the state to enjoy some time in the mountains.

For their honeymoon, John and Stella were given the privacy of the entire house and farm. Despite taking on the responsibilities of both Mr. and Mrs. Hall for the week, the couple couldn't have dreamed of a happier time. Their first week as husband and wife was spent in the place they preferred above all others, and with the joys of work to add to the joy of their love. John helped Stella care for her chickens, holding her steady when she stumbled as the birds ran willy-nilly beneath her feet. He stayed close in the kitchen as she prepared their meals, lifting lids from steaming cookers of stew, carrying dishes to and from the table, and either washing or drying them when the meal was done.

He treasured the feeling of her fingers brushing lightly against his when she handed him a steaming cup of coffee each morning. His heart beat faster at the sway of her hips as she moved from room to room, making sure every piece of furniture gleamed with a fresh coat of beeswax and oil. At other times, she went with him as he tended the stock, holding a newborn calf to its mother's udder until he was nursing strongly. She held tightly to the end of a long board as John sawed it the proper length to fix a broken place in the pasture fence. After he milked each evening, he helped her pour the milk into a tall metal can and carried it to the cellar to cool. He traded seats with her when her arms tired of churning butter, up and down, over and over so they could enjoy fresh butter on biscuits the next morning.

Almost every evening as the shadows lengthened, they filled a hamper with food and headed to the lake, but not to fish. There Stella seated herself between the roots of the old elm while he stretched out at her feet where he could look into her eyes with all the love a man could show. They talked of the same things as on so many other evenings and enjoyed the same comforting silence. They made a fire in the stillness to enjoy the meals Stella packed in the hamper. To end each evening, they curled together to watch the stars turn overhead.

"John," said Stella after one of their thoughtful silences, "did you ever wish you weren't an Indian?"

"Yes, many times," he laughingly replied. "I remember the first time the thought ever came to me. It was on my first day in Carter Heath's schoolroom, when I wished I could be like him. I wished it many times on the journey from the reservation to Carlisle when I saw for the first time the enormous number of white people. They were so interesting, and I wished that I could be like them and be a part of their world. But I do not wish it anymore, because if I weren't an Indian, I wouldn't be your husband, and I would rather be him than anyone else in the world."

"Then you wouldn't have had me for a wife if you had not been an Indian, or if I had been a white girl?" she asked.

"No, silly, it has nothing to do with the color of your skin. It is because if I hadn't been an Indian, I wouldn't have gone to an Indian school, nor would you had you been white. I have thought often that the Great Spirit made us just as we are in order that we would come together."

"Yes," she added, "and it makes no difference the color of our skin if we try to live as the Great Spirit directs us, and to do good."

"I would much rather be a worthy Indian than an unworthy and discredited white man," he said, "but did you ever wish that you were not an Indian, Stella?"

She sighed with a touch of sadness in her voice, "I am not an Indian—not as you are. But I've wished many times that I was what my appearance led others to think I was, because to be neither one is infinitely worse than being either one. So many times, my heart was torn by the thoughtlessness of others who didn't know there was more to me than my appearance. Because the people around me often thought I was white, I was privy to their deepest-rooted feelings about Indians. That's one of the reasons why I could never be the wife of a white man. I would always fear his friends and family were bitter towards me in their hearts, no matter what words they spoke. Because of what I've heard, I sympathize with those on the reservations."

"And yet," John stated, "human nature is the same the world over regardless of the color of our skin. Iron Horse understood that very well. He used to tell me that men's hearts were the same regardless of color. There are good men and bad men wherever we go, and there are good Indians and bad just as there are good white men and bad. He told me always to choose the good—and I've tried, although sometimes it's hard to tell one from the other."

"You've done very well from what I know of the people in your life," she commented as she thought of the major and the Halls.

He smiled, reaching to take her hand warmly into his. "Yes, very well when I chose you."

Stella looked demurely down at their entwined fingers. After a long silence, both watching the fire flicker before subsiding into a bed of glowing coals, she inquired in a whisper, "What is my husband thinking about now?"

His eyes twinkled as he smiled. "I was thinking of you and your questions, of course. I was thinking how some people might say we enjoy sitting around a fire in the open because we're Indians. Yet I've never seen anyone who didn't enjoy the same thing. Papa and Mother Hall and Major Mack all enjoy it. In fact, I don't believe that in all the millions in the great cities we could find many who wouldn't enjoy it. I think it proves how much we're all alike. Every human's nature is partly primitive, and if everyone had the opportunity to build a fire and get to the goodness that comes with closeness to nature, the world would be a better place."

"John, you speak so beautifully!" she said, taking his hand in both of hers and gazing with pride into his eyes as he helped her to her feet.

When they returned to the house, she laughingly led him out to the porch, where they sat together, very conscious of their closeness. When they finally went in, she led him to the front room and turned up a dimly glowing lamp. She seated herself at the upright piano and played the first measure of "Love's Old Sweet Song." They sang it together as they'd done many times before with the Halls, but it had never expressed the understanding or sentiment it did now. Tears welled up in her eyes as she said, "May it always be so."

He returned simply, "It will," as he bent to kiss her cheek.

The days passed swiftly. John and Stella learned that their love—great as they felt it before—could increase; that their understanding—perfect as it seemed—could deepen; and that their companionship—as close as they'd grown—could yet be closer.

One day, John stole softly into the kitchen where Stella was kneading dough on the table. Placing his arms around her, he said, "Wifekin mine, I hate to remind you, but our honeymoon will soon be over. Mr. and Mother Hall are coming home tomorrow, and our time to ourselves will end."

"Oh, John, I'm so sorry!" she exclaimed impulsively. "No, no! I don't mean that. Selfish me. Of course I'll be glad to see them, but it's been wonderful with only the two of us here alone."

When Mr. and Mrs. Hall returned the next day, the four of them resumed the life they enjoyed together. There was a difference, however, in that they all felt a new closeness to each other that made their lives more complete. A few days later, Mr. Hall stayed so late in the village that at Mother Hall's request, John and Stella walked down the road to meet him. It was not that she was concerned over his tardiness, but she understood the couple would enjoy a slow ramble along the picturesque road by themselves.

They strolled hand in hand without meeting him, happy to be by themselves as lovers are, until they came to what was known as the Old Indian Burying Ground. It was just a small square tract at the top of a rocky ridge above one of the streams that crisscrossed the farm. Its surrounding fence had long rusted away, and the burial mounds had been obliterated by the elements. The entire space was overgrown with trees and dense underbrush, but because of its name, it held a particular interest for John and Stella. They sat together to wait for Mr. Hall.

Looking over his shoulder at the massive tree trunks, John pondered aloud, his brows upraised, "Stella, do you think this place might be the original Indian country? In truth, where my family lives on the reservation now might not have known the tread of Indian feet when the land where we're sitting supplied every need for our race a hundred years ago. Perhaps some of my relatives lived here—perhaps some of yours."

"I've often wondered if anyone knew who was buried here," Stella replied. "Papa Hall told me that he remembers his grandfather, who was very old at the time, say the place was always like this, overgrown and unkempt, as far back as he could remember."

"I think I'd like to come one day and clear away the underbrush and see what we could find," mused John. "Perhaps there's something deep within the brush that would give evidence of the story." He continued, "When these graves were dug, this country was a vast wilderness, possibly even the very edge of civilization at the time. The dead might have been members of tribes long gone from here now, who moved further west to where my father lies buried. Every time I'm here, I think of that other burying ground at Potato Creek. Is there a connection between those lying here and those out there and me?" He thought of Annie and Iron Horse.

"I am content to know that we're going to live here and die here and sleep the long sleep here among these beautiful hills. I dreamed of serving our people at some point in my life. I believed it was my destiny to try to improve the lives of those who remained on the reservations. Perhaps, instead, it's my destiny, and yours, to make this place back into Indian country," Stella returned, laughing.

"It may be indeed, wife of mine. We're going to be happy trying to make the world a better place," he stated, raising his hand in greeting: "Welcome home, Papa Hall!"

Mr. Hall pulled the buggy to a stop, inviting them to join him for the ride back to the house. Stella pretended to chide him for being late, and he in turn implored John laughingly to protect him from the nagging of "these women" in his life.

When they returned to Carlisle six weeks after their marriage, it was with the understanding that they would return to Becket at the end of John's final year.

CHAPTER 44

Carter's Journal

Winter 1899 to Spring 1900

Wind River Indian Reservation, Fort Washakie, Wyoming

At Lillian's passing, I asked for an indeterminant leave of absence from work. I needed time to grasp how I could possibly raise my children properly while continuing my career to retirement with the bureau. For my lost love and my own goals, it was unacceptable not to remain in service to the Indian people she'd held so dear. I despaired of finding a way to cope with Father's tirades, although his loss and advanced age seemed to have mellowed his temper somewhat. At this point, he had no choice but to accept, if not approve of, my past choices and the difficulties they caused for my children. Much to my surprise, he welcomed the children into his home and planned for Mrs. Cooper to continue in their care as well. Liz—or Sissie, as she was called by everyone in New York—would return to an excellent school in Ithaca, and the boys would be doted upon by their grandfather in his retirement.

I remained with the Indian Field Service on paid leave. Despite being on leave, I was sent to investigate records regarding lands in the Wind River Valley that were in dispute between the Northern Arapaho and Shoshone tribes. Many years ago, our government had provided for a large number of hungry Arapaho by settling them near Fort Washakie, regardless of the fact that the Shoshone held treaty rights to the area. The two groups had been sworn enemies for many generations, and such close proximity at a time of limited food supplies had done nothing to settle old grudges.

There was rumor of an Arapaho missionary who intended to convert all the Indians to Christianity even if it required forcing Indian children to attend Christian schools. He'd supported the cession of much of the original reservation land to white settlers, a policy I vehemently opposed. There was little enough land available for the Indians, and the whites encroached on the wildlife as well as the oil and mineral resources of the area.

Not long after my arrival, I received a telegram appointing me as the federal prohibition agent for the area. Though the salary was sufficient and even allowed me to wire money for the children's support, the responsibilities I was given had nothing to do with teaching. Instead, I found myself investigating the sale and consumption of wine, liquor, ale, or beer to or by the Indians, a problem that had arisen on many reservations. I was also expected to investigate any sale of alcohol to Indians off the reservation. I quickly found myself negotiating with the worst nature of both races. There was great need for this work since many of the Indians resorted to alcohol to escape the destitution of their lives. However, local judges seldom fined or imprisoned either the sellers or the buyers, and I was never able to have much impact on the use of alcohol.

Besides a delayed letter from John notifying me of his marriage and of their plans to return to the Berkshires at the end of his school contract, the only bright spot in my position in Wyoming was the local postmistress in Casper. Her name was Jessie. Besides being quite lovely, she had a pert nature and happy countenance, cheerfully handling her duties with the mail and still finding time to spend with me. I was extraordinarily lonely. Her husband had been killed within days of their arrival in a fight over a gold claim. Having passed the civil service test before departing their home in Connecticut, Jessie applied for a job in the post office and quickly rose to the position of head of the facility.

I called on her a number of times. Having no children of her own, she expressed a willingness to become a mother to my four, and I responded by making her my second wife. I knew it was the only way to reunite my family in the West. Jessie was petite and kind, willing to help during my times of belly pain by preparing hot baths and assisting with my responsibilities in the office. The doctors had finally diagnosed the pain as resulting from a fistula in my lower intestine. Besides hot baths and a strict diet, surgery was the only treatment. Although this part of Wyoming was highly populated,

I hardly considered it civilized enough to plan surgery. I hoped to return to good health with rest and Jessie's assistance.

While researching an allotment claim near the hot springs on the northern end of the valley, I discovered the Arapaho had participated in land deals with both the government and private individuals regarding Shoshone lands despite having no right to do so. A significant dispute had arisen over the right of the government to sell such lands. It was my judgment that only the Shoshone could have legally made such deals, but the value of the land had increased exponentially, and my decision counted for nothing in the settlement of the matter.

When I returned to my office, I discovered the superintendent had opened an investigation into an incident that occurred while I was away. There had been an anonymous report of drinking and reckless behavior on the reservation. The report also alleged that I not only allowed but endorsed the behavior. I found the entire affair was conjured up by a gentleman I'd fined for selling alcohol to the Indians. He'd convinced some of his customers to testify against me, and I was required to defend my reputation to officials in Washington.

With the help of Mr. Huber, the local hardware store owner, and Mr. Garber, an officer of the savings and loan in town, I was able to send letters on my behalf to Washington. It was then I learned that a letter suggesting I take early retirement had been forwarded to Mr. Rhoads of the Interior Department. It implied I was in poor health, perhaps even drinking, and I was forced again to call in several favors from political constituents in Washington. It was clear I was interfering with some local politicians' plans for Indian land. I was certain a transfer from this duty was in order and offered to accept any position at any location in need.

I'd been remiss in responding to the news of John's marriage and penned a quick letter to him.

Dear John,

It brings my heart joy to hear of your marriage to Stella and hope for your forever happiness in the future. I've struggled with the care of four children as well as the underhanded treatment of your people that I constantly find at the hands of government agents. As you well know, it is an on-going battle, and there is no limit to the desires of my race to own the land that rightfully belongs to yours.

I applaud the Halls for their wisdom in offering you a position on their farm and congratulate you for honoring the wisdom of your father in choosing to return east upon completion of your school contract. I pray the memories of your mothers' songs and the stories of your youth will give you strength as you work in the white world. Your father's words to speak the truth and to do good to all men will serve you well.

I will seek a way to come by the farm to visit you and your wife in my travels to New York when I am able to bring my children to my newest post. I've put in for a change but know not at this time where I'll be.

With my highest regards,
Carter

P.S. I've remarried to a woman who promises she won't be burdened by four children gifted to me by my first wife. I'll bring her and the children when I visit.

Pretty Woman with Charles

CHAPTER 45

Retribution

Fall to Winter 1900

Carlisle Indian School, Pennsylvania

John and Stella applied themselves wholeheartedly to their responsibilities in what they believed to be their last year of service at the school. She was maturing into a quiet woman who showed compassion for all in need, whether student or employee. He had grown as a leader among his peers, listening to their concerns about family, salaries, or future openings and advancements. John was willing to carry these directly to the major, making him a spokesman for all the Indian employees of the school.

Following the midwinter holiday season, it was customary for the school to host assemblies where speakers with interests in "the Indian" came to be heard. They ranged from officials from the nation's capital to people who gave to one of the many organizations claiming to uplift the Indian. Public appearances rewarded donors with feelings of importance, which in turn guaranteed the schools an ongoing source of donations.

Sometimes there were alumni who'd been successful because of their education, but more often it was missionaries or church groups who had no presence on reservations but believed wholeheartedly in their Christian cause. Often, the speakers had little experience and no real interest in the Indian people themselves. They wanted a few moments in the limelight to advance their own image in the news or religious publications in the East. So it was that Judge Castle was granted an opportunity each year to inflict his own brand of pain on the assembled students and staff, who had no choice but to attend.

The man had gained the title of "judge" years before when he resided in two states that counted not a single Indian in their population. By some political mischance, he'd been appointed to a lower court judgeship and went to Washington seeking a higher appointment or more important federal position. Defeated, he turned to the Indian cause as an avenue for gaining public notice and celebrity. He was skilled in the art of flamboyant oratory, using grand gestures, hushed and trembling emphasis, and timely tears to impress his listeners. He'd rarely visited reservations, knew nothing of Indian culture, and made absolutely no effort to gather facts about those whose needs he spoke of so freely.

The judge was just emerging from middle life, rather below average in stature with a pudgy figure to which he attempted to give distinction and dignity by every artifice he could command. His baldness, of which he was rather proud, served only to reveal the roundness of his head. Were it not for the absence of hair on the top of his head, his brow would have been low, and his eyes were protuberant and fishy. A prominent nose shaded a short upper lip concealed by a closely cropped mustache. His mouth was habitually pursed, giving him the appearance of having just tasted something unpleasant. He delighted in the title of judge, and many had experienced his reproof when they addressed him as Mr. Castle, which to him was a personal affront. He rarely smiled, except in self-complacency, for he seldom responded to anything good that emanated from sources other than his own.

The judge's visit followed the regular order of things. He received the customary platitudes, beginning with an introduction from the major. He spoke first to the students, unsubtly reminding them how grateful they should be for his contributions to the education they'd so freely been given. Later, he spoke to the employees, reminding them how pitiful their lives would be without the generosity of such as himself and how humbled they should be that his donations allowed for their employment at the school. Following the judge's comments, it fell on John, the employees' representative, to voice the appreciation of those Indians present.

The young man began with his usual facility but, confident in his future, quickly digressed to words of soft-spoken mockery.

"I'm sure the Indians of America are thankful for the support provided by such as yourself, Judge Castle. As children, we were challenged to learn the English language because we were forbidden to speak in our native tongues. Today, we can proudly converse with any white person we encounter on our many trips off the reservations. While away from our families at the boarding schools, we learned to celebrate important Christian holidays such as Thanksgiving and Christmas with songs of the Savior and feasts beyond anything our families on the reservation have partaken of in many years."

His anger gathering, John ventured onto dangerous ground when he continued with only slightly veiled sarcasm, "I'm sure all my mothers' friends will be happy to purchase a punched tin chandelier for their tipis and perhaps several rolled tin cake stamps to shape their frybread. For certain, all the women of the tribe will be modeling the latest fashions of flimsy cloth stitched delicately by the girls who return to raise their families on the reservation. No doubt, the girls will be able to purchase the scissors and sewing supplies they need, and the dresses will look especially wonderful when tainted with the colors of the muddy stream banks and dusty floors of our homes."

John's final comments on the advantages he felt sure would accrue to the Indians of the country through the judge's sympathetic donations ended with the entire audience sitting in open-mouthed surprise. Some knew there would be retribution from the judge. The major almost trembled as John spoke, fearing the judge would bound to the stage and strike the young man down.

When they returned to their quarters, Stella exclaimed with a gasp, "How could you?"

"How could I not?" he replied.

The following morning, John was summoned to the superintendent's office. He walked slowly, dread dragging at his heels. He'd come to regret his commentary from the evening before and couldn't help being somewhat fearful of what might come of it. As he entered the office, he was reassured by the major's cheery "Good morning, John," only to have his apprehension return when the major looked down, shuffling papers on his desk and stating simply, "Judge Castle wants to see you in the inner office. Please go right in."

John entered the major's office to find Judge Castle engaged in cutting from the previous evening's newspaper a notice about the visit of a "distinguished patron of Indian education" to Carlisle. He made it a practice to visit the newspaper office immediately upon his arrival in every city to ensure that they not only knew of his visit but also were keenly aware of his political importance to all things Indian.

He looked up as John entered and abruptly snarled, "Take a chair," continuing what he was doing without so much as another glance at John. When he finished meticulously snipping every edge of the clipping to his satisfaction, he settled back in the chair, removed the wire-rimmed glasses he seemed to affect rather than wear, and with a portentous clearing of his throat grunted, "Iron Horse"—slowly, as if he were cutting off the man as he cut off the syllables of his name. John bristled at such a curt address using only his family name but waited without saying a word.

"Ah, Iron Horse," he rasped again. "I have watched your progress since I heard your words during the commencement service last year. Perhaps, in you, we have a somewhat exceptional Indian," he continued, cocking his left eyebrow scornfully.

"Major Mack tells me you've been an unusually good student and a desirable employee. I was particularly, shall we say, impressed by your remarks last evening, and I need to have a heart-to-heart talk with you this morning."

And you'll do the talking, thought John without uttering a word.

"Major tells me this is the last year of your contract here. With your insight into the needs of the Indian, you should return to the reservation for that year rather than spending it here. We need educated Indians such as yourself on the reservation."

John responded with finality, "I have no plans to go back to the reservation."

"No plans to go back?" mimicked the judge, his bristly eyebrows raised in mock astonishment. "Why, the very spirit of Indian education and the policy of the non-reservation schools is to educate young Indians and send them back to the reservations to civilize the old. What do you propose to do, Iron Horse? You can't expect a life tenure in your job here. Neither the government nor the school should be expected to give employment to all the Indians," he finished contemptuously.

"I don't expect to work at the school after this year. I plan to remain in the East to work and take my place in the community, the same as any other citizen," John asserted.

Judge Castle's eyes narrowed. Cunningly changing his approach, he queried, "But don't you think you owe the government for the education that's been given to you so freely?" It was obvious the judge resented John's presumption that he could just venture into the world of the white man rather than stay in his place and do what was expected by those to whom he should feel indebted.

There was something remarkably close to a glitter in John's eyes as he replied, "No, Judge Castle, I don't feel I owe anything to the government for my education. I was forced to attend their schools, not to better myself but to carry what I learned home to my elders. If I've obtained an education better than that received by many Indians, it's because of my own efforts. I believe the government owes every young person an education, especially the Indians, for whose condition it alone is responsible. But that education should be for the betterment of the individual, not for the repression of our past."

"I suppose that is what you believe, Iron Horse," returned Judge Castle, uninterested in arguing the point. He continued, "Do you not think you owe something to your people, to your relatives and friends back on the reservation? Do you believe you have a right to abandon them in their need?"

John felt compelled to share something of his personal history. "I survived the massacre of hundreds of my people at Wounded Knee and have recently lost Iron Horse, the father who adopted me when there was no one else to take me in. My adopted mothers loved me as their own and now live on the reservation in the old ways. They depend on others for support such as food and firewood. Even well-educated students who return struggle to survive. There's no game to hunt, no tools to farm, and no jobs. What can I do for my mothers that isn't already being done?"

John went on with confidence, "I don't believe there's a white man in the country who could go to my reservation as I would be expected to go, without horses, stock, implements, seed, or money, and exist through a single growing season if he had to depend on the land for his subsistence.

Yet that's all there is to depend on there. As to the education and civilization of the older Indians, they are more civilized than many white people. They want to live in the way they know, speak their own language, and worship the Great Spirit in their own way. I feel their wishes should be respected, for that's all that is left to them as compensation for what they've lost."

"Perhaps," conceded the judge, "but don't you feel you owe something to those two old women who saved your life? Don't you believe that if Iron Horse knew you could help his people, he'd say that you owe it to them to go back and do what you can?"

Despite the fact that Iron Horse had expressed nothing of the sort, instead urging John to enter the white man's world, the question hit home, and John didn't reply at once. He'd already questioned if he was deserting his people.

Seeing the young man's hesitation, Judge Castle smiled slyly and continued, "I can assure you a position at the agency until you can get otherwise established if you agree to go back and serve your people as a good leader would."

No job on the reservation offered as much for the future as his position at the Halls, but suddenly John found himself wavering between what had been his fixed purpose and what might be his duty.

As if to convince himself, John argued, "But I promised the major I'd remain at the school for my last year. I've also promised Mr. Hall I'd return in the summer. Furthermore, I can't insist my wife enter into the isolation and hardships of the reservation unless she chooses to go, and even then, I don't like to think of doing so, for she has no idea of the conditions there."

"I'm sure Major Mack can release you for such a worthy purpose," the judge replied, ignoring John's concern for his wife and extending his hand to end the discussion. "Mr. Hall won't question the major's decision. Shall we call your wife here and talk it over with her?" Before John realized what was happening, the man had stepped to the door and asked Major Mack to send for Mrs. Iron Horse.

"Iron Horse," he continued guilefully as he resumed his seat at the desk, determined to punish the young man for what he considered insubordination, "the education of the Indian is a great and noble work, and my heart is in it. When I think of the worthy purpose of educating the young to take our civilization back to their ignorant elders, a feeling of great satisfaction comes to me because of my ability to assist in such excellent work."

John listened without hearing until Stella's appearance put an end to the judge's self-glorification. As she entered the room, a questioning look on her face, John rose and placed a chair for her, while the judge remained seated behind the desk.

Shifting his pudgy body forward rather than standing respectfully, Judge Castle recited to Stella his previous conversation with John. He meticulously described the conditions under which the older Indians lived on the reservations. His words were based on a three-day visit two years before. He hadn't bothered to visit since. He blamed it all on the Indians' lack of "enlightenment" as he espoused the obligations all educated Indians were under to return to their tribes. As he described their duty to lift the veil of ignorance and savagery from the old ones' eyes, the tears he so easily commanded flowed, for, as he said, he could not restrain them when his sympathies were so stirred by the needs of the people for whom he'd made himself a guardian.

He went on to explain how John and Stella could serve as models of what the Indian had the potential to be. He played artfully on Stella's sympathies, flattering and then browbeating in turn. He reminded them that duty demands sacrifice and pressed upon John that any other course of action would be deserting his people. He even threatened that their own lives would be empty if they refused this call to service and reminded them of the righteousness of a worthy purpose.

Finished, his voice trembling and full of false emotion, the judge looked directly at Stella. She turned to John imploringly. "We've spoken of this before, John. I've always wanted to serve the Indian people. We can't be selfish, John, not after we've been blessed so richly to find each other and to have a home with the Halls. I want to go, John, please, and dedicate some part of my life to helping our people. We can be done by summer's end and return to Becket."

John sighed, thinking back to the happiness he'd seen in the Heaths while they served at Potato Creek. Turning to the judge, who was smiling smugly, knowing he'd successfully played the girl's heartstrings, John conceded.

"Judge Castle, you've said only one thing to induce me to go back to the reservation and undertake what countless returning students have failed to do: your suggestion that I will have deserted my people's cause if I do not. That and my wife's wishes to give back to our people. No one, especially she, knows better than I the futility of this undertaking. However, I'm willing to make the effort conscientiously if Major Mack will approve and Mr. Hall will release me for the summer. When we've proven the futility of our effort there, we'll return to Becket and live as we have planned. I accept your promise of employment, and if the arrangements can be made satisfactory to all, we'll be ready to start on the first of April."

John's words stole all feeling of triumph from the judge, who felt the contempt glaring at him from the younger man's eyes. He'd wanted to dictate the terms of their agreement but instead had been dictated to, and it stung deeply. Despite his anger, he rose with a show of satisfaction, stepped to the door, and asked Major Mack to join them.

"Major," he began arrogantly, "these two have decided to return to the reservation and engage in the work of uplifting their people. Of course, you must agree and secure from Mr. Hall a release from their obligation to him." He went on in the tone he always used when reminding anyone of his donations, "I'm certain you'll approve and make satisfactory explanations to Mr. Hall." His voice barely hiding his hypocrisy, the judge finished, "I'm deeply gratified by their decision, for in it I find justification for the excessive cost of Indian education."

The major's face showed distress as he responded, "I hardly know what to say, Judge. I wasn't expecting this. If John and Stella have decided to go back, I can only agree it must be for a particularly good reason. I'll explain everything to Mr. Hall."

With assurances from Judge Castle that he'd provide employment for the couple at the agency boarding school on Pine Ridge, John and Stella agreed to enter into their duties on the first day of April. The couple left Judge Castle and Major Mack, she to return to her schoolroom with hope in a new purpose, he to his work and near despondency, for in his heart he knew the difficulties that lay ahead.

Judge Castle settled himself that evening on the train ride home. Despite having penalized John for his outburst, the man failed to find the self-congratulatory satisfaction he usually enjoyed after such encounters. Deep in his arrogant soul, he felt the kind of dissatisfaction that often grows to resentment.

The major waited several days to write Mr. Hall, hoping he could break the news more dispassionately, but his use of the words "hypocrisy" and "meddlesomeness" in his letter bore testimony to his true feelings. He tried to share what good might come from their current disappointment, and he closed his letter with:

> Tom, perhaps this will prove to be the one experience that John and Stella need to make their lives complete. Let's hope they'll be content when they return to us and pray that they safely will.

IV

The Reservation

CHAPTER 46

Carter's Journal

Winter 1900 to Spring 1901

Cherokee Indian School, Qualla Boundary, Cherokee, North Carolina

Over a period of several months, I sent numerous letters and telegrams indicating I was willing to report to any duty other than one so inclined to intrigue, backstabbing, and rumors as Wind River. My requests went unacknowledged, despite my reaching out to numerous contacts in Washington. Interestingly, as soon as the physician from Wind River sent my health report to Washington, informing the commissioner of my diagnosis of high blood pressure, I was called to return to Washington immediately and begin paperwork for my early retirement.

My refusal to accept a forced retirement, assisted by a letter from Senator Zucker giving me his strong recommendation, resulted in my appointment to the Cherokee Indian Agency in the Southeastern United States. Attached to my transfer orders was the physician's recommendation for a less mountainous appointment. Strangely, I found myself in the mountains of North Carolina and, based on my initial impressions, not too far removed from the same scheming and collusion I'd dealt with in Wyoming.

My assignment as superintendent included a salary commensurate with my previous positions, less deductions for my quarters, fuel, and light. There were further deductions made for space for the children and Mrs. Cooper, but I was sure my family would be content to join me in the beauty of the mountains. The land was unlike anywhere I'd ever been. The lush, thick Carolina forests included ferns, flowering shrubs, tumbling waterfalls, and deep rifts filled with leafy vines that were almost impossible to pass through. When the atmosphere was exactly right, wisps of clouds rose from the treetops and drifted across the forest like smoke rising directly from the mountains themselves. It was little wonder former soldiers had failed to find the Cherokee who hid in the forests to escape removal from their ancestral homes. The dense woods, the forest sounds, and the swirling mists lent a feeling of enchantment that easily led one to believe there were spirits protecting the Indians.

The agency itself was located in a small valley and included an administrative building, which was a very spacious wooden structure with a wide wraparound porch, and our quarters, which were spacious as well with wide porches and large, sturdy, square-cut stone steps. Across a grassy square were the classroom buildings and dormitories for the students, as well as several barns and a shop. The surrounding land consisted of well-established farm fields where the Indians grew corn, squash, and beans as well as sweet potatoes, flax, and cotton. A well-built road curved around the entirety of the village, following the course of a beautiful but raucous river that spread softly over wide, flat areas near the town but roared wildly in the narrow gorges of the mountains. The women were skilled basket makers and weavers, and the men were successful at herding not just cattle but also hogs in the local woods. They were capable builders, and many supplemented their income by working on local farms off the reservation.

Among my list of tasks to be completed was to secure a nanny and tutor for the children so that Mrs. Cooper could assist Jessie with our household affairs. I was also allotted accounts to hire a mason, a cook, and a clerk to assist in my office. I made a point of going by Carlisle in the spring on my way to Ithaca to pick up my family and was devastated to learn that John and Stella had chosen to return to the reservation rather than to the Berkshires as we'd discussed. I was certain there was more to the story than what was explained to me, but berating the major's receptionist would have accomplished nothing. I decided to wire Mr. Hall in hopes of receiving an explanation for what to me was unexplainable.

We settled in at Cherokee and got busy with the business of the Indians. Jessie applied for a position in the post office, but it took time for her to be confirmed. The Qualla Boundary was not a federally operated reservation as all the others where I had served. Instead, the land was part privately owned and part held in trust, a system set up by individuals who escaped the tribe's forced removal to Oklahoma on what was called the Trail of Tears.

Some one thousand individuals had hidden out in these vast, inaccessible mountains and later formed, with the help of an attorney, a corporation that could own land. After purchasing a large tract of their ancestral home, the attorney helped them add to their holdings, allowing them to resist removal and to establish a community much like the white communities that dotted the area. The Indians had recently lost their right to vote based on a court ruling about timber sales that identified them as wards of the government in addition to being citizens of the state. Obviously, I had much to learn regarding the complex attributes of this group.

Despite being recognized as a new tribe with their own lands, the Eastern Band of the Cherokee still found themselves at the mercy of the government, including the exclusion of Indian language and culture from the school curriculum. The families living on this reservation had given up their rights as members of the original Cherokee tribe and lived as citizens of both the United States and the state of North Carolina. This led to a great deal of infighting, resulting in a troublesome state of tension not conducive to the proper management of the Indians' affairs.

The official report from the previous superintendent, Mr. Christy, attempted to explain the factions with which I'd be dealing.

There were two groups within the staff of the agency. One consisted of several teachers and the cook, and the other was made up of several other teachers, a counselor, and a local farmer. It took much unscrambling of stories and insinuations, but ultimately, I learned that one group of teachers set out to despoil the reputation of a new, attractive teacher who was well liked by the majority of students at the school. As if petty female jealousies were not enough to deal with, there was also a missionary who for at least seven years had caused difficulties by inciting the Indians against anyone of the Catholic persuasion, including turning the staff against a female doctor and embarrassing her publicly with rude and vulgar comments. Though I had no wish to confront anyone, I had no intention of tolerating such behavior and immediately penned a letter to the secretary of the interior, requesting the missionary's removal.

I was worried about John and wired to the Pine Ridge Agency to inquire of his and Stella's arrival.

"*Hope you are well* STOP *Why* STOP *Encourage return to Halls* STOP."

Weeks passed with no response from John as I struggled with my own disappointment in the government system.

CHAPTER 47

Going Back

Spring to Summer 1901

Pine Ridge Agency School, Pine Ridge Reservation, South Dakota

The first of April found John and Stella at the agency boarding school on Pine Ridge, the very school where John had excelled when he left Potato Creek. Their journey from Carlisle had kept them occupied with the sights and sounds of the trip, and the accommodations at Pine Ridge were comfortable. John appreciated the miles his little trunk had traveled and was thankful it had secured both his and his wife's belongings to their new home.

For Stella, everything was new and exciting, from the bustle of the Midwest to the beauty of the vast outdoors. Her enthusiasm for their venture increased steadily the further west they traveled. John was surprised to realize the things that had impressed him the most about the white man's world before didn't seem so impressive now, and those things he'd previously taken for granted now seemed incredibly important. He'd seen massive structures from Dubuque to New York and suddenly found himself yearning for the solitude of the vast stretches of grasslands from his childhood. Yet despite outwardly maintaining a lighthearted spirit for Stella's sake, he felt an intense foreboding for acting so opposite of the guidance of his father and Carter Heath.

Upon their arrival, they entered the duties of positions similar to what they'd held at Carlisle as teaching assistants and advisors. Their zeal and interest prevented them from feeling any regret or loneliness. It seemed strange to John that only one of the present employees, Mr. Gamble, had been there when he was a pupil at the school. He'd served as a clerk, and John's only memory of him was that his squinted eyes and tight lips made the students think he was always angry.

John was grieved to learn from Mr. Gamble that Good Heart, Annie's mother, had died the preceding year. He'd recorded her death in the tribal records himself. John reminded himself to reach out to Aaron Moss so they could share news of the changes in each other's lives.

It wasn't long before the couple was completely wrapped up in life there. There was an unsettling difference in the atmosphere compared to back east, but it was nothing they could identify, just something they sensed. They attributed their uneasiness to the new location and the absence of their loved ones. As time made them more familiar with the setting and the people at the school, the differences became clearer. Unlike John and Stella, the remainder of the staff seemed drained by what they considered to be the pointlessness of their duties. They took no joy in the children, nor in the value of what they were providing to the Indian people.

If they had overheard the conversation between other teachers at an event one evening, they might have understood. Stella was teaching several children a game she'd learned at Carlisle. John was helping, laughing, and clapping as the children played. Two elderly ladies stood apart from the others.

One remarked snidely, "Who do they think they are? The students always return so conceited and self-important. They think their jobs are special, but we'll see how long these two last, humph."

Her companion replied with a smirk, "Don't worry. When the job's gone, they'll slip back into the old ways just like all the others."

"Yes," returned the first, grinning, "we know what's coming. And then we'll be back to running the school just like we want."

John and Stella enjoyed their first three months at the boarding school. They focused their energies on the children, enjoyed the vast spaces of the reservation, and made frequent excursions to various points of interest. Along the little creek that flowed a mile below the school were many delightful nooks and retreats shaded by diamond willows and fragrant redbuds. Some two miles to the south were the Shark-Tooth Hills, a geological formation similar to the Bad Lands, where fossilized shark's teeth could be found, remnants of a great sea that once covered the area.

To the west an equal distance were moss-agate hills where fragments of colorful stone could be gathered, each showing the colors of the moss that had grown along the waters of the ancient sea. On the top of another hill not far away were graves so old that no one knew their history, and scattered around the adjoining prairies were buffalo horns and other reminders of the more immediate past. All these combined to launch any number of stories about the creation of the world or the history of their people, which John shared with Stella. He enjoyed the memories stirred by the stories immensely.

Indian life whirled about them in ever-changing variety. Beyond the agency itself in every direction were Indian homes they could visit when they had an opportunity, and Stella found endless fascination with the world around her. On a June evening following a perfect, sun-filled day of rambling, John and Stella returned to their cabin from several hours in the solitude of the great prairie. The prairie was where they felt closest to each other and the place that John had loved deeply as a child. They had turned towards the school, walking hand in hand along the smooth trail, when Stella looked up at John and said, her voice trembling with joy, "I have a wonderful secret for my husband."

"Wifekin mine, don't you know that I love you so much I know your very thoughts? You can have no secrets from me."

"Oh! But this is different," she teased. "No one can know this but me."

"But I do know," he insisted, "and I can prove it. I'll tell you your own secret." Putting his arm tenderly about her, he whispered into her ear so low that even the prairie swallow hiding in a grassy clump nearby could not hear what none but they might know.

Stella beamed as she hugged John even closer. "And his name will be John."

Like Iron Horse before him, John hoped for a man-child, never considering the babe might be a girl. For the remainder of the evening, they planned as the young so often do, incredibly happy with their secret.

Several days later, they were both loath to see the school year end and the children return to their homes. Stella had developed an abiding affection for each child and would miss them over the summer. John knew that by summer's end, most of the year's learning would be forgotten, and the boys and girls now leaving clean and healthy would return in the fall dirty and hungry, willing to attend classes to secure their families' rations for the winter.

The day brought an unexpected highlight for John, for among the many wagons that arrived to pick up students was the same one that had brought him to the school years before. It rumbled closer, driven by the last person on the reservation for whom John felt a deep and abiding love. The couple had not yet visited his mother, for John was unsure of how she would react to his wife's lighter skin and hair. She'd heard her son was at the boarding school and made the long trip alone, driving the same colorful ponies that Iron Horse had loved so dearly. Throughout the trip, she'd imagined she would bring the boy of her memories home, and life would be good again.

John and Stella continued waving to the departing children as Moves First approached. Her steps were uncertain, and she peered questioningly at all who passed her by. As she came closer, John realized her clouded eyes could not recognize him and put his hand out to stop her, exhaling, "Mother" with all the love that welled up from his heart. It was a term of respect among Indians young and old, and at first, she thought it was no more than a casual greeting from a youngster walking by. When his voice finally penetrated the fog of her understanding, a look of doubt crossed her wrinkled face. She grasped his face with both hands and peered into his eyes, afraid she was mistaken, but he said again, "Mother," and his voice pierced her heart.

She replied in a quavering voice, "My husband's son."

To the casual observer, it might have seemed a commonplace incident, but to John and Moves First, the meeting brought a flood of emotions. He felt the depth of his love for the woman who had saved his life, and a great pity for her loneliness in her declining years. The meeting brought her great happiness at the thought that her boy and the son of Iron Horse had come back. But as her grip slipped from his face down his arms to his hands, and she looked more closely, she noted how little he showed himself to be an Indian in his dress and speech and mannerisms, and disappointment entered her heart.

John took his mother's hand and placed Stella's within it, saying, "This is my wife." Instantly, he saw disappointment give way to shock as the old woman looked into the smiling face of the pale-skinned girl. Moves First saw nothing but sympathy in the girl's eyes, and her anger grew. Straightening her stooped shoulders as best she could, the woman pushed away Stella's hand, muttering words the young woman didn't understand but John recognized all too easily. "White squaw" spat again from his mother's lips as she turned and walked stiffly to her wagon.

John stood unmoving, arms hanging at his sides as she climbed with difficulty to the seat. Stella watched his expression and felt the hurt in his heart without knowing how such a special moment had gone so wrong. Moves First clucked to the ponies, turning them towards Potato Creek, and the low, plaintive song that John had heard as his family drove away from the boarding school so long ago wafted back to him.

The next morning, the superintendent called John and Stella to his office to inform them that their positions were ended as of the close of that very day. He added firmly that there would also be no employment for them for the coming school year. He regretted the situation and promised to try to secure their reemployment, but it didn't seem likely. He appreciated the work they'd done at the school, but since receiving the curt letter of their dismissal from the judge of the area circuit, he held little hope of finding funds for their renewed position. He agreed for them to stay in their home at the school until they secured another place but emphasized they must be out of it before the fall. He recommended they reach out to any friends for assistance.

Upon learning it was a judge's letter that upended their lives, John confessed to Stella, "I should have foreseen this from such a disingenuous man as Judge Castle. I've failed my father in not expecting the enemy to come from every side as the judge has done. My respect for my father, my loyalty to my people, and my love for you—he used it all to trick me into coming back to the reservation. Now that we're here, he can manipulate us at his will."

Stella interrupted his rant: "No, John, it was I who said I'd always wanted to come. I spoke with childish dreams in my heart and aided the judge in his duplicity."

"No, wifekin," John argued. "I said nothing to dispute the judge's claim to the major that we'd decided to go back to the reservation. I should have spoken the truth as Iron Horse taught me. Instead, I was arrogant and thought only of myself. I'm afraid I'll never be the wise leader my father was."

CHAPTER 48

Carter's Journal

Summer 1901

Cherokee Indian School, Qualla Boundary, Cherokee, North Carolina

Though the school was picturesque and gave the appearance that all was well, the facility itself had troubles beyond the frivolity of staff gossip and intrigue. From what I learned from school records, the tribe had been incorporated since 1889. It was difficult for me to grasp that a corporation had been established in North Carolina that guaranteed legal status to the entire Cherokee tribe one whole year before the killing of Indian women and children at Wounded Knee. Land ownership, both tribal and individual, had been legal here for over thirty years. The Cherokee had paid property taxes to the state of North Carolina no different than my family had paid in New York. This tribe was far advanced in their understanding of white civilization and had even taken a land-ownership case against the state of Georgia to the Supreme Court.

Despite being so advanced in some ways, the people repeatedly dealt with variables in leadership within the white bureaucracy. They'd been given virtual autonomy, including voting rights for the presidential election in 1884, and then reduced to being wards of the government by 1890. All voting rights had been taken away from them by 1895. Through the use of corporal punishment, boarding schools had expunged the use of the Cherokee language over just a few generations.

The Indians were governed by a council made up of representatives from the surrounding townships, each of which had special relationships with local communities. There were groups who strived to assist those in need and to hold the culture of the tribe intact. The Indians had exceptional knowledge of local medicinal plants, which they shared among themselves and their white neighbors, and for the most part supported themselves well with farming and logging.

I worked hard to explain to Washington that the land records offered their own challenges here. For years, many of the Indians held parcels that had been deeded to them according to their custom, but current law addressed only ownership granted by the federal government. The tribe agreed to honor the previous deeds since the individuals had lived there many years and, in some cases, had deeded portions of their land to family. This frequently put me in a quandary since the practice was at odds with departmental policies.

In addition to the maze of land records I dealt with on a daily basis, the previous agency clerk had been derelict in his duties regarding staff salaries. There were several doctors, a carpenter, my own office assistant, and the school's disciplinarian who had been advanced to higher field grades than what had been submitted to Washington, and their salaries had been paid from monies allocated to the Indians. As newly appointed superintendent as well as special disbursing agent, I found myself short of the necessary funds to operate into another year. I decided to reconcile the accounts. Despite multiple communications with the chief clerk of the bureau, a Mr. Menger, there were some busybodies in Washington, and locally, who demanded an investigation of the shortfalls.

In the midst of these struggles, I learned of my father's passing by note from a shift foreman at the gun plant and requested leave to travel home for his funeral. I'd lost touch with Father for the most part since Uncle Charles's marriage to a woman of questionable character named Fanny. Charles had immediately moved to the Finger Lakes to focus on increasing his real estate holdings. Since then, I'd heard little of my New York family. For what I expected to be my last trip to Ithaca, I planned a detour through Washington to personally sort out the disparities in the agency monies. I bought round-trip tickets for the trip and submitted everything in triplicate, a burdensome but obviously necessary new policy that was pushing me and my clerk to exhaustion.

Jessie was appointed as the postmistress for the agency. As soon as she began receiving her funds, she secured a tutor as well as a housekeeper, releasing Mrs. Cooper to focus most of her energies on the boys. At nine, Liz was annoyingly inquisitive at times and well advanced in her studies. Her time in New York had ingrained in her both the most proper English discourse and the femininity that demanded dresses and curls rather than dungarees and baggy shirts. There were few riding horses in Cherokee, and none of them were owned by the school or its staff. Without her beloved horses, the outdoors lost its attraction for my daughter, a fact for which I was grateful considering the dense forests surrounding us. Liz was content to read or draw for hours after her lessons and dreamed of being a nurse in a large city hospital.

On the other hand, at six, Ralph, was precocious and wandered off frequently to find polliwogs and frogs in the numerous creeks and streams that meandered across the valleys and ravines towards the river. On more than one occasion, we had to call for a hunting party to find him before darkness settled in. It wasn't that Mrs. Cooper was remiss in her duties; the boys were like wood sprites—here one moment and gone the next. While she focused on one, the others could always find a way to get into or out of something.

I had little time to visit the classrooms of the school but took a firm stance against the use of corporal punishment. I informed the teachers I expected daily lessons to include more than rote memorization and made it clear I expected them to encourage their students to seek higher education at places such as Carlisle, the Hampton Institute in Virginia, or the Chilocco Indian School in Oklahoma. These schools would open doors to the world off the reservation.

I budgeted for travel to visit and build relationships with the superintendents of these schools, not only to ensure our students would be accepted into their programs but also on the scant hope that I'd learn more about the fate of John and Stella along the route. There'd been little time to write him with news of my transfer, and even if he'd written to me, I doubted the letter could have followed my path to the hills of the Cherokee. There would have been no happier news for me than to receive notice they'd returned to the Halls' and were starting a family in the Berkshires, and I hoped to hear so every day.

As to the future of the Cherokee, there were already many travelers to their reservation who came to see the colorful leaves in the fall, to hike the trails to the waterfalls and scenic areas, and to purchase the high-quality baskets and other items made by the women of the tribe. Some of the younger council members hinted they wanted tourism to provide a new source of income for the future, but most of the council elders were opposed to such ideas.

CHAPTER 49

Reality on the Reservation

Midsummer 1901

Pine Ridge Reservation, Pine Ridge, South Dakota

The Fourth of July celebration was held on the Big Flats of Wolf Creek, a few miles east of the agency. It was an exceptionally large affair. Thousands of visiting Indians from other reservations were there as participants, and hundreds of white people from settlements near and far took advantage of the chance to view the great pageantry of Indian life. Many who lived in remote camps went directly from the closing of the boarding school to the campground, eagerly waiting for an opportunity to gather with others and celebrate the solstice with dance and song. Every day brought more people until, by July 2, there were more than ten thousand Indians present.

It was an extravaganza of Indian life. For those who looked upon it as a spectacle, it offered a wealth of the picturesque. To those who looked more closely, it showed a panorama of Indian life from the aboriginal to the modern that could never be reproduced. To those who were able to see and then feel through sympathy or interest, it revealed in detail the sordidness of the life to which the Indians had been forced by confinement on the reservations.

On the morning of Independence Day, John and Stella traveled by wagon with a group from the boarding school to Wolf Creek to witness and participate in the celebration of the season. John was interested in showing Stella all he could, good and bad. He prepared her as best he could for what she was about to see, and for what she might be called upon to do. He'd instructed her on some of the customs she might observe and had particularly cautioned her to show no evidence of curiosity or surprise, for those were not Indian attributes.

"In fact, Stella," he said, "you'll see much that I'd rather you didn't have to see, but I want my people to embrace my wife as long as we live among them. Perhaps it will be easier for you to act in ways they'll most approve of if you do as I do while we're in the camp."

Stella was excited; she hoped to see authentic Indian life, partake of its ceremonies, and live it as she'd dreamed. When they reached the camp, they left the others to keep the day's experiences for themselves only. Passing through the encircling tipis to the great central area, John and Stella observed and absorbed the details of reservation life. They attracted no particular attention, and though John frequently saw people he knew, no one recognized him. Because no one knew who he was, he felt at ease and was inclined to enter the spirit of the celebration just as Stella did.

As they mingled with the crowds and strolled among the tipis, John had frequent reason to be glad she didn't understand the language of his people. Now and then, he heard just enough remarks—such as "the young Indian with the ways and dress of a white man with a white squaw"—to know that what the Indians might be saying behind their backs was anything but complimentary. Sometimes the words came from a circle of blanketed old men seated in the shade of a tipi flap, passing the pipe of fellowship from one to another. Sometimes the words came from a group of older women gathered around a fire where they were preparing some part of the coming feast. The women especially ridiculed "the white squaw" with her airs and dress, while Stella wondered to herself how their beaded moccasins would have served their owners on the paved streets of Chicago or New York.

She was amazed at the enormity of the camp and the number of inhabitants, but she focused on the simpler details—the beauty of the painted tipis and the diverse colors of the ponies. Here and there, the covering of a tipi was raised so that the interior was exposed, showing the mounded sleeping blankets and an occasional infant slumbering peacefully away from the hubbub. These things and the ever-burning fires over which continuous cooking went on claimed her attention. Slowly, she began to notice the condition of the furnishings of the tipis and the personal appearance of the men, women, and children. It became clear to her that even in their best attire, the people were disheveled. The food being prepared over the fires might have been savory to smell but was being cooked with dilapidated castoffs of white civilization.

As they went along, John eventually met several people who recognized him. Stella was heartsick at meeting one of their old schoolmates from Carlisle, now barefoot, her dress torn and faded, and a sickly baby on her back. The girl spoke broken English but talked easily in Lakota, sharing with John that she remembered him from school and hoped he could meet her husband, who had been in carpentry class with him.

As they spoke, Stella grasped John's sleeve, turning him towards a commotion behind a tipi. "Oh! Look, John!" she exclaimed. She pointed to two older Indian women who were standing on either end of a tipi pole as it pressed down on the neck of a dog, which was slowly being strangled. "Oh, how awful!" she cried out. "What are they doing? Is it mad?"

"No, Stella," he responded sadly. "That's one of the things I'd rather you hadn't seen. They're preparing a feast, and the dog will be the choicest part. That's the preferred way of killing dogs that are to be eaten. Now that the buffalo are gone and game is scarce, they're as frequently eaten among our people as turkeys are at the Halls'. It's part of reservation life, and now that you've seen this much, we'll see the preparations completed."

"No!" she said firmly, looking away. "I've seen enough."

He directed Stella to a small, age-faded tipi on the outer edge of the camp. He'd been gradually steering their steps in that direction as they walked, and now they approached his mother's home quietly. As they looked through the uncovered opening, they saw Moves First sitting in characteristic Indian fashion, alone, her hands resting idly in her lap as though she were in deep thought.

At the sound of John's "How are you, Mother?" she started in surprise, got to her feet with effort, and came into the sunlight, her hand shading her eyes.

She took his hand and looked affectionately into his face, as if their encounter at the agency school had never occurred. "My son, my heart is glad to see you again."

Releasing his hand and turning to Stella, his mother extended her hand again to warmly grasp the girl's. Moves First spoke in her native tongue, which John interpreted happily to his wife as "My son's wife is my daughter." He was thankful his mother had reconsidered her judgment and knew she would honor the tradition of accepting her son's choice. He was certain she'd welcome them both into her home.

It was late, and John and Stella had been so engrossed in the sights and sounds of the day that they'd given no thought to themselves. Stella asked if she could have a drink of water, which John repeated to his mother. The old woman filled a battered tin cup from a covered keg and handed it to the young woman. The cup was bent and had obviously not had a good scrubbing in quite some time. The water within was the color of a puddle on their school playground and warm from the sun's heat. Stella regretted her request but drank it politely and returned the cup to John with a smile. Moves First went to the fireplace, a depression cut into the prairie sod close by the entrance of the tipi, and fanned the coals into a blaze. She added some dry wood and busied herself with several blackened vessels that served as her cooking utensils.

"What's she doing, John?" asked Stella apprehensively. "We should leave."

"No, wifekin mine." John smiled. "Her action is an invitation for us to stay for dinner. To go now would be to grievously offend one of the sweetest natures I've ever known. What she has to offer will not be much, but it will be flavored with enough love to make up for whatever it lacks in every other way."

"Of course." Stella looked down at her hands in her lap. "I'm ashamed of my words, John. I pray they caused no hurt to your mother," she added in a whisper. Though she feared the meal might contain a portion of the dog she'd witnessed being killed, Stella resolved she would enjoy it and be thankful.

After being told by John that any attempt on her part to help his mother would not be fitting for Indian proprieties, Stella made herself sit idly by and watch. From her larder within the tipi, Moves First brought forth a piece of fatty, thick salt pork wrapped in a cloth that had long ago lost its original color. Cutting several slices from the slab, she put them in an iron skillet and placed the skillet near the edge of the fire, then brushed a swarm of flies from a handcrafted wooden bowl.

In the bowl, she used her hands to mix flour, water from the keg, and baking powder into a thick batter. She removed the underdone meat from the skillet and fried the batter, handful by handful, in the smoking grease. While the batter cooked, she placed a chipped enamel coffee pot on the fire, added some coarsely ground coffee to the dregs already in the pot, topped it off with more water, and soon had a pot of coffee vigorously boiling. Stella watched these preparations with both interest and misgiving. Finally, the meal was complete.

Moves First placed a generous portion of the partially cooked meat and Indian bread on a tin plate, handing it to Stella with a smile. Stella swallowed hard as she accepted the plate, glanced at her husband, and gingerly raised the bread to her lips. Closing her mind to what she'd seen, Stella chewed bite after bite, washing the bread and meat down with small sips of boiling coffee served in a bent and handle-less cup. Glancing between her husband and his mother and seeing the love in his eyes, she managed to partake enough from her plate to convince Moves First she appreciated her meal.

Stella enjoyed conversing with her mother-in-law while John interpreted back and forth between them. Time flew by. After hearing stories about Annie, Iron Horse, and Potato Creek, the young woman realized how much love for her husband they shared. When they finally prepared to leave, the sun had all but disappeared beneath the horizon. Moves First showed she'd overcome any disappointment from their first encounter by her lingering grip on their hands and the feeling with which she said, "My children, it would make my old heart glad to see you both again, soon." Stella felt a new regard for the one to whom she felt indebted for the life of her husband.

They were walking swiftly to catch a ride home with the school group when Stella heard someone call her name from within a tipi as they passed. Pausing, they saw the woman inside settling a baby into the folds of a sling on her back and rising to her feet. As she stepped through the opening, they both recognized Julia American Horse. It was obvious she was glad to see them. She started by asking about school. John left Stella and Julia to reminisce while he went ahead to find their group.

Julia wore a calico dress cut after the fashion of white women and shoes instead of moccasins, but both looked worn and frayed. Her hair flowed loosely instead of being braided. The blanket with which she carried her child was dull and dirty, and the baby began to cry. Julia and Stella stepped back into the tipi, and when they were seated on the blankets, Julia pointedly asked, "Stella, why did you and John come back?"

Stella replied, "We didn't plan this. After a meeting with the school employees, Judge Castle tricked me into believing we should return, saying we owed it to the Indian people to help them better their lives. I wanted to see the old ways. I've never seen anything like what I've seen today. The Indians among whom I lived as a little girl lived more like the whites in the settlements. I was taught to pity the Indians who followed the old ways. I wanted to feel good that we were helping others. Now we've lost our jobs, and I see how difficult reservation life is. I'd love to go home to the farm in Massachusetts. For now, though, we have no money to purchase tickets for the train, and John is too proud to ask the Halls for help. He's sure he'll find work on a ranch soon. I won't argue with him again about what we should do."

"Go, Stella, before it's too late," urged Julia. "The longer anyone remains here, the harder it is to leave. Abram and I had jobs at the agency too, and our parents didn't want us to go, so we put it off. Then, like yours, our employment ended. Abram couldn't find work, and we had no money. Now we have two babies, and it's harder than ever to hope for anything better than reservation life."

John returned and informed Stella their group had left them behind.

"Shall we walk? It isn't that far," he encouraged his wife.

Before Stella could reply, Abram Lone Bear stepped into the tipi, and the four old friends found so much to talk about that it was dark before they realized it. At John's suggestion, he and Stella decided to go back to his mother's tipi and spend the night with her. As they bade their friends good night, John commented casually, "A night in the camp might prove an invaluable experience in case the schoolhouse isn't available for us at the end of summer."

Although his comment was said in jest, Stella shuddered. "Yes, the agent only promised us through the end of summer. Let's hope this isn't an omen." For a moment, memories of her dream of John standing at the base of a hill across from a schoolhouse and waving to her as if from a distance flashed across her mind.

When they reached Moves First's camp, the flap door was closed. John called to his mother in hushed tones, and she let them in, pointing to some blankets piled against the far wall before returning to her own pallet on the ground. She slipped immediately back to sleep. After securing the door closed again, John spread the blankets on the ground as best he could with Stella's help in the pitch-black darkness. The bed was surprisingly comfortable, despite smelling of smoke and fry bread, but before long, the air within the tipi became oppressive. Hearing a deep sigh and sniffle from Stella, John knew she was fighting tears.

She was fatigued from the activities of the day, yet she couldn't relax. Images from the day passed repeatedly in her mind—the squalor of the camp and the wretchedness of the people, both young and old. For hours, she lay awake; like all dreams of childhood, reality was vastly different from what she'd imagined. Stella resolved that since she'd been the cause of her husband's return to the reservation, she would also be the reason for his leaving.

John felt Stella toss and turn throughout the night. Like himself, she slept fitfully, and when the tipi's interior lightened with the daybreak, she grasped John's arm, holding him close as they listened to the crier's proclamations of upcoming events.

"John," she whispered, "despite your presence and knowing the people of Iron Horse are all around us, I can't help feeling lonely so far from our family in the Berkshires. The darkness is so black, and I don't feel that your people have welcomed us. I feel like running home with all my strength, not to the agency school but all the way back to Snow Hill."

As John shook himself free of the tangled blankets, Stella hastened their departure by quickly folding and stacking them back against the wall of the tipi. Emerging into the chill of the early morning, Stella wanted to plead, "John, please, can we find a way to return to the farm in Massachusetts now?" But she held back, knowing it would injure his pride.

As they turned in the direction of the agency, John knew his mother would accept their leaving when she awakened. It was the way of the Lakota not to question the actions of others. They passed through the outmost edges of the site, and he reflected on the hopelessness of the old ways and wondered why so many were unwilling to open their eyes and see it. Once clear of the camp, the couple settled into an easy distance-covering gait that came to them as experienced walkers. Suddenly, John stopped, pointing to a man some distance out on the prairie.

"Stella, I believe that's Aaron Moss." Aaron was walking towards the area they'd just left, leading two ponies. They waited until he drew near enough for John to confirm his identity before running to intercept him. Aaron recognized John and, although he'd never seen her before, knew who Stella must be immediately. He'd heard John was back and had taken a bride. Aaron invited them to breakfast with him and his wife back in camp. "Come on, you two. I'll return to the agency later and can give you a ride."

Arriving at the Mosses' camp, Stella was delighted to see not a tipi but instead a large wall tent with many of the conveniences of an established home. Giving no thought to the support he received from the church, she wondered to herself, *How have they returned to the reservation and built a successful life, unlike so many others here?* She immediately felt a closeness to Mrs. Moss, for she was soft spoken and gracious like Mrs. Hall. Yet it was apparent to Stella that while the woman accepted their life on the reservation, it was only on her own terms. She helped her husband minister to their people, but she didn't accept the old ways to do it.

After a breakfast of biscuits, blackberry jam, and sweet black coffee served from a porcelain pot, Aaron harnessed the two ponies to his wagon, and the group headed back to the agency. As they rode, Stella felt the negative images of the celebration being totally offset by her introduction to the Mosses. She saw that Mrs. Moss managed to maintain a level of cleanliness and comfort that inspired Stella to believe she could provide the same for her husband if she only worked hard enough. What she failed to consider was that a small salary was infinitely better than no salary at all.

CHAPTER 50

Desperation

Late Summer to Fall 1901

Pine Ridge Agency School, Pine Ridge Reservation, South Dakota

The agency superintendent did everything he could to find money to reemploy John and Stella for the fall. Unfortunately, he had no friends in Washington and no contacts among the politicians in the state capital to pull the necessary strings for additional funding. As the young couple's savings dwindled, John sent a letter to Judge Castle, explaining that their superintendent wanted them to continue at the boarding school, even hinting at Stella's pregnancy and sharing his concern about taking her away from the safety of the agency and school.

John knew better than to wait on the bureaucracy and wasn't about to leave their destiny in the judge's hands. He called on each of the nearby traders' stores and traveled south among the ranchers, seeking employment. There was nothing available. He went as far as Rushville to see if the railroad company was hiring, but everywhere there seemed to be far more people looking for work than there was employment to be had.

In early August, the superintendent was notified by telegram, "*Conclusive action regarding Iron Horse employment* STOP *No* STOP."

The man dared not risk angering his superiors by asking them to reconsider. When he told the couple they wouldn't be given a position at the agency, he assured them of the use of their present quarters with a stern reminder that it was only through the end of summer break.

At the same time, John received a response from Judge Castle, short and formal, in which he informed John,

It has been deemed inexpedient to continue the positions held by yourself and your wife for your special benefit. There are plenty of Indians returning to the reservation who deserve the same opportunities you were given. By now, you should be prepared to begin your work as apostles of civilization with no further assistance from or dependence on anyone other than yourselves. Furthermore, I wish to remind you that your term of education will not be considered fulfilled until April of next year. The major sends his regards but expects you to remain in service on the reservation until that time.

As John read the lines, a bitter smile crossed his face. His intuition that the judge had little interest in himself or his people had been right. He doubted the major would try to force the judge to keep his word regarding their employment even if he knew about the letter, which John doubted. Funding for the school was paramount in the major's eyes.

Begrudgingly, John admitted to himself that he'd known all along the judge had manipulated them for spite. Having seen the truth of life on the reservation, Stella suggested writing for funds to return to the Berkshires, but John had more than one reason for not sending a desperate plea for money. At least, not yet. He had to find answers to questions of his own. However disingenuous the judge's appeal had been, it struck a chord of self-doubt in John. One of his goals was to be a leader like his father. Looking back over his and Stella's time on the reservation, John admitted to himself that he'd failed to go out among their people and encourage them to do better. He'd taught a few English words to children who were forced to attend school, but at the first hardship he and his wife faced, they were ready to quit and go back to the comforts of the white man's world.

John was certain Annie would be disappointed if he gave up. He also knew he had to come to terms with his own pride. He had failed to humble himself and had spoken arrogantly. He wasn't the leader his father had been if he couldn't admit he'd made a mistake; and he couldn't live with himself if he conceded defeat too soon.

In his youth, he'd frequently been asked to carry mail for the agency post office and had earned the friendship of Mr. Lawson, the storeowner who operated the post office. One day in early August, Mr. Lawson sent

John a message that one of the regular store clerks was going out of town and asked if he would help in the store for a month or so. John was elated, for his family's financial needs were beyond urgent. Because goods at the trader's store were expensive, they'd developed the routine of eating only two light meals each day, a habit John prayed would not impact the health of his developing child. He saw the offer as confirmation that his father's spirit was watching over him.

Not long after John began at the store, Stella secured employment as an assistant seamstress at the boarding school. The position was authorized internally; therefore, the judge had no control over the hiring or firing of whomever was chosen. Her skills as a seamstress were exceptional, and the work made her feel she was contributing to her family's income, alleviating a depression that almost overwhelmed her some days. After weeks of forced idleness and dealing with the anxiety caused by a lack of income, the couple enjoyed their new positions. At the end of each day, however, they acknowledged that their work did nothing to benefit the Indians on the reservation, and they still had no home to return to at the end of summer break.

A second turn of fate came the day before John's month with Mr. Lawson was to end. A trader from Medicine Root inquired if he and Stella would be willing to help on his farm for the winter. John was well acquainted with the man from his days as a boy on Potato Creek and knew him to be honest and hardworking. As Stella's employment would soon end as well, taking this job would provide them with an opportunity to earn hard currency.

John and Stella packed their possessions into the little tin trunk and set it in the wagon that would transport them away from the agency and school. They would miss the students and worried about the new teacher, doubting his employment would last any longer than theirs had. Sitting dejectedly in the back of the wagon, cramped by the boxes and crates of supplies for the store at Medicine Root, the couple prayed this was the beginning of a new opportunity.

Dick Roacher, the trader who had hired John to work on his farm, also owned a small trading post that included a store, a post office, his family residence, a number of small storehouses, and a day school, all within a quarter mile of each other. Several Indian camps stood along the creek, and the area immediately above the store included several well-established ranches that belonged to white families. There was usually bountiful grazing and an abundance of water from Medicine Root Creek and its tributaries.

Mr. Roacher was a fifty-year-old white man who'd lived among the Indians since childhood. He'd been there so long that his English carried the same inflection as that of the many Indians who had not perfected the language. Years ago, he'd married a mixed-blood girl who was well educated and accomplished in business. They were respected by all their neighbors, both Indian and white. John and Stella fit in immediately. With the aid of some half-curtains and a colorful quilt from Mrs. Roacher, Stella made their quarters in the rear of the store as attractive and homelike as possible. They took their meals with the family, and Stella welcomed the opportunity to help with housekeeping when travelers stopped overnight or came in to avoid the worst of the storms that frequently blew through the area.

John was excellent help to Mr. Roacher in the store, but his main responsibility was his employer's 150 cattle that grazed an adjoining prairie allotment. Mr. Roacher had acquired them recently, so they did not know the range and had to be rounded up daily to keep them from wandering off. It was a big responsibility; John dedicated himself to checking them often, moving them to and from water, and familiarizing them with the presence of horse and rider. By the first snowfall, the cattle were in the habit of being brought in each evening. John enclosed a section of pasture near the store where they could be gathered and fed when necessary and repaired a log corral that protected the stacks of hay Mr. Roacher had purchased for winter feeding.

The autumn season was delightful on the prairie, and Stella found herself enjoying the beauty of the grasses and the changing leaves of the cottonwoods along the creek. A close friendship developed between her and Mrs. Roacher, but when time permitted, she visited Indian homes along the creek. She relished the long walks and was slowly learning the herbs that grew wild on the prairie. She watched as the women broke the stems and laid them over rocks in the sun before hanging the dried bundles for use over the winter. Back at the store, she crushed those she collected into the bland soups and stews that Mrs. Roacher served in a watery gravy. More than one traveler commented that the food at the post was among the best they'd had anywhere and wanted to learn the secrets of the flavoring.

In return for the women teaching her the use of the herbs, Stella took her sewing kit when she visited to stitch up the tears and ripped seams of the cotton dresses most of the women now wore. She reminded them that it was more sanitary if they took the government-issued iron pots down to the creek and scrubbed them with sand after each use. A few of the younger women who'd been to the bigger schools off the reservation resented Stella's expecting them to use what they'd learned when life here was so different, but she continued to remind them that even simple things could improve their lives.

John's occupation with Mr. Roacher's cattle didn't prevent him from finding time to renew his acquaintance with his people. Frequently, he traveled with Stella to visit the families, always carrying a small pouch of tobacco he purchased at the store. While she read to the children from her Bible or listened to the elders' stories, John sat around the embers of a fire and listened to the men talk of how hard it was to feed their families or how dry the season was or how expensive supplies had gotten at the trading post. He remembered the importance of keeping the government rolls updated and tried to encourage them to keep their own records of rations and cattle they'd received.

CHAPTER 51

Carter's Journal

Fall 1901

Cherokee Indian School, Qualla Boundary, Cherokee, North Carolina

Despite my making several trips to Washington to share documents that showed where positions had been allocated but not budgeted for at the agency, the assistant commissioner of Indian affairs suggested that I had "not measured up to the requirements of a responsible administrator." In fact, he wrote that my previous service had never been satisfactory and recommended I be dismissed or at the very least forced into early retirement.

I was disgusted, for I had merely exposed disparities within the previous accounts with my diligent review. Any discrepancies had nothing to do with misappropriation on my part, and I was prepared to provide more than ample evidence to that fact.

In addition to questions about funding, I struggled on a day-to-day basis with infighting in the staff. A preacher whose enrollment as a member of the tribe was being contested worked diligently to disrupt business at the agency. His testimony against other members of the staff was so vile and divisive that it was impossible to get the employees to work together. Each had his own supporting group—some white, some Indian, some full-blood, and some part-blood—and each group had its own reason for keeping their fingers in the agency's business. Much of the trouble was about the rights of tribal members to sell or lease land. There were significant monies to be made by whoever gained the upper hand in these affairs, and I was caught in the middle.

Jessie was a stalwart force of support, listening to the gossip and complaints of various members of my staff, which I refused to do. She worried that the two sides would join forces to end my career, but I'd been clear to the bureau that I wouldn't tolerate threats nor be forced into the loss of my pension. There was no evidence of misappropriations, and I had a number of connections in Washington who would attest to my work record and conduct.

The stress of it all gave Jessie severe headaches. She took frequent rest breaks from her duties at the post office each day, which angered her superior. Keeping up with the needs of a household of six added to her issues, but if she gave up her position, we would be forced to choose between paying either the tutor or the nanny as I was unable to cover both salaries from my own. Jessie would have been required to take on the responsibilities of whichever we let go, leaving her quite possibly more stressed every day.

In the best interest of the Cherokee, and to escape what was rapidly becoming an untenable situation, I recommended that Mr. Peavis, superintendent of Indian education, direct the transfer of not only myself but of every individual involved in the infighting as well. It was the only way to clean up the corruption that had evidently carried over through several administrations. I requested a transfer to any school near my beloved Pine Ridge.

Uncle Curtis had made a significant fortune in real estate and agreed to advance me the funds to send Jessie and the children to join my sister Margaret and her husband, Donald, in Denver. Margaret yearned for children to care for. They'd moved to Denver and purchased a large home in the Edgewood community after the silver crash. Donald had been remarkably successful in multiple food-processing ventures but not equally successful at producing children of their own, and their house echoed with emptiness. It would be a wonderful setting for my family until I could establish myself in a new position.

Margaret found an opening at a small parochial school for Liz. My daughter loved to write poetry and was especially good at putting funny stories to rhyme. She no longer played the piano or organ but wrote to me that she hoped to find a nice pony in Colorado. I encouraged her to take formal riding lessons because Margaret had noted that my daughter was a crybaby and needed to stop pouting and hiding in her room. I knew

Margaret would spoil her if Jessie allowed, but I felt time with others in a riding arena and caring for her pony would build Liz's confidence and stamina. I was thankful for the opportunities a growing city might provide.

Ralph, James, and Charles, my rowdy three musketeers, would have a governess. Mrs. Cooper had declined moving yet again, so Margaret found a widow woman in Denver, Frau Lauxman, who sounded quite suitable for the position. She was well educated, spoke very proper English, and was of a stout constitution and stern manner. She oversaw the boys on a daily basis and tutored them in arithmetic, English, reading, and writing to prepare them to join Liz at school in the future. This allowed Jessie time to rest and decide whether she wanted to join me on my mission to serve the Indian people near Pine Ridge.

As I was adamant I wouldn't accept a disability severance, I sent word to a professional associate that I was willing to relocate immediately; it mattered not whether it was in heirship work, funds disbursement, or as superintendent of an agency, even directing an educational program at a larger school if he knew of any openings. He sent a wire that they'd been notified that the young man recently sent to serve as superintendent at Fort Berthold in Elbowoods had vacated his post unexpectedly. I was suggested as a candidate for the position and notified to report posthaste to assume the duties.

I requested authority to ship all my household belongings, such as books, music, dishes, and clothing, by freight on a government bill of lading so that I could travel unencumbered to my new position. The office agreed to cover the cost from available funds in support of my rapid arrival. Mr. Dixon advised me that I had also been designated a special disbursing agent, so I forwarded bond along with the appropriate signature cards to Clark and Sons in New York.

I heard nothing of the transfer of any other persons from Cherokee, so I had to be thankful for taking my leave so quickly. I missed my family immediately but was sure they were adjusting happily to life *not* on an Indian reservation. I prayed every day that Jessie, if not my entire family, could join me at Fort Berthold, but she was content in Denver and unwilling to return to work. She knew she'd be the beneficiary of my pension when I passed on.

Liz with Little Dog's wife

A sunny afternoon reading in the crooked elm

CHAPTER 52

FIRE!

Fall 1901

Medicine Root Creek, Pine Ridge Reservation, South Dakota

John and Stella frequently drove the trader's wagon over to Potato Creek to visit Moves First in the cabin she'd shared with Iron Horse and her sister. It was about sixteen miles, and John insisted Stella ride in the back on a mound of quilts for the baby's safety. He enjoyed renewing relationships with some of the families in the camp, and Stella was interested in spending time where her husband had made his first memories as an Iron Horse. He showed her the creek bank where he and Annie once sat and practiced their lessons, always speaking English out of earshot of his mothers. He also took her to the dance house and shared details of the feast and storytelling he remembered from the night he was adopted.

One afternoon, John sat chatting with a young man she didn't recognize; he took every opportunity to seek information on the fate of his beloved Hantaywee. Stella strolled towards the day school where John had attended classes from Carter Heath. The school had apparently been abandoned for several years; the red paint was faded and chipped, the front door hung ajar, and birds darted past her head when she disturbed them as she entered. There was neither a rope nor a bell in the belfry, and the floors creaked as she stepped into what had been the boys' classroom. The chalkboards hung crooked on the walls, and the long, hard benches that had been the only seating for countless students stood in tumbled disarray about the room. A few old books lay tattered and torn on the floor, their pages flipping back and forth with the breeze wafting through the open windows.

John had told her stories of Lillian's beautiful beds of flowers and herbs, of the chicken coops and the barn and root cellar. Grasses and flowers grew all around the base of the building with the same abandon they grew on the prairie when it rained, but Stella found no trace of the rock borders that had defined Mrs. Heath's beds. The roof of the coop had fallen in, and much of the wood had been stripped from the sides of the barn.

The former shop consisted of nothing more than poles cut or broken at varying lengths, most likely for firewood for the local families. A few board remnants dangled from what had once been the walls where tools had hung, neatly cared for. Not a tool or table or bench remained, and not a single cedar shake that the boys' classes had diligently made could be seen lying in the yard, let alone on the collapsing roof. Stella dared not venture through the crumbling roof of the root cellar for fear a rattler might have made a bed there, and above the corrals, she found only ruts and eroded soil, remnants of the pasture stream after several years of drought.

Finally, Stella decided it was time for John to walk with her up the hillside to visit Annie's grave. He had refused on previous visits but agreed that, with the birth of his own child approaching, it was finally time. Holding hands, they ambled slowly, giving John time to absorb every detail as they approached. He thought he remembered where she should be, but the land had changed. There were no mounds, no markers, only slight indentations in the soil. It was clear no one was tending the final resting places of Annie, Iron Horse, and Good Heart. John sat down, his face in his hands. Stella placed hers lovingly on his shoulders from behind, supporting him as he grieved the loss of his family.

"It was not their belief to be memorialized with statues," John commented. "I hold their memories in my heart."

Then, he stood and pointed towards the butte where Iron Horse had stationed himself high above the camp to make announcements or to stand in solitude to reflect on events in their lives. "I believe Iron Horse's spirit rests there," John finally whispered, "and that he still looks over us today. I feel his presence."

Stella reached her arm about his waist, pulling him closer, and added, "I too feel a presence of peace here. I did not know your father, but I know he loved you and that his spirit stays with you."

With each visit they made to Moves First's home, Stella grew distressed by what she saw. On their first visit, they'd found no furnishings other than the dilapidated cookstove and the decrepit remains of the kitchen table of John's childhood. If he noticed the lack of amenities, it didn't show, for he was more concerned with the uncovered windows and broken door hanging loosely on its leather hinges. With winter fast approaching, his mother would be cold. Stella strolled around the cabin, mentally noting things she felt they could address.

At first, she dedicated herself to bringing some source of comfort or cleanliness to her mother-in-law's home. She insisted John walk down to the old schoolhouse and gather any wood that could be repurposed in the cabin. While he did that, she found a deteriorating stick broom and set about whisking dead leaves and dried grass stems from every corner. As she worked, she prattled like a magpie, knowing Moves First had no idea what she was saying but that chatter was normal for two women in a household. The elderly lady sat quietly beside the cookstove, holding her hands towards the meager fire John had built. When the couple prepared to leave, she grasped Stella's hands, nodding wordlessly and smiling her thanks.

The next time they came, John brought tools from Mr. Lawson's shop and set about repairing the door and making new shutters using wooden parts and pieces he brought from the school. He escorted his mother out the door to a thick pallet of blankets so she could rest and nap in the afternoon sunshine as he and Stella worked. On this day, he genuinely appreciated his years of carpentry lessons as he crafted two new chairs for his mother from the old school benches. He'd become a skilled craftsman, and the seats were sturdy as well as beautiful in their simplicity. Stella bundled the remaining blankets from the house and carried them far enough that the breeze couldn't blow dust back towards the cabin, then shook them vigorously and laid them out to be disinfected by the rays of the sun.

On another trip, Stella carried dainty curtains she'd fashioned from one of her old dresses. She'd rediscovered the delicate, flowery thing in the bottom of the tin trunk and realized immediately that it wasn't suitable to wear through the winter. Besides, with her increasing girth, she doubted she'd ever fit into it again. Once the uncomplicated design was complete, she ran heavy thread through the pocket at the top. John drove tiny nails above the corners of each window, and Stella tied off the thread, drawing her fingers lovingly down the fabric and smoothing the wrinkles and kinks until the curtains hung smoothly to cover the now shuttered spaces. Memories of the last time she'd worn the dress, in the gym with John, lingered until she remembered whose house she was caring for and thought about how much she owed the old woman for saving John's life.

No matter how much they did in the cabin each trip, Stella was invariably disappointed to find it cluttered and unkempt on their return.

She had the same experience in many of the homes on Medicine Root Creek. The Indians always seemed glad for her to visit. The younger ones with whom she could actually converse appreciated the attention she paid to their babies and understood her discomfort from her pregnancy. She showed them how to shake out their blankets as she had done those at Moves First's, clouds of dust rising from the flapping fabrics. She bought new corn brooms for several households with her earnings from Mrs. Lawrence and showed them how to sweep away the grit that seemed an ever-present part of living so close to nature. But upon her return she always found conditions as they'd been before. She couldn't comprehend their hopeless acceptance of their lives.

Following one of their visits, John seemed overwhelmed with the sordidness there. Stella had found his mother's home more disordered and ill kept than usual. As John turned the team towards the trader's home, she leaned awkwardly to rest against the sides of the wagon. Her shoulders slumped with despair, and she lamented, "John, what are we doing wrong that we can't convince them to strive for the same cleanliness we seek? Neither of us can work any harder, yet we don't seem to be making any difference."

"Not any, Stella, you're right. I'm finally coming to understand why Carter and my father were so resolute that we not come back to the reservation. They knew the Indians could do no better. Nor could white people under the same conditions. No one can. To have hope of a change brings courage. To have seen nothing change except for the worse and to face hopelessness day after day has paralyzed our people," her husband rejoined as he realized it was time to make peace with his father's and Annie's spirits and decide what he was going to do for his living family.

"I sometimes wish we were back home," she stated.

"We're almost there," he mumbled, deep in thought.

"No, John!" Stella said impatiently. "I don't mean there. I mean back at our true home with the Halls. The home where we plan to spend our future."

"Whoa," John said, pulling the wagon to a stop. Turning to face his wife, he looked deeply into her eyes before asking, "Stella, are you sure that's what you want? I know that Iron Horse is with me in spirit no matter where I choose to live. Annie encouraged me to be like Carter Heath and make changes. When we get back to the trader's, I'll count our savings carefully. You're in no condition to travel by stagecoach, and I know there isn't enough for two train tickets to Massachusetts yet. We'll need to find ways to conserve or to make additional money."

Stella thought back to all the trivial things she'd bought to help the families she'd been visiting. It was never much, and she enjoyed giving, feeling she was making a difference. John had enjoyed celebrating his visits with the elders of the tribe by sharing tobacco in the tradition of his father. They hadn't stopped to consider that each penny spent was one less to pay for their return home. They'd been thankful to find jobs and felt confident in their own abilities.

Turning once more towards their current home and staring briefly at his hands on the reins, he replied quietly, "But if you want to leave as soon as possible and think we should, we'll plan to leave here in time to be home on Christmas day. I'll write to Mr. Hall and ask for the money for our tickets to be advanced against my salary when we return."

Understanding her husband's desire to provide everything she'd ever asked for and knowing it would hurt his pride terribly to ask for money, Stella responded emphatically, "Oh, John, I didn't intend to let my feelings go so far. It was a selfish thought. The baby's strong, and I'm healthy and active. We'll save more carefully and return home as soon as possible."

At her words, John's shoulders slumped further, and Stella realized the pain he'd felt in admitting he was unable to provide for his family.

Pulling herself up from her seat on the blankets, she hugged him tightly and whispered, in an attempt to sound brave, "There's still much work to be done, and Mrs. Roacher depends on me."

Taking hope from her words, John replied, "I feel as you do, wifekin. If we're going back east, we must make plans and ensure our obligations to the Roachers are fulfilled. I'll let Mr. Roacher know he'll need to find another employee to take charge of the cattle. And I'll send a letter to Mr. Hall to let him know we'll be returning soon."

"Let's make our plans carefully," Stella replied. "Perhaps you can find extra work on one of the other ranches. All the cattle must be moved closer to their homes as winter approaches. I'll watch our spending carefully and not be so generous with the Indian families. Between us, we should be able to increase our savings."

"We'll wait," John said fatefully as they drove onto the ridge from which they could see Medicine Root Creek, their thoughts and conversation turning to things that would soon become unimportant.

Two days later, as John and Mr. Roacher were riding home for the evening, his employer remarked, "We need to watch that smoke to the north, John. It looks like a prairie fire. It's still a long ways off, but it's been burning since morning. That's the vicinity of Jack Lambert's ranch, and it may be they're burning off their hay meadows. The prairie's awfully dry, and a stiff wind could cause the fire to burn out of control."

"Yeah," replied John, "I've been watching it all day. I believe it's a prairie fire. Although there isn't much more smoke than there was this morning, it's moved considerably to the south. What will you do with the cattle if it comes this way?"

"I don't know," acknowledged the rancher. "I've been wondering that myself. They'll have to be taken out of the pasture, but we can't turn them loose on the prairie. Perhaps we'll burn a fireguard if the wind allows. That way, if the fire comes towards us, we can turn the cattle into the big corral until it passes or burns itself out."

As they went to bed that night, they each took a last look at the ominous glow in the sky to the northwest. When they arose in the darkness of early morning, they hurried outside to look again. The glow had grown to a more intense red, and by daylight the single column of smoke had extended into a long, thin veil that trailed to the south and hung heavily along the horizon.

"If the wind doesn't increase, the fire may burn itself out against the trail to Porcupine Creek," suggested Mr. Roacher as they watched the fire before going in for breakfast. "But I believe we ought to get help and burn some fireguards."

After breakfast, they saddled several horses. While John hitched the others to the lumber wagon holding three barrels of water from the creek, Mr. Roacher walked to the agency office to confer with the superintendent about burning a series of fireguards around the little community. Unfortunately, the man was one of those who didn't take suggestions from others in a kindly way. Brashly, he told Mr. Roacher he thought they had plenty of time to plan for fighting the fire if it headed their way. He wasn't a plainsman or he'd have known better. When Mr. Roacher saw him ride away an hour later, he knew they couldn't depend on his help.

Later that morning, Mr. Roacher and John, assisted by a passing drover, set back fires against the trail that ran along the creek. By midday they'd succeeded in burning a strip three or four miles long and wide enough that there was little danger of the fire jumping it. While it would help, it afforded them no protection from their greatest danger, which was along the creek itself, where the growth was so heavy and dry there was no way to burn a fireguard.

By midafternoon, it was clear the fire had grown. They could estimate the location of the fire itself by watching the smoke. Finally, Mr. Roacher called to John, "This guard will give us somewhere to fight from if the fire gets to us. I think we'd better get the cattle out of the pasture and into the big corral. I'm afraid we'll have fire all around us by morning. Every man, woman, and child should be burning fireguards the entire length of the creek, but the superintendent rode away, leaving the district with no one in charge. The Indians won't leave unless he orders them to. This is frightening, John. I say we quit worrying about others and try to save what we can of our own."

They rode to the pasture and rounded up the cattle. By sundown, they were safely in the corral where they could reach the hay and get water from the creek that flowed through a corner of the enclosure.

"The cattle won't need anything else for now," remarked Mr. Roacher as they fastened the logs that secured the entrance. "But it's the worst place in the world for them if the fire gets into the heavy brush along the creek."

They abandoned their plan to extend the fireguard as the wind grew stronger. Their manpower was limited. "I see no chance but that it'll be with us before morning," predicted Mr. Roacher, watching the bright-red glow in the dark. "The only chance is that the wind might change. We'll leave the horses harnessed and ready for an emergency. I wish we had more help."

"I'll ride through the camps and see what I can do," announced John, running towards the stable. He rode the area between the local schools, warning the families to beware of changes in the fire. When he returned, he found Mr. Roacher still watching the northwestern sky. With him were two drovers who'd arrived from Jack Lambert's ranch, where lightning had started the fire two days before. They told how every man had helped fight it, but now it was completely out of control. They shared that it'd already burned a wide stretch of prairie and crossed the trail leading to Porcupine Creek. They volunteered to stay with the Roachers for the night, certain the fire would reach them before morning. Together, the four men agreed the best plan would be to station themselves along the creek trail with water and wet sacks to whip the fire out.

As they prepared, the day school teacher, the missionary who lived up the creek, and two Indians from the nearby camp arrived to help. They gathered in front of the store and watched the fire creep over the tops of the distant hills. Knowing there was nothing more to be done for now and that the evening chill would get even more uncomfortable, the men went inside and rolled themselves in blankets on the floor around the woodstove to get a good night's sleep. Stella and Mrs. Roacher stacked whatever fabric items they could find nearby to use as sacks to fight the fire.

The following morning, John and Mr. Roacher donned their heaviest coats and went out to watch the oncoming fire. The line of flames extended several miles as it topped the distant ridge, and if the wind held as it was, it would be even wider by the time it reached them. They beheld the great sinuous fire rolling towards them with the awe and fear that fire on the prairie brings to the heart of a plainsman. There was a savage beauty in the color and size of the blaze, but Mr. Roacher knew it was a portent of disaster. Behind such a fire lay devastation over an expanse of prairie larger than many cities.

Ahead of the flames, the prairie was clothed in a rich mantle of native grasses, beautiful in the soft browns of their winter coloring. But that tinder burned hot, leaving the beauty and every living thing in the path of the flames in danger of total destruction. Everyone who gathered to fight the fire was aware that large herds of cattle were scattered over the vast grasslands. The men feared that as the animals sought to escape the danger, they'd drift into the corners of multiple strands of barbed wire fencing, where they'd stand in helpless fear until the fire caught them. After the fire passed, they'd be found wandering around the blackened wastes in an agony of seared bodies and sightless eyes and would have to be put out of their misery.

Standing transfixed, the two men saw the first forked tongue of flames lick over the ridge. They watched it advance along the slope that led into their valley and march across an area carpeted with low-lying buffalo grass, where it moved from one clump of thickly matted bunch grass to another in bursts of radiance.

They turned towards the store to rouse the others as the first, faint light of day emerged in the east. Mr. Roacher deployed the other men along the road to the south. He hoped they could fight any side fires that came up the trail. Another group of Indians from nearby camps arrived to help. As the sun rose, John and Mr. Roacher recognized a new danger as they felt the wind begin to shift direction. All the men worked persistently, beating down the dry grass along the trail with water-soaked bags and towels. Mrs. Roacher drove the wagon up and down the line for the fighters to saturate the sacks over and over, and at noon, she and Stella delivered hot coffee and a substantial meal to the men.

As the day advanced, it was evident the wind was changing to the west. The fire burned more fiercely, fanned by wind, and the trail offered less and less protection for the settlement. It was only a matter of time; all they could hope for was to keep it from catching the thick growths along the creek until it was as far south as possible.

Just as John and Mr. Roacher returned to the line after having a drink of water, the two drovers came racing back, yelling, "It's no use, Dick. The fire's crossed the trail in a hundred places ahead of us, and the creek bottom's burning."

"All right, there's only one thing to do," Mr. Roacher called out to his wife. "Drive along the line and tell the men to go try to save their own homes." Turning to John, he added, "We must get back to the house, John, for it won't take the fire long to run down the creek. In fact, if the wind changes again, it might beat us back."

They raced for the store, but to their consternation, when they gained the top of the rise, they spotted a sinister, wedge-shaped trail of black from the road to the creek bottom. The fire had already grown considerably and was burning fiercely between them and the barns and corrals.

As his wife caught up with them in the wagon, Mr. Roacher jumped on and grabbed the reins from her hands. John hopped onto the back and shoved the water barrels off. Dick whipped the horses to a gallop, determined to release the cattle from the corral if they had time. Although there was an expanse of bare ground around the corral that would offer some protection, the wind carried burning fragments that would light additional fires everywhere they landed.

As the two men hurried to the corral, they saw flames leaping from the thick, tangled growth along the creek less than a quarter mile away. They removed the heavy logs from the entrance as glowing sparks shot through the air above, working desperately as the fire moved towards them with incredible speed. When the last log was moved, they raced into the corral, shouting, jumping, and flapping their arms and legs in an attempt to drive the cattle out. Tragically, the fear that fire brings to dumb animals was already strong in the herd. Rather than run, they stood huddled against the wall of the corral farthest from the fire. The men were afoot, and the cattle were accustomed to being driven by someone on horseback. All efforts to move them were futile. As the flames leaped closer, the cattle stampeded against the corral in a frenzy. The ones closest to the wall went down while those in the back surged forward, climbing on top of others that were already standing on fallen ones. Their bellowing and the roar of the inferno made communication among the men impossible.

Finally, John, Mr. Roacher, and the two drovers ran to escape the searing heat. The tops of the haystacks were ablaze, and flames whipped and shot all around the gate. Realizing there was little hope of escape through the opening, the men tried to scale the wall of the corral on the other side. Just as John reached the top, Mr. Roacher lost his footing and crashed backward, landing with a thud in the center of the corral. John jumped down and ran to where the fallen man lay with flames roaring close above him. He lifted the unconscious form over his shoulders and started back for the gate. Despite the raging fire, it was his only path to get himself and the man out of the inferno. He crouched low and plunged through the opening, running towards a point where he was finally visible to the others outside the corral. He carefully laid Mr. Roacher away from the flames before collapsing into unconsciousness himself. The drovers extinguished their burning clothes and carried them into the house.

Mrs. Roacher immediately began to care for her husband as Stella tended likewise to John. She cut his charred boot from one foot, and as she gingerly removed his trousers, a long, narrow strip of skin peeled from his leg with the garment, exposing the quivering flesh beneath and sending John quickly back into unconsciousness.

Meanwhile, the cattle breached the corral wall in one last, frantic surge. Most escaped to the blackened prairie beyond, but fifty or so lay where they had been trampled to death or suffocated in the great pile. Suddenly, a gust of wind whipped the flames directly towards the shingled roof of the store. The remaining men, white and Indian alike, formed a line, passing the store contents from person to person to a place of relative safety near the house. They kept working, even when the entire building caught fire, for these were food goods and items that might help them all get through the winter. As they removed the last of the goods, blazing pieces of the roof began dropping to the floor beneath, and soon all that remained of the building was smoldering rubble.

Dusk fell across the remains of the store, the corral, and the seared prairie beyond while the fire burned into the distance. It would eventually be extinguished by passing thunderstorms. After thanking everyone who'd come to help, the drovers entered Mrs. Roacher's kitchen, looking closely at one another for the first time all day. Slowly, wide grins split their faces, and a sparkle of amusement appeared in their eyes. Their faces were blackened with soot and smoke so that only their teeth and eyes showed white, and their lips were parched and cracked. Mrs. Roacher thanked them profusely, not just for fighting the fire but also for saving supplies that might prove invaluable in the near future. They brushed aside her thanks, joking briefly with each other to distract from their pain.

"Ramsey, if you're not a black man, I'm a pure-blooded redskin."

To which the other replied, laughing, "If you're not blacker than me, I must be as white as a fresh snow in January." Remembering those more seriously injured, they both turned to inquire, "Mrs. Roacher? How are Dick and the young Indian doing?"

"I'm not sure, but it's bad, boys," answered Mrs. Roacher. "Dick is unconscious, but I'm sure he has more injuries than just the burns. John is suffering such pain that he's out of his head, moaning and thrashing madly. Stella has tied his hands to the bed rails but has no idea how to treat the raw, open skin on his leg. We need a doctor desperately, but the telegraph line to the agency must have been destroyed by the fire. I can't reach anyone."

"Mrs. Roacher," comforted Ramsey, the taller of the drovers, "there's nothing I'd rather do than ride to the agency right now. I'll get the doctor here if I have to hog-tie him and ride my pony double. I was just telling Red that I feel the need of some light exercise, and it's only forty-five miles to the agency." He smiled and winked as he spoke, trying to make light of the situation.

Mrs. Roacher could not restrain a chuckle, but she answered, "Ramsey, I hate to think of your doing it, but it may be a matter of life or death. I'll get you some supper before you start."

A short while later, Ramsey nonchalantly rolled a cigarette, mounted his horse, and shouted, "So long, Red" before galloping hard into the night. He reached the agency in the early-morning hours, threw open the unsecured door of the doctor's quarters, lit the lamp that sat ready by the bed, and shook the sleeping man vigorously. "Hey, Doc, wake up!" to which the doctor rolled over and muttered, "Do I have to?"

Ramsey jerked back the covers, picked the doctor up, and stood him upright on his feet in the middle of the room. "What's the big idea?" asked the doctor, slipping his feet into a well-worn pair of slippers.

"We've got to get to Medicine Root now," replied Ramsey. "There was a fire, and two men are burned badly. They need you." With a smile wrinkling his blackened cheeks, Ramsey jested, "Of course, if you go nice and easy, it'll be better, but you're going one way or another."

When the doctor finished gathering what he thought he'd need, he found Ramsey draped across a chair in his living room, his head hanging heavily to one side, sound asleep. He opened his medical kit, applied a soothing ointment to the burns on the drover's face, then carefully removed the man's shoes and outer clothing and placed him on the bed. Never once did Ramsey rouse from his exhausted sleep.

After banking the fire in the stove, the doctor grabbed his medical bag, extinguished the lamp, and headed out the door. He'd been on the reservation long enough to know the trails, so he threw the harness on his team and hitched them to the wagon, heading out on the most direct path to Medicine Root. He'd soon have daylight to help him find the way.

It was still a long and agonizing night for Mr. Roacher and John Iron Horse. Mr. Roacher drifted between awareness and complete unconsciousness while his wife applied cooling compresses to the burns on his face and hands. John stayed awake most of the time and watched as Stella wrapped the raw skin of his leg with a poultice Mrs. Roacher had given her. At that, he again lost consciousness from the pain. His last thought was how much he wished his wife had been able to learn more about the plant medicines his mothers had used, for he was certain there were several pain relievers among their remedies.

CHAPTER 53

Carter's Journal

Winter 1901 to Spring 1902

Fort Berthold Reservation, Elbowoods, North Dakota

Thirty-two hundred dollars a year! It was a long way from where I'd started as a teacher. I also had a travel allowance and hoped by spring to feel the joy of being astride a quality horse to travel as necessary on the reservation.

Once again, though, I found myself surrounded by the inefficiency and waste of bureaucracy at its worst. Having arrived at Fort Berthold, I determined my first duty was to set the boys to repairing broken and abandoned beds. It was ridiculous that boys were sleeping two to a bed in the dormitories while so many in need of minor repairs rested in the dump piles. I also found an extraordinary shortage of clothing, books, and medical supplies and planned to rectify these deficiencies as quickly as possible. The girls were perfectly capable of remedying the clothing needs once their teachers were admonished for not putting them to these tasks prior. I penned requests to Commissioner Rhoades and Mr. Peavis of the bureau as well as to Senator Cameron. Although much of the need was caused by poor management on the part of the school staff, I wrote numerous letters to ensure the delivery of sufficient materials for the efficient and effective operation of this institution.

In addition to the shortages, there was significant illness among the students as well as the staff, with countless cases of bronchitis and the hacking cough of those infected echoing down the halls. It was little wonder there'd been so much illness; life at Fort Berthold had evidently been run according to a strict military regimen for some time. The schedule posted by the former superintendent revealed there were eight roll calls with inspection for the students daily, beginning at 5:45 each morning and ending at 9 each night. Daily conduct reports were kept for each and every student. Among those reports, I found records of forced outdoor marches that were assigned to all children if any individual chose not to adhere to the code of conduct. The marches appeared to have been assigned regardless of the season or weather, including on several sub-zero winter days. From the same records, I derived there had been a number of runaways each week. It was little wonder, and I was incensed.

As to the education provided for the Indians, the children experienced far more forced labor than academics. I discovered the boys mined coal, dug wells, cut wood, and painted the school buildings as part of their training. The girls performed all the duties needed to run the kitchen, dining halls, and laundry as well as sewing all the fabric items needed by the school. They sewed aprons, towels, sheets, and window curtains and regularly made, for sale, bonnets that were popular among the white women in town. Proceeds from the sales supposedly went back to the school, but I could find no evidence the monies had been used to purchase food or necessities for the students.

I certainly considered all the skills being taught valuable, but I didn't consider them marketable for jobs that would lead to successful lives off the reservation. It was clear that what I considered the vocational portion of the curriculum had barely operated for some time. It should have included skills that were marketable to the communities around the reservation, such as carpentry, ironworking, and livestock management.

Mr. Shipe, assistant director of field services, sent funding for me and the agricultural instructors to attend the Mid-Winter Fair at Poplar, Montana, and mandated our attendance. He went so far as to require attendance by our extension supervisors as well, including sending a carbon of the order to the extension director for emphasis, so that they would also be up to date on the latest techniques and expectations for our teaching the Indians about farming. He instructed me to spend as much time as possible with the Indian farmers so that I could determine how many were leasing land off the reservation and to ensure that farm implements and stock were not traded for whiskey.

By reading over records that had been boxed for storage, I learned the facility had a history of intestinal disorders among the Indians, as well as pneumonia and tuberculosis, including the deaths of numerous children. The climate might have been partially to blame for the pneumonia. However, since the Indians had been living in the area for some time, I believed it to be more related to a lack of sanitation and insufficient nutrition. I understood that few of the ration cattle survived the Montana winters if they arrived at all. There had to be a way to dry the meat to preserve it for use over the winter without it becoming leathery and inedible.

I investigated the procedures in use by our farmers to see if there was any reason for insufficient food at the school. I also reviewed the budget to determine if a reassignment of funds would free up monies that could be used for the purchase of needed equipment. It might increase the harvest both at the school and for the families of the reservation if the lending of the equipment was meticulously organized and recorded.

I was remiss in communicating both with my family and John and could only hope that all was well. Liz wrote regularly, sometimes including a poem about things she thought important.

> The White Pony
> Here in Denver where we live
> There's a beautiful house where we stay
> We go to school and then to the park
> And find wonderful places to play
> But my brothers are mean to me all of the time
> And my father lives with the Shoshone
> I wish he would come to punish these boys
> And bring me a beautiful pony.

I knew I was missing important milestones in my children's lives. I could only hope that by this last year of his program, John would be well established in the East—if not with the Halls, then with another successful business of his choosing. I thought about the possibility that he'd decided to become a teacher at Carlisle, a choice that had brought me immense joy in the past. I should have written to him more often, but my duties were strenuous, and there was much to be done.

CHAPTER 54

Healing

Winter 1901 to Spring 1902

Pine Ridge Reservation, South Dakota

Dick Roacher couldn't leave his bed for two months after the fire. The doctor determined his spine was damaged by his fall from the corral and put him in a body cast flat on his back for the entire time. The doctor initially held out little hope that Dick would walk again. He advised the Roachers, as well as John and Stella, to wait patiently until nature did what only nature could do.

John's injuries were uglier but less serious. His face was severely burned, and for a time Stella feared he'd be permanently disfigured. His lower leg and foot were useless for several weeks, but his recovery progressed until the doctor determined the disability wouldn't be permanent. Healing would take time, but as soon as he was able, John hobbled around the yard, assisting with everyday chores despite his leg and foot not being fully healed.

Once the doctor removed the cast from Mr. Roacher's spine, he was able to reassure the man that there was a good chance for a full recovery—warning him, though, that his progress would be slow. People from surrounding ranches and nearby Indian camps organized the goods from the burned-out store and placed them in a vacant building near the superintendent's office. Cattle owners gathered their animals into one great herd and drove them to a portion of the prairie that hadn't burned. Each ranch agreed to take turns caring for them until spring, when it would be possible for them to return to their home ranges.

John's leg healed gradually, requiring hours of stretching and messaging to keep the muscles from atrophying. He refused to accept payment for what little work he could do while Mr. Roacher was bedridden, and he and Stella saw their dream of returning to the Berkshires by Christmas fading away. As if conditions in the Roachers' three-room cabin were not crowded enough, an elderly Indian woman arrived on their doorstep with two children in the midst of one of the worst blizzards Mr. Roacher could remember. The woman was wizened and bent, and her grandchildren, a boy about eleven and a girl who couldn't have been more than five years old, were thin and pitiful. Her daughter had died recently of pneumonia, and their home had been destroyed by the fire. They'd been living with a family at Medicine Root until supplies ran low. When it became clear there wouldn't be enough food for everyone, the old lady and her grandchildren walked to the trader's store in hopes of finding food and a warm place to sleep.

No one had the heart to turn the family out, but the closeness of the living arrangements, the forced inactivity from the men's injuries, Stella's progressing pregnancy, and the harsh winter weather put a strain on everyone's emotions. As January drew to a close, Mr. Roacher was able to move about a little without assistance. He began to plan for the reconstruction of his store and the return of his cattle to their home range. He talked these plans over with John and seemed to take for granted that the young man would be on hand to assist.

On the first morning they ventured outdoors for a short walk, Mr. Roacher began a conversation as they headed back to the cabin. "John, my boy, it won't be long before we can begin hauling lumber for the new building. I hope we can have it completed by the time the grass is green enough for the cattle to return."

Listening to Mrs. Roacher and Stella at work in the kitchen, John dropped an armful of firewood beside the stove and turned to warm his backside. Just as Mr. Roacher lowered himself to the cot where he'd slept many nights, John shared a plan that distressed the older man greatly.

"Mr. Roacher," John said, "you know Stella and I planned to return east as soon as possible. Although it would be good for us to remain with you and Mrs. Roacher until we can make that trip, you can't deny there isn't room in this cabin for seven people. I know it'll be better when the weather warms and the children can go outside, but even then, there aren't enough beds. Stella's belly continues to grow rounder every day, and it's harder and harder for her to get around, especially in the cabin.

"It'll be a month or more before you can do anything towards rebuilding. You and Mrs. Roacher don't need us taking up space that can be used by others. And Stella is extremely uncomfortable. She doesn't want to complain, but she's not sleeping well, and her back hurts much of the day. We appreciate everything you've done and will always count you among our friends. The old lady is frail, but the children can help you with daily chores, and the three of them can share a bed. My wife and I have decided to move to Potato Creek with my mother, just for a month or so until I can secure the funds we need to return east."

Without replying directly to John, Mr. Roacher rose and called to his wife in a tone that suggested anger and astonishment mixed with no small amount of fear. As Mrs. Roacher came from the kitchen, he informed her, pointing at John, "Mother, do you know what they're planning?"

After hearing John's proposal, she declared, a pained expression on her face, "I've heard something of this from Stella, but I couldn't believe my ears. John, your plans are beyond reason! Don't you know that in Stella's condition this could be dangerous for her and the baby?"

"Yes, Mrs. Roacher, I realize that all you say is true, but Stella and I have agreed. You have a giving heart, but there's not enough room for all of us in your home. My wife and I have an alternative; the others do not. It will only be for a little while," he finished determinedly.

"Stella!" Mrs. Roacher called out, much like a mother would call her own child. "Come in here."

When Stella joined the group, Mrs. Roacher continued, vexed, "Surely, Stella, you don't mean to do as you and John are suggesting and go to Potato Creek now. Child, can't you see what it might mean to you?"

"Yes, Mrs. Roacher," replied Stella firmly. "I've thought about it a great deal. You helped us through the winter and John's injuries, but you have three more people to care for. I'll be unable to do anything but care for myself, and we'll be getting ready to travel back east just when you're needing help the most. You and Mr. Roacher have been exceedingly kind to us, but you'll be busy rebuilding your own lives and don't need to worry with John and I."

Not giving up, Mrs. Roacher retorted, "Surely you've seen how wretchedly John's mother lives. It'll be impossible for you to be comfortable there. She has practically nothing, and I believe you'll be taking an unwarranted risk by going to the camp."

"I know she has little, but I was hoping you might be willing to let us take a few things from the store," Stella pleaded. "Just enough to make the place comfortable for a little while. We'll return to the Halls' as soon as possible. John's written for an advance against his salary to purchase tickets out of Rushton. The rains will end in plenty of time for us to make the trip before the baby's born. I'm healthy and strong from my work over the winter, and there's a nurse in the camp if I need her. John and I will leave the reservation as soon as we're able."

She tried to end the evening's discussion with confidence. Shrugging and smiling, she stated, "We don't plan on staying until the baby's born, but if that happens, it's done every day. I don't see why I should be the exception. Other women have their babies in the camp and get along very well. It's John's home, and his mother is there. We'll be fine."

"But, child," Mrs. Roacher declared, "there's such a difference! They're Indians, and they live there all the time. Conditions are harsh, and the doctor isn't always close by. A young girl who's taken nursing isn't the same as a nurse. If you insist on going, you must promise you'll send for me if you even think you might need help."

"We'll be comfortably with the Halls in a few weeks, but of course, if anything happens, I'll send for you," Stella consoled her, "and knowing you'll come makes me even more confident that everything will be okay."

The following day, the Roachers drove them to their new home. The lumber wagon was piled high with things their friends had insisted they glean from the trader's store. When the wagon pulled up to the low-built log house, the men off-loaded a number of extra blankets, a solid bed frame they'd built, a mattress filled with fresh straw, two newly crafted chairs, and several armloads of canned meats and fruit. It was a bright, warm morning that hinted it wouldn't be long before the summer heat parched the plains dry once more.

John's mother welcomed them warmly, kissing John's cheeks and then holding his hand tightly while patting his arm as if to reassure herself he was real. Then, she turned to Stella and hugged her tightly before laying her head against the young woman's belly with a smile, as if behind her clouded eyes her mind registered the sound of her grandchild's heartbeat. With plenty of sweeping, shaking, and dusting, Stella and John converted the simple quarters into a place of reasonable comfort.

One of the first evenings in their new home, after the old woman had retired to her pallet in the corner, John and Stella sat near the cookstove and spoke quietly. Cracks in the stove allowed light from the fire John had stoked to filter out and soften the room's crudeness with flickering shadows. Sitting side by side before the stove, the couple reflected on the year that had gone before and pondered the future that lay ahead. In muted tones, they found bits of humor in the trials and disappointments and laughingly admitted the wealth of experience and friendships they'd gained. Most of all, they shared their anticipation to return to their real home in the Berkshires, imagining all the projects they and the Halls would begin as soon as they arrived.

John pondered aloud, "Just think, wifekin, we'll be riding through the peach orchards, counting our fruit, or bringing a new crop of calves to the barn this time next year. But for now, we're in this predicament, and I'm sorry to have once again allowed my pride to lead me into a foolish decision. I felt sure we'd be able to save enough money for the train, but we couldn't have known about the fire. I didn't watch from all sides as my father taught me."

"Please, John, don't degrade yourself," Stella admonished him. "I'm sure this time spent with your mother will be an experience we look back on with joy. I'm content. We're comfortable, and even though I wouldn't look forward to an entire life like this, I feel sure that our being here is for the best. We'll be on our way as soon as the money comes from Mr. Hall and the sun dries the trails."

Placing his arm around her shoulder and gently patting her swollen belly with the other hand, John murmured, "Wifekin, you remind me of that wise, gentle man who once lived in this cabin. Like him, you see the good in all things and reassure those around you that whatever happens is always as it should be."

"But it's from your strength," she returned, "that I've gained my faith that such is so."

CHAPTER 55

Passages

Spring 1902

Potato Creek, Pine Ridge Reservation, South Dakota

The last dreary days of February gave way to the blustery days of March. John regretted not going to the agency to wire his request to Mr. Hall rather than sending a letter. He tried to have faith the funds would arrive any day and they'd be on their way. Stella reassured him the baby wasn't due for several more weeks, and she was enjoying the simplicity of their life on Potato Creek. She stayed active, making the little house more attractive with tiny touches of her own. Whether it was a bouquet of wildflowers in an old can on the table or a cross braided from strips of cedar bark and hung over the doorway, her efforts made the house more cheerful. Each day, John added to a pile of firewood he'd gathered from along the creek, hoping to provide for his mother's needs after they were gone.

Stella grew irritable when rain confined her inside the cabin for several days. On the first sunny day, they walked to the day school up the creek.

The couple currently assigned there, Mr. and Mrs. Marcus, had come to the Indian Service with a sense of pomposity rather than servitude. "Indian" was a word that stood for people in whom they had little interest except to look down on. They'd actually come seeking adventure and were quick to establish their superiority, at least in their own minds, by word and deed. Mr. Marcus looked at John with contempt when he heard John's clear enunciation of the English words of greeting. Mrs. Marcus didn't so far as offer a seat to Stella, nor a steaming cup of coffee to either guest, and made it clear she felt they were intruding into "her" world. The lack of warmth at the dwelling house ensured the couple's visit was brief.

As they walked back towards Potato Creek, John reflected on the place where he'd first encountered formal schooling and where he'd enjoyed his first intellectual triumph by mastering the white man's tongue and the written word. When they arrived at their cabin, Stella collapsed onto the bed, declaring the woman's arrogance had drained all her strength. John determined that as soon as they returned east, he would seek out his former teacher and renew the relationship that had given him a wealth of knowledge as well as wisdom.

The next morning, John checked again at the trader's store to see if funds had arrived by mail or wire. Upon his return, empty handed, he was greeted at the door by Stella asking him to bring a bucket of fresh, cool water from the creek. She looked pale, so he hurried to do her bidding. When he returned, Stella hadn't moved and stood propped against the doorway with a smile of relief tinged with suffering. She spoke softly, holding tightly to his hand.

"Husband, I think my time has come."

Setting the bucket on the bench he'd crafted from broken school desks, John drew her to him. Kissing her forehead reverently, he whispered, "Oh, wifekin, I am glad, And yet . . ."

"And yet?" she queried, taking a long, deep look into his eyes.

"And yet," he continued, "I feel so different than expected." After a pause, he smiled his peculiar, rare smile and finished, the smile spreading to a wide grin, "I think I'm afraid I'll miss the countless hours I've had you to myself."

"No, my husband, you won't have time to miss me, for soon I'll give you a little boy that we will share and love," she replied. "Now help me to the bed, my dear, and send for Lillie."

He hurried towards the camp, looking for messengers to send to Mrs. Roacher and Mrs. Moss. He summoned Lillie Lone Woman, who'd come back from the Indian School at Carlisle with some experience in nursing. When he returned, Stella met him at the door with a questioning smile, her brows knitted together in fear.

"Oh, John, I'm so glad you're back. I'm afraid."

A chill caused him to shudder. Wiping a trace of fear from his mind, he put his arms around her for support and led her back near the stove. "I'm here, wifekin mine, and will not leave your side again," he reassured her. Moves First had summoned an old Indian woman from a neighboring house who was skilled in the Indian practices of birthing, and soon Lillie Lone Woman arrived as well.

John sat stoically outside the door, waiting in an agony of suspense, seeing nothing and hearing nothing as he listened for the sound that did not come. The sun reached its zenith, pouring its warmth down on the cabin, but he was unable to find it comforting as he remembered the chill that had passed over him that morning. His mother offered a bowl of hot broth, but he shook his head, and she placed it on the bench by his side.

Stella sensed his presence as she advanced through the degrees of pain that accompany childbirth. She knew it was the tradition of the Indians not to cry out, so with respect for his people and her great love for him, she gave no sound that could reach him and cause concern. As the sun settled towards the horizon, John realized an entire day had almost passed, and suddenly he couldn't shake the fear from his mind. He looked to the west where Mrs. Roacher would come from Medicine Root, and then to the south where Mrs. Moss would arrive from Corn Creek. As the sun sank in the west and still they hadn't come, his worry grew.

At last, he heard the tremulous wail that told him his child had been delivered. He remained seated just outside the door, waiting, his fear growing. He dared not walk in on the women; he had not been summoned. As tension tightened every muscle, he waited for someone to come, to answer what he dared not ask. One of the women passed in and out of the door without saying a word. He looked for some assurance in their activity and allowed the faint wailing of the child to bring joy to his heart.

Suddenly, the pitiful crying stopped, and trepidation crept slowly back into his soul. Realizing he hadn't heard the sound of his wife's voice, John shivered as his stomach knotted with dread. The silence behind the closed door continued, adding to his growing unease. When his mother came out to gather more firewood, he questioned with a whisper, "Mother?"

The old woman replied simply, "She sleeps."

"And the child?" John added.

"She sleeps in her mother's arms."

At least he knew his child was alive. Looking towards the west once again, he saw a speck coming along the road from Medicine Root, but the shape was still a long way off. He prayed it was Mrs. Roacher and that all would be well. As he stared mindlessly at the moving speck, one word wormed its way into his consciousness. It was a word he'd heard without comprehending and which he'd temporarily pushed aside.

Suddenly, he realized his child was not a man to be called John as Stella had foretold, but a girl instead. Like Iron Horse in his younger years, John's first thought was the disappointment at having been denied a son. And then, he remembered once again the words "And tell him my spirit will always be with him." A feeling of calm passed over John as he thought, *Oh, Iron Horse, to have more of your goodness and faith!* He thought of the girls and women he'd known, the good old mother who had told him of the birth of his child, the gentle Annie who slept now beside her mother on the hill across the creek, and of his wife inside the house, who had just become a mother. With these comforting thoughts, a great peace settled on him, and he thought, *Yes, I am glad.*

He bowed his head as his mother stepped silently out to stand beside him. He was seized again, now with shivering and a sweat that seemed to stop his breathing and the beating of his heart. She placed her hand on his head, and in that touch, he felt all the tenderness of the woman's heart. He asked again in a voice that reflected his suffering, "How is she, Mother?"

She replied softly, "She sleeps, my son," then added after a pause, "in her long sleep."

John's head sank to his chest, and a dark numbness overcame him. He had no idea when Mrs. Roacher arrived and went inside, nor when she came out and took his hand in a gesture of compassion. He didn't feel when his mother came out again to sit beside him, stroking his hair and holding his face with a touch intended to soothe his pain. At last came the subdued murmur of their death chant and later the plaintive melody of their lament as they went up on the hill to share their grief.

As if from a distance, he heard the tentative cry of the tiny child again. With an expression of aversion mixed with distress, he entered the house, the dying light of the stove fire flickering across the still form lying on the bed. The newborn lay squirming in her mother's arms. Covering his face with both hands, John raced away from the scene, out the door and across the open land to the south.

When he gained the crest of the nearest ridge, he sat facing home, where his beloved lay in death. Engulfed with grief and anger, he lingered. At one point, he stood, his hands clenched into fists and a fierce expression on his face. Thinking he could hear the weak wail of the girl-child who had taken his wife from him, he lurched in the direction of the house; then, remembering the scene that awaited him there, he turned again to the south. As the distance grew between that place and himself, he stopped less frequently and squeezed his hands over his ears to silence the echoing words "And tell him my spirit will always be with him."

The eastern sky glowed with the first light of day when John staggered into the home of Aaron Moss on Corn Creek. It was clear Mrs. Moss hadn't received his message about Stella's labor, for they were seated comfortably, enjoying an early breakfast. They rose instantly and reached for John as he stumbled towards the table. He was pale and worn. His hair was disheveled, and his face showed lines of grief and despair. His dry lips parted, and his eyes glowed with anguish as he cried out brokenly, in agony, "Aaron, Aaron, she's gone away."

They guided him to sit and rest, but he shook his head. Aaron started, "John, we're so sorry. We were traveling on the other side of the reservation yesterday and didn't get your message until late last night. We heard only that Stella's labor had begun."

Mrs. Moss added as she cleared the table and reached for her shawl, "But it's clear we must go back with you this very minute. Hurry, Aaron, we must get to Potato Creek!" John rode silently beside the couple as the wagon bounced along. In his mind, it was the last time he would go to the place where he'd found immense happiness yet had lost his greatest joy.

As the miles passed, he determined he wouldn't look upon his beloved wife again, and when he left, he would leave her there—a sacrifice to the manipulations of those who pressed and coerced him to go back without caring what it cost him. He remembered his anger towards the young doctor who came to help Annie, recalling that even with the knowledge of the white man, the doctor had failed to help his beloved sister on the reservation. He remembered the nurses in the school infirmary where the shelves were stacked with clean, white bandages and bottles of medicine. He couldn't help but wonder if Stella would have lived had there been a doctor on the reservation.

A chill ran up his arms as he remembered the foreboding that had crept over both of them when they'd returned to the camp just a year ago. John found himself questioning every decision he'd made. Why hadn't he followed his father's long-ago admonition never to go back? Why couldn't he recognize the feeling as a message from Iron Horse's spirit?

He chided himself, *You certainly aren't much of a leader if you don't heed messages from the spirit world. Are you so arrogant that you can ignore the spirits' guidance?* And finally, he realized that he was going back to his mother's home with absolute proof that his people could never succeed until they learned not to go back to the meager life of the reservation.

CHAPTER 56

Lost

Spring 1902

Potato Creek, Pine Ridge Reservation, South Dakota

Late that afternoon, Stella was given to lie with the others on the hill across the creek. Those in attendance found some measure of comfort in knowing she'd be near gentle Annie and Good Heart and close by the man she had loved without ever knowing—a wonderful father and wise leader, Iron Horse. Aaron read the burial rites, his full voice deepened by the sadness he felt. In a way that everyone present could understand, he shared the spiritual lesson of life after death and the hope of seeing loved ones again in eternity. Not all those present had adopted his faith, but the words of comfort assured those left behind that Stella's spirit would be at peace.

It was clear to all once the service was over that John could take no more. As people wended their way sorrowfully from the place, he remained with her for yet a while, saying nothing and standing alone beneath the heavens. On the brow of the hill that had taken to itself so much from his life, he bowed his head in reverence and folded his arms across his chest as if to restrain the breaking of his heart. Finally, he walked despondently away and returned to the cabin by the creek.

The Mosses were waiting to return to Corn Creek. After taking time to kiss his mother's head gently, John climbed into their buggy and stared ahead, hollow eyed. He hadn't seen the preacher's wife take a tiny roll from Moves First and place it snugly on her lap beneath the robes. As they drove away to the south, he sat rigidly on the seat, holding tightly to his grief and loss.

His mother, now alone, gazed after them, her hand shading her age-dimmed eyes until she knew they had passed from sight as well as hearing. Only then did she make her way slowly to the top of a nearby hill. Moments later, everyone around the camp heard her lament as it rose to the heavens. Long after the sounds of her sorrow had quieted, and far to the south at their home on Corn Creek, Aaron jumped down to assist his wife from their wagon.

It quickly became clear that John had no idea until that very moment that Mrs. Moss had taken charge of the child and brought her along, bundled in one of his mother's cleanest blankets. When she held the bundle towards him before turning to climb from the wagon seat, his face grew distressed, and he looked away, jerking back his outstretched arms as if he'd been burned. Aaron quickly reached out to accept the little bundle, cooing and murmuring sounds of comfort as John turned and walked stiffly away.

Mrs. Moss prepared a late supper, and John forced himself to eat, choking down the food with repeated urging from Aaron and his wife. When the baby cried more frequently, Mrs. Moss prepared a warm bottle of goat's milk for her to suckle. Her cries seemed to devastate John, his eyes growing wide with both terror and anger, until he rose and disappeared outside. After the baby suckled and settled into a peaceful sleep, the Mosses whispered between themselves.

It was clear that John was not prepared to take the child at this point, and the couple had no idea how long he would need to come to terms with his loss. Since they'd been settled for some time and the minister was well supported by both the native families and the church, the Mosses determined she should remain with them until the time was right for her to return to her father.

Aaron walked outside to find John sitting dazedly on the porch.

"John, Mrs. Moss and I feel it will be better for the baby to remain with us for a little while. Of course, you'll be able to get her whenever you're ready, and the two of you can build a future in the East."

Much to Aaron's surprise, John shook his head and responded with a deep sense of melancholy, "I fear I'll never have enough of the goodness and faith of my father to regard the child as I should. It is through her coming that the light has gone out for me, and I don't know that I can find it in my heart to forgive her for that."

Speechless, Aaron didn't try to disengage John from his grief. He understood that time alone could bring about a reconciliation. Later, John came back into their home and informed the couple of his plans to go to the main agency the following morning.

"From there I'll leave for my home in the East," he continued. The minister offered to travel with him, leaving as early as he wished, but John said, "As long as I knew my father, he encouraged me to look beyond the old ways of the reservation and build a new life in the white man's world. Although my beloved felt an obligation to serve my people, the old ways took her life. It was our dream to raise a family and grow old together on the farm in the Berkshires. It is the only real home I have left where there is a future. If I'm not here for breakfast, I'll be somewhere on the road to the agency. Thank you for taking this girl-child into your home."

The Mosses urged him to get the rest he so desperately needed.

"I'll try, and hope to see you both in the morning, but at times it seems as though I cannot command myself any longer."

He went to bed early, saying he'd seek the sleep his body craved. But his thoughts of Stella back on the hill insistently crowded his mind so that he could only lie in the torment of sleeplessness. An hour later, the young man slipped out to the porch. When the child cried again, John heard nothing but a reminder of his irreparable loss. He headed brusquely into the midnight chill, walking across the prairie and towards the southwest.

The next morning, when Aaron caught up with him, John was well on his way to the agency. He climbed into the buggy and sat silently the remainder of the trip. Later that afternoon, he gathered the savings he and Stella had set aside. He took the stage to a small town to the south, from which the evening train east would depart. He left Aaron without a word, wringing his hand in a way that conveyed the depth of his emotions. As John turned away to climb into the stage, Aaron prayed fervently, "God bless you, my boy," but the young man never looked back to see the tears of respect, sympathy, and love in his old friend's eyes.

After a journey during which he cared not whether he ate or slept, John found himself at the familiar station in the Berkshires. Out of habit, he looked for Mr. Hall, before remembering he'd not sent notice he was coming. With only a cursory glance through town, he started on foot over the familiar road, glad for the opportunity to be active again. Walking briskly, it required no longer for him to cover the distance to the big white house with its wide-pillared porch than if he'd driven with Mr. Hall. He turned up the lane between the rows of maples with conflicting feelings of joy at his return and a renewed awareness of the emptiness he'd find in Stella's absence from this place.

Mr. and Mrs. Hall were seated at their supper table when he appeared—a disheveled, haggard, and careworn specter of himself as they'd known him. They both rose in astonishment, which at once gave way to expressions of grief and sympathy as Mrs. Hall recognized that what she had dreaded had in fact come true. She put her arms around John's neck and tearfully kissed his cheeks. Mr. Hall pressed his hand with silent understanding.

"Oh, John," said Mrs. Hall, "we are so grieved for ourselves and so deeply sorry for you," and he knew he had no need to tell them of Stella's passing. He seated himself without speaking and rested his drawn face in his hands. For the first time, he felt the sense of relief that comes through tears as they coursed through his fingers and dropped to the floor. A fleeting time later, when their mutual grief had been shared, Mrs. Hall brought out a letter and handed it to John.

Stella had written the letter to the Halls just before she and John had left Medicine Root to go to the cabin on Potato Creek. It was filled with expressions of love for John and for the child they would share.

In conclusion she wrote:

> And we are going in a day or two to the home of John's mother, which we will make very snug and cozy with the things that Mr. and Mrs. Roacher are going to let us take. It will not be long until we are all at home again. And yet, at times, dear Mother Hall, I feel a great fear, a premonition that I may not see you again. Surely, all expectant mothers must feel the same, and yet, I have had this

foreboding before. I want so much to come back, my dear Mother Hall, but if I do not, my husband will have the greatest gift a woman can give, and hopefully our child will also be yours. If I come back, we will all be happy together, and if I do not, you will each have to love my child all the more for my absence. In any event, I shall be content. With love to all of you and to my husband and child, and may He who knows best keep and guard you all.

Yours affectionately,
Stella

CHAPTER 57

Carter's Journal

Spring 1903

Fort Berthold Reservation, Elbowoods, North Dakota

After two years of challenging work, I felt I'd finally reached the pinnacle of my career in North Dakota. We'd enrolled our highest number of students, seventy-eight boys and girls, and I was told the school had never looked better. There had been no epidemic over the winter and, for the first time, only a few cases of pneumonia. Not a single child had died of rubella or diarrhea, and there'd been a decrease in cases of tuberculosis over the entire reservation. The number of runaways had been reduced to zero, and I felt many of the students were seeing new hope in our education program.

Much of the drudgery work I'd forced on the students until we got the school back into good operating condition was finished. More of the students appeared to enjoy their academic work and applied themselves regularly to lessons in writing and spelling. A number of our farming families competed successfully in local fairs, and we hoped to host our own event in the fall. I'd hired an excellent clerk who was well organized and set up a system to inventory the school's supplies and materials. Thanks to his orderliness, we got all of our necessities in a timely manner and had no shortage of books or medical provisions for the year.

As usual, there were a few dustups—as I called them—with local ranchers who wanted to influence the affairs of the reservation, mostly when it came to land transactions. There were more men willing to take advantage of the uneducated and trusting Indians than not, unfortunately.

However, our extension directors and farm agents became adept at recognizing discouragement in the Indians and helping them get back on track with producing crops rather than leasing or trading away their allotments. I required all my teachers, both industrial and academic, to spend time out among the Indians, and I was certain the practice enabled us to keep down the amount of whiskey that came onto the reservation.

Although my blood pressure remained high, my overall health improved. The doctor occasionally found symptoms of inflammation in my intestine, but regular walking and hot baths kept the pain under control. I was content in my position at Fort Berthold. I didn't want surgery, nor did I have enough years in the system to retire, so I worked to find positive results in everything around me.

Despite its remoteness, the school received both posted mail and telegrams regularly. I was able to read much about Liz's life as a soon-to-be teenager in Denver. She and Margaret were already planning her coming-out party. My, how time had flown! The boys were all in school except Charles. Margaret complained the governess spoiled him terribly but insisted he was a brilliant child who'd quickly catch up with his siblings academically. On the other hand, she worried he might choose to remain at home with Frau Lauxman forever.

Although I missed my children, I was thankful I no longer had to worry about my situation when it came to their care. Margaret treated them as if they were her own. Jessie enjoyed the social life of a growing city and chose to remain in Denver where there was a thriving financial district, lavish restaurants, and a number of museums. Like my father, she'd come to enjoy a life of ease rather than service, and as long as she enjoyed the benefits of my government position, I knew she was happy to exchange the commissary and summer celebrations on the reservation for the excitement of society.

North Dakota was where I experienced one of the highlights of my career, but it was also where I experienced my second-greatest heartache. At the end of my first year at the school, I was presented with a War Bonnet from the tribe's elders, a great honor, and asked to become a member of their tribe. They were grateful for the efforts I'd made in improving their children's school as well as the food supply for all.

Only days later, I received a note from Thomas Hall with the most devastating news. It had been hard enough to comprehend how John and Stella were manipulated into returning to the reservation. But to learn that it had cost the young lady her life, John his beloved wife, and a child her dear mother was almost more than I could bear. As much as I wanted to journey back to Massachusetts to see John and grieve with him, I was too fatigued, and there was too much for me to do to get the school in good running order for another year. I couldn't leave. I prayed John would find solace from the loss of his wife but worried he'd never find peace without his child at his side.

Almost a year later, Mr. Hall wrote that he and his wife planned to travel to Pine Ridge to get the baby as well as to bring Stella to what they considered her home. Knowing they planned to carry the child to her father was an answer to my prayers. Despite any anger he had towards the child for the death of her mother, I never doubted that John would remember his father's teachings about the importance of family and heritage and do what was right for both Stella's memory and for his daughter.

V

The Berkshires

CHAPTER 58

Family
....
Spring 1903

Snow Hill Farm, Becket, Massachusetts

A busy year followed John's return to the farm in Massachusetts. He spent much of the time reconciling himself to the loss of his wife and rebuilding his relationship with the Halls and the home where he'd always found acceptance and love. Each passing day, he felt more keenly the distance that separated him from where Stella lay. His heart ached with loneliness, making him wish almost nightly they'd laid her to rest on this very land as she'd described not so long ago. He was certain he'd feel her presence more closely.

He read her final letter over and again as the days passed into weeks and weeks into months. Gradually, he came to terms with the fact that he had to accept the child who was a living part of her whom he loved so dearly. The more he contemplated her, the more often he felt as if she were reaching out to him, calling for him to bring her home. Finally, the time came when John and the Halls could speak of Stella without tears interrupting their words.

John spoke softly. "Mother Hall, Stella made my mother's house on Potato Creek a beautiful place. With nothing more than simple curtains and a handful of prairie flowers, she did her best to decorate our home as you do here. The cabin was filled with love and hope for our family and the possibilities for our future."

Hesitantly, but hopefully, Mrs. Hall queried, "Don't you miss your daughter?" And because she couldn't help chiding John just a little, she added, "Your beloved gave her to you with great sacrifice. I don't believe she rests peacefully knowing your child isn't here with you."

"Yes, Mother Hall. My heart breaks with the conflict. Stella died giving life to our daughter," John replied sadly. "Yet I cannot forget that if it were not for the child, my beloved would be here now. Were it not for her coming into the world on the reservation, I might now be celebrating her birth with her mother and her adopted grandparents in this house. It was no fault of her own, and it's true that I love this tiny girl whom I don't even know. My heart tells me she holds within her a part of Stella, and that part calls out to me every day," he went on. "Still, I can't forgive her for the loss of my beloved wife."

Papa Hall had already planted a seed in his wife's mind, saying firmly, "Mother Hall, this can't go on. I don't know who needs whom the most, the father or the child. But I know we'll all regret if the child is lost to the reservation. We must act as we know John's father would act, as he acted all those years ago when he took in a wounded little boy."

Mother Hall arose as if she might begin packing right away. "You're right, Papa. A little girl is waiting, and we must go," she said, excitement and joy in her eyes.

A few evenings later, as they sat together after supper, Mr. Hall knew the time was right. He announced as if to an entire room, "John, I'll be shifting the entire responsibility for things here to your shoulders for a time. Day after tomorrow, Mother Hall and I are starting the trip of a lifetime. We're going west and will be gone for several weeks, perhaps a month or more. We'll see the land of your people, visit those who remain, and meet with Aaron Moss. He placed a hand-carved cross for Stella's headstone and will guide us to the site. We'll pay our respects to your father's spirit and place a cross on Annie's grave. When we return, we'll arrange for Stella to come home, and the baby as well."

John bowed his head to conceal the tears that sprang to his eyes. After a moment, he looked into the tender faces of those he considered his family. "Mr. Hall, you're more than kind. I feel Stella's spirit has shared with you the feelings I cannot express. I've wronged not just my wife's memory but our child as well. I'm eager to make amends. Travel safely, and return hope to our lives."

Lying anxiously in his bed later that night, he felt a spark of renewed hope. He drifted into his first restful sleep in almost a year as he prayed sincerely that all would be set right again.

After the Halls left on their journey, John came to know what utter loneliness was. He tried to distract himself by filling every waking hour with arduous work and painstaking attention to the business of the farm. The many broken boards, sagging fences, and weed-filled pathways through the orchards made it clear Hiram hadn't returned to help with the upkeep of the farm. In spite of all, when he wasn't too exhausted to notice the silence that surrounded him, he reviewed the memories of his life. He envisioned Stella on the evening he first saw her in that wisp of a dress, and his heart beat quickly at the memory of their closest moments. His mind replayed his stuttering awkwardness every time Stella had turned her attention towards him. Frequently, cherished thoughts of the kindness of Mr. and Mrs. Hall arose, and he worried he could never show enough appreciation for their presence in his life.

Inevitably, each evening when day's end settled over the farm, John's thoughts turned to the child he'd refused to look at, whom he had, in his bitterness, held responsible for Stella's going away. Try as he might, he could no longer feel the resentment he'd first known. As the nights rolled by, he felt a growing sense of anticipation. He yearned to hold her close and adore her as he had her mother. John wondered how it would be to know that Stella was resting peacefully in the corner of the orchard, where he could visit every day. He wondered what the child was like and how he would react to her whose name he did not know.

On the evening the Halls returned, John distanced himself from the house, preferring to greet his wife's spirit before making himself known to his daughter. Stella's coffin was immediately interred in the far corner of the orchard, close beside the place where the Halls' infant son lay in eternal rest. The weathered cross was once again positioned at her head. Their labor of love was finished just as the sun settled on the horizon, much as it had when she was first given back to the earth at Potato Creek.

Later, when John went alone to seek her presence, his thoughts went back to the evening under the apple tree when he'd first perceived her grace and beauty. Tears coursed down his cheeks as the memories of another evening crept into his mind. He and Stella had come into the glow of the fire, enveloped in the folds of an imaginary courting blanket. It had felt so real at the time that he could almost feel its weight on his shoulders now.

Then, a second memory washed over him, that of another evening, on the prairie, when a great promise had been given to them to hold and to cherish as their secret. As waves of pent-up emotions washed over him, John experienced a sense of contentment in knowing she was now nearby to comfort him. He grew confident Stella would guide and strengthen in him the love he felt for their child. Finally, peace settled slowly over his heart.

The next morning, as he worked on the shelters that protected the chickens Stella had treasured, John heard Mrs. Hall calling from the kitchen door, concern and curiosity in her voice, "John! A moment, please."

As he entered the house, he saw her seated by the stove, the baby in her lap, fresh from the bath and wrapped in a blanket. Her expression was the same as any grandmother's. "Look here, John, you never told me about an accident to our baby," she chided, moving the blanket aside to reveal a long, narrow mark on the child's chubby leg.

"She had no accident, Mother Hall," he replied, hiding his surprise. Reaching down and pulling his own pant leg almost to his knee, John pointed out a scar of which the baby's was almost an exact replica. "It's the mark of the fire at Medicine Root," John went on, accepting the mark on his daughter's leg as a sign of their destiny. A great lump came into his throat, and he took the child into his arms and held her close.

"Mother Hall," he added, choking back tears, "it's the mark of the reservation that binds me to her. I believe it's also a rebuke from the Great Spirit for my lack of courage. It's evidence of the capacity to love that Stella gave to our daughter and thus to me. I'm ashamed of the selfishness I've shown, and now I know I love this baby as Stella would have me love her."

"John," Mrs. Hall replied, smiling warmly at those she loved as completely as if they were her very own, "as you grow older, you'll find that all things in life are ordered for the best."

John reached out to embrace Mother Hall, squeezing the child between them until she squealed loudly. Releasing the older lady and holding the little girl off from himself, he noticed as if for the first time the wealth of dark hair curling around her shapely head—just like her mother's. As he sat her on his lap and peered into her deep-brown eyes, he realized they shone with a luster and depth that reflected her mother's intelligence and capacity to love, and that her nose and mouth were a pleasing compromise between his own and Stella's. Rubbing his fingers delicately over the baby-soft skin of her chubby arms, he noted the clear, deep-copper color that would have defied the efforts of a master colorist to replicate. But best of all, in John's mind, was the sound as the child chortled at the bouncing ride he gave her on his knees.

As the days passed, the child enchanted them all. To Mr. and Mrs. Hall, she was the greatest joy that had come into their lives since the loss of their own tiny babe long ago. To John, she was life itself, a constant reminder of his love for Stella, as well as an opportunity for him to experience the meaning of fatherhood as Iron Horse had shown to him. Although Stella had promised long ago on the prairie that their firstborn child would be called John, Aaron and his wife had deemed it inappropriate for a girl-child and given her the name Johanna instead.

Now John lovingly whispered what they had chosen to call her: "Hannah, my sweet, you are the image of your mother and the embodiment of our love. We'll look now only to the future as your grandfather advised." And he hugged her tightly.

EPILOGUE

The Orchard
....
September 1911

Snow Hill Farm, Becket, Massachusetts

John sat propped against the base of an old apple tree, its gnarled branches laden with fruit soon to be harvested. His gaze skimmed over the grassy knoll, taking in the neat rows that arched gracefully away to the horizon. Nine years. His beloved had gone to the spirit world nine years ago. Forcing his mind back to this tranquil corner of land, he focused on four marble gravestones standing silently just a few feet away. His long legs stretched outward from his seat, one booted foot almost touching the smallest of the stones. It was carved in the likeness of a tiny angel and marked the resting place of a child John had never known but whose fate had played a profound role in his future. Two larger markers stood resolutely over a husband and wife, one of New England's finest couples, who had given John a home not just in their hearts but also in a new world on land far from the open vistas of the reservation where he was born.

He rose and slowly approached a smaller gravestone, pale blue gray in color and topped with a carving of roses. Leafy marble vines trailed down both sides and wrapped around the single name chiseled in its center. The marker replaced a wooden cross worn smooth by loving hands and was the focal point of all John's visits here. Gently caressing the roses that would bloom forever, he inhaled deeply, closing his eyes as memories converged from among the fields and trees, memories that marked the happiest times of his life. His chin slumped to his chest, his breath leaving until he gasped to inhale again, knowing he had much to live for but that his life was about to change in ways he had yet to comprehend.

Shaking his head to clear away his worries of the future, John focused on a cloud of dust moving along the tree line. A colorful group of cattle emerged over the horizon, closely followed by a spotted pony, its rider perched atop its bare back with all the grace a nine-year-old could muster. The fingers of one hand were locked deep in her pony's mane, her spindly legs gripping its sides as she "Yahooed" her encouragement for the herd to hurry to the security of the barn. She whooped and giggled in that strange combination only childhood exuberance can display, her auburn curls bouncing in unison as her body bobbled atop her mare, Ehawee.

Papa Hall had arranged for her to be shipped to the farm from South Dakota for his granddaughter's eighth birthday. John imagined her colorful coat derived from one of the ponies from his father's herd, which he hoped still grazed the prairies of Pine Ridge. John smiled, thinking how well the pony's name fit, for it meant Laughing Maiden. It was hard to tell who was having more fun on this brisk New England evening, the girl or the horse. A yearning grew in his chest, for the scene reminded him of days spent racing his own pony, kicking his bare heels against his trusted Hantaywee, streaking across the grasslands in abandon. Forcing his mind back to the present, he watched the group disappear into the cavernous structure, whispering a prayer of thanksgiving that his daughter enjoyed a life so full and free.

Turning away from the cemetery, John strolled towards the barn, listening to the girl's laughter as she brushed her pony's coat and poured the evening's ration of oats into a bucket. He entered the open expanse of the door just as she reached the loft above and began tossing forkfuls of hay to the cattle.

His daughter's life had been vastly different from her mother's. He was thankful she had been dearly loved by the elderly couple she knew as Papa and Unci Hall, her grandparents. If she'd ever noticed any difference between the deeper tones of her skin and their pale ones, she never commented. Besides himself, they'd been the only family she knew, and John understood her animals brought respite from her grief.

Only the mention of tuberculosis or typhoid could have been more frightening than the word influenza a year ago when the doctor arrived, pounding on the door. Papa Hall had done everything from garlic and peeled onions to camphor and mustard plasters. Nothing had eased Unci's breathing, and the fever sapped her strength. When the doctor tiptoed from the room with word of their loss, Hannah had run sobbing down the hall and out the door to the solace of her pony. For weeks, she'd wept unconsolably, curled in a ball while Papa Hall rocked her to sleep. Later, he'd taken her hand and strolled with her around the farm, reminding the child of all the things they had to be thankful for in their lives.

John had struggled to find a way to console his daughter. He'd never embraced the Christian concept of heaven, never accepted a religion that allowed its believers to massacre families like his own and go about building their houses and farms on land where Lakota blood ran deep. Over weeks of grieving, John had turned to traditions and beliefs that welled from within him, long-buried memories of stories and song.

Night after night, he'd held his daughter and crooned the singsong lullabies of his people until she drifted off to sleep. When the weather was cold or damp outside, they shared a cup of steaming, honey-sweetened elderberry tea in the kitchen, Unci's favorite place. This was their private time, when John told the old stories of his people, Black Corn, Why the Leaves Fall, and Brave Woman Counts Coup, for they were the stories that would give his daughter wisdom and courage. Hopefully, one day, she'd pass them to his grandchildren.

And then, suddenly, Papa Hall was gone. Whether his heart stopped beating from old age or from shattering into pieces over the loss of his beloved wife, the doctor couldn't say. Whatever the cause, Hannah had once again dealt with her grief by slipping away to an imaginary world with her four-legged companions. She'd reach to the underside of her horse's belly and scratch that secret spot that made the pony lift her nose high in the air and wiggle her lips as if she were laughing out loud.

"Oh, my friends, what will I do now when others at school make fun of my red skin? Unci and Papa Hall always said that names couldn't hurt me. Father tells me to be strong. It's easy for him to be strong, but not for me," the girl whispered to the fuzzy ears cocked her way. Overhearing his daughter's words, John's eyes burned as he realized his daughter understood far more than he realized about the world. Tears ran freely over his cheeks until, slowly, his frown reversed into a grin as he heard Hannah close out the one-sided conversation.

"I don't care about those girls at school as long as I have my father and you, Ehawee, and you, Red Bull, and you, Spotted Mother." Her voice faded to a whisper as she murmured her abiding love to each of her four-legged friends.

Listening to the peaceful exchange, John knew his daughter had inherited her mother's strength and allowed his mind to drift to other concerns. The upcoming week would be busy with the reading of the will. Reviews of the farm accounts were scheduled with a barrister. Carter Heath would be arriving to support his former student as the estate was settled.

Carter had been made an examiner of heirship on the Pawnee Reservation in Oklahoma, dealing with the intricacies of Indian inheritance. He'd traveled to Washington many times regarding policies of the Office of Indian Affairs he disagreed with. Though no longer a young man, he sometimes took a circuitous route through the Dakotas to get updates on the goings-on at Pine Ridge and then traveled on to the Berkshires to visit with John and the Halls. He'd brought news that Moves First had joined her husband and sister in their long sleep just three years ago. Whenever he arrived at the farm, he enjoyed a cup of tea on the back porch with the adults before spending the remainder of his time with the little girl he considered his goddaughter.

On this trip, Carter and John were both thankful Mr. Hall had been a stickler about integrity in his business dealings. Carter explained, "There may be a few delays from the court since this is a significant bequest. The community knows you well, but the court does not. Still, I'm confident a judgment supporting the Halls' gift will be upheld."

John shared what he'd already learned. "The barrister had some questions since I'm not considered a citizen of this country. He's already interviewed several business owners that Mr. Hall dealt with. This part of Massachusetts has a history of inclusiveness, and they've assured him nothing will change with my ownership. Hiram Parker filed against the estate, asking for compensation for the years he worked here. He claimed to have been promised a portion of the land as compensation for his time away from his father's farm. There was no such agreement, and Hiram has nothing in writing, so the barrister is certain the grievance won't be upheld. No other claims have been filed."

Having seen so many challenges to Indian ownership in other places, Carter commented, "Excellent. I'm glad the barrister's done his work. Obviously, the townspeople know you're very much like Mr. Hall and your integrity and dedicated work are more important than the color of your skin."

Hesitating just a moment and then laughing loudly, John replied, "Stella and I used to imagine what it would be like to make this farm into what we could call Indian land."

Carter's Journal

Fall 1911

Snow Hill Farm, Becket, Massachusetts

Looking around as we strolled up the lane, I was thankful that fate had provided so well for the adopted son of Iron Horse. The chief had been as fine a gentleman as I'd known in all my dealings over the years. His vison for his people had been astonishingly accurate. He'd done the best he could for his family, both those who stayed on the reservation and the one who went boldly forward into the world of the white man. With that thought foremost on my mind, I knocked softly to let John know we'd arrived.

He looked worn when he opened the door, a smile of relief lighting his face as I reached to take his hand. I offered my condolences with the only words I could find. "John, your father would be proud of the man you've become—not of the things you have but of the son and father you are."

"And who is this you've brought with you?" John asked as Liz emerged from behind me to extend her hand in greeting.

"John, you remember Elizabeth, mine and Lillian's daughter and the oldest of my children. She's Liz to me, and she insisted on joining me here to be company and perhaps comfort to your daughter during the hours we'll spend dealing with the estate."

John took her hand, speaking warmly. "Thank you for your thoughtfulness." Looking more closely, he added, "You have your mother's eyes. You're as beautiful as she. I can't wait for you to meet my daughter."

While Liz blushed and shuffled her feet, I reminded John, "She was born on Pine Ridge, if you remember. Just before you left for boarding school at the agency."

John replied softly, "I remember. So much has happened, hasn't it?"

"Yes, John, so much has changed except our friendship. I've taken a leave of absence and can stay as long as you need me."

For the next few hours, we meandered through the house, John pouring out his memories from room to room. He was sure Mrs. Hall would be proud the floors shone like newly minted pennies and every piece of furniture gleamed with a fresh polish of linseed oil. Watching him, I could see John was still confident, his stride purposeful and balanced. Yet I sensed he was overwhelmed by the enormity of the demands placed on him by the death of Thomas Hall. I knew he was dedicated to being both mother and father to his daughter, but until now, I hadn't given any thought to the hours Mr. Hall put into the bookkeeping and management of his business. Those responsibilities had now fallen to John alone. I was confident he was as capable of continuing the business as he had been of being my most exceptional student.

Finally, we stepped out on the back porch and settled into the rocking chairs that had seen it all. John leaned his head to rest on the carved chair back, letting out a sigh as if embracing the relief my arrival brought. Seeing the horses in the corral, Liz asked impatiently, "May I go out to the barn? I can't wait to meet Hannah! We can visit with the animals while you men talk."

"Certainly, Liz, just don't forget your manners. And don't spook the cattle," I finished as she darted off around the corral.

John whispered, "It's so good to have you here and to meet your beautiful daughter. I remember when she was born there on Potato Creek. Sometimes, I can almost see my Indian family—Annie, Iron Horse, Moves First, and Good Heart—overlooking the little schoolhouse that my sister loved until her last breath. I close my eyes and feel the warmth of the

Dakota sun on my face and smell the wild grass of the prairie."

He continued, "I know they'll forever guard that place and their spirits guide me wherever I go. I'm happy here, but sometimes, I miss the land where I was born."

"I too have often missed the happiness we found at Potato Creek. Like yours, my life's been filled with family, travels, and hardship. We have come full circle, my friend."

At that moment, the barn settled into a peaceful silence. Hannah and Liz appeared in the doorway, laughing, then approached the porch stride for stride, holding hands and chatting like old friends. As they joined us, Liz leaned against the rail, and Hannah perched lightly on the arm of her father's chair, hugging him closely.

Turning to me, John whispered, "Thank you. With your help and my father's spirit to guide me, I'll build a home for my daughter. And perhaps, one day, you and I will return to the Indian land we knew and find hope for the future."

Acknowledgments

Thank you to the following people:

Abby Hoverstock, senior archivist at Denver Public Library, for researching family records in the midst of the pandemic and securing for me permission to use some of their archived material for this book.

Tom Williams and Kellen Cutsforth, digital image collection administrators of the Denver Public Library, for their assistance with accessing archived family photos. I hope to see the whole collection one day.

Fran Lebowitz for her unique ideas, enthusiasm for the story, and dedicated editing. And to her daughter, Sadie, for her insight into my characters.

Quinton Maldonado for his inspirational ledger art and his support as I tackled this project.

My great-grandfather, who didn't survive to collect his pension but gave us true insights into the evils of greed and prejudice and the power of commitment.

My family for allowing me time to continue this work.

My Place—original ledger art by Quinton Maldonado

Author Bio

Writing has allowed J. Stanion to express her feelings through the depths of depression and unrequited love, to exchange joyful poems with her father over a lifetime, to succeed at being named a National Board Certified teacher of science, and to research and complete the application of her family farm for listing on the National Register of Historic Places (McPhail Angus Farm). Most recently, it has allowed her to publish her first novel, a story of tragedy and triumph that begged to be told. www.jstanion.com

www.ingramcontent.com/pod-product-compliance
Lightning Source LLC
LaVergne TN
LVHW041743060526
838201LV00046B/890